The Judge

Farin Powell

iUniverse

THE JUDGE

iUniverse books may be ordered through booksellers or by contacting:

iUniverse
1663 Liberty Drive
Bloomington, IN 47403
www.iuniverse.com
1-800-Authors (1-800-288-4677)

ISBN: 978-1-4917-9684-9 (sc)
ISBN: 978-1-4917-9694-8 (hc)
ISBN: 978-1-4917-9693-1 (e)

Library of Congress Control Number: 2016911009

Print information available on the last page.

iUniverse rev. date: 08/18/2016

To Richard, Bobby, and Jimmy

Friday, July 2, 4:00 p.m.

Judge McNeil assumed that the only sentencing on his court's docket would not take more than ten minutes of his time. He was anxious to go back to his chambers and review several defense motions filed in the triple-murder case. He wished he could transfer the case to another judge. Whenever he was handling a high-profile case, he cringed every time he read the *Washington Post*'s coverage of his decisions.

At the defense table, attorney Amanda Perkins was seated next to her client. The young defendant was accompanied by a deputy US marshal and wore an orange jumpsuit—the DC jail's uniform. McNeil hoped Perkins would not repeat her usual bombastic allocution. It was a well-known fact that he didn't like her, and the feeling was mutual. Over the past five years, he had held her in contempt of court twice, each time imposing a heavy fine on her—and he was convinced his rulings were fair. She could have faced jail time.

After his courtroom clerk called the case for the record, McNeil turned to the prosecutor and asked, "Is the government ready to proceed?"

A young male prosecutor jumped to his feet and nodded. "Yes, Your Honor."

"Go ahead."

"Your Honor," the prosecutor said, addressing the court, "Damian Lewis is seventeen years old, and although we've charged him as an adult, we agree with the presentencing report of the probation department and Attorney Perkins's request that he should be given credit for the nine months he has spent in jail and be placed on probation for two years under the Youth Rehabilitation Act."

"The fact that you all have agreed doesn't mean that I should follow your proposal," the judge replied. He then directed his gaze toward the defense table. "Ms. Perkins, I've read your report and the three letters from members of the community submitted on behalf of your client, so you don't need to repeat them. I'm ready for the concluding part of your allocution."

McNeil moved in his black leather swivel chair and shuffled some papers around in a folder on the bench. Then he turned away, staring at the pictures of the retired judges on the wall.

"Your Honor," Amanda said as she stood and addressed McNeil, who didn't shift his gaze from the pictures on the wall. "Damian Lewis was abandoned by his mother three days after he was born in DC's General Hospital. He lived in different foster homes and group homes until he became eligible for the independent living program. He has three juvenile delinquencies, but he stayed out of trouble for a long time until this recent—"

McNeil swiveled his chair quickly and looked Amanda in the eyes. "Ms. Perkins, those were significant adjudications: theft one, assault with a deadly weapon, and carrying a pistol—"

"Your Honor, he was only twelve years old when—"

"Ms. Perkins, do not interrupt me when I'm talking," McNeil said, raising his voice.

"I apologize, Your Honor."

"Your client possessed a gun at age twelve."

"Your Honor, that was due to lack of supervision by his foster parents. After his last court adjudication, he stayed clean for five years. We have objected to the government's charging him as an adult. He's only—"

"Your client had a hundred Ziploc bags of cocaine, a scale, and other tools for measuring drugs."

"Your Honor, you remember we argued during the trial that the drugs and all the other incriminating evidence were planted in his closet by another individual."

"The jury didn't buy it."

"We're appealing the jury's verdict and—"

"And I suppose all of my procedural rulings."

"Yes, Your Honor."

"Good luck. I'm ready to sentence your client. Does he have anything to say?"

"Your Honor, my allocution is not finished."

"I've heard enough," McNeil said impatiently. He turned to the defendant. "Mr. Lewis, stand up. Do you have anything to say before I sentence you?"

Damian Lewis stood, looking frightened. He lowered his gaze. "No."

McNeil saw the surprised expression on Perkins's face. He knew her style during sentencing—she always had her clients prepared to tell the judge they were remorseful.

"Mr. Lewis," the judge said, addressing the defendant, "in case felony number 237, I sentence you to four years of imprisonment. I'm obligated by law to order at least one hundred dollars to be paid to the Victims of Crime Fund. You can pay that within four years."

"Your Honor," Amanda pleaded, "the government agreed to probation under the Youth Act, which expunges my client's criminal record. I urge the court—"

"Ms. Perkins, I've ruled, and you're still talking."

"Your Honor, with all due respect, this is a harsh sentence. You know what happens to a seventeen-year-old in jail while—"

"The law allows me to give him up to thirty years."

"Such lengthy jail time is intended for drug czars, not a seventeen-year-old—"

Judge McNeil stood and pointed to a young deputy US marshal who stood at the court entrance. "Could you please escort Ms. Perkins out of my courtroom?"

* * *

Amanda paced the hallway outside Judge McNeil's courtroom for a few minutes, not knowing what to do. Her face was flushed. Like a wounded tiger, she was ready to attack anyone who appeared in her path. The judge had kicked her out of his courtroom and had not even allowed her to explain his harsh sentence to her client. She stopped pacing and stood for a few seconds and then ran to the escalator in the atrium, heading for the court's criminal division on the fourth floor. After filing a notice of appeal with the court clerk challenging the jury's decision and the court's rulings, including sentencing, she rushed to the lawyers' lounge. She sat at one of the computers and drafted a short two-page motion asking the judge to reconsider his sentencing.

When she returned to the court clerk's office, the clerk was surprised to see her again. "Ms. Perkins, it's almost time to go home. What have you got this time?"

"It's a Rule 35 motion; I'm asking him to reconsider his sentencing."

"Good luck," the clerk chuckled as she stamped the copies of the motions.

Amanda knew what the clerk meant, but she was in a hurry. She took her copies and headed for Judge McNeil's chambers.

She stood in front of the door in the corner of the second-floor hallway—the secured entrance to the chambers of many judges. The security guard, who could see her through the surveillance camera, opened the door electronically and allowed her in. She found the chambers quickly and knocked on the door. Amanda was surprised when McNeil opened it himself.

"Ms. Perkins, what do you want now?"

"Your Honor, this is your copy of my Rule 35 motion. I'll be serving the prosecutor as soon as I leave the courthouse," Amanda said as she handed the motion to the judge.

"You know I'll deny it," McNeil said with a snarl, slamming the door in Amanda's face.

Amanda stood in disbelief before the closed chamber door for a few moments and then walked away quickly. Before reaching the exit, she heard her name. She turned around and found Detective Manfredi.

"Hey, where are you going in such a hurry?"

"I have to file an urgent motion at the US Attorney's Office."

"What kind of motion?"

"McNeil just gave my seventeen-year-old client four years in prison."

"I have an appointment with him. Do you want me to say something to him?"

"Just tell him to go to hell."

Chapter 2

McNeil opened his eyes and found himself on a bed in a narrow, hospital-like room inside a moving vehicle. He tried to get up, but his wrists and ankles were tightly fastened to the bed, and an IV was inserted in his right arm. At first he thought he was in an ambulance, but the presence of the two individuals who had held him in the black Pontiac at the foot of his bed reminded him of the kidnapping.

"Who are you, and where are you taking me?"

"Never mind who we are. You're in a mobile home, hundreds of miles away from DC," responded the shorter kidnapper.

"Whom are you working for?"

"Stop asking questions."

"What day is it?"

"It's Sunday, the Fourth of July. The court is closed even on Monday."

"What do you want from me?"

"Stop asking stupid questions. We'll introduce ourselves properly once we reach our destination," said the light-skinned kidnapper, who McNeil noticed was holding a syringe.

He had a severe headache, his mouth was dry, and he couldn't move. The last thing he remembered was his trip to the cemetery and an encounter with attorney Amanda Perkins on Friday before the Fourth of July holiday. He also remembered that he had been reviewing the defense motions filed on behalf of Keshan Walker—the accused in the triple-murder case. He tried to figure out why he was being kidnapped. He was not rich and didn't have anyone who would pay ransom money for him. He was a widower whose only daughter had run away from home four years ago. He had a sister who hated him. So why was he being kidnapped? He watched the light-skinned kidnapper put something into his IV. He fell asleep before he could ask another question.

* * *

McNeil heard two people talking and moving things around, but his eyelids were too heavy to open. He ignored the pain in his neck and listened to their conversation. One voice belonged to the short kidnapper, the other to the heavy mustachioed man who had asked for directions to Union Station. The two men were talking in hushed tones, but McNeil could still hear them clearly.

"When do we get the Pontiac?"

"One of my men will drive it from DC."

"You said nothing to nobody?"

"No. I trust the dude. I've paid him enough not to ask any questions."

"How much is this gonna cost me?"

"Nothing, man. This is on me."

"Where's Doc?"

"Next door, doing something with his computer."

"Ask him to come and get the judge up."

"Hey, Doc, we need you here."

McNeil heard a third person enter the room.

"Time to wake him up." McNeil believed this was the voice of the big kidnapper.

He felt two hands grab his shoulders and shake him gently. "Time to wake up," a voice said.

He ignored the order, but when his kidnapper shook his shoulders harder, he reluctantly opened his eyes. For the first time, he saw the faces of the three African American kidnappers around his bed. The tall, heavy man with a mustache and broad shoulders resembled a football player. He was the passenger who'd approached McNeil with a map in his hand and asked for directions. The light-skinned kidnapper was slim and about five feet ten. His goatee gave him a handsome appearance, and he wore his long hair in dreadlocks. The short kidnapper—who always carried a gun in his hand, McNeil had noticed—was less than five feet four. He had a chubby body, a big nose, and small eyes. He wore a bandana, like the ones worn by actors in pirate movies.

The light-skinned kidnapper, whom they called Doc, untied the judge's arms and helped him sit up in his bed. The change in position made him dizzy. He looked at the tray of food they had brought him, but he didn't have an appetite. In fact, he felt nauseated when he looked at the thick corned beef sandwich they had prepared for him. He took a spoon and tried a small portion of his soup, but the soup didn't sit well in his stomach. He felt bloated and vomited instantly.

The large kidnapper turned his head away in disgust. "I don't need this shit. Clean him up," he ordered the other two kidnappers. "If he gives you trouble, show him his grave in the backyard," he added as he left the room.

Chapter 3

Gloria Sanders, Judge McNeil's courtroom clerk, kept looking nervously at the clock on the wall. It was 9:55 a.m. on Tuesday, July 6, and there was no sign of the judge. Unless he was on vacation, every day for the last sixteen years, Judge McNeil had always taken the bench at 9:30 a.m. She called the judge's secretary.

"Hi, Maureen. Sorry to bother you. Have you heard from the judge?"

"No, we're worried too."

"Can I talk to his law clerk?"

"He hasn't received any call either."

Ms. Sanders said a quick good-bye and looked at the faces of the twelve impatient attorneys in the front row of the courtroom. At least twenty other people were present, including the defendants who had been released on their personal recognizance. The deputy US marshal had transferred the incarcerated inmates to the cellblock behind the courtroom. Their family members were anxiously waiting for the judge, hoping he would release their loved ones.

"I don't know what has happened to him," Ms. Sanders mumbled. "He's never late."

"Why don't you check your voice mail?" the deputy US marshal suggested. "Maybe he left *you* a message instead of calling his secretary."

Ms. Sanders looked at the telephone on her desk. The message light was blinking, as usual, which she always ignored in the early morning. She knew there would be at least a dozen messages from attorneys and defendants who were late, the court reporter's office, and other divisions of the superior court. She never had time for those phone calls until her lunch break. Typically, before the judge's arrival, she had time only to review the docket and to make sure that all defendants' file jackets had been brought to the courtroom. She then would have to page the tardy attorneys who had trials before the judge since their cases had priority over the others.

She pushed the message button on the phone. Sure enough, the judge had left a message. He sounded sick and agitated. "I'm out of town, taking care of a family emergency. Please ask Judge Bowen to handle my calendar for the next few days."

Judge Fredrick Bowen was a childhood friend of Judge McNeil. They were both forty-seven years old and from Madison, Wisconsin. They both had attended Harvard for four years, had received their law degrees from Stanford Law School, and had been appointed associate judges in the Superior Court of the District of Columbia by the president a few months apart. But the similarities stopped there. The two had very different personalities. Whereas McNeil was a strict and harsh-sentencing judge, Bowen hardly ever sent a defendant to jail. Almost every defendant got probation from him, except those who had committed dangerous or violent crimes.

When Ms. Sanders announced that Judge Bowen, next door, would handle Judge McNeil's calendar, the attorneys cheered. Some even clapped.

* * *

After everyone left the courtroom, Gloria Sanders checked the rest of the messages on her voice mail. The courtroom door opened, and a good-looking African American woman—in her early forties, Ms. Sanders guessed—walked in.

"Can I help you?" Ms. Sanders asked the woman.

"When is the judge coming back?"

"Do you have a pending case before him?"

"No. Judge McNeil was supposed to come to our charity last Friday evening, but he never showed up and didn't—"

"What charity?"

"The one at the First Baptist Church on Benning Road."

"When he's not in trial, Judge McNeil goes to St. Mathews, and I'm not aware of any Baptist church charity on Benning Road ... but hold on. Let me ask his secretary," Sanders said. She called McNeil's chambers.

"Maureen, this is Gloria again. Was Judge McNeil supposed to go to First Baptist Church last Friday?"

"No, he sometimes goes to St. Mathews during lunch recess."

"I know that. Let me know which day he plans to come back."

"Will do, but he may call you first."

Sanders looked up to share the information with the woman, but she had already left the courtroom.

Chapter 4

After several days of vomiting, McNeil felt better. He didn't know what kind of drugs they had pumped into his body, and he still didn't know where he was. His captors had shown him a big hole in the backyard and made sure he understood that it would be his grave if he didn't cooperate. Standing at the edge of his potential grave had reminded him of how many times he had told defendants during sentencing, "You dug your own grave." He wondered whether he had now dug *his*.

While his captors kept threatening him, McNeil tried to figure out where he was. One day, when they allowed him to walk outside, in the front yard, he saw the size of the house for the first time. It was not a mansion, but it was a huge ranch-style estate seated on an acre of forest. The unique white stone masonry, the stylish patio, and the four-car garage suggested the house had been designed by an architect and probably belonged to someone wealthy.

Though it was still July, the air was not hot or humid; it was rather comfortable. He thought maybe they had taken him to Arizona or Nevada—but why?

Because he had followed their orders and called his courtroom clerk, that evening they rewarded him with a good meal—steak and a baked potato. At the dinner table, they tied his feet to a chair but left his hands free so he could eat. He cleaned his plate and thanked his captors for the meal. "When are you going to tell me what you want from me?" he asked, his voice shaky.

"You'll be with us for a few months," answered the short kidnapper, his gun pointing at the judge, as always. "Next month, there's a hearing on the triple-murder trial before you. We want you to favor the motions filed for Keshan Walker."

McNeil didn't need to ask what they were talking about; he had been reviewing those motions in his chambers on that fateful Friday he was kidnapped. "How can I make a decision away from my chambers?"

"Don't worry—you were carrying your laptop in your briefcase when we stopped you," Doc, the light-skinned kidnapper, answered.

McNeil looked at the faces of his kidnappers. He was more afraid of the heavy man with big muscles. It seemed that this man hated him more than his cohorts did. Every time he talked to the judge, he avoided eye contact.

"You may not know this, but I have a reputation for denying defense motions—"

"You're full of shit, you son of a bitch!" the big kidnapper said, unexpectedly running at the judge and punching him in the face several times.

The short kidnapper jumped to his side and pulled him away. "Hey, man, be cool. We need him," he said.

Doc brought some gauze over, stuck it in the judge's nostrils, and told him to lean his head back.

"Even if I write what you want, no one's going to believe it. Besides, the prosecutor will ask for a hearing, and I have to be there."

The big kidnapper, whom the other two called Boss, raised his fist and charged toward the judge again. "You motherfucker, you still think you're calling the shots?"

Doc stopped Boss and took him out of the room. When he came back, he pointed his finger at the judge. "Look, either you write the motions and send the e-mails we ask you to, or we do it ourselves."

"Lawyers write motions; judges make decisions. Even if I make a favorable decision, how will you know where to send it?"

"Don't worry about that. We know your law clerk's e-mail, and we know yours, even your password."

"How could you? Only my daughter knows my password, and she's been missing for years."

"I told you not to ask any stupid questions. Are you going to write your decision and e-mail it to your law clerk, or do you want me to write it?"

"Are you a lawyer?"

"No, but I'm gonna pretend I'm you and tell your law clerk that I've decided to approve the defense's motions to suppress Keshan Walker's confession. I'll ask him to do the research and cite legal cases. He's a lawyer, isn't he?"

"He's a third-year law student."

"That's good enough for us."

"Okay, I'll write the decision you want."

After the judge's nose stopped bleeding, Doc untied his feet and walked him to a large room that looked like an office. McNeil recognized his own briefcase, cell phone, and laptop sitting on a huge desk at one end of the room. He sat in the comfortable brown leather chair and opened his laptop. Doc tied his feet to the chair and adjusted his laptop for him. He stood behind the judge in a position that enabled him to read everything the judge typed.

The puzzle was solved for McNeil. The kidnappers were trying to change the outcome of the triple-murder case he was handling. He also knew that the prosecutor would appeal his decisions immediately. He was not worried about the furor his rulings would create at the US attorney's office, but he was worried about his safety and freedom.

He had wondered many times whether anyone had witnessed his abduction, but he knew too well that after 8:00 p.m., Indiana Avenue and the areas around the courthouse turned into a ghost town. Only a few homeless or drunk individuals frequented the street.

He wondered why the kidnappers had not abducted him in front of his house. Then he realized how difficult it would have been to move out of the cul-de-sac, especially when neighbors were sitting on their porches and kids were playing or biking outside.

It was alarming to him that his staff believed him to be out of town handling a family emergency. How could he let them know he was in danger? He only hoped that Detective Manfredi and Attorney Perkins, whose appointments he had missed, would question his absence.

Boss's words rang in his ears: "You still think you're calling the shots." Had Boss been one of the many defendants he had sentenced? He tried to remember the significant cases he had handled. In one case, the defendant had attacked his lawyer and broken his nose. He still remembered the attorney's bloody face. He also remembered a defendant who had killed his mother while on PCP. He had cried during his entire trial and then, on the last day of the trial, had committed suicide by jumping from the courthouse's fourth floor to the lobby. That day when McNeil left the courthouse at five, three individuals were still washing the blood off the lobby's floor.

Boss's face did not resemble that of any defendant he had sentenced before. And for what it was worth, he had always thought he was fair in his decisions.

McNeil began typing; he knew how to tell his law clerk the decision was not his. He smiled, knowing that Doc could not understand his complicated legal argument.

Chapter 5

Attorney Perkins showed up in Judge McNeil's chambers for her four-thirty appointment on Friday, July 9. McNeil's secretary informed her that the judge was out of town.

"I'm sorry. When I gave you the appointment, I didn't know he'd left town to take care of a family emergency."

"I still would like to stay. He may show up or call you to reschedule my appointment."

"I'll be leaving at five. You're more than welcome to wait in his office," the secretary said.

Still bitter about McNeil's courtroom behavior, Amanda entered the judge's office but did not sit down. From McNeil's office on the second floor, one could see the court's entrance on Indiana Avenue. She walked to the window, hoping to see the judge's face among the individuals entering the courthouse. Amanda remembered how many times she had dreamed about this meeting—the meeting in which she'd finally tell the judge what a horrible person he was.

She had practiced in the superior court for only five years, but since her early days, she had heard terrible stories about Judge McNeil from other attorneys who had known him longer. She herself had experienced the judge's temperament each time he held her in contempt of court. Every time, she believed she was just doing her job—being a zealous attorney. The judge treated all attorneys poorly and sent their clients to jail for even low misdemeanor cases. While a group of attorneys were detailing their unpleasant experiences with the judge one day, they had all agreed that he had become worse four years ago. "Something terrible happened to the man," one attorney had said.

"What?" Amanda asked.

"The judge's daughter—his only child disappeared."

"You mean she hasn't been found yet?"

"No. After his wife's death, his daughter was everything to him."

Unlike some lawyers who showed sympathy for the judge's ordeal, Amanda detested McNeil and the way he embarrassed attorneys in front of their clients and colleagues. Now that she was leaving DC and the judge did not have any power over her, she was dying to tell him, "Judge McNeil, go to hell!"

It was 4:55 p.m., and the judge had not called to leave a message. She walked around the room and noticed two large framed pictures on the bookshelf behind the judge's desk. One photo showed a blond woman; the other was of a teenage girl. The two women were extremely beautiful and resembled each other. Obviously, these were pictures of the judge's wife and daughter.

As she was leaving the judge's chambers, Amanda ran into Detective Aristo Manfredi. "Are you following me?" she asked him. "Any time I'm here to see McNeil, you show up."

"Oh, no. I had a five o'clock appointment with the judge. They tell me he's out of town."

"I had a four-thirty appointment."

"The buzz is that you're leaving Washington. So who's gonna crucify me on the witness stand?" Manfredi chuckled.

"There are plenty of other attorneys around."

"But no one as feisty as you!"

After the judge's secretary confirmed there were no messages from the judge, Amanda and Manfredi left the chambers together.

"Why are you leaving us?" he asked. "And I'm eager to know where you're heading."

"I'm going back to Denver—my hometown."

"Practicing criminal law?"

"Yes. My uncle practices criminal law in Denver. He was getting ready to retire, but he couldn't resist when he got a complicated class-action case against a big pharmaceutical company. He needs me to handle his cases and eventually take over his practice."

"Is that the only reason?"

"Detective, I know my ex's scandal was covered by the *Washington Post*, and you read those articles—"

"But nothing has changed my attitude toward you. You should know that the officers and the detectives at DCMPD, and the prosecutors at the US attorney's office, have the highest degree of respect for you."

"I appreciate your kind words. Let's say that I'm leaving because I've had enough of Washington—and Judge McNeil."

"Now that you're going so far away, can I buy you dinner?"

"I'm sorry. I'm too upset with McNeil to enjoy any dinner."

"I insist."

"Maybe some other time."

Amanda said good-bye and left Manfredi, but she was not ready to go home. She walked to the Italian restaurant near the courthouse to have a drink. Just as she was sitting down at a booth, one of the superior court attorneys entered the restaurant. After a quick hi, he sat on the opposite side of Amanda's booth without asking her permission.

She didn't say anything, even though she had planned to be alone. *I'm leaving town; I don't have to put up with them anymore after this.*

"So when are you leaving?"

"In a few days."

"I heard about McNeil's behavior. I'm so sorry."

"How do you know?"

"You've been in superior court long enough to know that attorneys gossip too. Besides, this is more like protecting each other from judges like McNeil."

"Well, I don't have to see or deal with him anymore."

"The man has had a sad life. First, his young wife dies, and then the missing daughter—"

"That doesn't give him a license to be cruel."

"He's a character. Did you know he goes to church during the lunch recess and does charity work?"

"You're kidding?"

"No, that's true."

Amanda excused herself and walked to the bar to get a drink and was surprised to see Detective Manfredi standing there, staring at her with a naughty smile.

"Detective, you've got to stop following me."

"I came for a drink. You know this restaurant is a favorite place of the detectives."

"No, I didn't know that."

"You rejected my dinner invitation, but who's the guy you're having—"

"Oh, he's a lawyer from the superior court. He just indulged himself and sat there."

"I'm still jealous."

The attorney joined them at the bar, pointed to his cell phone, and said, "Ms. Perkins, I'm sorry, I have to run; this is an urgent matter."

He was already running out as Amanda said, "That's okay."

"May I join you now?" Manfredi asked.

"Okay, why not?"

Manfredi had barely sat down when his phone vibrated. He ignored it and asked Amanda if she'd like some wine. The phone vibrated again. After the waiter took their order, he apologized to Amanda and walked outside to listen to his voice mail.

The call was from Judge Bowen: "I need to see you immediately. I believe Judge McNeil has been kidnapped."

Chapter 6

Manfredi was not going to ignore Judge Bowen's shocking message, but Amanda was leaving Washington, and he didn't want to lose the only opportunity he had to tell her about his feelings.

After the waiter took their dinner orders and left, Aristo poured more wine for Amanda and himself. "Now that you're leaving Washington, I have to confess," he said as he sipped his wine. "I have had a crush on you since the day I met you in Judge McNeil's courtroom. After your divorce, only God knows how many times I tried to work up the nerve to ask you out."

"It wouldn't have worked, Detective," Amanda said, smiling. She took a gulp of her wine.

"Why not?"

"We were *always* on opposite sides. You were the prosecution witness in every case, testifying against my client ... don't you remember the attorney who got suspended for one year by the DC bar because her boyfriend was the cop who testified against her client? Even though she defended him brilliantly, the bar counsel ruled that she should've disclosed her relationship to her client."

"Does that mean that if I were not *always* a witness for the prosecution, you would've gone out with me?"

"Still, it wouldn't have worked. Look, you're a cop with a different mentality. You put people in jail, and you like Judge McNeil, for God's sake."

"Well, I like him because he tries to clean up the streets of Washington by putting the criminals in jail. But you get them out anyway," Manfredi said with a chuckle.

"It's my job to help them. Besides, as a citizen and a member of this community, I feel responsible for those so-called criminals."

"How's that?"

"If the community had afforded them a good education, jobs, and housing, maybe they wouldn't be stealing or selling drugs."

"I can't believe you're leaving DC."

"I'm not going to disappear. Washington is home to all national associations and hosts many conferences. I'll be back to attend some of those conferences, at least a few times a year."

"I don't participate in those conferences, and even if I *do* bump into you when you're in town, that's not enough," Aristo said, touching Amanda's hands and looking deep into her eyes.

They had finished their meals when Aristo's cell phone vibrated again. As much as he hated to take the call and interrupt his conversation with Amanda, he pulled out his phone from his pocket and opened it anyway. "Excuse me. I have to answer this call," he said to Amanda.

It was Judge Bowen again. "Detective Manfredi, could you please come and see me right away?"

"Where are you?"

"I'm still in my chamber. Judge McNeil's law clerk has received a strange e-mail from him."

Manfredi encouraged Amanda to accompany him to Judge Bowen's chambers. "It'll be short, I promise. I want to continue our conversation."

"We've been talking for an hour."

"That's not enough. You're leaving the city in a few days. I want to take you on a boat trip around Washington. Maybe you'll change your mind and stay." He chuckled. Manfredi saw Amanda's reluctance. "I promise, it will be short."

Amanda accepted Manfredi's offer and accompanied him to the courthouse. She stayed outside Judge Bowen's chamber, waiting for his return.

* * *

As soon as Manfredi entered Judge Bowen's chamber, the judge pointed to a three-page document laid out on his desk. "This is the most bizarre decision I've ever seen. He never throws out a confession, especially in a murder case."

"Which murder case?" Manfredi asked.

"Oh, I'm sorry. I forgot you handle only some of them simultaneously. This is the case of *United States v. Keshan Walker*."

"I'm not handling that case, but I know it's high-profile—the seventeen-year-old who's being tried as an adult for killing three girls."

"That's the one."

"What can I do for you?"

"Judge McNeil called the other day. Told his courtroom clerk he had to take care of a family emergency. Normally, he would've called me too. We've known each other since elementary school. I introduced him to his wife. We have lunch at least two or three times a week. And since his wife passed away, my wife and I have been inviting him to dinner every Friday."

"Your Honor, I still don't know how I can help you."

"McNeil's secretary told me that you had an appointment with him today. I know you cannot break your ethical rules, but I think the judge is in danger, and I need to know what he wanted to talk to you about."

"Judge, you know the confidentiality of—"

"C'mon, Detective. I know all about that. McNeil never grants a motion to suppress confessions, even in a simple theft case—much less in a triple-murder case that's covered by the media 24-7. Not only has he dumped the research and the writing of his opinion on his law clerk, which he never does, but he's also asked him to use a case that is so irrelevant. He cited a California Supreme Court case that involves a kidnapping of a police chief by a gang."

"You're sure the judge has been kidnapped?"

"I don't know. That depends on what he was going to talk to you about."

"He wanted me to locate a missing person."

"Oh my God—his daughter, Daphne. She disappeared four years ago. The judge hired two retired detectives, but no one could find her, not even the FBI."

"Do you think there's a connection between Daphne's disappearance and the judge's recent family emergency?"

"I don't know. The judge has only one sister. They don't have a good relationship. I called her today, but she hasn't heard from him since their dispute over Daphne's disappearance."

"So no family member has received any call asking for ransom money or anything?"

"No. McNeil is not a rich man. He only has a house in DC with a heavy mortgage, a beach house in Rehoboth, again with a mortgage, and maybe some twenty thousand dollars in the bank. *Rich* people get kidnapped."

"Maybe the kidnapper is trying to use the judge for other purposes."

"Like changing the outcome of Keshan Walker's case?"

"Exactly." Detective Manfredi paused to think over what the judge was suggesting. "Why don't you give me the name and address of the judge's sister? And some information on Daphne's relatives on her mother's side?"

"Fiona, McNeil's wife, was an only child. She had several cousins, but I don't know who they are or where they live. At this point, our best family contact is Margaret, McNeil's sister. She lives in Madison. I'll find her address."

"Madison, huh? I grew up in Minnesota, but my parents moved to Madison when I was in high school. I know the city well."

"That's wonderful," Judge Bowen said as he shuffled through some papers on his desk to find Margaret's address. "Here, this is the street address." He handed a piece of paper to Manfredi. "If you know the city, you won't have any problem finding her."

Manfredi looked at the address and smiled. "Not at all. She lives near the college campus."

Chapter 7

Leroy Walker had arrived at the Lorton federal prison in Virginia as a frustrated twenty-six-year-old who had never spent time in jail. He was angry with the judge who had sentenced him to eight years for selling two Ziploc bags of cocaine to an undercover agent. He was infuriated with his attorney. Not only had he failed to make a strong argument to get Leroy probation, but the attorney also had misled Leroy by reassuring him that because his prior drug convictions had been misdemeanors, he would most likely receive probation. He was angry with himself for insulting the judge by using profanities in his courtroom. The judge had originally sentenced him to four years, but with every "fuck you" Leroy uttered, the judge had added another year.

During his orientation at Lorton, his case manager informed him that with good behavior, he would probably serve only a few years in jail. Leroy promised himself that he would be on his best behavior and finish his term of incarceration without any problems. He felt lucky when they housed him in a minimum-security facility that had dormitories rather than cellblocks. Like other inmates, his work involved farming the land, rethreading tires, and even knitting sweaters. The pay was twenty-one to forty-five cents per hour. Although the working conditions were harsh, he did not complain.

He was a good cook and had always dreamed of opening his own restaurant. He had learned how to make delicious food from the master—his adoptive mother, Doris Walker. From the very first day he walked into Doris's home, he had followed her around the kitchen. Doris was surprised and extremely pleased that her twelve-year-old adopted son had an interest in the culinary arts.

Over the years, she had taught him everything she knew about cooking. Doris's specialty was chili beans. Some of her friends even said that Doris's chili beans were as good as Ben's chili—from Washington's famous restaurant on U Street.

Leroy made use of his cooking skills, befriended the chef in Lorton, and eventually became his assistant. Life in jail was not as horrible as he had imagined, yet he was worried about Doris, who had to go through kidney dialysis twice a week. And he worried about his five-year-old daughter, Samyra, and three-year-old nephew, Keshan. He missed the days when he would sit his daughter on his lap and read children's books to her. Samyra had given him a sense of real family. She had washed away Leroy's pain of not knowing his biological parents. Samyra was his blood, his world, and the reason he got out of bed every day. His girlfriend—Samyra's mother, Yvette—had reassured him that she would take care of their daughter, his mother, and his nephew, but Leroy didn't believe she was strong enough to keep the family together. Besides, where would she get the money? Her job as a part-time waitress didn't pay much.

Throughout his incarceration, he thought a lot about Doris. He remembered the first day they met. He was in a group home that housed juvenile delinquents. Doris Walker, a widow whose husband had been killed in Vietnam, adopted Leroy despite his lengthy juvenile record. When Doris began the adoption process, Leroy had already been arrested five times for unauthorized use of a motor vehicle, or UUV—a fancy legal term for stealing a car. Because he was always the passenger in the stolen car, the prosecutors had always dropped the charges, or the judge had given him a period of probation, ordering him to live in a group home.

Leroy had spent most of his life in different foster homes. Neighbors told him that before foster care, an old woman had raised him. The day his adoption papers were approved by a DC family court judge, Leroy felt for the first time that he had a family. Doris owned a nice, large house in northeast Washington. She offered Leroy a clean room, good food, decent clothes, and an education. Doris's older son acted like a young father, keeping Leroy out of trouble.

After finishing high school, Leroy found a job at the deli department of a supermarket near their home. Six months later, he started dating Yvette—a sexy brunette who had just started working in the deli. A year later, they had a daughter. Although she was a churchgoing woman, Doris didn't object when Yvette moved in.

Two years later, Doris's older son brought his baby, Keshan, home after his girlfriend dumped the baby on him. Doris loved children, and her five-bedroom house was large enough to accommodate her new family. And when Yvette quit her job, Doris had enough help to care for her grandchildren.

Leroy enjoyed a happy life until his brother was killed in a hit-and-run accident. A few months later, Doris was diagnosed with a kidney infection. Leroy panicked—he was the breadwinner, taking care of a family of five. When Doris saw the worried expression on Leroy's face, she sat him down and said, "Look, the mortgage is totally paid. With my husband's pension and your salary, we're gonna manage just fine."

"But my salary is not enough."

"Don't worry—God will provide."

Leroy felt in his gut that Doris was wrong. He lost his job at the supermarket a month later. Despite his efforts to find employment for months, he didn't have any luck finding a new job. But then he discovered how easily he could make money selling drugs. He was arrested twice for possession of narcotics—a misdemeanor charge that got him short periods of probation and a lecture from the judge. But the third time, he sold drugs to an undercover agent. The charge was felony distribution.

His attorney told him, "These undercover cases are hopeless. If we go to trial, you'll lose, and then the judge will be mad at you for wasting his time. Why don't you plead guilty? You'll probably get probation because you've had two successful probations before."

"But you told me the penalty for distribution was up to thirty years' jail time or five hundred thousand dollars, or both. Suppose the judge gives me jail time," Leroy said, confused.

"I've never seen anybody get the five-hundred-thousand-dollar fine or the thirty years. This is your first distribution. He can't give you more than a year."

"Hey, man, I cannot be in jail, even for one month. My family needs me."

"You won't get jail time." Leroy's attorney was new and had just started practicing at the DC superior court. He had never had a case before McNeil.

Leroy assumed that if he told the truth about his mother's kidney dialysis and explained that he was the only provider for the family of five, the judge would show some sympathy and give him a lenient sentence. He was wrong.

After Leroy finished his plea for leniency, Judge McNeil shook his head. "You expect me to let you stay in the community and sell drugs because you're supporting your family? Millions of people are supporting their family without breaking the law."

Leroy looked back to the audience in the courtroom and saw both Yvette and his daughter, Samyra, crying. He took a good look at Judge McNeil's face before he was taken to the holding cell behind the courtroom. *McNeil, one day you're gonna pay for this*, he thought.

Chapter 8

After he e-mailed his decision granting Keshan Walker's motion to suppress his confession, McNeil expected to receive a series of e-mails from his law clerk. After all, out of all the people who had worked with him, his law clerk would be the first one to be alarmed. McNeil had never granted any defense motion. When he didn't hear from anybody, McNeil panicked. *Where are they? What if everyone really does believe I'm out of town handling a family emergency?*

For days, he had expected FBI agents to storm in, knock down the door, arrest his kidnappers, and set him free. Though masking his anxiety, he was becoming more fearful for his life as his captivity continued. Now the only hope he had was his law clerk. As the triple-murder trial date approached, his law clerk was bound to contact him. He was puzzled as to why his secretary and Judge Bowen had not noticed that he had been missing for so long.

That night, after his kidnappers brought him his meal, he asked them how long they planned to keep him captive. Boss and Shorty laughed, but Doc, who was untying the judge's hands and feet, responded, "We told you. You're gonna be here for a few months."

"What about my murder trial, my cases?"

"Eventually, the murder trial will go to your good friend Judge Bowen. And that's exactly what we want—for *him* to handle the case."

"Are you guys related to Keshan Walker?"

"None of your damn business," Boss shouted from another corner of the room.

"Come on, Judge, loosen up. We're gonna show you a good time tonight because you granted Keshan's motion," Shorty said.

After McNeil finished his meal, Shorty pulled out a few marijuana cigarettes and offered one to the judge.

"I'm not a smoker," the judge said.

"Don't worry, this is *weed*. Take a few puffs."

"If I do that, will you let me walk in the yard and get some fresh air?"

Shorty looked at Boss, who nodded in agreement.

"Yes," he said.

The judge's first attempt at smoking marijuana was not successful, so Shorty taught him how. In a few minutes, McNeil felt high and began giggling for no reason. His kidnappers' conversations seemed hilarious. He had never felt this relaxed in his entire life. For a moment, he saw images of his wife and his daughter. The images faded soon, and he started laughing again.

He told his kidnappers he needed to go outside and get some fresh air. Shorty and Doc helped the judge walk to the backyard. At first, everything seemed hazy to him. But when his eyes got used to the moonlight, he noticed a wall of identical tall trees around the yard. He knew the name of those trees. He tried to remember it but couldn't.

After ten minutes of walking outside, the judge asked Shorty to take him back inside the house. On his way back to the building, he noticed that a big tarp now covered the hole that was supposed to be his grave.

Once inside, as his kidnappers joked and laughed, he dozed off in his chair several times. He finally rose and walked toward his room—the windowless room that looked like a walk-in closet. He collapsed onto his narrow folding bed and looked around for a few minutes. Unlike previous nights, he was too exhausted to think about the size of the room, which looked like the cellblock adjacent to his courtroom, or about his future in the hands of three criminals. The sound of the turning doorknob and the key signaled that Shorty was locking the door as he did every night. For the first time, McNeil didn't mind the screechy bed and didn't think about his missing daughter.

Chapter 9

Leroy was eager to get out of Lorton, but he was not complaining. Yvette visited him as often as she could. Sometimes she even brought Samyra and Keshan along. She assured him that his mother's kidney dialysis was going successfully and that she was feeling better.

When the Lorton facilities closed, Leroy and many inmates were transferred to a federal correctional facility in Hazelton, West Virginia. He felt lucky that the Bureau of Prisons did not have authority to transfer the DC inmates to a facility more than five hundred miles from their residences. Besides, he had only ten months left before he'd be eligible for parole.

As he counted the days until he'd be a free man again, he realized that Yvette had stopped visiting him since his transfer to Hazelton. She had not written a letter or attempted to contact him by phone. He called his home telephone number but found it disconnected. Another week went by, and there was still no visit from Yvette. He placed a collect call to his friend Montrel Johnson, who lived in Maryland, and asked him to check on his family and report back to him. "I wanna know what the hell is goin' on," he demanded.

A few days later, Montrel drove to Hazelton to visit Leroy. After a quick hug, they sat down on opposite sides of a table, and Leroy anxiously shot questions at his friend. "What's with Yvette? Why ain't she visitin' me no more?" He noticed that Montrel looked uncomfortable. "Hey, man, you seem scared. What's up with you? The guards ain't gonna handcuff you here. Sit down and tell me, how's Doris and everybody?"

"I don't know how to tell you. Doris died two days ago. I thought someone must have called you and told you."

"That bitch Yvette never calls me." Leroy banged his fist on the table, fighting tears.

"Yvette has been gone for a long time."

"What do you mean, 'has been gone'?"

"You know I live in PG County, and I don't go to DC no more. I just heard stuff."

"What stuff?"

"Rumors."

"What rumors?"

"Yvette wasn't waiting tables no more. She was bringing men home … Hey, man, why should I be the one to tell you this?" Montrel seemed agitated.

"To tell me what? Monty, don't fuck with me."

"One of her johns messed with Samyra and gave her HIV."

"*HIV*? She's only ten years old! Who's the motherfucker? I'm gonna kill him when I get out of here! I'm gonna kill that bitch first, then her john."

"Leroy, Yvette disappeared with Samyra. No one knows where they are."

"So who's watching my nephew Keshan?"

"Yvette found his mama and dumped him on her."

"So who's living in my house?"

"Yvette sold the house to some white folks from out of town. They've renovated it. It ain't lookin' like your house no more."

"That was Doris's house—my inheritance."

"Your neighbors tell me that Yvette fooled Doris into signing some papers, telling her that she was selling the house to buy her a kidney. But the papers said Doris was giving the house to Yvette. Doris died in a shelter."

Leroy could not hear any more. He felt like he was in a horror movie as he stared down at the table, weeping quietly. Suddenly, he stood, wiped his tears with his right sleeve, and took Montrel's hands. "You've got to help me go to Doris's funeral."

"How? Man, you're locked up."

"Go to the public defender's office. They're near the courthouse. Get an attorney to file a motion for me to go to my mother's funeral."

"What are you talking about?"

"Go, man. Don't waste time. The PDS attorneys know how to do this. I'm sure they can get the judge's permission to let me go for one day. Last month they did it for another inmate here."

* * *

A day passed, and there was no news from Montrel. The next morning, Leroy paced in his small cell, waiting for the warden to allow him to make a collect phone call. He was grateful that there was sympathy for people who had lost their loved ones. Growing impatient, he pounded on the walls once in a while, until his fist hurt and inmates in the two neighboring cells began yelling.

Around noon, he was taken to the warden's room. Montrel was waiting for the call. As soon as Leroy heard Montrel's voice, he asked, "When do they come to pick me up?"

"The attorney did everything, but I'm sorry, it takes time," Montrel said, his voice cracking.

"What do you mean, it takes time?"

Montrel explained that the PDS attorney had immediately prepared the necessary papers and gone to the superior court judge responsible for reviewing emergency motions, but the judge did not have power to sign the order.

"What the fuck does that mean? He's a judge, ain't he?"

"Because you're in a federal correctional facility, only a judge in a federal court can order your release."

"Why didn't she go to a federal judge?"

"She wants to do that, but because it's the weekend, it has to wait until Monday."

"Man, the funeral is tomorrow. I've got to get out of here today."

"I'm sorry. I don't know what else—"

Leroy banged the telephone on the wall before Montrel could finish his sentence.

* * *

Late that afternoon, Leroy reported to the kitchen as usual to help the cook prepare dinner. Luckily for him, the food deliveryman had just arrived. As part of his kitchen duties, Leroy was tasked with helping the driver carry cartons and boxes of food items from his truck. He had a good relationship with the deliveryman, but on that afternoon, after greeting him, Leroy jumped him and punched him in the face many times.

The unexpected attack shocked the man to the point that he couldn't defend himself. Leroy's final punches knocked him unconscious. He yanked the duct tape off a box and pressed it against the man's mouth. He then took off the man's uniform, which fit him perfectly, and perused the deliveryman's wallet—a credit card, a picture ID, and fifty dollars were inside.

Leroy grabbed the deliveryman's keys and baseball cap and climbed into the huge truck. He pulled the cap low enough to cover his face above his eyebrows. His heart pounded when the guard took the delivery papers at the prison gate, but the guard didn't even raise his gaze to look at him. He merely stamped the papers and opened the gate.

Leroy was a free man with no sense of direction. Knowing he had to get rid of the truck, he drove aimlessly until he found himself in a quiet residential area. It was getting dark when he parked the truck near a small playground. During his teenage years, some older kids had taught him how to steal a car by hotwiring the ignition. He scanned the vehicles parked in front of the houses, eliminating the new models equipped with modern security systems. An old, dirty station wagon caught his eye. While hotwiring the car, he didn't notice the young boy watching him about seventy feet away.

As soon as he reached Manassas, Virginia, he found a cheap department store. Using the deliveryman's credit card, he bought himself a new suit, a shirt, a hat, a pair of sneakers, and dark sunglasses. After changing into his new clothes, he abandoned the station wagon in a remote area of the department store's parking lot and hailed a cab. He asked the cab driver to take him to the nearest metro station.

By the time Leroy arrived at Latisha's place, it was after midnight. He trusted that Latisha, his nephew's mother, would help him. He sneaked into the basement through one of the windows with no difficulty, but he was hungry and tired. He tiptoed to the kitchen upstairs and fixed a sandwich. After he finished his meal, exhaustion took over, and he fell asleep in one of the basement's large closets.

The sound of hurried footsteps woke him in the morning. He heard Latisha's voice and a man's voice. When he put his right ear close to the closet door, he realized the man was Montrel. The conversation revealed that his mother would be taken to the nearby cemetery where his brother was buried. After everyone was gone, Leroy sneaked out of the house and walked toward the cemetery.

With his large hat, bearded face, and dark glasses, he was certain that no one would recognize him. When he arrived at the graveyard, he stood in front of a stranger's gravestone, far away from the funeral crowd that had gathered around Doris's grave. With his sad face and tearful eyes, he was sure every passerby would be fooled into thinking the tombstone before him belonged to a loved one. However, Leroy's concentration was on everything happening seventy-five feet away, near his mother's coffin.

He recognized Doris's relatives and friends who had come to pay their last respects. Everyone was there except Samyra and Yvette.

The absence of police officers put him at ease. He wondered how he could get in touch with Montrel, who could help him escape town. In Hazelton, Leroy had befriended a drug kingpin. The man had a large ranch he wanted Leroy to look after when he was out. Since Leroy had only ten months left on his incarceration, the kingpin had given him the address. At first, Leroy had been suspicious of why a powerful man would ask him for help, but when the kingpin explained that he was making a deal with the government and going into a witness protection program for a period of time, Leroy decided to trust him. The man had given Leroy the location of the keys to his ranch too. All Leroy needed was Montrel's help.

When Doris's coffin was lowered into her grave, Leroy felt a rage he'd never felt before. He longed for revenge, but to his surprise, neither Yvette nor the man who had molested their ten-year-old child was at the top of his list. The first target to come to mind was the man responsible for all his miseries—Judge McNeil, the judge whose harsh sentence had destroyed his family.

Leroy stared at the grave under his feet, but his mind was millions of miles away. He would kidnap McNeil, take him to the kingpin's ranch, and torture him. Leroy's daydream was interrupted when he heard a voice behind him.

"Freeze! Don't move. Put your hands on your head." In a moment, someone grabbed Leroy's hands from behind and put him in handcuffs. Two deputy US marshals escorted him to a police cruiser hidden behind a large structure in the cemetery. He saw four more police officers waiting for him.

Chapter 10

Because he had been arrested on a Saturday afternoon, Leroy had to spend two nights in the DC jail before he could be arraigned as a fugitive in the DC superior court. His court-appointed attorney advised him that since the offenses had occurred in another jurisdiction, a DC judge didn't have authority to decide on the merit of the case.

He would only look at the charging documents, the seal of the West Virginia authorities that had issued extradition, and the accompanying affidavit.

The attorney also explained that if Leroy challenged the fugitive documents, he would have a right to an extradition hearing before the chief judge of the DC superior court. In order to get that hearing, though, he would have to wait for thirty days in the DC jail.

Leroy didn't waive his right to an extradition hearing even though he knew the authorities from West Virginia would come get him as soon as they could. The thirty days in the DC jail would allow him to have visitors like Montrel and other friends. He needed to gather information about Judge McNeil, Yvette, and his daughter.

Montrel and a few of Leroy's friends retained an attorney to represent him in the West Virginia court. They paid the attorney five thousand dollars cash in advance to negotiate a pre-indictment plea bargain with the prosecutor.

According to the terms of the agreement, Leroy had no choice but to plead guilty to a charge of felony escape from a federal correctional facility. All his attorney could do was break the single felony charge of robbery against the deliveryman into two misdemeanor charges of assault and theft in the second degree.

Leroy was back in jail again. But unlike his previous stint, when he spent his jail time in minimum security, this time he had to spend the first six months of his incarceration in maximum-security solitary confinement. Living in solitary confinement was not easy, but it gave Leroy a lot of time to think about his life and his future. He promised himself that this time he would finish his term without any incidents and find his freedom. The thought of revenge gave him the patience to endure the harshness of a captive life. Leroy had only one wish—to live long enough to get his revenge. Judge McNeil had to pay for what he had done to him and his family.

During the last year of his incarceration, Leroy met two other inmates who had also been victimized by Judge McNeil's harsh sentences. Darnell Lewis had been a first-year med student at Howard University. His world fell apart when he found his father bleeding in bed one night. Darnell's father told him that he had killed a man, and if he went to the hospital, he would be arrested.

Darnell pleaded with his father. "You can tell them it was in self-defense."

"No, you don't understand. They're a gang. They'll kill you. Please go and get me some medicine."

Darnell then broke into one of the medical labs at Howard University Hospital and stole several vials of morphine and other medications he needed. He also forged the name and signature of one of the hospital doctors he knew and wrote a prescription for antibiotics. He was on his way out of the lab when a security guard stopped him and asked him why he was there after midnight. His explanation was not good enough. He attempted to escape, but the three-hundred-pound, six-foot-four security guard overpowered and detained him. When the police arrived, the security guard handed them the stolen morphine and the forged prescription.

During the sentencing, Judge McNeil had laughed at Darnell's attorney when she commented, "He's a medical student with a bright future. This was a terrible mistake."

McNeil retorted, "This community is better off without a future doctor who breaks into a hospital lab, steals medication, and writes a prescription by forging a doctor's name."

When Darnell didn't come home that night, his father sought the help of a friend, who removed the bullet from his shoulder and got medication for him from a drug dealer on the street. He survived the gunshot wound but had a heart attack when McNeil sentenced Darnell to ten years in jail. He died of another heart attack during Darnell's second year of incarceration.

Melvin Hill's experience with Judge McNeil was part of yet another heartbreaking story. He had been released on parole after three years of incarceration for distribution of cocaine and PCP. The rumor in the neighborhood was that his wife had slept around while he was in jail.

"I confronted her, but she denied it," Melvin told Leroy and Darnell. "When I tried to fuck her, she refused, so I slapped her a few times. When I finished fucking her, she ran out. I thought she had gone to her mother's house, but she showed up in our bedroom with two cops."

"For assault?" Leroy asked.

"No, for rape or whatever they call it now ..." Melvin paused and tapped on his temple. "First-degree sexual assault."

"How much time did McNeil give you?" Darnell asked.

"Ten years. When I kept telling him she was my *wife*, he told me he could've given me life imprisonment. I'm telling you, those bitches out there, they've learned how to get rid of their men. They call the cops. They always believe them bitches."

"That was a tough sentence," Leroy commented.

"That's not the only beef I have with McNeil. When I was incarcerated, the neighborhood gang got my sixteen-year-old boy involved in selling dope. One night, a deal went bad. Guys started shooting at each other, and my son got killed. As far as I'm concerned, McNeil killed my son. When I was out in the community, no drug dealer dared get near my boy."

The three men whose lives had been destroyed by Judge McNeil formed a pact. With Montrel's help, Leroy gathered information about the judge and shared it with Darnell and Melvin. He never told Montrel why he needed the information; he didn't want to implicate him. Montrel was like a younger brother, always ready to help. Leroy knew that if something happened to him, Montrel would take care of Samyra and Keshan.

When Leroy was released, the first item on his agenda was to find Judge McNeil and get his revenge. But he had to wait a while longer for Darnell and Melvin to finish their jail sentences.

He failed in a series of attempts to locate Yvette and his daughter, so he concentrated on his nephew, Keshan, who was now thirteen years old.

He also needed to find a job. With the money he had earned in jail doing various jobs, he could get by for only one month. He remembered he had two hundred dollars in his savings account, so he made a trip to the bank near Doris's old house to collect his money. The bank teller shocked him when he said that Leroy had twenty thousand in his account.

"Where did the money come from?" he asked.

The bank teller traced back the transaction. A check signed by Doris Walker had been deposited in Leroy's savings account several years earlier. When Leroy saw the date on the screen of the teller's computer, he held back his tears. The deposit had been made a few months before Doris's death. Leroy thanked the teller, took a bag full of hundred-dollar bills, and left the bank.

* * *

Latisha Williams, Keshan's mother, had always been attracted to and had a good relationship with Leroy. Her opinion of Leroy hadn't changed, even when he hid in her basement and caused the DCMPD to go after her. She had faced criminal charges of hiding a fugitive, aiding and abetting a fugitive, and obstruction of justice, but the charges were dropped later when the prosecutor couldn't find any evidence connecting Latisha with Leroy's escape.

As soon as she heard that Leroy had been released, she called him and offered a room in her house. "I need someone to keep an eye on Keshan," she said. "You're his uncle and the only one he listens to."

Leroy had spent a few weeks in Montrel's house in Silver Spring, but he had been born and raised in DC. Latisha knew that he missed the city because all his friends and Doris's relatives lived there.

Leroy accepted Latisha's offer and kept encouraging Keshan to focus on his education. "I want you to be the first Walker to go to college and get a degree, you hear me?" he often said.

Leroy was careful not to blow Doris's money. He spent two thousand dollars to buy himself a nice truck. It was summertime, so he figured he could easily make money mowing lawns. He bought a used lawn mower and a leaf blower. He targeted rich homes with big yards in fancy northwest areas of the city.

On the weekends, he sometimes took Keshan with him, which got his nephew interested in the business. His intention was not to leave any free time for Keshan to get involved with drugs or any other criminal activities. He felt he had failed his mother and daughter, so he wasn't going to fail Keshan.

Latisha welcomed Leroy's supervision of her son. To show her gratitude, she prepared delicious meals for him, cleaned his room, and acted like a girlfriend. But she soon found out that Leroy was not interested in her and considered her more a sister-in-law than anything else.

* * *

Finding Yvette and Samyra had become an obsession for Leroy. Every time someone gave him a lead, he got behind the wheel of his truck and drove to the location, hoping he would find them.

The last lead took him to Baltimore. He spent several hours looking for the address he had been given, but at the end of the day, he realized Yvette was smarter than him and had managed to get the support of her family members. The address in Baltimore belonged to her cousin. The relative pretended he hadn't heard from her in years. Leroy sensed he was lying, but he didn't know that Yvette had just escaped an hour before his arrival.

There was nothing he could do. He couldn't risk getting into a fight and finding himself back in jail again. Years of incarceration had taught him something—to control his anger and play it cool. He would have loved to kill Yvette, but he had decided that he would not even touch her. All he wanted was to get his daughter back.

After a dozen futile trips to various cities, as close as Baltimore and as far as South Carolina, Leroy stopped searching. It was time for him to concentrate on his other obsession—finding Judge McNeil. It didn't take him long to find McNeil's home address. He simply followed him one day. McNeil took the Red Line train at the Judiciary Square metro station on a daily basis. He got off at Van Ness and walked to his house located at the end of a cul-de-sac near Connecticut Avenue. The house's big yard was an attractive place for a man with a lawn mower.

Leroy left fliers in the judge's mailbox, as well as the mailboxes of his neighbors, who also had large yards. He used a phony name for a nonexistent company and a long list of services. He was not surprised when he received several job offers, and before long, he was servicing several of the judge's neighbors. He had intentionally lowered the price to tempt the home owners to call him.

Then one day, Leroy's dream came true: McNeil called. "The old man who mows my yard is sick. I need to hire someone new. Can you provide some references?"

Leroy gave the names and telephone numbers of five others he serviced in the neighborhood.

"These are my neighbors. I'll call them, and if they are happy with your services, you're hired."

Leroy was hired by the judge the following week. He soon found out that McNeil was living with his only daughter, Daphne. She was a beautiful girl with large blue eyes and thick lashes. She always wore her blond hair in a ponytail. She was fifteen—just like Samyra, his daughter, who had been raped at age ten and diagnosed with HIV, the daughter he had not seen for many years.

Leroy knew the judge left the courthouse daily at 6:00 p.m., so to avoid face-to-face contact with him, he informed him that he worked only during weekdays until five o'clock. The judge resisted the idea at first because he preferred weekend services, but when he learned that all his neighbors had agreed to Leroy's afternoon services, he agreed too. Leroy suggested 3:00 p.m. because this was the time Daphne would get home from school.

Kidnapping Daphne would be the best revenge—he wanted the judge to taste the agony he had felt when his ten-year-old was raped—but Daphne always came home with one or two of her classmates.

McNeil also had an African American maid named Tonya. She was light-skinned and in her early forties. Her straightened shoulder-length black hair enhanced her cheekbones. Leroy asked her out the very first day they met, but she informed him that she had a boyfriend who worked at the courthouse. Leroy lost his interest in Tonya when he felt she had an attitude and acted like a white woman. Yet he prodded Tonya as much as he could to gather information about the judge. He befriended Daphne and chatted with her whenever Tonya was working inside the house. He often wondered how he could kidnap and rape a sweet girl who brought him cool lemonade when he was hot and thirsty. But he had to punish and torture the judge.

Chapter 11

McNeil felt too drowsy to get up; Boss had to drag him to the kitchen to eat his breakfast. He didn't have much of an appetite, but Boss encouraged him to eat some of the oatmeal he had prepared. The judge ate a few spoonfuls and drank half his coffee. When he began walking back toward his room, Boss stopped him. He took the judge to the computer room and pointed to his laptop.

"You have to write another motion for us," he said.

"Motion?" the judge said mockingly. "Attorneys write motions."

"He means a decision," Doc said.

"What decision?"

"Keshan's public defender has found a witness who can testify that Keshan's codefendant lied to the police," Boss said. "She has written a second bond-review motion asking for Keshan's release to a halfway house."

Doc showed the judge a copy of the motion he had printed from his computer.

McNeil skimmed the two-page motion and shook his head. "The prosecutor will run to the DC Court of Appeals, screaming all the way, to stop the release of a defendant accused of killing three people."

"The motherfucking codefendant killed the three girls, not Keshan!" Boss shouted. "He lied to the police because he had heard that juveniles didn't get more than two years' jail time. You've read the police report. Don't you remember what it said?"

"No, I don't. I have a headache, and everything seems fuzzy to me right now."

Boss looked accusingly at Shorty. "You gave him too much weed last night."

"Hey, man, you're a judge. Do you really believe a thirty-year-old man was afraid of a seventeen-year-old kid?" Boss continued. "The codefendant told the police that Keshan invited the three girls to dinner. He said when the girls refused to have sex and decided to leave, Keshan gave him his gun and told him to 'kill the bitches,' and he did because he was afraid of Keshan. Does that make sense to you?"

"If what you're saying is true, why did he confess?" McNeil asked.

"Because Keshan was afraid of what his codefendant would do to him or his mother," Boss responded.

"C'mon, Judge. No one was holding a gun to the codefendant's head, ordering him to kill," Shorty said, angry. "The man had the gun. He could have turned the gun on Keshan and threatened to kill him."

"If the case is that strong, why don't you let the jury decide?" the judge asked Boss.

"The codefendant has cut a deal with the prosecutor. He'll testify against Keshan and another defendant in another murder case. Then he goes into ... what they call 'em ... a witness protection program."

"How do you know?"

"We have people in jail who report to us."

"If I write this decision, will you please let me go?" the judge pleaded. "I'll send my resignation to the chief judge, and I will never give your physical descriptions to the police. I'll tell them you wore masks the whole time."

Boss laughed. He pulled out a chair and sat opposite the judge. "You haven't been punished for what you did to us," he said.

"What did I do?"

"I think it's time to tell him," Doc suggested.

"We'll tell you about us. By the time you're in jail, we'll be in Mexico anyway," Boss said.

Over the next twenty minutes, McNeil heard details about how his harsh sentences had ruined the lives of his three kidnappers and their families. Sometimes he closed his eyes, unable to look at the faces of his victims anymore. Sometimes he wished they would stop talking. He kept looking at the design on an old rug in the room. He sensed that his face must have shown his internal pain because his kidnappers suddenly stopped talking.

"I'm sorry. I'm terribly sorry," he said, still avoiding eye contact with the angry men.

"You gave me ten years for fucking my wife," Shorty said.

"You could've gotten up to—"

"I know. You told me before. Up to life," Shorty said. "You told me that. But what kind of stupid law is that?"

"I don't make the laws. I apply them when—"

Shorty jumped unexpectedly from his chair, rushed to the judge, and hit him hard in the head with his closed fist. McNeil lost his balance and fell to the floor.

"I hold you responsible for my boy's death. If I wasn't in jail, no one would have dared have my boy dealin' drugs."

Doc pulled Shorty away and helped the judge get up from the floor. He sat him back in his chair again. McNeil massaged the top of his head with both hands. The pain of the blow was surely visible on his face.

"How do you explain my sentence?" Doc asked. "My attorney made a deal with the prosecutor that would reduce my sentence to only two years. When you asked me three dozen questions, I made a mistake answering one, and you tore up the plea agreement and forced me to have a jury trial, knowing damn well I would get ten years in jail."

"I didn't think the jury would convict you."

"I saw your face when they read the verdict. You were happy with it."

"That's not true. Judges are not supposed to show any reaction when the verdict is read."

"I hold you responsible for my father's fatal heart attack. The man couldn't bear seeing me in jail for ten years. He expected me to become a doctor and have a good life."

"I wasn't responsible for your stealing medicine from a medical lab, or forging a prescription, or assaulting a security guard."

"You're right. You weren't. But you could've accepted my plea. You could've acted compassionately and let a medical student fulfill his dream."

McNeil didn't say anything; he felt like his brain was exploding and stared at the rug again, attempting to find his balance. Doc and Shorty left the room. McNeil's heart raced. He was scared to be alone with the man they all called Boss.

"Look up, Judge!" Boss ordered. "You don't remember me, do you?"

"I've handled thousands of cases. I can't remember every case," McNeil responded and then immediately lowered his gaze.

"So a defendant is just a file number to you, not a human being with a face, huh?"

McNeil continued staring at the rug. Fear crawled along his skin.

"Look at me when I'm talking to you."

McNeil looked up and saw Boss's angry face.

"What do you have to say about my sentence?" he demanded. "You could've given me probation or short-term jail. You gave me four years for selling two lousy Ziploc bags to an undercover, and every time I said 'fuck you,' you added one more year to the original sentence. What kind of monster are you? I told you my mother was on kidney dialysis. I had a daughter and a nephew to support. You didn't give a shit. I lost my home, my baby mama became a prostitute, and one of her johns raped my ten-year-old daughter and gave her HIV. My baby mama has disappeared with my daughter. If I hadn't been searching for my daughter every day, Keshan, *my nephew*, wouldn't be facing murder charges now."

"I'm so sorry. You're right. I was wrong in my—"

"A human being can be wrong. You are a monster. Admit it!" Boss shouted.

"When my wife died, a part of me died too. I had so much pain I couldn't see other people's pain. I'm sorry. I understand your pain. I have a missing daughter too. I've been searching to find her for the past four years now," the judge said as he lowered his gaze and stared at the rug again.

Boss became quiet, letting McNeil bask in Boss's hatred for a few moments before he left the room. Once he closed the door behind him, he flashed a satisfied smile. *McNeil, your real punishment will come soon.*

Chapter 12

As she was packing her books and clothes, Amanda reminisced about the night before—the unexpected, pleasant dinner date with Detective Manfredi. After what she had gone through—her husband's embezzlement, her much-gossiped-about divorce—she had really needed that relaxed, romantic boat trip on the Potomac River. Although there had been dozens of other couples around them, she felt like the boat, the river, and the night had belonged to her and her detective admirer. The man was seriously interested in her. But as usual, the timing was wrong. She was leaving Washington in two days. History was repeating itself. Amanda couldn't help remembering other occasions when she'd had to leave behind the man she liked.

She remembered how painful it had been to say good-bye to her high school boyfriend in Colorado Springs. When her uncle accepted a job offer from a large law firm in Denver, Amanda had reluctantly accompanied him. Uncle Frank and his wife had cared for her since she was sixteen, when she had lost both parents in a multiple-car crash on I-70.

Then, after graduating from Boston University, she'd had to leave her college boyfriend behind. When the UCLA Law School offered her a three-year scholarship, she was thrilled with the news, but he didn't have any interest in living on the West Coast. She had faced the same dilemma once more after landing a job at the prestigious law firm of Carter and McDougal in Washington. Her native Californian boyfriend hadn't wanted to leave Los Angeles.

Finally, she had accepted that she was too ambitious to sacrifice her career for men. Why couldn't she meet Mr. Right at the right time and in the right place? But as she delved into her past, she realized she *had* met the right man in the right place and at the right time.

Or at least she thought she had.

* * *

In her early days in Washington, Amanda had admired everything about the city. With its museums, art galleries, theaters, and the Kennedy Center, Washington seemed as cultural as New York City—Amanda's favorite town on the East Coast.

She rented an apartment in a high-rise building near Dupont Circle and used the metro to commute to work. Her law firm, Carter and McDougal, one of the top large law factories in town, occupied an entire building in downtown Washington.

From the outside, the building looked like any other commercial structure, but inside, it was more like a mansion. The partners' offices and their conference room were located on the top floor of the building, giving them a view of the Washington Monument, the White House, and the Capitol.

When she arrived in Washington, she knew only one person: Gabrielle, a former classmate at Boston University and the daughter of the Argentine ambassador. In less than a month, Gabrielle had taken Amanda to a dozen diplomatic receptions and events held on Embassy Row. Amanda soon found out why Washington was known as the city of lobbyists, lawyers, and politicians—many former congressional representatives, senators, and diplomats had stayed in the city and now worked as lobbyists or consultants. She met dozens of them during those embassy events. Fascinated by the politicians' wives, she wondered why these highly educated women had decided to stay in the shadows of their husbands—something Amanda could never do.

When she first started working for Carter and McDougal, she was surprised by the limited number of female attorneys in a law firm that boasted three hundred lawyers. She was only the twentieth woman hired. Before her arrival, the firm had also promoted a female attorney to the rank of partner after she brought a ten-million-dollar client to the firm. The only female partner, however, didn't make any effort to promote other women. She didn't even acknowledge Amanda's frequent hellos when they passed in the hallways.

Amanda noticed that the male attorneys in the firm exhibited a certain air of superiority over female associates, who mostly helped the firm's partners. During conferences and meetings, legal arguments or suggestions by female attorneys were either ignored or not taken seriously. Amanda promised herself early on that she would not allow them to ignore her.

Instead of hanging her degrees on the walls of her office, she placed a small, framed cartoon on her desk that reflected the firm's attitude. It depicted a bulky middle-aged male attorney shaking hands with a woman in her twenties and saying, "So you got a law degree. How cute!"

Because of her major in criminology and several essays she had published in prestigious criminal law journals, Carter and McDougal assigned Amanda to work with the senior partner who handled only white-collar crime cases. One day, when the partner came to Amanda's office to express his appreciation for her work on a difficult case, he noticed the framed cartoon on her desk. "That's cute," he said. "Oh, I'm sorry. I didn't mean to use the word *cute*. I meant funny."

Amanda only smiled. Pretty soon, that partner as well as every other attorney in the firm had to take the young female associate from Denver, Colorado, very seriously.

Amanda didn't have much of a social life and didn't go out too often, except for the few parties she accompanied Gabrielle to, and she resented the male attorneys she met in Washington because of their arrogance. Later, when she had to work with attorneys in the firm's branch in New York City, she decided that every male attorney in a major city must consider himself one of God's gifts to humankind.

After living in Washington for a short time, she stopped dating attorneys altogether. She had grown sick and tired of hearing about their triumphs. She had also noticed that anytime she won a case, she lost a male attorney admirer. It seemed to her that every attorney she dated ended up competing with her. So when the firm's accountant asked her out, she accepted with no hesitation.

Brian was six feet tall, and with his wide shoulders and chest, he looked more like an athlete than an accountant. He had intelligent brown eyes and a dimple in his square chin. Maybe it wasn't his charm or sense of humor that attracted Amanda. It was possible she was attracted to him simply because he was not an attorney.

After three months of living together, they got married. Amanda couldn't believe her luck. She had finally found a man she loved, and this time, unlike her previous relationships, they both lived in the same city and worked for the same firm.

But Amanda's fairy-tale marriage didn't last very long. One day, two uniformed officers knocked on her door, showed her an arrest warrant, read Brian his Miranda rights, and took him away in handcuffs.

Chapter 13

Carter and McDougal fired Amanda when she chose to represent her husband in the ten-million-dollar embezzlement lawsuit the firm had brought against him.

"Surely you understand," a senior partner told her. "He's stolen millions of dollars from us. We'll have a conflict-of-interest issue if you represent him against the firm."

Amanda believed Brian at first when he claimed that he was innocent and that there was a conspiracy against him created by the firm's junior accountants. But as the evidence gathered by her private investigator piled up on her desk, she discovered not only Brian's illegal transactions but also his secret love affairs. He had paid two million dollars in cash for his house on Massachusetts Avenue. He had deposited millions of dollars in different banks in Aruba, Bermuda, and the Bahamas. He had also been paying the expenses of one woman living in DC and another in Aruba for several years, even after his marriage to Amanda.

She was in shock for the first few days. She kept questioning her own intelligence. How could she be married to a man for three years and not know he had love affairs with two other women? Why had she trusted him and never questioned his frequent business trips?

After a period of self-pity and a lot of crying, she realized this was not the time for her to feel like a victim. She had to act like a lawyer. She realized that Brian needed her. Years of legal training and practice had taught her how to suppress her emotions and solve the problem. In her mind, Brian was no longer a cheating, lying husband. He was a client who needed her as a lawyer, not a vengeful wife.

She hired the best white-collar-crime law firm in town to represent her husband and promised the attorneys she would work with them anytime they needed her assistance. She continued visiting Brian in jail and holding his hands, but during her last visit, she gave him the divorce settlement agreement she had drafted. In it, she had not asked him for anything except his consent to divorce. Brian realized he couldn't save his marriage when Amanda showed him incriminating documents that proved he had two mistresses.

"Please, at least take the house on Massachusetts Avenue," he said, acting ashamed.

"You need that to pay your attorneys' fees."

"I want you to know that I've never loved any woman in my life the way I love you."

"Thanks."

* * *

Amanda had read somewhere that there were nine women available for every single man in DC and that the ratio of lawyers to DC residents was three to one. She was divorced and without a job in a city full of lawyers and single women. Because of the notoriety that Brian had brought to her life, the majority of lawyers in town had read about her in the *Washington Post*.

After receiving a dozen polite rejection letters, she stopped applying for jobs in big law firms. She finally found a job working for the Federal Criminal Defense Program. Financed and supervised by Congress, FCDP paid for court-appointed attorneys who represented indigent defendants.

After her first meeting with the chief director of the program, Amanda felt that he was a godsend, an angel there to help her. Within her first few months of work at the superior court, the director had given her so many cases that she didn't have time to ruminate over her failed marriage or the loss of her job with a famous law firm.

She found most of the judges in the criminal division of the DC superior court to be fair, if not compassionate. But then there were a few hardliners she couldn't tolerate. The worst one in that group was Judge Walter McNeil. At first, Amanda had believed the judge was mean to her in particular because she defended her clients zealously. But she soon found out that her disdain for the judge was shared by other attorneys who had known him longer.

She was astonished when she heard that Fredrick Bowen—her *favorite* judge—was McNeil's best friend. She found the two judges to be so different, not only in their appearance but also in their personalities. McNeil stood at five feet eleven—Amanda's height. He was a slim man with thinning brown hair who always looked bored, or perhaps tired. His unsmiling tight lips and arched eyebrows seemed to suggest he didn't trust anyone. When he wrinkled his forehead, it was as though he saw himself as the wise guy, the senior player in the criminal justice system. With him, it seemed, the defendant was always guilty until proven innocent. During trials, he couldn't forget his prosecutorial background. Sometimes when he made a procedural ruling or sentenced her clients harshly, Amanda imagined that he had just disrobed himself and taken a seat at the prosecutor's table.

Then there was Judge Bowen. Standing six foot three with a wide torso, Judge Bowen resembled a college football player. His light-hazel eyes were friendly. His thick ash-blond hair, although grayish at the sideburns, gave him a youthful look. His constant smile and sense of humor entertained the attorneys and put their clients at ease. Unlike Judge McNeil, who upon graduation from law school had joined the US attorney's office as a prosecutor, Judge Bowen had spent a few years at the DC Public Defender Service and had represented hundreds of indigent defendants. Attorneys dreamed of appearing before Judge Bowen. Not only did he know everyone by his or her name, but he also respected and helped their clients beyond their expectations.

One day during one of Amanda's trials, when the prosecutor told Judge Bowen that a 911 tape recording was not available, the judge stood from his chair and said, "Let's go next door to the police department and see why, after so many months, Ms. Perkins cannot have her discovery."

As the judge (still dressed in his black robe), Amanda, and the prosecutor headed toward 300 Indiana Avenue, the prosecutor's cell phone vibrated. He answered it promptly and then turned to the judge and said, "Your Honor, we don't have to go to DCMPD. My supervisor just authorized me not to use the tape against the defendant." The judge smiled, turned around, and headed back toward the superior court.

Getting used to every judge's policies was not Amanda's only problem. She never got used to the living conditions of some of her clients. Most of them lived in dangerous, drug-infested areas in Washington. Once, a cab driver refused to drive Amanda to an address on the southeast side of town, even at two in the afternoon, in broad daylight.

"In Southeast, even some residents are scared to come out of their homes at night," a client once told her.

Amanda felt lucky to receive the assistance of Mike Franklin, one of the most experienced investigators who worked for the FCDP. Mike, a tall, good-looking man who resembled a basketball player, was always available to take Amanda to the DC jail or to do crime-scene investigation in dangerous places. Mike was the one who taught Amanda that when an African American client introduced someone as his cousin, chances were he was not his real cousin. "When African Americans are close or feel someone's like family, they call them a cousin," he said.

Mike also had to comfort Amanda every time they visited a client at the DC jail. She felt the jail was located in the most depressing part of the city, near a hospital and a cemetery. She never got used to the place. She had witnessed political, financial, and social powers in Washington, but her new job was exposing her to the other face of the city—the face of the powerless and the poor.

The tale of the two cities became more of a reality when, one day, Gabrielle stopped by Amanda's apartment and insisted on taking her out. Amanda pleaded with her for a rain check, wanting to stay home. She was tired after long hours of crime-scene investigation and visits with three clients in the DC jail.

"I'm not going to take no for an answer," Gabrielle said.

Amanda knew that Gabrielle would take her to another embassy reception, so she put on an evening gown. Japan's embassy was their first stop. Amanda saw a small, artificial, indoor lake for the first time in her life. She gazed at the fish and the lilies while trying to forget her day.

At their second stop, at the Dutch embassy, the building's large foyer and Washington's social elite—the A-list—resembled glamorous scenes from Hollywood movies. Despite her elegant gown, Amanda felt she didn't belong there. She couldn't forget the DC jail, the deafening sounds of the metallic bar doors closing behind her, and the faces of her clients—clients who would never get invited to an embassy event.

* * *

Amanda looked down from her window seat on the plane and whispered good-bye to the city of politicians, diplomats, lawyers, and lobbyists—the city she had called home for ten years. Her painful divorce and the embarrassment she had felt after she was fired had washed away any good memories she had in Washington, except one—her boat trip on the Potomac River and the romantic dinner date she'd had with Detective Manfredi. *Will I ever see him again?*

Chapter 14

Aristo had already promised his mother that he would fly to Madison and spend a few days with her when his father left for Italy to visit his aging parents. Aristo's new assignment to talk to McNeil's sister and investigate Daphne's disappearance in Madison expedited his trip.

He sensed that the judge's abduction had some connection with Daphne's disappearance a few years ago. He planned to start his investigation after spending a day with his mother. The visit became overwhelming, though, when Mrs. Manfredi celebrated her son's arrival by throwing a big party and inviting all their relatives and friends. Now, in addition to his mother, every relative and family friend was asking him about his love life.

Aristo took his mother to a corner of their kitchen, out of their guests' earshot. "Mom, I know you care about my future," he said, "but I came here to spend a little time with you, not people I haven't seen in ages. Besides, I have to investigate a kidnapping."

"So you came on a business trip, not to visit me."

"No. I wanted to spend some quality time with you, but so far I've spent more time with other people than you."

"What do you expect? These are the relatives who haven't seen you since you became a hotshot detective in Washington and buried yourself in your job."

"I love my job."

"I know you do, but you should also think about a wife or a girlfriend. Since Mary—"

"Mom, do we have to go through this every time I visit you?"

"I'm the only woman of my relatives and friends who doesn't have a grandchild. Every time we get together, they show their grandkids' pictures on their cell phones. Do you know how that makes me feel?"

"Okay, if it's going to make you happy ..." Aristo hesitated for a few seconds and then continued. "I'm interested in someone."

"Who? *Who?*"

"You see, that's why I can't talk to you about my personal life."

"After all these years, I have a right to know."

"Okay, she is a very attractive lawyer. But she lives in another town. I've had only one date with her."

"So you finally find a woman you like, but she lives in another town. I'll never have a grandchild." Mrs. Manfredi shook her head and left the kitchen.

Aristo waited for a few minutes and then joined everyone in the living room. He found them all chatting, joking, and enjoying the party. *They won't even notice I'm gone*, he thought as he snuck out of the house.

* * *

Manfredi's Greek mother had named him Aristotle, but when the kids in school teased him constantly, she allowed him to shorten his name to Aristo. While his mother, a librarian, had encouraged him to study Shakespeare, Greek mythology, and philosophers, his Italian father had taught him how to play soccer.

"Literature is for girls. He's a boy. He should play soccer," his father nagged.

In college he majored in philosophy, and when he wrote his thesis about the impact of Montesquieu's doctrine on modern government, his mother shrugged. "He was no Plato, Socrates, or Aristotle," she said in a thick Greek accent. "But I suppose he was the best the French could offer."

"Mom, the man introduced the theory of legislative, executive, and judicial branches of government as early as the eighteenth century."

"So what?" she responded.

During his first year of law school, Aristo fell in love with Mary—a girl from a small town in Wisconsin. And she returned the love. They got engaged, moved in together, and planned to marry after finishing law school.

During his second year in law school, encouraged by Mary, he took a seminar on the philosophy of law. Disappointing his mother once more, he ignored the Greek philosophers and wrote a paper about Immanuel Kant. Mrs. Manfredi didn't know Mary had been the one to introduce Kant's Copernican Revolution in philosophy to her son.

Aristo and Mary wrote several joint papers together. The more they spent time together, the more they found that Immanuel Kant was not the only common interest they had; they both enjoyed the same books, the same food, and the same movies and dreamed of a future practicing law.

At the end of his second year, Aristo got an offer to intern in Washington at the office of one of their congressmen from Wisconsin. He and his fiancée moved to DC and rented the basement of a townhouse near Capitol Hill. Life could not have been more exciting and promising for Aristo until one night when he and Mary were walking home.

He saw two young men walking fast toward them. He greeted them, but suddenly, one snatched Mary's handbag. When she screamed, the second robber shot her in the chest twice. Aristo froze. He couldn't even open his mouth to cry for help. Mary died shortly after the ambulance arrived at the emergency room of George Washington University's hospital.

Mary's murder changed Aristo's life. He quit law school and stayed in Washington to help the police find the robbers, whose faces he couldn't forget. He went to 300 Indiana Avenue, Northwest—DC's Metropolitan Police Department headquarters—every day, as though he had a job there. The sluggish investigation of Mary's murder frustrated him to the point that one day he walked into the DC Police Academy and signed up. At five feet nine inches, he was the shortest officer in his cadet class.

To find Mary's murderer, he patiently put up with all the jokes and teasing from his fellow classmates. They called him Aristotle the Philosopher and sometimes even Shakespeare, because they had seen him reading Shakespeare. He was an outcast—he drank wine, not beer; he played soccer, not football; and he didn't use any four-letter words, whereas his fellow colleagues uttered them as often as they said hi or hello.

After passing all the difficult tests and trainings, he became a detective faster than anyone else in the history of the DCMPD. Being a successful detective didn't confine Aristo to his office or to the interrogation room, though; he still searched for Mary's killer in the streets of southeast DC, having concluded that the killer must have lived somewhere in the neighborhood. Despite his diligent search, it took him five years to find the twenty-three-year-old who had ended the life of another twenty-three-year-old—Mary. The murderer was twenty-eight now.

The jury's guilty verdict and the judge's thirty-year sentence completed Aristo's mission. He then grew his black hair long and wore it in a ponytail. The unusual hairstyle made his round, tanned face more noticeable. He was the only detective allowed to wear his hair in a ponytail because the chief of police loved the way he resolved many of the department's unsolved homicides—the cold cases.

Since Mary's death, he had buried himself in his work and his books. Although he dated many women, he never fell in love again or even became serious with another woman. Then one day he met a criminal defense attorney named Amanda Perkins. As she was cross-examining him on the witness stand, he sized her up. She was five feet eleven, which was intimidating to a man two inches shorter, but she had the sharpest blue eyes he had ever seen. Her chin-length straight black hair accentuated her pale skin.

While she tried hard to impeach him on the witness stand, he kept his cool and promised himself that one day he would ask her out. But back in the office, he discovered that Amanda was married to an accountant.

* * *

Margaret McNeil and her husband lived in a three-bedroom townhouse near the campus of the University of Wisconsin at Madison. Aristo's investigation had confirmed that Margaret's husband was a college professor, but that information didn't matter to him. He needed to talk to Margaret, not her husband.

Margaret refused to talk to Aristo, even through the chained door. When he emphasized that the lives of both her brother and her niece were in danger, though, she reluctantly let him inside the house.

She was an average-height brunette with short curly brown hair. Her thick eyeglasses made her look like a teacher or a librarian. She showed

Manfredi to a chair and, as soon she sat in a chair opposite him, started talking. "I have very limited information. I don't think I can help you. I don't know where Daphne is. I've told the same thing to the FBI people. Daphne showed up here one day and told me she had a fight with her dad. He had kicked her out because she slept with her boyfriend."

"Everyone knows how much Judge McNeil adores his only child. You believed her story?"

"Yes, I did, because I know my brother."

"Did she tell you how she got here from Washington?"

"She said a friend drove her here."

"And you believed that a fifteen-year-old had a friend who would drive her from DC to Madison?"

"Detective, I was hoping to see her leave in a week."

"You didn't like her?"

"No, I didn't like my brother, and I didn't want to have anything to do with her because of him. I called Walter, and I told him that Daphne was here with me. He asked me to take care of her until she was ready to go back home."

"Did you agree?"

"I reluctantly did—until Daphne started going out with college boys, partying until two in the morning, and drinking."

"How could she find college boys so quickly?"

"My husband teaches at the university here. As you see, we're a few blocks away from the campus. Daphne had apparently crashed one of the many Saturday-night parties on campus. She had told them she was eighteen. When I objected to her behavior and set some rules for her, she left my house and moved in with three college boys. When I confronted the boys and threatened to call the police and bring statutory rape charges against them, they panicked and told Daphne to move out."

"Did she move back in with you?"

"No, she left town."

"How?"

"I asked her three roommates. One of them had seen Daphne with a large African American man."

"Did he give you any specific description?"

"No. He said he looked like a football player, and when I asked for a more detailed description, he said that all black people looked alike to him."

"Did you report that to the police?"

"No, I called Walter and told him his daughter had run away. I didn't want to deal with the police or the FBI. I didn't want to have anything to do with the mess my brother had created."

Chapter 15

Upon his return to Washington, Aristo spent a few more days finishing his investigation before making an appointment with Judge Bowen. They met at Aristo's favorite Italian restaurant on Pennsylvania Avenue—the same place he had dined with Amanda before her departure.

Judge Bowen was more eager to hear about Aristo's talk with Margaret than about any other part of the investigation he had done. "Did you get any leads?" he asked as soon as Aristo had sat down.

"The short answer is no. But I found some significant information in Madison that might interest you. But before talking about Madison or Margaret, I want to tell you what I've done here in DC."

"Go ahead, I'm listening."

"I wasted a lot of time going through the list of those who have received harsh sentences from Judge McNeil." Aristo chuckled. "As much as I love the man, he was brutal when it came to sentencing. Over the past sixteen years, he has sentenced approximately nine thousand two hundred individuals. If we go with the theory that the suspect might be one of those people, we're looking at a pool of thousands of defendants."

"What else did you do?"

"I watched the videos from the security cameras on the second-floor hallway near his chambers, to see whether there were any suspicious activities going on. I didn't find any."

"Okay, what else?"

"First, I have a question for *you*. Have you called McNeil on his cell phone?"

"I only get the voice mail. I haven't left any messages. In case my theory is correct and he's been kidnapped, I didn't want his kidnapper to know we suspect anything here."

"Has he contacted you at all?"

"No. He's been away for two weeks now. The only message he's left is the one for his courtroom clerk, telling her that he was out of town handling a family emergency. Oh, I forgot to tell you—in addition to his bizarre decision to throw out Keshan Walker's confession, he sent a new one. He has agreed with the defense that because their two newly discovered witnesses will testify that the codefendant killed the three girls in cold blood, Keshan should be released into a halfway house."

"Even you wouldn't grant a motion like that."

"No, I wouldn't ... now tell me about the trip."

"I found Margaret, but she didn't want to see me at all. I have to tell you, I've never met a sister with so much animosity toward her brother. I don't know what Judge McNeil did to her for her to hate him so much."

"McNeil told me once that his sister hates him because their parents gave him a larger share of their inheritance."

"Well, somehow I managed to talk to her for two hours. She told me that one day Daphne showed up at her door and told her the judge had kicked her out."

"Why?"

"Apparently, she had slept with her boyfriend."

"Judge McNeil is a disciplinarian, but he loved Daphne to death. He would never do that to his only child."

"I said the same thing, but apparently, Margaret believed her."

"So if her aunt was on her side, why did she leave *her* house?"

For the next ten minutes, Manfredi told Judge Bowen about Daphne's involvement with college boys and her final disappearance after being seen with an African American man.

"So what's your next move?"

"I talked to the judge's courtroom clerk and asked if she had seen or heard anything unusual after the judge's disappearance."

"And?"

"She says there's a woman who comes to court around noon every day and asks if the judge is back in town. I'm going to follow her tomorrow. But we have to get the FBI involved."

"The FBI has not been able to find Daphne for years. I really don't want to get them involved. What if McNeil has been kidnapped by the same people who kidnapped his daughter? Or maybe he has found his daughter and is trying to bring her home. Besides, I don't know whether he's been taken out of DC. When he cites those kidnapping cases, I don't know whether he's telling us *he's* being kidnapped or he's telling us about Daphne's kidnapping."

"I'm going to investigate the mystery woman, but his decisions on Keshan Walker's murder case make me wonder whether I should investigate Keshan and his family first."

"Please hurry. If we cannot find out where the judge is in a day or two, we *will* have to get the DC police and the FBI involved."

* * *

Before he could start anything new, Aristo was summoned by his supervisor, who complained that Aristo had been neglecting two significant homicide cases he had been handling. Aristo explained to his boss that it had been necessary for him to take a few days off to take care of a family matter and that he would resume the investigations immediately. As he was leaving the supervisor's office, Detective Preztacnik walked in, and Aristo suddenly knew why his supervisor had lectured him. Krzysztof Preztacnik was a younger detective whom Aristo had trained. He was a tall, sandy-haired Polish American with a college degree in criminology. When he first joined the DCMPD, his name had made him the target of all kinds of jokes. He had painfully tried to teach other detectives and cops how to pronounce his first name. When they refused and continued calling him Chris, he tried to teach them how to pronounce his last name: Pasheh-tach-nik. The detectives and cops laughed at him and settled for Prez, using the first four letters of his last name.

After learning Aristo's techniques, Prez had become very competitive with him. He wanted to be involved in every homicide case assigned to Aristo. At the beginning, Aristo had been sympathetic because he had seen similarities in Prez and himself: they both had immigrant parents, and they had unusual first and last names. He remembered how detectives and cops had called him Man or Fredi instead of Manfredi. Aristo had stopped being supportive, though, when he realized that Prez was after his job.

He assumed Prez had brought his absence to the attention of their supervisor. At first, he felt the urge to punish Prez by kicking him out of the two cases they were investigating together, but then he realized he was more interested in finding McNeil. Resolving McNeil's mysterious disappearance had become an obsession for him—similar to the time he'd spent searching for Mary's killer. Finding McNeil and his daughter had priority over everything else. So Manfredi gave Prez what he wanted. He wrote an e-mail to him, assigning him to take over one of the two cold homicide cases they had been working together.

* * *

Manfredi followed the mysterious woman who had come to court every day asking about Judge McNeil and found out she lived in a high-rise building near the zoo on Connecticut Avenue. He showed his badge to the building's security guard and asked about the woman.

"Her name is Tonya Henderson. She lives in apartment 716."

"Is there someone else living with her?"

"No, but there's a Caucasian gentleman friend who visits her once in a while. I haven't seen him for the past several weeks."

By the time the security guard finished describing Tonya's friend, Manfredi was certain the man he was referring to was Judge McNeil.

Chapter 16

At first, Tonya refused to provide any information about her relationship with Judge McNeil. But when Manfredi said the judge's life might be in danger, her face showed deep concern. "Is he okay?"

"We don't know where he is. We're hoping you can give us some leads that can help us find him."

"I don't know where he is either."

"I know that. But I have some questions, and your answers may be crucial."

"Go ahead. I'll do anything to help you find him."

"How do you know the judge?"

Tonya started telling the detective her life story: she was from a small town in South Carolina, and after her boyfriend was convicted for robbery and went to jail, she found out she was pregnant. "So I ran away and came to DC to live with a cousin I had here."

Manfredi was losing his patience. "Ma'am, I don't mean to be rude, but I need to know how you know the judge."

"Okay, I know I'm rambling. This is what happened. Some years ago, I did a stupid thing. I hit my sixteen-year-old daughter with a TV cable for not doing her homework. She called the cops. They arrested me, but after arraignment, because I had no prior record, they released me on personal recognizance. But Child and Family Services took my daughter. I was shocked—she was *not* a child."

"Didn't you say you had a cousin here? Why couldn't she stay with your cousin?"

"When my cousin retired, she went back home. All of my relatives were and still are living in South Carolina."

"What happened next?"

"I was lucky because Judge McNeil was handling neglect and child abuse cases that year. He called the judge who had the criminal assault case and convinced him that the case belonged to the family division."

"But a judge cannot drop charges against you; only the prosecutor can."

"I don't know. I'm not a lawyer. All I know is that six months later, he also dismissed the neglect case after I finished an anger management class."

"Were you reunited with your daughter?"

"My daughter moved to South Carolina with her boyfriend and later got married there."

"So that's how you know Judge McNeil?"

"I think he took pity on me because my boyfriend had abandoned me, and then everything happened with my daughter. One day he showed up at my doorstep and offered me a job supervising his teenage daughter. On even days, Daphne would come home from school at three. On odd days, she came home after Judge McNeil had come back from the courthouse."

"So with the salary of a babysitter, you could afford a two-thousand-dollar, one-bedroom apartment on Connecticut Avenue?"

Tonya hesitated. Manfredi moved closer to her. He knew how to make people talk. In good-cop, bad-cop interrogations, he always played the role of the good cop and always got the result he wanted. "I know it's painful to talk about your private life, but I need to know the whole story. You can't leave anything out."

"Okay. Once a month, he came here, and ... I kind of ... comforted him."

"Okay, I need to know about the people who visited him at his house."

"There were fancy uptown people—judges, lawyers, and some politicians."

"What happened to Daphne?"

"One afternoon, I went to the judge's house as usual, but there was no Daphne. Instead, I found the judge in his office, looking like he was in mourning. He was devastated."

"Did he explain why Daphne had left?"

"He said they had a fight over Justin, Daphne's boyfriend."

"Did the judge talk to Daphne's other friends?"

"Oh yes. Judge McNeil talked to everyone to find out about Daphne. Then we heard she was visiting her aunt in Wisconsin. But when she disappeared for the second time, the judge hired two retired detectives to find her. When they couldn't, he handed the case to the FBI."

"Did the judge have a cleaning lady?"

"Since the judge was paying my rent, I volunteered to clean the house. But I have to be honest with you—he never asked me to clean anything. I think his friends and neighbors thought I was his part-time housekeeper."

"So you didn't see anyone else in that house except the judge's friends and Daphne's friends."

"Oh, I forgot—there was this lawn man who always talked to Daphne. I didn't like him. He got fresh with me the first day he came to work."

"How long ago was that?"

"He was recommended by neighbors a few years back."

"How long did he work there?"

"Come to think ... he stopped coming about the same time Daphne disappeared."

"What did he look like?"

"He was a big black dude, with a mustache."

* * *

The next day, Aristo talked to Keshan's mother, Latisha Williams, who told him that Keshan had been very much influenced and supervised by his uncle—Leroy Walker.

"If Leroy looked after him, how did he get into trouble?" Aristo asked.

"He was not here when Keshan got into trouble."

"Where was he?"

"He was searching for his baby mama, Yvette. She took his daughter, Samyra, and ran away some years ago when Leroy was in jail."

"Do you know where Leroy is now?"

"I don't know. Probably still looking for Yvette and his daughter."

"Do you have a picture of Leroy?"

"Oh yes. Over the fireplace, there's a picture of Keshan with his uncle."

Aristo approached the fireplace. There was a picture of Keshan with a large mustached man who looked like a football player.

"May I borrow this picture?"

"Is he in trouble?"

"No. We're also trying to find Yvette—for Samyra's kidnapping." Aristo took the picture and left Latisha's house, smiling.

Chapter 17

Every day that Shorty unlocked the door to Walter McNeil's room and dragged him out of his bed at gunpoint, McNeil expected it to be his last. He knew his decisions to throw out a murderer's confession and to release him into a halfway house would be appealed by the prosecution in a heartbeat. He also knew they could ask the court of appeals to review his two rulings on an emergency basis and reverse them immediately. Still, Judge McNeil couldn't understand why no one seemed shocked by his recent decisions! It seemed as though no one had even noticed he was gone.

That morning was not the last day of McNeil's life. Shorty gave him the choice of having breakfast or walking in the yard for fifteen minutes. "I'll have some breakfast first," he responded. He was purposefully delaying his walk in the yard because he wanted to see his surroundings better.

After breakfast, he walked outside with Shorty close behind, pointing a gun at his back. When he got about fifty yards from the house, he realized that the walls created by the tall trees were enough to completely isolate the house. He saw a range of steep hills beyond the trees in the distance, and he felt the July heat on his skin.

"What incredible trees. Do you know what they're called?" McNeil asked.

"I dunno ... something spruce."

Suddenly, McNeil realized where he was, or at least he thought he'd found a clue. His wife had loved Colorado blue spruces. She had ordered one every Christmas until 1997—the year she died. The trees, the dry heat, the hills, and the fact that he hadn't seen or heard any raindrops suggested one place—Colorado. But which part?

"Have you heard from Keshan's attorney?" he asked Shorty.

"What about?"

"My decisions."

"No. But it better be good. Otherwise, you're in big trouble."

"Are you planning to kill me?"

"I dunno. Only Boss makes that decision."

McNeil had gotten used to his kidnappers' nicknames. It was obvious to him why they were not using their real names. The one they called Boss was presumably the head of their operation. Doc apparently had been in medical school prior to his arrest, and Shorty's nickname was an obvious reference to his height. Out of his three kidnappers, McNeil feared Doc the least. For some reason, he sensed that Doc was a reluctant participant. He also knew that he owed his life to Doc; he was the one who knew how much sedative to give to put him to sleep without killing him. If they had taken him to Colorado, they must have driven hundreds of miles. McNeil remembered a law clerk he'd had once from Aurora, Colorado, who boasted he had driven for twenty-six and a half hours to get to DC.

The judge's uneventful morning didn't last long. As soon as he stepped inside the house, Boss grabbed him, pushed him toward the wall, and banged his head against it several times. "You son of a bitch, you fooled me. Another court threw out the garbage you wrote."

Doc ran toward the judge and rescued him from Boss's attack. "Hey, man, how could he stop the prosecutor from going to a higher court? McNeil listened to us and did what we told him to do."

"He should've made it clear for us about the other court and its power!" Boss shouted.

"He did! You weren't listening," Doc said while taking McNeil to his room.

After putting McNeil in his bed, Doc examined his head. "Don't move until I make an ice pack," he instructed as he left the room.

Minutes later, he came back with an ice pack, placed it on the back of the judge's head, and put some pillows around his head. "Try to rest."

"You can still pursue your dream and become a doctor, you know," McNeil whispered, hiding his pain.

"You should've thought of my dream when you tore up my plea agreement and forced me to have a jury trial. They convicted me, and you gave me ten years," Doc reminded him, covering the judge's body with a blanket.

"I didn't think the jury would convict you. I had no choice but to sentence you the way I did. My hands were tied; the law required those ten years. I'm so sorry. I was wrong not to accept your plea."

Doc left the room to calm Boss, who was still ranting and raving in the kitchen.

"Hey, man, you could've killed him," Doc said as soon as he entered the kitchen.

"I don't give a shit. You've already dug his grave."

"I thought your plan was to put him in jail, to let him feel the humiliation and the pain we went through. Killing him or winning Keshan's case was not on the top of your agenda."

"Putting him in jail was the idea before Keshan got into trouble. Right now, winning Keshan's case has priority over everything. Maybe you weren't paying attention when I talked about my plan."

"Why don't you let Keshan's lawyer win his case?"

"I don't trust those white lawyers."

"She's one of the best lawyers from the Public Defender Service."

"I don't care. She's paid by the city. To me, she works for the prosecutors too."

"Now you're really being paranoid. PDS attorneys are the best. I'm going to get some medication for the judge—"

"What medication?"

"He may have a concussion. Please, don't hit him again while I'm gone."

When Doc came back, Boss was in a better mood and didn't mind when Doc checked McNeil's head. "So your patient didn't die of concussion, huh?" He chuckled.

Doc didn't respond. He was happy that the swelling in the back of the judge's head had not worsened.

"I need to send two e-mails to my staff," McNeil said, seeking Boss's approval.

"What kind of e-mail?" Boss asked.

"I have to let the chief judge know I'm retiring. The second e-mail goes to Judge Bowen, so that he can deliver a package to another judge. His name is Judge Fletcher. He and I were writing a book together before you brought me here. He needs to get the research I've done."

"Can this wait another week?"

"No, you don't know Judge Fletcher. He's a retired judge who has no life except writing. If he doesn't get the materials I've prepared within the next few days, he'll call everybody and everywhere to find out where I am."

"Doc, let him send his e-mails. But make sure he doesn't pull any shit," Boss ordered.

"I also need to shave. My beard is getting too long and makes me itch," the judge told him.

"You need that beard. Next week you're gonna start selling drugs. You need to hear those words—'You're under arrest'—and you need to stand in front of a judge feeling helpless, like a piece of shit."

McNeil didn't say anything. He accompanied Doc to the computer room, opened his laptop, and sent his e-mails while Doc stood behind him and read every word he typed.

McNeil could hardly wait to sell drugs and get arrested. He knew he had a right to make one phone call from jail. He was certain that his phone call to Detective Manfredi would put him and several FBI agents on the next plane to Colorado. But he was still not sure which city he was in. He could only guess it was Denver. He also didn't want Doc to get arrested. After he closed his laptop, he looked at Doc for a long time and whispered, "You're not a criminal. You're educated and—"

"Shut up, man. Don't try to mess with my head."

"How can you do this? You did your jail time. You could've started all over again."

"Sometimes you reach a point in your life where you don't care anymore. You've suffered so much that you're numb. You don't feel anything, and you don't care what happens to you next."

"I suppose using drugs helps you get that feeling."

"I only smoke weed."

"You have enough medical education to know what marijuana does to you."

"It relaxes me. Shut up and don't lecture me."

"Do you know that in 1977, a medical marijuana user got ninety-three years in jail in Oklahoma for growing marijuana plants? You're a good-looking man. Why can't you relax with a girlfriend?"

Doc laughed, but McNeil just stared at him.

"First of all, I'm not growing weed. Secondly, you haven't tried heroin yet. Man! That stuff will give you the best orgasm you've had in your life. You don't need a woman!"

* * *

The next day, Keshan's attorney called Leroy and told him that Judge McNeil had resigned and that Keshan's murder case had been officially assigned to Judge Bowen. "With Judge Bowen handling the case and the two new witnesses we've found, I'm confident we'll win the case," she said.

Leroy was all smiles when he gave the news to Melvin. He had stopped sharing information with Darnell, though. He resented the way Darnell was showing concern for the judge's life. "As soon as the police arrest him, we're on our way to Mexico," he told Melvin.

"What about Darnell?"

"I've told him I'll give him money to go to medical school down there. But it seems to me right now he cares too much for the man who fucked up his life."

For the next ten days, Leroy and Melvin injected different drugs into Judge McNeil's veins. Sometimes they forced him to snort cocaine. They watched him get high and then vomit, shiver, and tremble. They enjoyed watching him in pain when he exhibited withdrawal symptoms—when the cocaine's euphoria had worn off. And they laughed at him when he screamed and told them there were spiders climbing all over him.

After they injected heroin into his vein, they kept asking, "Did you feel the rush? Wasn't that the best orgasm ever?"

Every day, they ignored him for hours when he begged for more heroin, but then they'd give it to him, knowing he would ask for more.

Darnell kept to himself anytime Leroy and Melvin forced the judge to use drugs. He pretended he was busy at his computer doing research, but he treated the judge with some over-the-counter medications to stop his vomiting, diarrhea, and muscle pain.

McNeil tolerated all the pain because Boss had promised him that once he sold drugs and got arrested, they would be out of his life, and he'd never see them again. McNeil had never been incarcerated, but right now, the word *jail* sounded like paradise. He knew that as a first-time offender, he wouldn't get jail time, and with all the drugs in his system, any judge in any jurisdiction would send him to an inpatient drug treatment program.

He planned to tell his arresting officer and other authorities immediately about his kidnapping and the torturous days he had endured. His plan didn't include telling them about Doc, however. He hoped Doc would be smart enough to escape before the police and the FBI could catch him.

* * *

Under Boss's careful watch, Shorty dressed the judge and put several Ziploc bags of marijuana, cocaine, and heroin in his pants pockets. He also put three twenty-dollar bills in the breast pocket of the shabby jacket the judge wore, giving the police enough evidence to believe he'd already sold some dope.

"With that beard, long messy hair, and dilated eyes, you really look like a drug addict," Shorty commented.

McNeil was blindfolded and guided to climb into a vehicle that had steps. He sensed that this was the same mobile home they had used when they abducted him from Washington, DC. After a few steps, he was ordered to sit down. He was surprised his kidnappers had not gotten rid of the mobile home. He remembered the conversation he had heard between Boss and Shorty—someone had been paid to come and take the mobile home back to Washington.

After a short drive that seemed to last about twenty minutes, they stopped. Boss removed the blindfold and helped the judge out of the mobile home. McNeil felt the muzzle of a small gun in his back. Before he could turn around to read the license plate number on the mobile home, it was gone. He assumed Shorty had driven it away.

"Remember—your name is John Smith," Boss said. He put his left arm around the judge, like he was helping him. "You're an addict and homeless. Your drug supplier's name is Bo. You don't know nothin' about him. Give them whatever phony description of Bo you want, but don't try pullin' any shit. I'll be watching you from across the street, and I'll be watching you in the arraignment court. If you say a word about us to anybody, I'll kill Daphne."

McNeil nearly jumped out of his skin. He whipped around and faced Boss. "You bastard! So you're the one who kidnapped my daughter!" he shouted.

"Lower your voice. You threw her out, remember?"

"I could never do that to Daphne. I loved my daughter. She was my life."

"According to her, when you found out she was pregnant with her boyfriend's child, you kicked her out."

McNeil sighed. "Pregnant? What are you talking about?"

"Don't pretend you didn't know."

"You kidnapped my daughter and kept her hostage to take your revenge?"

"Because of you, my baby mama ran off with my daughter. I know what it feels like to look for a missing daughter. I'll have Daphne visit you in jail. If I wanted to take my revenge, I would've killed you by now. But I'm no murderer. Keshan is no murderer neither. I just want you to get arrested … spend some time in jail. So you can feel what I felt. That's my revenge—*not* killing you."

"Where's my daughter, and what are you doing to her?"

"We're friends. I helped her when she needed my help."

"If you harm my daughter, I'll kill you."

"You're in no position to threaten me. Just sell some of those zips. You'll see your daughter soon."

Chapter 18

Judge Bowen was waiting for Manfredi in his chambers. He had canceled a meeting about Keshan's murder case with the chief judge to spend more time with the detective. He had cleaned off his conference table like a general who needed more space for his war maps.

"Please give me some good news," he said as soon as Manfredi walked in.

"I have some good news, but I also have some bad news," the detective said. He scattered some papers on the table.

"Give me the good news first."

"I located the judge's female companion."

"What female companion?"

"The woman who was coming to court every day asking about the judge."

"Oh, now I remember. What about her?"

"Her name is Tonya Henderson."

"I don't know any Tonya Henderson."

"She was supervising Daphne three days a week after school before the judge got home. Neighbors thought she was the judge's maid."

"I've never met her. Who is she?"

"She was a mother who was accused of child abuse when Judge McNeil was handling family court cases a few years ago. McNeil closed the case after six months and started seeing this woman."

"You mean dating?"

"He first hired her to supervise Daphne, but he also rented an apartment for her near the zoo on Connecticut Avenue. That's where they had their dates."

"Did she have any information about the judge's whereabouts?"

"No, but I discovered that the man who cut the judge's grass back then, Leroy, was Keshan Walker's uncle. Leroy also had been harshly sentenced by Judge McNeil years earlier and spent many years in jail."

"McNeil would never hire a criminal."

"He must've used a fake ID. The judge couldn't have possibly recognized him because he had sentenced the man many years before. Besides, according to Tonya Henderson, Leroy was highly recommended by neighbors, and he would mow the lawn while the judge was in court. So McNeil never even saw Leroy. Only talked to him on the phone."

"Did you get this Leroy guy's description?"

"Here, this is his picture." Manfredi pulled a picture from his pocket and handed it to Judge Bowen. "This was the description I got from the student in Madison. He looks like a football player, doesn't he?"

Judge Bowen looked at the picture for a few seconds and then asked, "Where did you get the picture?"

"From Keshan's mother. So our suspect is Leroy Walker. He has a vendetta against the judge, and he has an interest in his nephew's murder trial."

"If your theory is correct and Leroy is our suspect, then what's the bad news?"

"No one knows where he might be. Keshan's mother and Leroy's friends think he's searching for *his* missing daughter."

"Well, I have some news too. You must have heard by now that McNeil has retired. But he's also sent me another bizarre e-mail." Judge Bowen retrieved his laptop from his desk, opened it up, sat next to Manfredi at the conference table, and clicked on Judge McNeil's e-mail. "Here, read it. Maybe you can make some sense out of it."

Manfredi pulled the laptop closer and read.

Dear Fredrick,

I have two favors to ask. As you know, Judge Fletcher and I have been writing a book. I have to send him the outcome of my research. I can't ask my staff to deliver the package because you're the only one who has the key to my house. Please go to my Den. There is a package there, labeled "Tennessee v. Fletcher," that should be delivered to the judge. His home is located at 7 2 Kolora Street, NW, Washington, DC. While you are at my house, please ask my gardener to trim my blue spruce tree.

Thanks,
Walter

"He calls you Fredrick, not Fred?"

"To McNeil, abbreviating a name kills its character, so Fredrick instead of Fred, Edward instead of Ed, Thomas instead of Tom. Now let me give you some information. The e-mail may seem normal to you, but number one, there is no Judge Fletcher, and McNeil isn't—nor has he ever been—writing a book. The only thing I read in this e-mail is that he's trying to tell us he's being kidnapped—because *Tennessee v. Fletcher* is the name of a case where the defendant kidnapped the man who had raped his daughter, drugged him, tortured him, and finally killed him. Two, I don't have a key to his house. I've never had one. Three, there is no Kolora Street in Washington. And four, he doesn't have a gardener or a blue spruce tree."

Manfredi read the e-mail several times. He then wrote different parts of it on a piece of paper. "When did the judge contact his staff about his family emergency?"

"I believe it was the day after the Fourth of July holiday. That must have been July 6."

"And he cited a kidnapping case when he told his law clerk to suppress Keshan's confession, and now again he's using another kidnapping case in his e-mail to you. He's definitely telling us he's been kidnapped. It seems to me that his kidnapping is linked to Keshan's murder case—*and* his daughter's disappearance."

"So you think the person who kidnapped him is also the one who kidnapped Daphne?"

"I don't know. At the present time, my suspect is Leroy Walker, and my priority is to locate him. But maybe Judge McNeil's e-mail has more clues. Look at the way he's put a space between the 7 and 2. It looks like

July 2. I think he's trying to tell us he was kidnapped on that date. Now, Kolora—do we have any similar street?"

"We have Kalorama off Connecticut. I don't know any other street, do you?"

"No, I don't."

"Let's see what a blue spruce tree is."

Manfredi Googled "blue spruce tree," and in a few seconds, a page of information and pictures of the Colorado blue spruce appeared on the screen.

"The man is genius," Manfredi said. "*Kolora* means Colorado. And look at the word *Den*, with a capital D and a period—Den. instead of den. He's telling us he's in Denver, Colorado. I'm going to call the FBI."

"Hold on, Detective," Judge Bowen said, raising his right hand like a stop sign. "We don't know about his daughter's situation. Let's get the Denver police involved first. I'll be taking a few days off. Will you come with me to Denver?"

"Yes, of course, and we're lucky to have a fabulous lawyer in Denver who can help us."

"Who?"

"Amanda Perkins."

"When did she move to Denver?"

"Recently."

"Too bad. I'll miss seeing her in my courtroom. She's one of my favorite attorneys."

"Mine too."

Chapter 19

McNeil was so preoccupied with the shocking news about Daphne's involvement with Boss—a criminal—that he nearly forgot Boss had put him on the corner of a busy street, expecting him to sell drugs. He felt relieved that Daphne had not told his kidnapper the truth about the *real* reason she had run away from home. But now he knew why Daphne had left Madison after only a few months—she hadn't wanted her aunt to know she was pregnant.

He wondered how his kidnapper knew Daphne originally and where he had kept her captive. Could she possibly be in the same house? The same city? Or did he have her in a different location? He now felt he was being punished for the crime he had committed some years ago. Only Daphne knew about his crime, and now she was paying for her father's sin.

He had read many books and articles to learn about drugs because 90 percent of the defendants who appeared in his courtroom had drug problems. He knew that marijuana had two hundred street names. He knew the physical and psychological damages of each drug. He knew how cocaine acted on dopamine, a brain chemical, and about the euphoria it created. He knew that cocaine came from coca leaves and that the Indians in Peru and Bolivia had chewed coca leaves for about twelve hundred years.

He also knew how LSD and other hallucinogens could create gruesome images for the user. So when his kidnappers had given him LSD back at the house, he had expected to see decapitated people or lizards chewing people's necks. And he *needed* a gruesome image to erase the horrible memory that had haunted him for years—the image of the crime he had committed. But the hallucination he'd experienced was more gruesome than what he had read about in the books and articles: he saw himself stabbing his victim's body repeatedly, splashing blood everywhere.

McNeil suddenly felt cold and started shivering, and the severe cramping in his stomach was getting worse. The shaking and trembling told him he was experiencing withdrawal, which caused him to panic. What would happen to him if he had diarrhea in the middle of the street?

The area around him looked more like a downtown, with busy traffic and people wearing business suits. While he scanned his surroundings with frightened eyes, a young man in blue jeans and a plaid shirt approached him. "What's up?" he asked.

"I think I'm about to throw up. I'm really sick."

"What you got?"

"Some cocaine and heroin."

"Give me some coke."

McNeil recognized that the man was an undercover. He wanted to get arrested, but he wasn't going to sell anything and be charged with felony distribution. He knew that possession of drugs was a misdemeanor offense, and the penalty could be six months or a year in jail. It couldn't be more than one-year imprisonment—even in the most conservative jurisdictions.

He could not see his kidnapper, but he knew that Boss was watching him from somewhere. He took a few Ziploc bags of cocaine from his pockets, showed them to the man, and said, "I'm not selling; these are for my personal use."

He was correct in his suspicion—the man pretending to be a drug addict turned out to be an undercover agent. In a quick move, he jumped behind the judge, brought the judge's hands together, and put him in handcuffs. The cop then read him his Miranda rights: "You're under arrest for possession of narcotics. You have the right to remain silent. Anything you say can and will be used against you in a court of law. You have the right to an attorney. If you cannot afford an attorney, one will be appointed for you."

McNeil looked across the street to see whether Boss had witnessed his arrest, but all he saw was a police cruiser and two police officers jumping out of it. When they approached him, he saw the logo on their jackets: Denver Police.

Chapter 20

Amanda had known some small law firms in DC where only a few attorneys practiced within certain areas of law. They were called boutique law firms. However, she had never imagined she would see a boutique courthouse.

Denver's Lindsey-Flanigan Courthouse was a large, modern building and an architectural work of art. Its multiangular design was covered in glass, reflecting Denver's blue sky and many of the downtown buildings. Yet inside, Amanda saw only a limited number of defendants and their families. She couldn't help remembering the long lines in front of the two major entrances of the DC superior court building. The hallways in the Denver courthouse were spacious but almost empty—another contrast with the corridors of the DC superior court, where people had to push others out of the way to reach their designated courtrooms. Walking in crowded hallways was even worse when hundreds of potential jurors were waiting in front of various courtrooms for jury selection.

The DC jail was located in southeast Washington, far away from the DC superior court, but Denver's Van Cise-Simonet Detention Center was across the street from the courthouse. It was a state-of-the-art facility that had just opened a few months before Amanda arrived in Denver. The exterior of the building, made of gray-tan Indiana limestone, seemed like an ordinary government building, but Amanda had been amazed when she first toured the fifteen-hundred-bed facility. Unlike the DC jail, the Denver detention center had thick glass windows, which invited sunlight inside. The facility had two arraignment courts and its own infirmary and was connected to the courthouse with a secured underground tunnel.

* * *

On Friday, July 30, Amanda had only one case to handle in the arraignment courtroom at 4:30 p.m. After that, she planned to go home, take a leisurely bath, dress up, and attend a welcome-home party being thrown for her by one of her high school friends. She was looking forward to seeing some old classmates.

The arraignment judge had ordered a drug treatment program for her client, and she was waiting for the courtroom clerk to finish the paperwork. When the clerk finally handed her the release papers, Amanda separated the attorney copies and put them in her case file before taking her client's copies and entering the cellblock adjacent to the courtroom. Her client was talking to one of the other two inmates in the block. Amanda noticed that the third inmate, who looked homeless, stood quietly behind the conversing men, staring at her. She called her client's name, interrupting his conversation.

"Mr. Pringle, these are your release papers and information about your drug treatment program. I hope you realize how difficult it was today to get you released on personal recognizance. You've assaulted your wife twice in a week. I'm going to negotiate with the prosecutor to get you an early favorable plea. However, between now and then, if you assault your wife one more time, I will not represent you. You will have to find yourself another attorney."

"The bitch asked for it," Pringle said as he took the papers from Amanda through the bars.

"Please don't use that phrase in front of me. My investigator tells me you have ongoing relationships with three other women. Don't you think your wife has a legitimate reason to complain about it? It's your life, your decision, but if you want to have four women, go live in Saudi Arabia where it's legal to have four wives."

"Listen, man," said the inmate who had been talking to Amanda's client. "This is God talking to you through her. Listen to her."

Amanda was surprised at the inmate's comment, but she didn't react to him. She said good-bye to her client and was about to leave the cellblock area when the other inmate—the quiet one—addressed her. "Miss, can I please have a piece of paper and a pen for a moment? I need to write something before I forget."

Amanda tore a page from her legal pad, folded it, and passed it with her pen through the bars. The man quickly jotted a few lines, folded the page, and returned it to Amanda with her pen. "Please read it," he said.

She returned to the courtroom to pick up her briefcase and leave. There was something about the homeless man in the cellblock that bothered her. She felt she had seen his face and heard his voice somewhere before. She assumed the man wanted her to call someone. Some inmates in the past had made similar requests. Amanda left the courtroom and sat in a chair in the hallway. She opened her cell phone and the paper the man had given her. She was looking for a number to dial, but there was no telephone number, only a note:

> Ms. Perkins,
>
> I have been kidnapped. The lead kidnapper is also holding my daughter in captivity somewhere. He is in the courtroom and will be watching me during my arraignment. Please help.
>
> Thanks,
> Judge Walter McNeil

"Oh my God!" Amanda said aloud, but there was no one in the hallway to hear her. She didn't know what to do. She ran back to the courtroom. Judge McNeil was now before the arraignment judge with his court-appointed attorney standing next to him. Amanda was about to ask the court's permission to approach the bench—she thought the Denver judge should know the true identity of the bearded defendant—but she stopped herself when she remembered that the judge's daughter had been kidnapped too. She looked around the courtroom. There were only seven individuals sitting in the audience. The man in the last row caught her attention. He was a heavily built African American who moved around in his seat several times to observe the court proceeding better.

After the court-appointed attorney for McNeil entered a not-guilty plea, the prosecutor asked for no bond, telling the Denver judge that the defendant had no fixed address and no job and couldn't even remember the name of the shelter he lived in. "He is a drug addict and cannot be trusted to come back for his next court date."

McNeil's attorney told the court his client didn't have any prior criminal conviction and could benefit from an inpatient drug treatment program during his pending case.

The arraignment judge agreed with the defense attorney and ordered the defendant released on personal recognizance. "Mr. Smith, I don't mean to lecture you about what you're doing, but I cannot help wondering what's going on in your brain. You hang out two blocks away from this courthouse and the detention center looking for customers. You have multiple Ziploc bags of drugs, which indicate you were attempting to sell. I know the prosecutor has dropped the felony charge of possession with intent to distribute to a misdemeanor possession, but I know you were standing there to sell. You have also tested positive for cocaine, heroin, and marijuana. I don't know what you're doing to your body. Are you committing suicide? If you had a prior criminal record, I would've sent you to jail with no hesitation. But you're a first-time offender, so I will put you on personal recognizance until your trial or disposition in your case. You have to report tomorrow morning to one of our inpatient drug treatment facilities and enroll in their program. Your lawyer will help you find the address. But Mr. Smith, I'm warning you—don't show your face in my courtroom again. Next time, you go to jail and stay there until your case is over. I'm not in the habit of lecturing defendants, but your case is very unusual. Okay, you'll be released as soon as the courtroom clerk finishes the paperwork."

"Thank you, Your Honor," McNeil said, his voice shaking.

Amanda knew how humiliated Judge McNeil must have felt. She looked around and saw the big man in the last row leave the courtroom in a hurry. He seemed agitated, as though he were ready to punch someone. She picked up her briefcase, left the courtroom, and followed the man. She lost him when an elevator door opened and took him away.

Amanda retrieved her car from a garage near the courthouse and drove it to the front entrance of the detention center, where she waited for Judge McNeil to show up. A black Pontiac with a DC license plate circled around the building several times. Amanda recognized the man she had seen in the courtroom behind the wheel.

As soon as McNeil appeared outside the courthouse, the man jumped out of the Pontiac, ran to him, took him by the arm, and shoved him into the backseat of the car. The traffic light turned red, so the driver of the Pontiac had to stop, but as soon as the light turned green, the car's tires screeched, and the driver took off. She followed the Pontiac, keeping enough distance to not arouse any suspicion. The car entered the southbound lane of Interstate 25 and then, to her surprise, exited onto 6th Avenue, going west toward Lakewood, where she lived. The driver continued west, passing through Lakewood and the exit Amanda would have taken to get home.

After several miles, the car entered Interstate 70 and continued west until it reached the steep foothills of the Rocky Mountains. A few miles farther, the driver exited I-70 and drove south on a two-lane road. After a short drive, Amanda noticed a few expensive-looking homes on very large lots, spaced far apart. This was an area where the home owners obviously preferred and could afford privacy. Most homes were built far back from the roadway and were partially hidden by the evergreen trees native to the area.

She noticed how sparse traffic on the road was and suddenly became nervous. She wondered whether the driver had noticed her car. About two miles from I-70, the Pontiac turned at a long, gated driveway and headed toward a house on the top of the hill. The house was almost completely hidden by the dense forest of trees.

Amanda parked her car far away from the gate, turned off the air conditioner, and rolled down her window to take some pictures with her cell phone. She needed to gather more information before talking to the authorities. She didn't know anyone in the Denver police department, and she knew her Uncle Frank would've forbidden her from getting involved in such risky activity. There was only one person who could help Judge McNeil—Detective Manfredi.

Amanda took a few more pictures and then dialed Manfredi's number. She got his voice mail and decided not to leave a message. Sitting behind the wheel, she tried hard to think of a way to help Judge McNeil and his daughter without jeopardizing their lives. At the moment, she had totally forgotten how much she detested the man. The shocking events of the last ninety minutes had numbed her brain to the point that she also hadn't noticed it was growing dark.

She decided to drive home and call Manfredi again. But before she could start the car, she saw the black Pontiac coming down the driveway. She froze for a moment and then locked her doors, started the car, and drove away quickly. She hadn't driven more than a few hundred feet before the Pontiac rear-ended her car and then immediately hit it again on the left side. She kept driving, but the Pontiac kept ramming her. Finally, it pulled ahead of her small Toyota, slowed down, and stopped, blocking her completely. The man she had seen in the courtroom and a shorter man with a gun emerged from the car.

Her heart was beating fast now. She knew she had to come up with some explanation of why she had been observing the house. The short man ordered her out of the car at gunpoint. When Amanda refused, he smashed the driver's side window with an object she couldn't see. She turned her head to the right to avoid the glass that sprayed inside.

"What do you want?" Amanda asked.

"Lady, the question is what do *you* want?" the tall, heavy-set man asked as he snatched her cell phone from her hand.

"I heard this is a nice house. I just moved to Denver. I thought maybe it might be for sale."

"Do you see a for-sale sign anywhere?"

"No, but sometimes people sell their houses online."

"I suppose that's why you took some pictures."

"Exactly."

"You can't see a damn thing from here except the gate, the long driveway, and the trees. C'mon, counselor, don't fuck with me. A good-looking white woman in a courtroom full of black defendants and their relatives stands out."

"Please let me go. I don't know you or your business."

"But you know Judge McNeil. You're his friend, ain't you?"

"I don't know what you're talking about."

"Sorry, lady. I don't buy that. You made a big mistake following me."

The shorter man dragged Amanda to the Pontiac, pressing his gun against her back, and pushed her into the backseat of the car. The larger man climbed into the driver's seat of the Pontiac and ordered his accomplice to bring Amanda's car inside the yard.

"All three garages are full."

"Put a cover on it until I can get rid of it."

* * *

McNeil killed a sigh when he first saw Amanda tied to a chair. He stayed emotionless, trying to convince his kidnappers that he didn't know their new victim or care what they had planned for her. But deep down in his heart, he knew that by asking Amanda for help, he had endangered her life. He was surprised Amanda had taken such a risk to help him; last he knew, they had both hated each other. He felt guilty for how he'd treated her during their last case together. He had practically kicked her out of his courtroom and had then slammed his chamber door in her face. He remembered how harshly he had sentenced her client. If his kidnappers were not holding Daphne as a hostage, he could have told the police or his court-appointed attorney about his kidnapping, but he couldn't jeopardize Daphne's life. And unfortunately, that had put Amanda's at risk instead.

Chapter 21

Detective Manfredi and Judge Bowen checked into a hotel in a nice area in Denver at 9:00 p.m. Bowen was anxious to talk to Denver's chief of police immediately, but Manfredi wanted to contact Amanda first; her number had appeared on his cell phone as a missed call when they landed. She had not called him since her departure from DC, so he was surprised and happy to have received a phone call from her.

"This is our first time in Denver. She's a native, and her uncle is a well-known lawyer here," he told Bowen. "They both know how things are done in this town."

Bowen agreed, but when Amanda didn't return Detective Manfredi's calls, the judge became impatient. "She may be out of town, or maybe her cell phone doesn't have good reception. We have to get moving."

Manfredi agreed with the judge, so they took a cab to Denver police headquarters. A sergeant told them the chief was at home and couldn't be disturbed.

"Please call him and tell him Judge Bowen from the District of Columbia's superior court is here to see him. It's urgent. We're dealing with a dire situation."

The chief met with them reluctantly. After he heard about Detective Manfredi's investigation, he paused for a moment and then asked, "If the suspect has transported a judge through several states, shouldn't this be handled by the FBI?"

"We don't know whether he came here on his own to rescue his daughter or whether he was kidnapped," Bowen said. "He has sent us some puzzling e-mails."

"We don't know where his daughter is," Manfredi added. "We're worried about her safety as well."

"Are you telling me the kidnappers have also kidnapped his daughter?"

"We're not sure, but his daughter disappeared four years ago at the same time the man who mowed the lawn for him disappeared," Manfredi said. "The man's name is Leroy Walker."

The chief asked his deputy to find out whether there had been any recent criminal activity involving a Leroy Walker in Colorado. A few minutes later, the deputy reported that the only prior convictions on Walker's crime sheet were his convictions in DC and Hazelton, West Virginia. The deputy also checked for recent arrests in Aurora, where most of the city's drug transactions took place. He couldn't find any arrest record for Leroy Walker in Aurora either.

"I'm sorry, gentlemen," the chief said. "If he has just passed through our town and is involved with a kidnapping that started somewhere else, we don't have any jurisdiction."

"Judge McNeil has sent us two e-mails citing kidnapping cases," Manfredi said, clearly frustrated. "He told us to go to his 'Den,' with a capital D, which we think means Denver, to deliver a package, and he has talked about a spruce tree, which can't mean anything but a Colorado blue spruce. I know he's here."

"I'll alert my department to look for any suspicious activities around town."

"If he hasn't come here on his own, they obviously couldn't have flown him," Manfredi said. "And they couldn't have driven him in a regular car in two days without stopping at some motels, though if they did stop, they could have given false names. In any event, we cannot check the records of the hundreds of motels located between DC and Denver. My gut tells me they transported him in a mobile home, so nobody could see what was going on inside. And there must be more than one kidnapper."

"Could you please have your men check suspicious mobile homes parked around town?" Judge Bowen asked the chief.

"Will do, but I still want to get the FBI involved."

"Can we wait to see whether your local police find anything first?" Judge Bowen asked. "McNeil hates publicity. He'd hate to see his picture or his daughter's picture all over the media or printed in major newspapers around the country."

* * *

After leaving Denver's police department, Manfredi kept calling Amanda, but he only reached her voice mail. During the last call, he left a message for her: "Amanda, when we said good-bye in DC, I imagined that my next visit with you would take place in a romantic restaurant in Washington or Denver. Believe it or not, I'm in Denver right now with Judge Bowen, but unfortunately for an investigation. We need your help. Please call me as soon as you get this message."

Chapter 22

Melvin took Amanda to a different room, pushed her into a chair, and tied her feet to it while Leroy pulled out the contents of Amanda's wallet. He examined several of her ID and membership cards, checking each one carefully and announcing the names of the agencies that had issued the cards. "DC Bar, Women's Bar Association, DC Criminal Defense Attorneys Association, Superior Court Criminal Defense Foundation ... oh, ACLU, interesting ... and you tell me you don't know this superior court judge?" Leroy asked. "You think I'm stupid or something?"

"I never told you that. I know him all right, and I wish he would rot in hell. Do you know how many lives he has destroyed? He gave lengthy jail time to my clients, and he denied every single motion I filed asking him to reduce his horrible sentences. Why would I care what happens to him?"

"So why did you follow me?"

"With his long messy hair, beard, and worn-out clothes, he resembled one of my homeless clients. And when you left the courtroom so angry, I thought he worked for you. I wanted to help him."

"So you thought he was one of my men? You bitch! You have the right answer for everything, don't you?"

"I'm telling you the truth. I hate this man because anytime he puts his damn black robe on, he acts like God, changing people's lives."

Melvin pulled Leroy's arm and took him to another room. "Boss, what do you want me to do with her?"

"Keep an eye on her for one more day, until the judge is in jail."

"He was supposed to be in jail today, but he's out."

"The local judge let him go because he was a first-time offender. But when he goes back tomorrow and starts selling drugs again in the same spot, he's gonna piss off the judge. He told him if he showed his face in his courtroom again, he'd go to jail. I'll put him in the same spot tomorrow with more dope. This time, he's going to get felony charges and serious jail time."

"What about the woman? We can't leave her here."

"She's smart. She'll find a way to get herself free."

"How? She's tied to a chair."

"She's a lawyer, ain't she? She'll figure it out."

"Boss, we have the judge's daughter, so he ain't gonna say nothin'. But this woman can tell the cops how we look."

"By the time she does that, we're out of the country. By the way, where's Doc?"

"He left right before you got here."

"Where?"

"He said he needed to buy a pair of shoes and a suitcase before the trip."

"Bring the judge here. I want to ask him some questions," Leroy ordered Melvin.

* * *

McNeil heard Shorty and Boss whispering in the far corner of the room while he watched Amanda, but he was not paying any attention to their conversation. He was worrying about whether Boss had found his note to Attorney Perkins. If he had, McNeil knew that either he or Shorty would kill him. When Boss didn't mention anything about the note, McNeil started making plans in his head. He assumed his kidnappers were keeping Daphne in either DC or Denver. He had also concluded that as a captive man he could never help his daughter. He was determined to find a way to free himself and Daphne; therefore, he was ready and eager to get arrested. His plan was to tell the police about his kidnappers the minute he was in their custody. He only wished he could call Detective Manfredi and get him involved. He knew his career as a judge was over, but he didn't care. He wasn't even concerned about the media coverage of his life, which he figured must be an effect of all the drugs they had forced him to take.

* * *

The door opened, and Doc walked in. At first he didn't notice Amanda, who was in the far corner of the living room, surrounded by Boss and Shorty. As soon as he saw Judge McNeil tied to his chair, he threw his arms out. "Aw, I thought you said he'd be in jail, and by the end of the day, we could hit the road!" he said to Boss, showing his frustration.

"The Denver judge had mercy on him. Don't worry, Doc. He'll be in jail tomorrow. But look who we've got here! A new guest. One of the judge's friends has come to rescue him."

When Boss moved back for Doc to see Amanda, Doc shouted, "Oh no! You can't keep her captive! She's the lawyer who worked on my appeal case for two years for free. She's got a good heart. She's helped hundreds of people like us. You can't do this to her. Oh God!"

Doc stormed out of the room, went straight to his bedroom, and locked the door behind him. He lowered his body to check the box under his bed; it was still there—untouched. In his closet, he took all his clothes off the hangers, folded them, and put them on his bed. Next, he opened the large suitcase he had bought and laid it wide open on the floor. He put his clothes inside first and then carefully pulled the box from underneath his bed. He hid each bundle of money, one by one, inside a different item of clothes until there was no money left in the box. After securing the closed suitcase under the bed, he climbed under his covers and willed himself to sleep—he had to travel in a few hours.

Chapter 23

The next morning, while Amanda was tied to a bed in a small room, Shorty brought McNeil to the kitchen and gave him a bowl of cereal. He then helped the judge into his homeless outfit. Boss finished counting the Ziploc bags of cocaine, heroin, and marijuana. This time, he put five twenty-dollar bills in the judge's right pocket and shoved the twenty Ziploc bags into his left pocket. "Remember," he told the judge, pointing his finger, "one word out of you to the police, and you'll never see your daughter again."

"When am I going to see her?"

"When you're in jail and we're gone."

"How can I trust you and your coconspirators?" asked McNeil, trying hard to mask his hatred. "Where's my daughter? Here? In DC? Are you treating her the way you're treating me?"

Boss and Shorty looked at each other and started laughing. "Wait a minute," Boss said. "First of all, *Your Honor*," he continued mockingly, "this ain't your courtroom. So, stop using fancy words like *coconspirators*. Secondly, your daughter is fine and very happy where she is."

"I don't believe you," the judge said. "Get her on the phone. Let me talk to her and determine for myself whether she's happy or not."

"Shit, you're wasting my time. I was going to let Daphne tell you all the juicy details, but since this is the last time I'm seeing you, I might as well tell you the whole story myself."

In the next few minutes, Boss shocked the judge by telling him about his phony lawn-mowing company and how he had befriended Daphne. He shared with him the details of how he had helped Daphne get to Madison and how he'd gotten her out of there when she found out she was pregnant. With every detail of his relationship with Daphne, Boss plunged a knife into the judge's heart. McNeil had let a vindictive criminal into his house, not knowing that he was after Daphne to take his revenge. He had ruined his precious daughter's future—his daughter, who had attended the best international school in Washington and had once planned to go to Oxford for her college education.

"I still don't believe you," he shouted. "What kind of happiness could you offer her? Have her call me. I want to hear my daughter's voice."

"Calm down, Grandpa. I have a picture to show you. Look at it and see for yourself if she's happy or not."

Boss stood from his chair, took his wallet out of his right pocket, and pulled out a picture. He looked at it for a few seconds and then gave it to Shorty and directed him to hand it to the judge. He went back to the table, sat in a chair, and munched on a long piece of bacon. When he first looked at the picture, McNeil sighed and fought back tears. Daphne had grown into a beautiful woman, resembling her mother more than ever. She was smiling and holding the hand of a little boy. Standing next to her was Boss, holding a baby in his arms.

"The little blond boy, Sean, is your daughter's baby with her ex-boyfriend, Justin. But Malcolm there is *our* baby."

McNeil froze for just a moment and then charged toward Boss, ready to attack him. "You raped my Daphne, you bastard! I'll kill you!"

Shorty jumped in between them and pressed his gun into McNeil's abdomen before he could reach Boss.

"Chill, Grandpa, I'm not a rapist. I allowed your daughter to go out with anyone she desired. We were together for a while, but since then, I've taken care of her like she was my daughter."

"What kind of a sick man sleeps with someone he considers to be like a daughter and makes a baby with her?" At that moment, McNeil hated Boss so much that he forgot about Shorty and his gun. "You raped an innocent fifteen-year-old girl. You bastard."

"Hey, she was not that innocent when we got together."

"Shut up. I don't want to hear anymore."

"As you see, Malcolm is only seven months old. Your daughter *wanted* to sleep with me. I think it was her way of thanking me for all the help I had given her. We only slept together a few months. Then she found a new boyfriend, and it was over."

"Shut up! You slept with a girl half your age!"

"Hey, you didn't bring any charges against Justin. Because he was white, right? He slept with your daughter when she was fifteen. Even I know what that means. That's called statutory rape. He even got her pregnant. She was eighteen when I slept with her."

McNeil grew quiet. He was surprised and relieved that Daphne had not given Boss the details of what had actually happened on the night before her disappearance. He also was relieved that this argument about Daphne seemed to be ending without violence. In the past, any unpleasant remark by McNeil had angered Boss to the point that he would run to the judge and punch him in the face or the head. *Maybe he is calm because he has accomplished his mission—he has ruined my life.*

* * *

When they arrived at the same intersection as the day before, Boss parked his Pontiac nearby, took off the judge's blindfold, and directed him to the spot where he'd been arrested. "As soon as the police take you in," he said, "I'm out of your life. Remember that."

McNeil felt an urge to put his hands around Boss's throat and choke him to death. But just as Boss was desperate to see him get arrested, he too was eager to go to jail—to free himself and maybe even Daphne. But he didn't know the location of the house where they had kept him. He hadn't seen the license plates of the mobile home or the black Pontiac, and he could only give physical descriptions of his kidnappers. He knew he had sentenced all three of them more than a decade ago, but he didn't know their names. And they were fleeing to Mexico, so there wouldn't be enough time for the police to investigate the case and find them. *If only I could make a phone call to Detective Manfredi.*

He knew Boss was watching him from across the street, but he didn't care anymore. He was preoccupied with the news about his daughter. He couldn't erase the image of Daphne standing next to a criminal, smiling as though she were taking a happy family portrait.

McNeil kept walking back and forth in the same limited space. He felt like screaming—so loud—for someone to hear him in the sky. How could Daphne sleep with a criminal and get pregnant with his baby? The mental images of Daphne with Boss were too painful to endure.

He took a Ziploc bag of cocaine out of his left pocket, opened it, poured it on the back of his hand, and began snorting it. He felt his rapid heartbeat and the rising of his body temperature. The heavy traffic obstructed his view of Boss's location, and his euphoria had just started when Boss showed up and pulled his right arm in a rage. "You son of a bitch. What the fuck are you doing? You're supposed to sell this stuff, not use it. If you mess this up again, I'm gonna kill both you and your daughter."

Boss yanked the judge's arm again, pulling him toward the curb aggressively. He tried to show him how to approach the cars when the traffic light was red and how to talk to the cars' occupants. "You stand right here. When the cars stop for the red light, you go talk to the passenger or the driver through the window. Tell them what you got."

"Leave me alone."

"You have a job to do here. Don't try to pull a fast one on me because there will be other people watching you even when I'm gone. If I were you, I'd watch my back. So no fancy ideas. You know I have associates who—"

"Leave me alone!" McNeil yelled as he shook his arm free from Boss's grip.

The judge's combative behavior angered Boss, who grabbed both of McNeil's shoulders and pulled him toward the curb again, backpedaling. McNeil felt a surge of energy he had never experienced before. He managed to free his shoulders, put both his hands on Boss's chest, and pushed him into the street.

Boss lost his balance and fell backward into the oncoming traffic. McNeil heard a loud thud and the screams of some bystanders who had witnessed the incident. He saw Boss's body fly up and over the hood of a car and land in the next lane of traffic. The next moment, he was run over by a large SUV, crushing his chest and head. McNeil covered his eyes with both hands.

Oh my God.

Chapter 24

Around the time Leroy was pronounced dead at 11:00 a.m. in a Denver hospital, Detective Manfredi and Judge Bowen were in a meeting with Denver's chief of police. The three of them had reviewed dozens of arrest reports and the tapes of 911 calls. At 11:20 a.m., a police officer interrupted their conference and asked them to listen to a call they had received at the police communications center. At first, it had seemed the caller was playing a prank because he used a device that masked his real voice, and the call was made from a pay phone. But the caller's message was too serious to ignore.

"A woman and a man have been kidnapped and held hostage at a place in the hills above Lakewood. The address is 72243 Cedar Street. The kidnappers are dangerous and carry guns. A homeless man might get arrested today. Take him seriously and pay attention to what he has to say. Don't laugh at him if he tells you he's a judge."

Manfredi looked at Judge Bowen with a smile. "I'd like to check out the Lakewood address," he told Bowen. "But I think you should stay here and look at the mug shots of the detained homeless individuals."

"What are you thinking?" Bowen asked.

"The kidnapped man and woman may be the judge and his daughter, Daphne. Or the homeless man could be our Judge McNeil."

"If the two of them are with the kidnappers in the house, then why is the caller talking about a homeless man who claims to be a judge?"

"I think the caller is referring to two individuals being kidnapped, but he's not sure whether both of them are going to be in the Lakewood house when the police raids the place."

"Why would they allow the judge to get out of the house, dressed as a homeless man, and be arrested?"

"Judge Bowen, we talked about Leroy and his plan, remember? Maybe this is part of a plan to get the judge arrested and sent to jail."

"For vagrancy?"

"I don't know. Maybe for selling drugs."

"Don't they know the judge will tell the police who he is?"

"Remember they have his daughter too. Maybe he's been trying to protect Daphne all this time."

"I'm still puzzled," Judge Bowen said, shaking his head. "If the judge and Daphne are in the Lakewood house, then what's the story about the homeless man being a judge? Is the caller suggesting three people have been kidnapped?"

"I have a question for you," interjected the chief. "Why aren't the kidnappers asking for ransom money? And I'm really suspicious about the call. This is not an accidental piece of information discovered by a Good Samaritan," he added. "The caller knows what's going on in that Lakewood house."

"It's not about the money," Judge Bowen said. "They have a vendetta against Judge McNeil. By kidnapping him, Leroy Walker—if he's one of the kidnappers—has been able to get Judge McNeil removed from a triple-murder case. But I agree: the caller knows what's happening in that house."

"The caller might have a vendetta against the kidnapper ... or kidnappers. I'd still like to check out the house," Manfredi said.

"Detective, remember you have no authority in this jurisdiction," the Denver chief said.

"I know, sir. But if the kidnapped man and woman are the judge and his daughter, your men need me to identify them."

"Based on the address the caller gave, this is probably the Jefferson County sheriff's jurisdiction. We need to get them involved immediately. I'll make a call to the sheriff."

"Would you please ask the sheriff to allow me to accompany his deputies? I've been working on this case for a long time and have tons of information. I believe they can benefit from my investigation. Look, I don't have a gun. I'll just accompany them."

"The sheriff is a good friend of mine. I'll ask him to deputize you temporarily and let you carry a gun," the Denver chief said with a smile.

* * *

Shorty knocked on Doc's bedroom door. When he didn't hear a response, he banged on the door. "Hey, Doc. Get up. It's eleven thirty. I need to shower and pack. You gotta watch the lawyer."

There was still no response, so Shorty pushed the door open and walked into the room. Doc was not in his bed. Looking around, Shorty saw that Doc's computer, his bags, and the new suitcase he had bought for the trip were gone. Shorty opened Doc's closet but found only empty hangers. He panicked and ran to the bathroom to discover that Doc had also taken all his toiletries. A note typed on a large piece of paper and taped to the cabinet door stopped him cold: "I can't help you torture people anymore."

"You motherfucker!" Shorty shouted as he dialed Boss's number. Boss didn't answer. He tried several more times, but he only got Boss's voice mail. He unlocked the door to Amanda's room and brought her out at gunpoint.

"I'll let you eat in the kitchen, but no funny business." He led her to the kitchen and sat her in a chair. He tied her feet to the chair but left her hands untied. He brought her a bowl of cereal and milk and then sat in a chair across the table to watch her eat.

Amanda had a migraine that wouldn't go away. She had not slept the entire night, and she didn't have any appetite, but she pretended she was eating, just to avoid her kidnapper's stare. She wondered whether she would leave the house alive. Her friend must have informed her uncle that she had never showed up for the party. Her secretary must have told Uncle Frank she hadn't come to the office. She assumed her uncle and aunt were worried sick. But what could Uncle Frank do? How could he guess about the kidnapping? *Maybe they've called the police at least*, she thought.

Amanda saw a shadow outside the window behind Shorty. "Are you going to kill me?" she asked him, hoping that the shadow belonged to a policeman.

"Shut up and eat. Boss will decide. I'm waiting for him."

"Is *he* going to kill me?"

"I said shut up. Didn't you hear him yesterday? You'll be here for a few days, until we're out of the country."

"Suppose I can't untie myself. I'll die in this chair—"

"Shut your fat ass up! Let me call Boss."

As Shorty pulled out his phone and dialed, Amanda saw the shadow through the window again. Then she heard hurried footsteps. Shorty jumped from his chair, closed his cell phone, and stood behind Amanda, his gun to her head. "One sound out of you, and you're dead."

Amanda's heart raced. She expected someone to knock down the door. She expected gunshots, but instead she heard a loudspeaker.

"The house is surrounded. Let your victims walk out unharmed."

"Shit!" Shorty muttered, pressing the gun to Amanda's head.

"Let your victims come out," the voice on the loudspeaker repeated.

Amanda's heart was pounding. There would be shooting and bloodshed at any moment, probably her own. Would her captor kill her, or would the rain of bullets from law enforcement get her first?

* * *

Manfredi had already snuck in through an open window and had immediately hidden in one of the rooms near the entrance. He was watching the hallway through the slightly ajar door when his cell phone vibrated. He answered it quickly. It was Judge Bowen.

"Detective, I have good news and bad news. The caller whose message we listened to in the chief's office was telling the truth. The arrested homeless man was indeed Judge McNeil. I just talked to him. But the other victim, the second kidnapped individual in the Lakewood house, is *not* Daphne—it's Amanda. Do whatever you can to save her."

"Okay," Detective Manfredi whispered. He was numb for a moment. His brain couldn't absorb the two shocking pieces of news. What the hell was Amanda doing in this house? He was about to call the leader of the county's SWAT team and advise him to change his message when he heard the loudspeaker again.

"This is our last warning. Your partner, Leroy Walker, has been killed, and Judge McNeil is in police custody in Denver. We're not going to shoot if you put your weapon down. Send Attorney Perkins out first. Then put your hands on your head and come out."

Manfredi heard footsteps in the hallway. When the sound stopped, he peeked through the doorway and saw a short man pushing Amanda quietly toward the door, a gun pressed to her back. The man opened the front door, pushed Amanda closer to the opening, and shouted, "If you shoot, she'll be dead. Give me the Pontiac in the garage, and I'll give you the lawyer."

"That's not negotiable. You have to surrender. If you cooperate, we can offer you a deal," the voice on the loudspeaker said.

Manfredi was afraid that if any gunfire were exchanged, Amanda would get caught in the crossfire. He had never worked with the law enforcement officers in Colorado and didn't know their tactics. Time was crucial. He had to do something fast. He emerged from his hideout, tiptoed quietly behind the shorter man, and in a sudden calculated move, pushed him away from Amanda and out of the house. The man lost his balance and fell to the ground on his face, but he managed to hold on to his gun. Amanda's scream and the sound of gunshots from the gate area dissuaded Manfredi from going after him. Instead, he pulled Amanda inside the hallway, closed the entrance door, and shoved her into the nearest room.

"Lock the door behind you and lie on the floor," he advised. Then he returned to the entrance door. Through the door's glass window, he saw the man with the gun running toward the garage and firing shots erratically. The man ignored the shots coming from the SWAT team that had been positioned at the front gate of the house. He managed to get behind the wheel of the Pontiac and drive it out of the garage. When one of his shots hit and wounded a deputy sheriff, the other members of the SWAT team fired a hail of bullets at the car, breaking the glass and striking him in the chest and head. The Pontiac swerved off the driveway, hit a large tree, and came to a stop. The man was no longer moving.

"It's safe. You can come out now," Manfredi called to Amanda. "It's over. He's dead now."

Amanda was still shaking when she came out. She stared at Manfredi for a few seconds and then threw herself into his arms. "I can't believe you're here. You saved my life."

Manfredi put his arms around Amanda's trembling body and kissed her on the cheeks softly. "For our next date, please choose a nice, quiet restaurant, will you?"

Amanda fought her tears and smiled. "I promise."

Chapter 25

Manfredi found Amanda's car key in the dead kidnapper's pants pocket. The little car still functioned, despite all the exterior damages it had sustained when the men repeatedly rammed the car. Amanda was still shaking, so Manfredi drove. For the first few miles, Amanda was silent. She only stared at her hero every now and then, giving him a silent "thank you." Once they were far away from the Lakewood area, she felt safe and spoke. "How did you know I was in that house?"

"I didn't. Actually, I came here to rescue McNeil and his daughter, Daphne."

Manfredi caught her up on his investigation in Washington and Madison. He told her how brilliantly McNeil had sent them clues through his e-mails, telling them he had been kidnapped and taken to Denver. He talked about Leroy, the judge's assumed lead kidnapper, and the call that had led them to the Lakewood house. "But a better question is, what in the name of God were *you* doing there?"

Amanda told him about the note she had received from the judge and how she had followed the black Pontiac.

"I thought you hated him. Why would you risk your life for him?"

"You should've seen him in those ragged clothes, with his long beard and unkempt hair."

"Did you know that the lead kidnapper was Keshan Walker's uncle?"

"You mean the juvenile in the triple-murder case McNeil got?"

"Yes, that's the one. We think Leroy had a vendetta against McNeil because of the harsh sentence the judge gave him many years ago. But after Keshan was arrested, Leroy changed his plans. First, he wanted McNeil to make favorable decisions on defense motions; then he wanted to cause McNeil's removal from the case by keeping him captive."

"McNeil is notorious for his lengthy sentences."

"Exactly. He gave Leroy eight years for selling two bags of cocaine to an undercover agent."

"He did that to several of my clients. I was infuriated with him. I filed—"

She was interrupted when Manfredi's cell phone rang. He answered it immediately; it was Judge Bowen.

The judge was happy to hear that Amanda was safe, but he had called Manfredi to give him bad news. "Judge McNeil was the one who killed Leroy. He's being charged with murder one. I'm waiting for you at police headquarters."

* * *

When the two arrived at police headquarters, Judge Bowen was pacing the hallway. He gave a firm handshake to Detective Manfredi but hugged Amanda, forgetting that a DC superior court judge would never express his emotions in public. "I'm so happy to see you unharmed," Judge Bowen said. "I'm also surprised … knowing the way you felt about Judge McNeil, how could you get involved like that?"

Amanda smiled. "Professional hazard!"

"Have you talked to Judge McNeil?" Manfredi asked.

"Yes, and it was painful to see him looking like a homeless drug addict. He is so grateful to you both, and counselor, he wants you to represent him," Bowen said, pointing his finger at Amanda.

"With all the hotshot lawyers he knows?"

"Yes, Ms. Perkins, he wants you, and he has asked me to write you a check for ten thousand dollars as your retainer fee."

"That won't be necessary."

"He insisted."

"What are they charging him with?"

"First-degree murder, distribution of cocaine, heroin, and marijuana—"

"Distribution? Are you kidding me?"

"They found multiple Ziploc bags of drugs and cash on him."

"Has the Denver district attorney ever heard the word *duress?* The man was *forced* to sell drugs."

"Well, I'm hoping you'll talk to the DA in charge and convince him or her to drop those nonsense charges."

* * *

After saying a quick good-bye to Judge Bowen and Manfredi, Amanda left Denver police headquarters in a hurry. She felt her face burning with fever. She knew it was not a real fever, and it was not because of Denver's summer heat either—this was a panic attack. Her feverish face was warning her that she should expect a period of anxiety. When she divorced Bryan, lost her job, and experienced her husband's scandal filling the pages of the *Washington Post* on a daily basis, she had endured three months of anxiety. A good family doctor had saved her with a nonaddictive anxiety medication.

She was desperate to go home, shower, and see her family—Uncle Frank and Aunt Julie.

* * *

When she arrived at Uncle Frank's house, it was five thirty. She had prepared herself for a rainstorm of questions from her aunt and a lengthy lecture from her uncle, but instead, she found them smiling and happy to see her. "Did my friend call you last night?" she asked them.

"No," they responded in unison.

"Uncle Frank, did you go to the office today?"

"No. I was taking depositions all day at the pharmaceutical company's attorneys' office."

"And you haven't watched the news?"

"No. It's not six o'clock yet."

"Oh, thank God," Amanda said with a sigh of relief.

She invited her uncle and aunt to sit down and told them the scary tale of what had happened to her.

With every detail, Aunt Julie cupped her face and said, "Oh my God." After Amanda reassured them she was not physically injured, Uncle Frank, who had listened silently, walked over to her and took her in his arms. "I've always admired your fearless approach as a lawyer, but I cannot approve of your detective work. You're my brother's precious daughter. How could I have lived with myself if something horrible had happened to you?"

"C'mon, Uncle Frank. I'm alive. Nothing happened to me."

"You were terrorized by three criminals, and you call that nothing?"

"I have to admit, it was terrible, but I'm okay."

Aunt Julie didn't allow Amanda to go back to her townhouse that night. She prepared a delicious chicken pasta dish that Amanda liked, and they decided not to watch the news until the next day. After dinner, Aunt Julie accompanied Amanda to her old room and sat on her bed. "You're the daughter I never had. I don't express my love as much as I should, but like your uncle, I'd be devastated if someone hurt you."

Amanda kissed her aunt and said good night. After her aunt left, Amanda realized that although Aunt Julie could never take the place of her mother, she was the closest and the best support she could dream of having.

Despite the happy ending, Amanda had difficulty falling asleep that night. The images of the events of the past twenty-four hours kept dancing in her head. But the last image helped her relax and fall asleep—the image of her detective admirer who had saved her life, the Prince Charming who had not ridden in on a white horse.

* * *

The next morning, accompanied by Manfredi and Judge Bowen, Amanda met with Judge McNeil in jail. A spacious room had been made available to them after the Denver chief of police alerted the warden that the prisoner was a well-known judge from Washington. It was hard for Amanda to see McNeil in the blue jumpsuit, or Denver County blues as they were known by inmates. Still, she acted professionally, staying calm and not showing any emotion.

The judge praised Manfredi for his genius method of figuring out the kidnappers had taken him to Denver. He then turned to Amanda to show his gratitude. "You're a true advocate. I didn't think you would even bother to read my note. You risked your life for me. How can I ever thank you?"

"I acted like an idiot; I should have gotten the police involved."

"Please help me get out of here."

"I'll do my best. But Your Honor, first, I need to apologize to you for those terrible things I said about you to the kidnappers."

"Maybe they were all true."

"Could we please talk about more urgent matters now?" Judge Bowen interjected.

"Ms. Perkins," McNeil said, "I don't want to give the description of the third kidnapper they referred to as Doc. I have no doubt that when he was supervising the writing of my e-mails, he figured out I was giving information about my kidnapping and the town where I was being held captive. Yet he let me write and send them. I'm also sure he was the one who called the Denver police and gave them the address of that house."

"I totally agree with you. When he saw me tied to a chair, he yelled at them and told them I had helped him with his appeal. I remember his first name—Darnell. But I can't remember his last name. I don't want to tell the police about him either. I'm alive because he called the police."

"Listen to you two, a judge and an attorney," Judge Bowen said, shaking his head. "You have to give the police all the details about the kidnappers. Suppose one of Leroy Walker's friends in Washington knows about the whole scheme and the fact that Darnell agreed with it. You'll both be charged with defrauding the police and the prosecutor, obstruction of justice, and God knows what else."

"I agree with Judge Bowen," Manfredi said, breaking his silence. "Amanda told me he had long dreadlocks. Just give the police his description as close as possible. I'm sure by now he has cut his hair short and is enjoying himself somewhere else, probably in Mexico."

"I heard the kidnappers say several times they were planning to go to Mexico," McNeil confirmed.

"Me too," Amanda agreed.

After Judge Bowen and Manfredi left, Amanda spent two hours with Judge McNeil, getting details of his kidnapping. The two talked about the pros and cons of various legal arguments against the murder charge. They discussed some of the Supreme Court cases that could help them.

At the end of the meeting, McNeil shook Amanda's hand and thanked her again. "I have to confess, counselor, I deserve to go to jail, not only for killing Leroy Walker but also for being a terrible father … my poor Daphne."

Amanda saw that the judge was tearing up and struggling with words. "I think we should concentrate on you first. Detective Manfredi and the Denver police are checking every name and telephone number on Leroy's cell phone. They're also searching his belongings to find more clues as to Daphne's whereabouts. Now that the FBI is involved, I'm sure they'll find your daughter very soon."

* * *

That evening, Amanda invited Aristo to a nice restaurant in Lakewood located in a hilly area with a spectacular panoramic view of the city. The dim lighting inside and the soft jazz music added to its ambiance—a perfect place for a date.

"This place is so beautiful. The city lights remind me of another city," Aristo said.

"Where?"

"Phoenix. I was investigating a case there once and had dinner at a rooftop restaurant. The view of the city was unbelievable."

"So you liked that view better?"

"No, I like this view better because you're sitting next to me to enjoy it. As much as I regret the loss of two lives and seeing a decent judge go to jail, I'm glad this tragedy brought us together. After we said good-bye in Washington, I was afraid I'd never see you again."

"Me too."

Aristo took Amanda's hands in his and looked deeply into her eyes. "Do you believe in fate?"

"Not really."

"Why not?"

"Maybe because I lost both parents at sixteen, and then I had to leave everyone I loved behind. And then there was my failed marriage, my husband's scandalous embezzlement, the humiliation of being fired, and my public divorce … Do you need more?"

"I know why you don't want to get serious about us, but things can change. A month ago, who would've guessed that I'd be working on a case *with* you and not *against* you? Don't forget, I've had my share of disappointments too. I was devastated when my fiancée was murdered. I changed my plans, quit law school, and became a cop. But after the last few days here, I've started believing in fate again."

"I don't know."

"You have always been in control of your life. Why don't you just sit back, relax, and let your destiny take over?" Aristo said as he kissed Amanda's hands.

"How can I sit back and relax when you act like Superman in an unknown territory? You could've been killed yesterday trying to rescue the judge and his daughter."

"Look who's talking! You followed a criminal and risked your life to help the judge."

"That won't happen again. If you're going to search for the judge's daughter, the kidnappers' associates could come after you."

"I'm trained to do this kind of police work. You're not."

"How are you going to find his daughter?"

Aristo's cell phone vibrated. He apologized to Amanda and opened it. It was Prez, the young detective who was after his job.

"The chief wants you back in DC," said Prez. "It's urgent."

Chapter 26

During the presentment, Amanda argued passionately to get Judge McNeil released on bail, but the Denver judge sided with the prosecutor. Amanda's subsequent bond review motion was also denied a few days later.

The assistant district attorney assigned to Judge McNeil's case was a well-known Denver prosecutor in his early thirties. During their first meeting, he immediately let Amanda know he had won every homicide case he had tried. Amanda realized that she had to deal with yet another arrogant male attorney, like some of those she had worked with at Carter and McDougal in Washington.

The prosecutor had convinced the Denver judge that McNeil should not get preferential treatment because he was a judge. "He could flee like any other defendant charged with murder," he had argued.

When Amanda offered the judge's passport, the prosecutor treated it as a joke. "Criminals know how to get to Mexico!"

Before leaving Denver, Judge Bowen accompanied Amanda once more to the district attorney's office at 201 West Colfax Avenue.

The DA laughed at Amanda when she suggested that the district attorney's office should drop all the charges against her client. He told her that the case had all the elements the prosecution needed to prove murder in the first degree. "Your client planned, plotted, and intended to kill his victim from the first day. So I have motive, intention, and premeditation."

"You don't care about the crimes your so-called victim committed against McNeil?" Judge Bowen asked.

"By the time I'm finished with this case, there won't be a dry eye in the jury box," the prosecutor said.

"Are you ignoring the kidnapping, the pumping of drugs into the judge's body, and all the other inhumane things Leroy did to him?" Judge Bowen asked angrily, his face showing his disgust.

"If Leroy Walker were alive, I would be prosecuting him, but he's dead—thanks to your friend. Your judge killed a man, and he has to be treated like any other murderer."

"What about vehicular homicide? Don't you think the driver of the car that hit him and crushed his skull bears some responsibility?" Amanda asked.

"I have five witnesses who will testify that your judge pushed Leroy into the heavy traffic and the drivers could not have avoided hitting him."

After a long, unsuccessful negotiation, Amanda realized not only that the prosecutor would *not* drop the murder charge but also that he seemed to be looking forward to trying a highly publicized case. After all, how often does a prosecutor have an opportunity to try a murder case against a judge?

"What if I advise Judge McNeil to waive his right to a jury trial and let a judge, and not a jury, decide his fate? With that scenario, we won't have to fight over which evidence is admissible before the jury, or which evidence isn't. We put all of Leroy's prior convictions and also the judge's sins—being a harsh-sentencing judge—before the trial judge and see what he has to say."

"Ms. Perkins, I want to reassure you that no judge in this jurisdiction would be willing or would dare to exonerate a murderer just because he is a judge."

"Even if he acted in self-defense?"

"If you have already come up with your best defense scenario, why don't you let the jury decide?"

At the end of a tense two-hour meeting with the prosecutor, Amanda was able only to get the drug charges dropped. "I'll see you in court," she said, leaving the prosecutor's office with Judge Bowen.

Bowen thanked Amanda for her negotiations as they left the building. "I have to get back to DC, but I know my friend is in good hands. Please talk to him and gather more information before you file a medical alert. I know he's ashamed to talk to you about his drug addiction, but they pumped so many different drugs into his body that he's really sick now."

"I'll try to find out whether there's a short-term drug treatment program available to him in jail," Amanda promised.

* * *

To expedite the jury trial, Amanda waived Judge McNeil's right to a preliminary hearing. She knew the hearing wouldn't provide any useful information to her; the only thing the prosecutor had to do was put an officer on the witness stand to describe what he had heard from witnesses in the street. The hearsay rule did not apply to the testimony of witnesses at a preliminary hearing. An officer could even use double hearsay—something heard by people the police had interviewed. Amanda knew that for a preliminary hearing the prosecutor would not bring his actual eyewitnesses to court and expose them to the defense's cross-examination. And the only thing the Denver judge had to do was decide whether the police had probable cause to arrest Judge McNeil.

She did not raise the bond issue again because she knew her argument would fall on deaf ears. But she renewed and emphasized her client's right to a speedy jury trial. She was not surprised when the prosecutor got a quick grand jury bill indicting Judge McNeil with first-degree murder; the grand jury process was a one-man show. Only the prosecutor had a chance to bring witnesses and ask them questions. The defense attorney was not invited to the grand jury proceedings. As a result, there wasn't any cross-examination of the prosecution's witnesses.

Despite her disappointing days and her failure to get the judge released on bond, Amanda had exciting evenings with her detective admirer when he returned from DC. She felt comfortable around him and had started calling him Aristo. During one of their dates, she revealed her fear about the judge's murder trial: "The prosecutor is planning to bring witnesses from DC to prove that Leroy was an innocent victim in this case."

"Don't worry. I'll talk to those witnesses before he finds them, and I'll let you know who they are and what they have to say."

"Aristo, it's so wonderful to work with you on this case."

"I like the sound of my name when you say it. I have to confess, it feels weird to work with you on this case because I've always worked with a prosecutor against you. But at the same time, it gives me such a good feeling."

"So now you see not all attorneys are that bad," Amanda said, smiling.

"I don't know about other attorneys, but I know I'm crazy about the one sitting next to me." Aristo smiled and moved closer to Amanda, put his arms around her, and kissed her passionately.

Aristo's cell phone vibrated, but he ignored it, assuming it was Prez calling to tell him the chief needed to see him immediately back in DC again. Prez had turned into his nemesis. He was taking advantage of Aristo's absence to get closer to the chief.

Chapter 27

Judge McNeil was embarrassed and reluctant to talk about his drug addiction, as Judge Bowen had assumed he would be. Amanda had to gather information from other sources to file a medical report with the detention center's infirmary. In her report, she indicated that the judge needed detoxification followed by an intensive drug treatment program.

Once they found the right program, Amanda had a long session with her client in which she prepared him for what to expect. "The program is tough, but its success depends on you," she said. "I know you've seen many drug addicts in your courtroom and have heard about various drug treatment programs. But you were a judge, not an addict. I'm sorry that it sounds like I'm lecturing you. But I want you to get well."

"I'm so ashamed to talk about this—"

"Please remember one thing: you didn't do this to yourself. I don't have to repeat this every time we talk about your addiction problem. You know better than anybody else that you were under duress. I hope you show your willpower and determination and finish the program successfully."

"What about my trial?"

"Let me worry about that. We have Detective Manfredi working on your case. Your good friend Judge Bowen has allowed me to call him day or night and seek his advice. So let the three of us take care of your trial. You just concentrate on your health."

After McNeil was admitted into one of the drug treatment programs available in jail, Amanda concentrated on her trial preparation. She bombarded the trial judge with defense motions. The first one was a motion to compel discovery, asking for more evidence from the prosecutor. The next category of motions was to suppress certain statements made by

Judge McNeil when he was arrested and those of the other witnesses the DA's office planned to use. The last motion she filed was a motion *in limine*, asking the judge to review, in advance of the trial, which evidence could be included or excluded from the jury.

Douglas Hutchinson, the trial judge, was known by the members of the Denver Bar Association to be a fair-minded judge. Overwhelmed by the number of defense motions, he summoned both Amanda and the prosecutor to his chambers. "Ms. Perkins, though some of your motions are legitimate, others are troublesome. This is not Washington, DC. We do things more cordially here. You should sit down with the prosecutor and try to stipulate as much as possible. Otherwise, this trial could go on for months."

He then turned to the prosecutor and admonished, "The fact that the defendant is a judge doesn't give you the right to walk all over him. I understand why you have considered the house above Lakewood a crime scene and denied access to the defense. But why aren't you giving her the picture of the judge's daughter with Mr. Walker? She believes she needs that when she talks to the jury about his daughter's kidnapping."

"First of all, Your Honor, we don't have the picture. Second, there is no evidence that Leroy Walker kidnapped the judge's daughter. This is just what Judge McNeil would like us to believe."

"Your Honor," Amanda said, addressing the judge, "I truly apologize for filing so many motions. Had the prosecutor provided me with the evidence I requested, I would not have been forced to burden you. I'm outraged that the prosecutor is not only denying the kidnapping of the judge's daughter but also preventing us from proving that the judge himself was kidnapped. He wants to start his case by telling the jury that Judge McNeil killed Leroy Walker for no reason and without any provocation."

Judge Hutchinson turned to the prosecutor. "The man has tested positive for several narcotics. Why on earth do you think that a DC judge who has been on the bench for sixteen years would come to Denver, use various drugs, dress up like a homeless man, and stand a few blocks away from our courthouse to sell drugs?"

"Your Honor," the prosecutor said, "Ms. Perkins wants to introduce all prior convictions and bad acts of Mr. Walker. He's dead and cannot defend himself. This is the murder trial of Judge McNeil, not the kidnapping trial of Leroy Walker—his victim."

"Unless you two stipulate on some of the unresolved issues you have, I'm going to rule from the bench as to the admissibility of each piece of evidence. I don't think you'll like that, but I won't allow you to argue back and forth and slow down the trial."

* * *

Over the next few weeks, Amanda stipulated to some of the undisputed facts in the case relating to pathology tests and other forensic evidence. She relied on Aristo to investigate the case in DC and gather evidence.

When Aristo returned to Denver and provided her with significant and valuable evidence—another picture of Leroy posing with Daphne and their son, Malcolm—she jumped with joy and embraced him in a long hug. "You're a godsend! Where did you get this?"

"From Keshan Walker's mother."

"The boy accused in the triple-murder case?"

"That's the one—Leroy's nephew."

Chapter 28

After finishing an intensive drug treatment program, Judge McNeil looked healthier, but he admitted to Amanda that he was still apprehensive about the outcome of his trial and the safety of his daughter. The FBI had now officially resumed its investigation of Daphne's kidnapping, and the media was covering the news about Judge McNeil's murder case on a daily basis. The stories varied from one newspaper to another, however. Whereas the Denver papers were more preoccupied with the ranch in the hills above Lakewood where the kidnappers had kept the judge captive and with the ranch's mysterious owner, the *Washington Post* dedicated two-thirds of a page in its Metro section to discussion of a harsh-sentencing judge who had ended up killing his captor. One of the *Post*'s reporters, who had an insider in the superior court, had come up with a creative headline: "Attorney Hates Judge but Ends Up Defending Him."

Amanda occasionally talked to McNeil about the media coverage of his case, but she never showed him any of the articles printed in the *Post* or the Denver papers.

As in any other jurisdiction, murder was a serious crime in Denver; therefore, those facing murder charges were housed in cells with little freedom. But with the help of Judge Bowen, who kept calling Denver's chief of police every chance he got, Amanda was able to get some privileges for Judge McNeil. He could receive books and use the library for a limited time. He could play games with other inmates or simply chat with them when authorized.

At first, McNeil was scared to talk to the other inmates, but he followed Amanda's suggestion and told them about his kidnapping, his daughter's disappearance, and his drug problem. He was surprised when he received their support. "My addiction problems make them feel like I'm one of them," he told Amanda. "They sympathize with me because I've gone through a drug treatment program and have had my share of family problems."

"I'm glad you've found some friends," she told him.

As the judge's popularity grew, many inmates were interested in getting his advice on their cases. Soon, he was nicknamed the Jailhouse Lawyer.

One day, Amanda discussed the judge's new title with him and asked jokingly how he felt about it.

"It feels good, actually. I'm helping people. Now I know how the attorneys feel because I never practiced law."

"Are you telling me that now you can see and appreciate a criminal defendant's behavior from a lawyer's point of view?"

"Precisely. Now I really see that you have a tough job. You're fighting against a giant—the prosecution's office, with all its money, resources, staff, and power. It's like a fight between an ant and an elephant."

"I hope you're not stepping on any attorneys' toes."

"No. I've been very careful. I didn't want anyone to sue me for practicing law without a Colorado license. I've asked those inmates who need my advice to bring a written note from their attorneys saying it's okay with them."

"And did their attorneys agree?"

"With the exception of a few who have instructed their clients not to speak with me, most of them have welcomed my help."

"And why not! I too would have welcomed a judge's legal research for me."

"That's exactly what I've been doing—legal research. I've told them that their attorneys should be the ultimate decision makers."

"I'm really happy that you've found something meaningful to do—using your knowledge and helping people."

"Me too. Now I understand why sometimes even good law-abiding citizens end up breaking the law."

"Like Darnell."

"Yes. I have to confess, I feel so guilty for not accepting his plea and forcing him to go to trial. In the end, I had no choice—I had to give him ten years because of sentencing guidelines—but he showed me who the bigger man was. He saved my life."

"Mine too."

"When you encouraged me to talk to other inmates, at the beginning I was so afraid. I thought they would hate me because I was a judge. But they support me. Some even tell me they're praying for me and my daughter when they go to the chapel."

McNeil's job as jailhouse lawyer didn't last long, though. One day, as he was kneeling in the prison chapel, praying, he felt a sharp pain in his neck and a strong hand pushing him down. He couldn't see the face of his assailant, but he did see the long kitchen knife that had been plunged into his chest. With every stab, he moaned. He saw his blood running as he lost consciousness.

Chapter 29

Detective Manfredi had to fly back to Washington; his job was in jeopardy. Prez was repeatedly telling the chief that Manfredi had neglected the two homicide cases they were investigating together. Manfredi went to his boss's office directly from the airport. After a minute of small talk, he quickly changed the subject to Prez.

"Either you trust me with these two cases, or you don't," he said bluntly. "Prez has been after my job since the day I finished his training. If you think he can handle these cases, by all means, I'll give him all I have discovered and wait for your next assignment."

"Take it easy, man," the chief said. "I just got worried. You're spending too much time on McNeil's case. I have to deal with the families of the victims in these two cases on a daily basis. They're on my back. I was afraid I was losing you."

"I've known the families for two years now. I can never forget their pain and agony."

"I know they trust you."

"The reason I spent time in Denver is because my sources working on the homicide cases here are doing some digging for me. If they'd had any news, I would have been on the next plane back to DC."

"You know how much we love your work and the way you're handling these cold cases. Just give me a short report from time to time."

"Get Prez off my back. Give me another detective to work with."

"He's smart. You told me so yourself. I can't remove him now. You two have spent two years investigating these cases."

Aristo said a quick good-bye and knocked on Prez's office door.

Prez opened the door, nodded in greeting, and asked, "How's everything in the Rocky Mountains?"

"Cut the crap. Either you work *with* me or against me. If you talk to the chief one more time about my activities, I'll give you both murder cases and let *you* find the killers." Aristo walked away without waiting for Prez's reaction.

* * *

Aristo was gathering evidence for Amanda in Washington, DC, when he first heard about the stabbing. He flew back to Denver immediately because he sensed Amanda needed him. His prediction was right. A tearful Amanda threw herself into his arms and kept repeating, "I can't take this anymore. They're going to kill him before his trial even starts."

The stabbing hadn't killed McNeil, but his surgeon announced that the judge's condition would be critical for at least several days. When Amanda was allowed to see him for the first time, she couldn't believe that the frail man lying in bed, connected to so many tubes, IV lines, and machines, had recently been a powerful judge in DC. She couldn't help remembering the day she had waited in his chambers just to tell him that he was a monster. She had rehearsed the line many times in her head: "Judge McNeil, go to hell!"

Now she felt like the pale man fighting for his life was more like an uncle than a villain. She tried to figure out why the judge she had detested for so long had become so important to her. Was it because he was vulnerable, like any ordinary person? Was she trying to prove to the judge that he was wrong about her and other criminal defense attorneys? She knew that not every attorney was ethical and honest. There were dozens of attorneys who got disbarred, suspended, or admonished every year by the bar associations in various jurisdictions all over the country. Many had done unethical, even illegal, things. Still, was she trying to teach the judge a lesson—how to be kind to attorneys. Had he become special to her because he had been victimized and tortured by Leroy? Or was it simply because he was a client who needed her help?

Amanda remembered how she had put aside Bryan's cheating and helped him with his embezzlement case because he needed a good lawyer.

In the end, she concluded that she was helping the judge because he was a client and because she liked him after all.

Overwhelmed by the pain that Judge McNeil had gone through, Amanda went to the prosecutor's office without an appointment. "Are you still planning to try the judge after all he's been through?" she asked, her tone angry.

"Ms. Perkins, I'm sorry about the stabbing, but that's not a reason for me to drop the murder charge against your client."

"Hasn't the man suffered enough?"

"Why is it so difficult for you *lawyers* to understand that it's my job to prosecute, not to psychoanalyze the one I'm prosecuting?"

"Who was the assailant?"

"I know your detective is going to learn this soon, so I'll tell you. The man knew Leroy from—"

"Aha!"

"Our office is going to get a grand jury indictment as soon as possible. If the judge dies, I'll be bringing a first-degree murder charge against his killer."

"So if the judge dies, he becomes a saint, like what you've been trying to make out of a criminal like Leroy Walker?"

"My job is to bring justice to the victim."

Amanda sneered. "I have news for you. By the time I finish this case, there won't be a dry eye in the jury box."

* * *

Going back to the crime scene was not as easy as Amanda had envisioned. When she arrived at the Lakewood house, she froze for a moment. The horror she had gone through rushed back to her mind. But the presence of Aristo and the homicide detective from Denver police headquarters made her confident that she was safe.

While Aristo was doing his routine crime-scene investigation, Amanda took pictures of the judge's closet-sized, windowless room. She then toured the other rooms and took pictures of the judge's laptop and cell phone. Pictures of the judge's potential grave outside in the backyard were the final important pieces of evidence she needed.

Back in her office, Amanda continued ruminating about her meeting with the prosecutor. She was not sure whether the judge could survive an emotional and lengthy trial. The man had been tortured for a month and then forced to use drugs, sell drugs, and get arrested—and now he'd been stabbed.

The telephone on her desk rang. She reluctantly picked up the phone. "Law offices. May I help you?"

"Is this Ms. Perkins?"

"Speaking."

"This is Daphne, Judge McNeil's daughter."

Chapter 30

Amanda couldn't persuade Daphne to visit her father at the hospital. She was not interested in the outcome of her father's trial either. She had called only to find out whether her father was dying.

"If you don't want to see your father, at least help me win his case. Your testimony will prove to the jury that Leroy kidnapped you to torture your father. Then—"

"Trust me, your case will be much stronger without me. If I testify, it may hurt your defense."

"How's that possible?"

Daphne hung up.

Amanda's caller ID showed a 202 area code. She dialed the number several times, but no one picked up the phone. Aristo later confirmed Amanda's suspicion: Daphne's call had come from a pay phone in Washington.

"Don't worry," Aristo reassured her over the phone. "The FBI will find her."

"In addition to the FBI, McNeil hired two retired DCMPD detectives. They couldn't find her. Apparently, she knows how to hide."

"During those years, a con man was helping her. Leroy is gone now. She's going to run out of money pretty soon," said Aristo.

"Maybe she was calling to find out how soon she could collect her inheritance."

"Was she that cold?"

"She didn't want to help her father by testifying against her kidnapper. To me, that's cold."

"Maybe she's scared of her new captors. Leroy must have had a lot of friends. You saw the crazy one who stabbed the judge and almost killed him."

"She can go to the FBI and ask for their protection."

"Let's not forget she has two children. Maybe her new captors have threatened that if she talks to the authorities, they'll harm her or her children."

"No friend of Leroy will harm *her* or Leroy's child," Amanda said, shaking her head.

"But they can harm her older son, who's not Leroy's child."

"I guess you're right."

After the call with Aristo, Amanda pondered whether she should tell her client about Daphne's call. He had just started to recover from the stabbing. On one hand, it would make the judge happy to know she was alive. On the other hand, it would hurt him to know she didn't want to help him in his murder trial. After debating the outcome in her head, she finally decided to tell McNeil about Daphne's call. As an attorney, she couldn't withhold information from her client.

Contrary to Amanda's expectation, when she told the judge about Daphne's call, he sighed in relief, and a glimpse of a pale smile appeared on his face.

"Thank God she's alive."

"But she's not ready to see you or to help you."

"That's fine. I just hope Leroy's friends won't harm her."

"They won't. They know that if Leroy were alive, he would've killed anyone who hurt the mother of his baby. Besides, they have already taken their revenge: they stabbed you."

* * *

After spending a month in the hospital, McNeil was released and sent back to jail. He had to be hospitalized again when one of his wounds got infected, though.

As soon as her client was healthy, Amanda began pressing the trial judge for a speedy jury trial. When the prosecutor objected to an early trial by making excuses—arguing that they had not found some of their key witnesses in Washington, DC—Amanda surprised the prosecutor by saying, "We can bring those witnesses to Denver and make them available to you."

The judge was sympathetic and agreed that because of the stabbing, Judge McNeil's case should receive priority. When a defendant in another murder case pled guilty, Judge Hutchinson's calendar opened up, and Amanda got a trial date in mid-April.

Manfredi had obtained a written statement from every potential DC witness who had been subpoenaed by the prosecutor. This would help Amanda impeach the witnesses during her cross-examination if they changed their stories. Judge Bowen traveled to Denver and discussed some of Amanda's defense strategies with her. He provided her with valuable criticism and offered some of his own suggestions.

During a pretrial meeting between Amanda, Judge Bowen, Detective Manfredi, and Judge McNeil at the jail, McNeil seemed withdrawn. He had no interest in participating in any legal discussion offered by his defense team. When Judge Bowen noticed his friend's indifference, he encouraged him to help Amanda by actively participating in every issue that she raised. McNeil's response was disappointing. "She knows what she's doing."

"You must have handled more than three dozen murder cases," Bowen said, emphasizing the word *murder*. "Don't you want to help your attorney?"

"She doesn't need my help. Besides, have you forgotten that my brain is half smoked after all those narcotics they put in my body?"

"First of all, you have gone through a tough drug treatment program, and I'm sure your brain functions just fine. Second, I trust that even with your 'half-smoked' brain, you can still come up with some brilliant legal arguments to beat this murder charge."

"I hope Ms. Perkins helps me get out of here, but if the jury convicts me, maybe I deserve to be punished for my crime. I cannot forget that I've killed a human being."

"That was self-defense, after all he had done to you!"

"Fredrick, I've committed another crime against my daughter."

"Every parent has had disputes or disagreements with their kids, but not everyone runs away from home."

"Yes, but I'm the reason that *Daphne* ran away."

* * *

Back home, Amanda was still worried about her client's state of mind and his self-imposed sentence of feeling guilty about both Daphne and Leroy at the same time. But she forgot about McNeil's agony when she found a handwritten note on her bed: "You bitch. We know where you live. Watch your back."

Chapter 31

Uncle Frank and his wife owned a nice three-bedroom townhouse not too far from their home in Lakewood. When Amanda returned to Denver, they had secretly fixed the place up for her and put her name on the deed. But they had decided to wait and give the house to her as a gift on her birthday.

Initially, Amanda had stayed with her aunt and uncle at their home, but then she began searching for an apartment near her uncle's law firm in Denver's downtown area. She claimed she didn't like to drive and wanted to be close to the courthouse. But in reality, she preferred to live by herself. Uncle Frank and Aunt Julie kept quiet until the day Amanda told them she had failed to find a nice place and asked for their advice.

"Living in the downtown area is not appealing to me anymore. The prices are high there, the area is noisy, and frankly, I don't have a whole lot of time to spend searching for a better area."

Aunt Julie smiled at her husband, walked to a bureau behind her, and pulled a thick envelope from the top drawer. "Here, this is for you," she said as she handed the envelope to Amanda.

"What is it?"

"Read it."

Amanda quickly opened the envelope. Inside, she found the deed to a three-bedroom townhouse. At first she thought it was a lease, but she quickly realized the document named her as the owner. "This is a very expensive gift. I cannot accept it."

"We wanted to give it to you on your birthday, but that's five months away," Julie said.

"Take the house and say thank you," Uncle Frank said, smiling.

"Thank you both. This is a very generous gift, but—"

"No buts. You're our only heir. This is a part of your inheritance. You would have gotten this after my death anyway. I wanted you to have it while I'm alive," Frank said.

"What about the tenant who lives there?"

"We didn't renew his lease when it expired two months ago. We didn't have the time or the energy to keep up with maintenance and repairs."

This was the first piece of real estate Amanda had ever owned. The house where she had lived with Bryan, on Massachusetts Avenue in DC, belonged to him. Even if he had put her name on the deed as a joint tenant, she still wouldn't have felt that it was hers. At an early age, Amanda had learned that she had to work hard to get what she wanted. She hadn't paid for Bryan's house, so it didn't feel like her property. She had a different feeling about the townhouse, though. This eventually would have been hers anyway.

She loved her new home but thought it was too big for a single woman—especially a workaholic attorney. After Aristo rescued her from the Lakewood ranch, she was tempted many times to invite him to stay at her house instead of a downtown hotel. But every time she thought more seriously about the offer, she ended up deciding against it. She enjoyed their dinner dates and the old-fashioned way he was courting her. She didn't want to complicate things by getting too serious. Her past long-distance relationships had all failed.

She had recovered from the terror she had experienced as a hostage and was about to move past the nightmare that McNeil's stabbing had created for her. But what if Leroy's friends were determined to kill *her* next? She didn't like living a fearful life. But the note on her bed terrified her enough to give some serious thoughts about asking Aristo to stay at her place. In the past, she had mocked women who needed the protection of men. "Show me a helpless woman, and I'll show you several men who are ready to help," she always joked with her friends. But the threatening note was too serious to ignore. She needed Aristo's help.

After ruminating for days, she finally built up the nerve to ask Aristo to stay with her whenever he was in Denver.

"How did I get to be so lucky?" Aristo said, hugging Amanda for a long time.

She pulled away nicely and handed him the note. "For selfish reasons," she said shyly.

"What the heck is going on? When did you get this?"

"A few days ago."

"We have got to get you a gun."

"Oh no. I'm so against guns, I don't know where to start."

"But Amanda, I'm not here all the time. How about a dog?"

"I love dogs, but having a dog is like caring for a baby. I'm working on McNeil's case like crazy. Sometimes I even forget to eat."

"Okay then. I'll just spend more time in Denver."

Aristo informed the Denver police, but all he got from them was a police escort for Amanda to and from the courthouse—nothing more. He bought and installed a sophisticated security system in Amanda's townhouse. He also bought her pepper spray in case she was accosted on the street by one of Leroy's friends.

Aristo's presence created a feeling of peace and security in Amanda's life that she had never experienced before, yet she was still anxious about her trial and Judge McNeil's fate. One evening, she confessed to Aristo over dinner, "I've won several murder trials using the self-defense theory; I don't know why I'm so worried about this case."

"I think you're nervous because your client doesn't show any desire to win his case."

"You might be right. Deep down, he feels he's guilty and that he should be punished."

"I don't understand the man. How can he feel guilty? Leroy kidnapped him, drugged him, and humiliated him by sending him to jail—not to mention he had also kidnapped his daughter."

"He talked to me once about Daphne and what he refers to as the crime he committed against her. I feel he wants to be punished for *that* crime more than the murder case. On one hand, he denies that he kicked Daphne out of his house. On the other hand, he keeps saying he's been a horrible father to her. But that's not a crime."

"Daphne told her aunt Margaret that her father kicked her out because she slept with her boyfriend. If that's true, what was Leroy's role?"

"I'm still going to tell the jury that Judge McNeil believed Leroy kidnapped his daughter."

"You have the picture to prove it."

"Thanks to an astute detective I know. I don't know what I would've done without you. I'm beginning to understand why I lost every case you testified in against my clients."

"You lost those cases because your clients were guilty as hell, and the jury saw it."

Standing from his chair, Aristo put his fork down, walked around the dinner table, put his arms around Amanda's shoulders, and kissed her on the cheek. "You're a brilliant attorney and a wonderful cook. Thanks for the most delicious meal I've had in ages."

"Do you think it's a good idea to put the judge on the witness stand?"

Aristo sealed Amanda's lips with a long, passionate kiss. "Enough about the judge," he said as he helped Amanda rise from her chair.

He took her hand and led her to her bedroom. Amanda didn't resist. For the first time in her life, she was breaking a lot of self-imposed rules: *Don't mix business with pleasure. Don't date a man who lives thousands of miles away.* She had lived by those rules for too many years. She was now ready to experience a long-distance relationship—and yes, Aristo Manfredi was the *right* man. He loved her, and anytime he kissed her, she forgot about Judge Mc Neil's murder trial. She even forgot that he was two inches shorter than she was.

Chapter 32

Amanda did not ask Aristo to do an investigation related to McNeil's stabbing because she knew that the prosecutor would object to any defense evidence related to the incident as irrelevant. The prosecutor had warned her numerous times that he would fight any evidence she attempted to introduce to the jury against Leroy. "As much as you hate to hear this, Leroy is the victim in this case, and your 'law-abiding judge' is the murderer," he had said.

As a detective, on the other hand, Aristo ignored the evidentiary rules and thought that the information about Leroy's connection with the judge's assailant would help the defense.

The prosecutor had not given any details about the judge's assailant, but with the data available to him at Denver police headquarters and from DCMPD, Aristo discovered the man's true identity. He was a twenty-five-year-old heavily built African American who stood six feet tall and weighed 280 pounds. He had obtained a fake name—Jeffrey Hughes—for his ID card and other papers. His true name was Lionel Warrenton. As a juvenile delinquent, Lionel had lived in different group homes during his teenage years. His record showed several adjudications for selling drugs.

Warrenton had met Leroy in Hazelton, West Virginia, while serving his sentence for aggravated assault while armed. After his release, Leroy had helped him find a job and a place to stay. He had acted as Warrenton's mentor, friend, and older brother all at once.

Amanda was grateful to Aristo for his investigation, but she didn't have any confidence that the information he had gathered would withstand the scrutiny of the rules of evidence. She could already hear the prosecution's objections in her head.

A week before the trial, Amanda received notice from the district attorney's office that Judge McNeil's murder case had been assigned to another prosecutor—Denis Gray. She panicked. She had heard from her uncle Frank that Denis Gray was the best prosecutor in the Denver area and one of the most successful in the country. She filed a motion objecting to the change of prosecutor. Judge Hutchinson, angered by the motion, summoned Amanda as well as the new prosecutor.

* * *

As soon as they sat down, the judge addressed Amanda. "Your frivolous motion is denied."

"Your Honor, it took such a long time for the former prosecutor and me to reach an agreement on the scope of the discovery, the list of witnesses, and other procedural matters. I don't think I have enough time to start the discovery process all over again."

"Ms. Perkins, your motion is as ridiculous as if the prosecutor had objected to Judge McNeil's choosing you as his defense attorney. As for your agreements with the former prosecutor, I'm sure Mr. Gray will honor them."

"Yes, we shall, Your Honor," Denis Gray said, nodding. "In addition to our office's prior agreements, I'm also going to stipulate to some of the items Ms. Perkins wanted to waive."

"So it's settled. You two should have several meetings before the trial and smooth out any issues and problems you have," the judge said.

Amanda knew that she wouldn't receive any favorable discovery from the new prosecutor. She also knew that her opponent was an expert in Colorado law, so she did a second round of research on the state's laws, including its procedural rules.

During their meeting, contrary to her expectation, Amanda didn't find Denis Gray arrogant like his predecessor. In fact, he was a soft-spoken, charming man. This was not a good sign. Amanda had been hoping that the bombastic approach of the original prosecutor would turn the jury against him. But now she was afraid that Gray was going to easily charm them.

"Ms. Perkins, as I understand, my predecessor never offered you a plea," Gray said as soon as he pulled out a chair for Amanda.

"No, he didn't."

The prosecutor sat behind his desk. "Well, as you know, Colorado has a death penalty. So I'm willing to offer you murder in the second degree, which has limited years of imprisonment."

"Mr. Gray, I know you can probably recite every provision of every Colorado law by heart, but I've done my homework too. Judge McNeil didn't have a deadly weapon on him. That's an affirmative defense to murder in the first degree. So the best you can do is get a verdict of murder two. Clearly, you're not offering me anything."

"But I can argue that your judge used the vehicles in a busy street as a deadly weapon, calculating that one of them would hit and kill his victim." Denis Gray got up from his chair and came around his desk. In a friendly gesture, he pulled out the other chair and sat closer to Amanda. "This is really a good offer. I think you should discuss it with your client."

"If you use the vehicles traveling in a busy street as murder weapons, then you'll have a hard time proving the essential elements of a murder-one case," Amanda said in a confident tone. "How can a defendant premeditate, plan, and assume that if he pushes someone in front of a dozen moving cars, one of them will hit his victim and fracture his skull at the exact moment he had intended?"

"That's my best offer."

"The best offer you can make would be manslaughter, but I don't think the judge is even ready to take that. This was a classic case of self-defense."

"Your judge knew that Leroy wasn't going to kill him, that he only wanted him to get arrested and go to jail. So your client planned to kill Leroy the first opportunity he got."

"He had used cocaine seconds before Leroy approached him. Mentally, he was not in any condition to form any *intent* to kill. He just wanted to be left alone."

"Ms. Perkins, you know that voluntary intoxication is not a defense."

"Of course I do. But Leroy had provoked the judge many times; every day, he added a little bit more."

"Provocation should be instantaneous. It cannot be delayed, continued, and accumulated until the right moment."

"What about battered woman syndrome?"

"I hope you're not going to use that argument, assimilating your client's situation to a battered woman."

"Why not? A typical battered woman takes the husband's physical abuse and brutality for days, months—sometimes for years. The provocation builds up continuously until one day, under particular circumstances and at a specific moment, she is provoked to the point that she loses all common sense."

"You better talk with your client about your theory. I don't believe Judge McNeil wants to be compared to a helpless battered woman."

"What about self-defense?"

"What self-defense? Leroy was not armed. Just because he pulled the judge's arms or shoulders doesn't mean he deserved to be killed. Remember the proportionality doctrine? Your judge should have used the same force used by Leroy. He could have pushed him back in self-defense, not thrown him into a street full of speeding cars."

Amanda stood, looked Gray in the eyes, and gave him a Mona Lisa smile. "I'll see you in court," she said as she shook his hand. She left the prosecutor's office, already feeling defeated.

As McNeil's attorney, it was Amanda's duty to take any plea offer to her client. She wasn't surprised when McNeil rejected the offer. "Murder two could give me up to twenty-four years in jail, right?" he asked Amanda.

"I believe so."

"So he didn't even offer manslaughter?"

"No, he didn't."

"I can't serve any long jail time. I won't even survive a short sentence for manslaughter. I've got to get out of here and find my daughter."

That afternoon, Amanda called Judge Bowen to discuss the day's events and asked for his advice.

"Ms. Perkins, it's Judge McNeil's life. He should decide. If he wants to have a jury trial, you know he's exercising his constitutional right."

"I know, but he's so passive. I feel he's trying to be a martyr. I sense he *wants* to be found guilty."

Later that day, Amanda walked toward the parking garage near her office building. It was dark, but she still saw the shadow of a man running away from the area where she had parked her car. Fear crawled under her skin, and she froze. She wished Aristo didn't have to go to Washington every few days; when she walked with him, she felt safe. For a moment she hated herself for acting like a helpless woman who needed a man's protection again. Before McNeil's case, she had never allowed herself to feel that need. Even at age sixteen, as both her parents were buried, she had stood courageously by their gravesite and held her tears back in front of the mourning crowd. But at night, she had sobbed from the moment her head touched her pillow.

She hesitated to enter the garage when she didn't see the garage keeper. This was a one-level open garage usually used by lawyers and office workers in the area. Everyone paid a monthly fee for business hours use, but other people were allowed to park after office hours, and the garage keeper charged them three dollars per day. Her car, though parked far away, was visible because most of the cars around it had already left for the night. Amanda was waiting for someone else to appear before she entered the garage when she heard a loud explosion. Moments later, she saw the fire and the smoke. She ran from the garage as far as she could and dialed 911, her hands shaking and her heart pounding. She had no desire to see her car in flames.

Chapter 33

The car insurance company paid Amanda a fair amount of money for her car, but she had no desire to buy a new one. Taking taxicabs to court or the office seemed the wisest thing to do. When Aristo returned from Washington, she was at first too scared to tell him about the car explosion. She didn't want to hear another lecture about the significance of having a gun or hiring a bodyguard. But eventually, she had to share the news before he found out on his own.

As she had expected, he was furious. "The police have to provide you real security, 24-7. I cannot stay in Denver until the end of the trial. I'll talk to the Denver chief of police," Aristo said.

Amanda now had to admit it—she needed protection. Having Aristo in Denver would give her more actual and psychological security than the Denver police ever could. She noticed how Aristo snuck out of the courthouse during her recess to do his investigation on the car explosion. She decided to let him do his detective work and concentrate on her trial.

Before the jury selection, Amanda participated in a meeting with Judge Hutchinson and the prosecutor to discuss voir dire. Judge Hutchinson advised them that he was aware of their concern over jurors' exposure to the media. "I'll make sure that none of them has formed any opinion based on what they have read, heard, or seen about this case."

Amanda and Denis Gray went over fifty pages of questions that the judge was going to pose to the potential jurors. With the judge's approval, each eliminated some questions or added new ones. It took two days to select a jury panel out of the pool of 120 citizens who had reported for duty. Amanda used all of the defense strikes to eliminate active or retired cops, security guards, police relatives, or anyone with a close connection to law enforcement authorities except juror number seven, whose cousin was a police officer. The prosecutor eliminated ten potential jurors, mainly because they were attorneys, were married to attorneys, or admitted they distrusted the police.

During the voir dire, Judge Hutchinson eliminated a dozen individuals because of their prior criminal records. Using his power to strike for cause, he also eliminated two other categories of prospective jurors. The first category included those who admitted they couldn't be fair to the defendant; they strongly believed that if someone was arrested, that meant he must be guilty. The second category consisted of individuals who could not sit in judgment of others because of their religious beliefs.

The night before the trial, Amanda had a lengthy conference with her client, Judge Bowen, and Aristo. McNeil insisted that at the time he pushed Leroy into the street, he didn't intend to kill him. He just wanted to get rid of him, to be left alone. He instructed Amanda to pursue the theory that this was just an accident. "If the jury doesn't buy that, then we can pursue the self-defense theory," he said.

"But Walter, I agree with Ms. Perkins. Self-defense is our best defense," Judge Bowen said. "I'm certain the prosecutor is going to attack you on your two defense theories."

"I can hear him now," Aristo interjected. "Ladies and gentlemen, the defense is not sure about this murder case. First, they want you to think that this was an accident, but if you don't buy that, then they want you to believe the defendant killed the victim in self-defense."

"I'm afraid I have to agree with Judge Bowen and Aristo," Amanda added.

McNeil reluctantly agreed to the use of the self-defense theory.

Aristo felt good about helping Amanda, but he was disappointed to learn he was not on the list of defense witnesses. "I'm the best witness to tell the jury how Leroy kidnapped you when he found out you were helping Judge McNeil. I was the first one who saw you through the window, tied to a chair, remember?"

"How can I forget?" Amanda said, looking at Aristo with admiration. "But I need you in the courtroom all the time to take notes, to observe every juror's reaction to every witness they hear and every piece of evidence they observe."

"I agree with her," McNeil commented. "If you're a witness, you can't sit in the courtroom until your testimony is finished. The prosecution has dozens of witnesses. You'd have to sit in the hallway until they are finished. Then the defense would start, and you could not come into the courtroom until your turn."

"The judge is right," Amanda agreed. "And you wouldn't even be my first witness. I'd lose a lot by having you as a witness."

"Even after Amanda is finished with your testimony, the prosecutor might prevent you from sitting in the courtroom by claiming that they might call you as their own witness," Judge Bowen said.

"Okay, I had totally forgotten about the witness rule. I remember now: being a witness means that I miss the whole trial," Aristo said, sounding disappointed.

The foursome continued their discussion about the trial, the witnesses, and the defense tactics until Amanda got tired. She needed to go home and prepare for her opening statement. She gathered her papers, put them in her briefcase, shook hands with both judges, and walked toward the door. But before opening the door, she walked back to the conference table and addressed her client. "Judge McNeil, I have to tell you something." She hesitated for a moment and then looked at Aristo. "I'm dating your detective. I hope that's okay with you."

Judge Bowen laughed and clapped his hands. "It's about time—two of my favorite people. I'm so happy to hear that," he said as he stood and hugged Amanda.

"I'm happy for you too," McNeil said, smiling. "But I'm also happy I have both of you on my side. You're my dream team."

* * *

Aristo drove Amanda home in his rented car. Since the car explosion, he had been renting a new car every few days to confuse those who were trying to hurt her. During the ride home, Amanda was quiet for a long time, but then she turned to Aristo and said, "I got his approval for the self-defense theory, but now that he has agreed, I'm scared to death."

"What are you worried about?"

"About the outcome. He says he didn't intend to kill. For self-defense, he has to admit to the jury that he did the killing but argue that he had legal justification for it."

"I'm sure he intended to kill Leroy several times during his captivity."

"But you can't transfer the intent from those occasions to the moment that Leroy was killed."

"Let's see how the prosecution's case goes first."

"I wish they didn't have the death penalty in Colorado."

"No jury is going to convict him of murder one after hearing what his kidnappers did to him."

When they reached the cul-de-sac, Amanda saw several fire trucks and police cars near her house. "Oh my God," she said, her voice cracking.

Stopping the car and jumping out, Aristo ran toward the police cruiser near the house. "What the hell?" he shouted.

"Someone threw a small handmade bomb through the window," the police told Aristo. "A neighbor called us when he heard the explosion and saw the flames."

Amanda stood frozen, watching flames rise from her living room. *How can I prepare for my opening statement now?*

Chapter 34

That evening, after a lengthy meeting at Denver police headquarters, Amanda accepted Aristo's suggestion and checked into a hotel with him instead of going to her uncle's. She persuaded her uncle and aunt that her presence in their home would endanger their lives—she couldn't do that to the two individuals she loved the most and considered her parents.

The next morning, Amanda was still shaken. The image of the flames coming out of her house had not allowed her to sleep well. After a quick shower, she put on the same clothes from the day before. She was glad her clothes consisted of a dull grayish business suit and a pair of flat shoes. She always wore flat shoes in court because she didn't want to intimidate the jury with her height. She knew she had to stand in front of them several times each day of the trial. She then pulled her hair into a French twist. She made sure that nothing about her appearance would distract the jury. In the past few years, she had noticed that during her trials some jurors paid more attention to her than to what she had to say. At the end of each trial and outside the courtroom, at least one female juror had commented on her nice shoes, chic pantsuit, or even her hairdo. She looked in the mirror once more; there was nothing extraordinary about her looks today.

She left a note for Aristo, who was asleep, grabbed a cup of coffee and a croissant from the hotel's coffee shop, and called a taxicab. She planned to arrive at the courthouse two hours before the trial—early enough to avoid the reporters, TV camera crews, and spectators who were anxious to get tickets and watch the most high-profile case in Denver.

Later that morning, when Aristo saw her in the courtroom shortly before the judge took the bench, he commented, "You look beautiful even in your nun outfit."

Amanda couldn't respond before the courtroom clerk announced, "All rise." She smiled at Aristo, ran to the defense table, and listened to the clerk's announcement.

Judge Hutchinson climbed the three steps, stood behind his bench, and looked at the numerous spectators in his courtroom. Then, with a hand motion, he asked everyone to be seated. He sat down, leaned back in his swivel chair, and addressed the spectators who had taken every available seat in his courtroom. "This is a public trial, so it's open to the public. However, we have a serious case here. The jury needs to concentrate on the testimony of the witnesses and the evidence submitted to the court. I expect to conduct this trial smoothly like any other trial. Therefore, any comment, noise, or gesture from anyone in the audience will result in his or her expulsion from the courtroom. I hope I've made it clear. I don't like to hear myself repeating this every day. And trust me—if any one of you disregards the rules in my courtroom, I will not hesitate to use my power and hold you in contempt. And last, if there's too much noise or disruption, I can clear this courtroom of spectators in no time."

The judge then turned to the bailiff and asked him to bring in the defendant. The bailiff brought Judge McNeil from the adjacent cellblock and helped him get seated at the defense table. Amanda looked at her client and was amazed at how the civilian clothes had changed his appearance. His trimmed mustache and beard made him look more like a college professor than a criminal.

Judge Hutchinson asked whether either of the attorneys had any preliminary matters to discuss outside the presence of the jury. When both answered, "No, Your Honor," he asked his courtroom clerk to bring the jury in.

While the jurors were taking their assigned seats in the jury box, Amanda whispered to Judge McNeil, "You look great. Please remember what I asked of you yesterday. Look the jurors, the judge, and the witnesses in the eyes. If you avoid eye contact, they think you're hiding something."

McNeil didn't respond. Instead, he looked at the audience, and when he located Detective Manfredi in the second row, he gave him a half smile.

Judge Hutchinson gave his usual forty-five-minute jury instruction while Amanda was sizing up the jurors. He explained the grand jury indictment for the jury and the fact that it did not mean that the defendant was guilty. He then told them what to expect from the prosecution and the defense. He warned them not to consider the attorneys' opinions as evidence. "Only the evidence that has been admitted by the court is to be considered as evidence," he emphasized.

He distinguished the role of the judge from the role of the jury by telling them that they were only fact-finders, and they had to leave the interpretation of the law and the procedural rules to the judge. He also briefly talked about the reasonable doubt standard in criminal law and the fact that the government had the burden of proof to convince them beyond a reasonable doubt that the defendant was the one who had killed Leroy Walker. He also discussed the right of the defendant in a jury trial. He promised them that at the end of the trial, he would give them a lengthier jury instruction before they started their deliberation.

As Amanda had expected, the prosecutor started his opening statement with the moment the witnesses saw Judge McNeil pushing Leroy Walker into the street. He summarized what each one of the prosecution witnesses was going to testify to. He boasted about the number of the prosecution's exhibits and evidence that would prove beyond a reasonable doubt that the defendant had planned and premeditated to kill his victim. He asked the jurors not to be intimidated by the fact that the defendant was a judge. He warned them that the defense was going to confuse them by concentrating on the kidnapping of the judge.

"Please remember—this is not the trial of Leroy Walker for kidnapping or his prior bad deeds. This is the murder trial of *this* defendant." He pointed his finger at Judge McNeil. "If you agree with the prosecution's evidence, then it's your duty to ignore Leroy's past convictions and to find Walter McNeil guilty of murder in the first degree."

It was the defense's turn now. Amanda did not waive her opening statement. She was eager to talk to the jury and let them know about the defense's factual and legal arguments. She walked toward the jury box and stood in front of the jurors. "Good morning, ladies and gentlemen. My name is Amanda Perkins, and I'll be representing Judge McNeil—"

"Objection," the prosecutor said loudly, jumping to his feet.

"Counselors, approach the bench," Judge Hutchinson ordered. Hutchinson looked surprised and not amused to hear an objection at such an early stage of the trial—and especially during the defense's opening statement. As soon as the attorneys approached the bench, he put the husher on and asked the prosecutor, "Mr. Gray, what are you objecting to?"

"Ms. Perkins's use of the defendant's title," the prosecutor responded. "In this courtroom and this trial, only *you* should be referred to as 'the judge.'"

The judge gave a don't-bribe-me look to the prosecutor and then turned to Amanda. "Ms. Perkins, please refer to the judge as Mr. McNeil or 'my client.'"

"Very well, Your Honor," Amanda said. She walked back toward the jury box. "I referred to my client as 'Judge McNeil' because I have known him as Judge McNeil for many years, but I was admonished by our prosecutor that he is a *defendant* in this courtroom.

"Mr. Gray has portrayed a picture for you that is not accurate. His story is not complete. We will give you the full story—the real story. In July of last year, my client was a superior court judge in Washington, DC, presiding over a triple-murder case. The accused murderer was Leroy Walker's nephew. Leroy Walker had a grudge against Judge McNeil— excuse me, my client—because many years ago he had been sentenced by my client to eight years of imprisonment for selling drugs to an undercover agent. You should know that the DC code allows a judge to sentence a drug dealer to up to thirty years in jail for selling drugs. During his imprisonment, Leroy's family members suffered. He held my client responsible for all their mishaps. He got into trouble again when he escaped from a federal correctional facility in West Virginia. During his escape, he committed robbery and stole two vehicles. Those convictions, of course, added more jail time for him.

"During the last years of his imprisonment, he befriended two other inmates who hated my client as much as he did. Those two also believed that my client had sentenced them harshly. So the three of them planned and plotted to take their revenge. Leroy was the first one who got out of jail. He started a fake lawn-mowing business targeting my client's neighbors and was eventually hired by my client. One night, my client had an argument with his fifteen-year-old daughter, Daphne. She disappeared the next day, and so did Leroy Walker. My client has not seen his daughter for the past five years. He believes that—"

"Objection," the prosecutor shouted.

"Approach the bench," the judge ordered. "What now, Mr. Gray?"

"Your Honor, Ms. Perkins was about to say that her client believes Leroy Walker kidnapped his daughter. We have evidence that his daughter left DC on her own volition and lived with her aunt in Madison, Wisconsin."

"Ms. Perkins, leave this for your closing argument if and when you have enough evidence to establish that your client's daughter was kidnapped by Leroy Walker."

"Very well, Your Honor," Amanda said, and she returned to the defense table.

"Ladies and gentlemen, last year, on Friday, July 2, my client worked late in his office. As a matter of fact, he was reviewing motions filed by the defense in the murder case of Keshan Walker—Leroy's nephew. It was 8:00 p.m. when he left his chambers. He had walked just a block away from the DC superior court when he was abducted by Leroy Walker and two other individuals.

"He was transported to Denver in a mobile home while under sedation and hooked up to an IV bag. When he woke up, he asked his kidnappers who they were and what they wanted from him. They kept him in a windowless, closet-sized room for almost a month. Every day, they showed him a large hole they had dug in the backyard and threatened that if he didn't cooperate, he would be buried in the hole. Leroy Walker forced him to rule in favor of his nephew Keshan Walker, whose murder case was pending before my client.

"They pumped all kinds of drugs into his body to get him addicted— to make him experience what addicts go through and the pain they endure. This was the collective revenge of the three kidnappers. But Leroy had two additional goals: first, to get favorable rulings by my client and eventually cause him to be removed from his nephew's murder case; and second, to force Walter McNeil to sell drugs, get arrested, and face lengthy jail time.

"Mr. McNeil was kept tied to a chair, even when he sent e-mail messages approving defense motions in Leroy's nephew's triple-murder case. His feet were also tied to a chair when he was allowed to eat. They untied his hands only so that he could eat or e-mail his decisions to his law clerk. All that time during his month-long captivity, at least one kidnapper always had a gun pointed at him.

"After my client became forcibly addicted to heroin, Leroy Walker forced him to stand a few blocks away from *this* courthouse, use a phony name, and sell drugs. He wanted my client to get arrested. His mission was accomplished—my client was arrested. But because he was a first-time offender and didn't have any prior convictions, the arraignment judge released him on his personal recognizance. This angered Leroy, since he and his cohorts had planned to escape to Mexico. He had to come up with another plan. He knew that the only way my client would get a lengthy sentence was if he got convicted for felony drug distribution.

"So the next day, Leroy and one other kidnapper dressed my client as a homeless drug addict and shoved dozens of Ziploc bags of marijuana, cocaine, and heroin into his pockets. To imply that he had already sold some Ziploc bags of narcotics, they put several twenty-dollar bills in his pockets too.

"Forty-five minutes before his death, Leroy Walker showed my client a picture of himself posing with my client's daughter, Daphne. In that picture, Leroy Walker was holding a seven-month-old baby, which he claimed he'd had with Daphne. He told my client that the baby was my client's grandson. My client couldn't erase the image of his daughter with Leroy and their baby. His daughter was only fifteen when she disappeared. This was statutory rape—"

"Objection, Your Honor."

"Approach the bench."

"Your Honor, the defendant's daughter had a child with her boyfriend. The age of Leroy's baby proves that by the time he slept with her, she was over eighteen."

"Your Honor, the age of Leroy's baby with Daphne doesn't negate the possibility that Leroy slept with her when she was fifteen. In any event, this was my client's state of mind."

"Ms. Perkins, please leave these arguments for your closing statement, provided you have proved all of your allegations," Judge Hutchinson ruled.

"Very well, Your Honor." She turned back to the jury. "Ladies and gentlemen, when my client was standing a few blocks away from this courthouse, looking like a homeless man, forced to sell drugs, all he could think of was his daughter, the daughter he had not seen for five years. Leroy had already threatened that if my client messed up the sale and didn't get arrested, he would never see his daughter again.

"The pain was too much to bear. My client opened a Ziploc bag of cocaine and snorted it in an attempt to forget his misery. Leroy, who was watching him from across the street, expecting him to make a transaction and get arrested, lost his patience. He became angry because my client was using the drugs instead of selling them. He made his way across the busy street and charged toward my client. He grabbed his arm and pulled him toward the curb, where the drivers and the occupants of the cars could see him. He threatened that if my client messed up, he would kill him and his daughter—"

"Objection."

"Sustained. Jury should disregard the last statement," Judge Hutchinson ruled.

"Ladies and gentlemen, my client thought that his daughter's life was in danger. Leroy's act of grabbing and pulling him toward the street created fear in him that his life, too, was in imminent danger. That's why he pushed Leroy into the street."

Amanda paused, looked at the faces of the jurors for a moment, and continued. "Ladies and gentlemen, this is called self-defense, a universally accepted norm that gives legal justification to homicide in every criminal code in every jurisdiction."

* * *

Aristo left the courtroom in the afternoon to search for the list of individuals who had visited Lionel Warrenton—Judge McNeil's assailant—in jail. With the help of the Denver police, he singled out two men who were good friends of Warrenton. Over the past month, each man had visited him every week, but separately. He also got the tape of the telephone conversations Warrenton had held with those two individuals. In one phone call, he had urged his friend, "You better get the bitch before she starts the trial."

Aristo asked the Denver police to get a handwriting sample from the men. A handwriting expert confirmed that one of the two men had written the threatening note Amanda had found on her bed.

After the Denver police obtained a search warrant for the arrest of the two individuals involved in the arson, Aristo let them handle their police work. He had successfully identified the suspects. Still, he was deeply concerned about Amanda's safety. Had this murder case belonged to anyone other than McNeil, he would have asked Amanda to withdraw from the case. But this was Judge McNeil, a man he had liked and respected for so many years. Besides, he realized that even if he did suggest the withdrawal, Amanda would not leave McNeil, no matter how often she was threatened.

Chapter 35

Judge Bowen invited Amanda and Detective Manfredi to dinner to review the first day of the trial. Amanda was not happy with her opening statement. "I was interrupted several times, and I forgot some significant issues I had planned to discuss," she said.

"Ms. Perkins, the prosecutor unintentionally helped your case by interrupting you so many times," said Judge Bowen.

"How do you know? You're my witness; you're not supposed to be in the courtroom."

"Your secretary, Molly, gave us all the details. She also told us some of the jurors really seemed angry at the prosecutor."

"He tried to tell the jury he had a strong case—he was the boss in that courtroom. How did that help *me?*"

"Ms. Perkins, he started with the victim's death, but you started from the beginning," Judge Bowen said. "The jury was listening to an incredible story, and every time he interrupted you, they felt deprived of hearing what had actually happened. They sensed Gray was trying to hide something from them."

"Judge Bowen is right," Manfredi said, nodding.

"Imagine you're watching an interesting play," Judge Bowen continued. "And the director jumps to the stage and interrupts the play several times because he doesn't like the way the story is unfolding, or he doesn't like the way the actors are portraying the characters. Ms. Perkins, you know well that the jury doesn't understand the evidentiary rules, so every time the prosecutor interrupted you, he only made the jury angry."

"I don't know what Judge McNeil thinks about today's proceedings," Amanda said.

"I went to the detention center to say good-bye," Judge Bowen said. "He was very pleased with your performance."

"Judge Bowen, I wish you didn't have to go back to Washington so soon. I could use your advice," Amanda said.

"I have to go back, but let me know when the defense case starts. I'll be here."

"What's happening with Keshan Walker's murder case?" Aristo asked Judge Bowen.

"We'll start the trial next month. Keshan's attorney is confident that she will win the case."

"Good for her," Amanda said. "I wish I had that much confidence."

"Look, for the first day, you scored a lot," Manfredi said. "First, you had a strong opening statement. Then with your cross-examination of the prosecution's witnesses, you established that the judge had been kidnapped. Witnesses also testified that there was a hole in the backyard, as you described in your opening statement. The jury saw the pictures of the house, the judge's windowless room, his laptop, cell phone, and attaché. Your cross-examination also proved that Leroy and two other kidnappers lived there."

* * *

Back in the hotel, after a glass of wine, Amanda seemed more relaxed. Aristo gave her a backrub and whispered in her ear, "You're gonna win this case."

"I wish I could believe that."

"Tomorrow, I'll talk to the crime-scene people to see whether Leroy had a gun on him."

"I asked the prosecutor in my discovery request. He said no."

"I'm gonna find out whether he hid it in his car, and if the car was near him, you can tell the jury that the gun was *readily* available to him."

"You're such a great help, you know that?"

"Thanks. Do I get a reward for my detective work?"

Amanda stood, put her arms around Aristo's shoulders, and kissed him. "How about a kiss for every new piece of evidence you bring me?"

"That's not enough, counselor."

Chapter 36

The next morning, the prosecutor introduced five eyewitnesses who testified that they had seen the defendant push Leroy Walker into the street. The testimony of each witness lasted between twenty-five and thirty-five minutes.

The witness stand was to the right of Judge Hutchinson and opposite of his courtroom clerk. The judge turned in his swivel chair and stared at the witness each time he heard the same repetitive statement: "I saw him pushing the man to the street." Amanda noticed that the judge was not amused.

On cross-examination, Amanda asked each witness a limited number of questions, aiming to get the same answer.

> Amanda: On direct examination, you said that you only saw the back of the man who was arguing with my client, right?
>
> Prosecutor: Objection. On direct, the witness didn't testify that Leroy was arguing.
>
> Court: Overruled.
>
> Witness: Can you repeat the question?
>
> Amanda: You saw the back of the man who was arguing with my client, correct?

Witness: Correct.

Amanda: Could you describe him physically?

Witness: He was a tall, big man.

Amanda: How tall and how big?

Witness: Maybe six three or six four and between 280 and 300 pounds.

Amanda: Could you describe my client physically?

Witness: Maybe five ten or five eleven, around 165 to 170.

Amanda: Because you only saw the man's back, you couldn't see his face, could you?

Witness: No, I couldn't.

Amanda: So you couldn't tell whether he was angry or talking normally?

Witness: No, I couldn't.

Amanda: By observing the two individuals talking, could you tell if they were having a friendly conversation?

Witness: I don't think it was friendly. It was more like an argument.

Amanda: Had you seen these two individuals before?

Witness: No.

Amanda: So you didn't know what kind of relationship they had?

Witness: No.

Amanda: So you didn't know the heavy man had kidnapped my—

Prosecutor: Objection.

Court: Sustained.

Amanda: On direct, you said you saw him pulling my client's arm, then his shoulders, correct?

Witness: Yes.

Amanda: Could you hear any part of the heavy man's argument with my client?

Witness: No. The traffic was heavy. I couldn't hear anything over the sound of the passing cars.

Amanda: Did you see my client pull a gun?

Witness: No.

Amanda: Did he have any other object in his hand that could be used as a weapon?

Witness: I don't understand the question. Could you explain it more?

Amanda: Did my client have a bat, a stick, or anything in his hand that could be used as a weapon to attack someone?

Witness: No, he didn't.

Amanda: You said you couldn't hear them arguing, so if the other man had said, "I'm gonna kill you," you couldn't—

Prosecutor: Objection.

Court: Sustained. The jury should disregard the last question.

Amanda: No further questions.

Through her cross-examination, Amanda established that Leroy Walker was several inches taller than Judge McNeil and many pounds heavier. In a self-defense case, she knew that the height and the weight of the assailant were important. She had to emphasize for the jury that Leroy was much taller and heavier than Judge McNeil.

She also had to let the jury infer that Leroy was the one who had initiated the fight and assaulted Judge McNeil by pulling his arms and grabbing his shoulders. She was hoping that the jury would conclude that it didn't matter what kind of argument Leroy had with the judge. The fact that the witnesses had observed his behavior of pulling the judge's arms and shoulders would prove that he had assaulted the judge first.

The prosecutor couldn't rehabilitate his witnesses on redirect. They gave him the same answers they had given Amanda.

Amanda's morning victory took a turn in the afternoon when the prosecution brought in its forensic scientist and the medical examiner who had performed the autopsy on Leroy. Amanda knew that Gray was anxious to give the jury a detailed description of the death, the exact time of death, and whether there had been any struggle before the death.

She approached the bench and complained to the judge about the prosecutor's refusal to stipulate. "Your Honor, I've informed Mr. Gray that we are ready to stipulate that Leroy Walker died of a cerebral hemorrhage, but the prosecution has refused."

"Ms. Perkins, I cannot tell the prosecution how to handle their case. They have the burden of proof. They should present their case any way they want, as long as they are not violating the evidentiary rules."

"Your Honor, the enlarged bloody pictures of Leroy are very inflammatory. Could you please at least tell Mr. Gray to take the pictures out once his witnesses have finished their testimonies? He should not be allowed to leave the pictures here permanently."

"Your Honor," Gray stated, addressing the judge, "our victim is dead and doesn't have a voice here. These pictures will remind the jury that we're not talking about a ghost. They should see who Leroy Walker was."

"Mr. Gray, you can present them to the jury once, and then you have to remove them from the courtroom. I agree with the defense. They're inflammatory," said Judge Hutchinson.

For several hours, Amanda sat patiently through the testimonies of the state's team of scientists. She endured the pain of watching Denis Gray show the jury the oversized photos of a bloody and bruised Leroy. She noticed how some jurors turned their heads, signaling that they couldn't bear seeing the pictures anymore. She looked at her client. He was staring at the pile of defense evidence. She turned around and found Aristo sitting in the second row. With the desperate look on her face, she sent him a silent message: *It's over. The prosecution won.*

Amanda had decided not to cross-examine the members of the scientists' team because doing so would give them additional time to strengthen the prosecution's case. But when she saw the impact of their testimonies on some of the jurors' faces, she changed her mind. She had already stipulated with Denis Gray that the witnesses were qualified to testify as experts and give their opinions on Leroy's cause of death, so she was not about to attack their credentials or their opinions. Instead, she thought some commonsense questions could strengthen the defense's case. She had to establish for the jury that despite all their education and expertise, the expert witnesses were not eyewitnesses.

> Amanda: You're a salary-paid employee of the state, are you not?
>
> Witness: Yes, I am.
>
> Amanda: And you said that you have worked in this job for more than twenty years, correct?

Witness: That's correct.

Amanda: How many times have you testified for the prosecution?

Witness: More than two hundred cases.

Amanda: And during these twenty years of providing your services, how many times have you testified for the defense?

Witness: None.

Amanda: On July 31, 2010, you were not present at the crime scene, were you?

Witness: No, I was not.

Amanda: So your knowledge about this case is based on the police report and the information provided by the prosecutor, correct?

Witness: That's correct.

Amanda: You read a report stating that my client killed Leroy Walker, but you don't have any proof of that, do you?

Witness: No, I don't.

Amanda: You did not observe what happened between Leroy Walker and my client?

Witness: No, I did not.

Amanda: You don't know my client, do you?

Witness: No, I don't.

Amanda: Actually, this is the first time you have seen my client, correct?

Witness: That's correct.

Amanda: You did not know the relationship between Leroy Walker and my client, did you?

Witness: No, I did not.

Amanda: So you didn't know that Leroy Walker had kidnapped my client, did you?

Prosecutor: Objection.

Court: Overruled. The witness can answer the question.

Witness: No, I did not.

Amanda: You don't know exactly what happened between Leroy and my client just before Leroy fell into the street, do you?

Witness: No, I don't.

Amanda: You don't know whether my client was assaulted or threatened by Leroy Walker, do you?

Witness: No, I don't.

Amanda: You didn't see my client push Leroy into the street, did you?

Witness: No, I didn't.

Amanda: Thank you. No further questions.

Chapter 37

Denis Gray's disclosed list of witnesses included Montrel Johnson and Keshan's mother—Latisha Williams. It was a mystery to Amanda why Denis Gray would risk exposing them to the defense's cross-examination. After all, if the two talked about Leroy's kindness and good traits, it would open the door for her to bring up all of Leroy's prior criminal convictions and bad acts.

She asked Aristo to check Montrel's prior convictions so that she could impeach his credibility on cross-examination. To her surprise, Montrel was clean—no prior convictions.

On the witness stand, Montrel told the jury that when he was growing up, his family had lived a few blocks away from Doris Walker's house, and when Doris adopted Leroy, he had become Montrel's best friend. "He was more like an older brother, keeping an eye on me," he told the jury.

Through a series of carefully selected questions, the prosecutor drew a picture of a kind, hardworking Leroy—a family man who would do anything for the people he loved.

Montrel told the jury about Leroy's brother being killed in a hit-and-run car accident. He told them about Yvette, Leroy's girlfriend, and how she had become a prostitute after Judge McNeil sent Leroy to jail for a long time. He told them how Samyra, Leroy's daughter, had been raped by one of her mother's johns when she was ten years old and how she had been diagnosed with HIV. He told them about Yvette's disappearance with Samyra and how devastated Leroy had been after his mother's death.

Through Montrel's testimony, Denis Gray told the jury that it was Judge McNeil's harsh sentence and its aftermath that had driven Leroy over the edge. It was as though Denis Gray was telling the jury that even if they believed Leroy committed the horrible act of kidnapping the judge and keeping him captive, he did that for only one month. But it was Judge McNeil who had kidnapped Leroy's life and happiness for many years.

Denis Gray finished his direct examination of Montrel by sending an indirect message to the jury that although Leroy had done some bad things in his life, he had not killed anyone.

Amanda saw some of the jurors wipe their eyes. She feared that they believed that the real monster was Judge McNeil. He was the one who had given Leroy lengthy jail time and destroyed his life and his family. Before her cross-examination of Montrel, Amanda asked to approach the bench. The judge granted her request. Denis Gray and Amanda walked to the bench.

The judge put the husher on. "What do you want, Ms. Perkins?"

"Your Honor, I believe the court should appoint an attorney for this witness. I have some questions that might create Fifth Amendment problems for him."

"Your Honor, our witness doesn't have any prior convictions," Denis Gray said.

"Your Honor, I have to ask this witness whether he had knowledge that Leroy Walker planned to kidnap the judge, and his answer might incriminate him."

"Mr. Gray, that's a legitimate concern," the judge said, agreeing with Amanda. "I'll break for lunch so that I can find a court-appointed attorney for this witness. We'll resume the trial at 2:00 p.m."

Amanda ignored the angry expression on the prosecutor's face. She was relieved that the judge had given her a long lunch recess. She hoped that the lunch would dry up the tears of the jurors who had heard Leroy's sad life story and who seemed to sympathize with him.

After the lunch break, Amanda saw a more relaxed jury. The judge also informed her that he had questioned the witness, and Montrel didn't have any knowledge of Leroy's plan, and therefore, there was no Fifth Amendment problem and no need for the presence of a court-appointed attorney.

The witness was duly sworn by the courtroom clerk.

Amanda: On direct examination, you put the blame on Judge McNeil for everything that happened to Leroy. In

1996, did the judge send him to the street to sell drugs to an undercover agent?

Witness: No, but Leroy had lost his job. He had to support five people.

Amanda: Was Judge McNeil the undercover agent who arrested Leroy?

Witness: No.

Amanda: Was he the one who prosecuted him?

Witness: No, but he gave him a lot of time in jail.

Amanda: Do you know the maximum sentence Leroy could've gotten for selling drugs?

Witness: Someone told me it was thirty years. But man, that's insane. Other judges would have given him probation. If he had stayed in the community, none of those bad things would've happened to him. Your judge is insane. Who adds a year to a sentence every time the defendant uses the f-word?

Amanda: Your Honor, I move to strike the editorial portion of this witness's testimony. Could Your Honor also direct the witness to answer my questions and to keep his opinions to himself?

Judge Hutchinson advised Montrel to answer yes or no and directed the jury to disregard the witness's personal opinion.

Amanda: You visited Leroy when he was in Hazelton, West Virginia, didn't you?

Witness: Yes.

Amanda: Why?

Witness: His baby mama had stopped visiting him when he got transferred from Lorton to Hazelton. He wanted to know what was happening to his family.

Amanda: In fact, you were the one who gave him the bad news that his mother had died and no one had told him, correct?

Witness: Yes.

Amanda: What was his reaction?

Witness: He was devastated. Wouldn't you be?

Court: Only attorneys are allowed to ask questions. Please don't answer the attorney's question by posing a question to her.

Witness: Yes, Your Honor. I apologize.

Amanda: When you gave him the news about Yvette, his daughter, and his mother, he banged on the table and threatened to kill Yvette and her john, didn't he?

Witness: Have a heart. The man had lost everything.

Court: Answer the question.

Witness: Yes, he banged on the table.

Amanda: You found a PDS attorney to get the court's approval for him to attend his mother's funeral, didn't you?

Witness: Yes, I did.

Amanda: Did the attorney get him a pass to go to the funeral?

Witness: No, because the attorney needed more time to find the right judge.

Amanda: What happened next?

Witness: The attorney couldn't find a judge to sign her motion.

Amanda: When you told him the news, he banged the phone against the wall, didn't he?

Witness: Yes, he was frustrated.

Amanda: What happened next?

Montrel paused. His face showed agony. Judge Hutchinson directed him to answer the question.

Witness: He got into trouble.

Amanda: He escaped from Hazelton, didn't he?

Witness: Yes.

Amanda: And during the escape, he robbed the man who delivered food to the federal facility; he stole his truck, his credit card, and his money. He also stole another man's truck, didn't he?

Witness: Yes, he wanted to go to his mother's funeral.

Amanda: And he committed all those crimes when he had only a few months until his parole, correct?

Witness: Yes.

Amanda: Had he stayed in Hazelton, he would've finished his sentence in a short period of time, wouldn't he?

Witness: Everything that happened to Leroy was because of that son of a bitch who is sitting next to you.

Montrel stood and pointed at Judge McNeil.

"No further questions," said Amanda.

Chapter 38

Denis Gray announced that he was about to wrap up the state's case-in-chief that morning. The prosecution had only one more witness to call—Latisha Williams, Keshan's mother.

As usual, Amanda had avoided the reporters by coming to court early. She had done that almost every day since the beginning of the trial. Unlike Gray, who talked to the reporters and was eager to stand in front of the TV cameras, Amanda refused to talk to them, and when she was caught off-guard in an unusual place such as the ladies' room, she would simply say, "No comment." When he was in Denver, Aristo always drove her from the courthouse at the end of each trial day.

Latisha Williams came to court dressed like a cocktail waitress. She wore a short skirt and a tacky top that showed much of her breasts. Amanda saw the surprised, somewhat-panicked expression on Gray's face. Apparently, he had forgotten to tell his witness to dress conservatively.

He asked Latisha a series of questions similar to those he had posed to Montrel. Amanda knew what the prosecutor was trying to do—rehabilitate Leroy Walker. He was actually asking the jury to ignore Leroy's prior crimes and concentrate only on his good deeds.

Latisha repeated some of the information Montrel had shared with the jury during his testimony. She then emphasized that Leroy had raised Keshan after Leroy's brother's death, like a father, not an uncle. She concluded her testimony by telling the jury that Leroy always helped the kids in the neighborhood by keeping them from using or selling drugs.

Denis Gray jumped to his feet, trying to cut off Latisha Williams's testimony, but it was too late. She had already opened the door for Amanda to impeach her with Leroy's drug-dealing days.

Amanda rose from the defense table, walked to the jury box, and stayed near its edge, facing the witness.

Amanda: How old was Keshan when Leroy started selling drugs?

Prosecutor: Objection.

Court: Overruled. The witness can answer the question.

Witness: I don't know about Leroy selling drugs.

Amanda: I remind you, Ms. Williams, that you're under oath. Let me pose another question. You said Leroy raised your son. How old was your son when Leroy started serving his jail time?

Witness: I don't remember.

Amanda: Isn't it true that Keshan was only three years old when Leroy got incarcerated?

Witness: I don't remember.

Amanda: Isn't it true that Leroy was in jail for ten years?

Witness: He was in jail, but I don't know for how long.

Amanda: Do you remember the funeral for Leroy's mother?

Witness: Yes.

Amanda: When he escaped, he hid in your basement, didn't he?

Witness: Yes, he did, but I knew nothing about him being there. The police cleared me.

Amanda: You said you don't remember how many years Leroy was in jail. Do you remember when he was released?

Witness: A few years ago.

Amanda: By my calculation, he had a total of seven years acting like a father to Keshan, didn't he?

Witness: I haven't been counting the years.

Amanda: How old is your son?

Witness: Seventeen.

Amanda: Where is he now?

Prosecutor: Objection.

Court: Overruled.

Prosecutor: May we approach the bench, Your Honor?

At the bench conference, Denis Gray argued that Keshan's murder charge was irrelevant to McNeil's case and the jury should not hear about the details of another murder case. "Your Honor, Ms. Perkins is trying to confuse the jury by bringing Keshan's murder case into *this* murder trial."

"Your Honor," Amanda said, "the prosecutor has opened the door by putting Leroy Walker's good character before the jury, and this witness is telling them what a good father Leroy was to her son. Besides, in addition to taking his revenge, Leroy kidnapped the judge to force him to rule favorably in Keshan's case. Your Honor, we have copies of all of the judge's e-mails to his law clerk and his rulings related to Keshan's trial."

"Mr. Gray, I have to agree with the defense; Keshan's murder case is relevant here because Leroy had planned to get the judge to rule in favor of his nephew. I'm sure you can damage-control all of this in your closing argument."

Court: The witness should answer the last question.

Witness: Can you repeat the question?

Amanda: Isn't it true that your seventeen-year-old son is in the DC jail facing a triple-murder charge?

Witness: Yes, but he didn't kill nobody.

Amanda: Was Leroy worried about Keshan's murder case?

Witness: Of course he was. He did a lot to get him off the hook. He always said he'd do anything to see Keshan free.

Amanda: Did his effort include the kidnapping of the judge who was presiding over Keshan's murder case?

Prosecutor: Objection.

Amanda: I withdraw the question. Did you know that Leroy had kidnapped the judge?

Prosecutor: Objection.

Amanda: I withdraw the question. Let me ask you this. Ms. Williams, when was the last time you saw Leroy Walker?

Witness: Maybe two months ago.

Amanda: Wasn't it strange to you that Leroy, who was so worried about Keshan's trial, all of a sudden disappeared?

Witness: I thought he was looking for his missing daughter and his baby mama.

Amanda: In addition to his daughter, Samyra, do you know if Leroy had another child?

Witness: I saw a baby boy with him a few times.

Amanda: Did he care for that baby?

Witness: No, his baby mama did.

Amanda: Do you know her?

Witness: Leroy brought her home once.

Amanda: Your Honor, may I approach the witness?

Court: You may.

Amanda: I'm showing you what has been marked as Defense Exhibit 27. Have you seen this picture before?

Witness: Yes, I gave it to that detective … I forgot his name.

Amanda: Detective Manfredi?

Witness: Yes.

Amanda: Could you tell the ladies and gentlemen of the jury who the individuals are you see in this picture?

Witness: There's Leroy holding his baby, Malcolm, and then his baby mama.

Amanda: Do you know the name of Malcolm's mother?

Witness: Yeah, her name is Daphne.

Amanda: Did you know that Daphne is Judge McNeil's daughter?

Witness: No.

Amanda: Could you point to Daphne in the picture?

Witness: She's standing next to Leroy.

Amanda: Your Honor, may I publish the picture to the jury?

Court: Yes, you may.

Amanda showed the 8-by-16-inch photo to the jurors, walking slowly from one end of the jury box to the other.

Amanda: You said the last time you saw Leroy was two months ago. Did you hear from him after your last meeting?

Witness: No.

Amanda: Wasn't it odd for someone who acted like a father to your son to just disappear and not even call you on the phone occasionally?

Witness: As I told you before, he was looking to find his daughter and Yvette.

Amanda: Isn't it true that Leroy disappeared because he was planning and plotting to kidnap Judge—

Prosecutor: Objection.

Court: Sustained.

Amanda: No further questions.

Amanda walked back to the defense table and looked at her client. McNeil gave her a nod, showing he was pleased with her performance. Amanda too felt she had done a good job, though she didn't care for Judge Hutchinson's ruling sustaining the prosecution's objections. She had wanted the jury to hear that Leroy had disappeared from Keshan's life because he was too busy with his kidnapping plan, despite the fact that the trial judge agreed with the prosecutor that some questions were inappropriate.

On his redirect, Denis Gray tried hard to establish for the jury that Keshan Walker was not the real murderer in the case in which he was charged. In fact, there was mounting evidence proving that it was his codefendant who had committed the crime and killed the three girls. Through Latisha's answers, he also brought to the jury's attention that Keshan was only seventeen years old, and despite the fact that he was facing murder charges as an adult, he didn't have any juvenile record.

Amanda sat calmly and let her opponent defend Keshan. Her goal was not to convict Keshan. It was to show the jury that despite Latisha Williams's testimony that Leroy had acted like a father to Keshan, Leroy had left him at a crucial time in his life to kidnap Judge McNeil.

When Judge Hutchinson told Latisha she was excused, she stepped down from the witness stand, but instead of walking by the prosecution table, she veered toward the defense table and stopped there. She looked at Amanda for a moment, with an expression of disgust on her face. "You bitch. I hope you and your client rot in hell."

Judge Hutchinson ordered the bailiff to escort Ms. Williams out of the courtroom. Amanda lowered her gaze. At that moment, she didn't want to see the jury's reaction. She was afraid some of the jurors might agree with the witness.

Chapter 39

Aristo took Amanda to their favorite Lakewood restaurant on top of the hill, where they could overlook the illuminated city of Denver. She was staring at the city lights when Aristo ordered two glasses of wine.

"You're so preoccupied. What are you thinking about?"

"The trial, Keshan's mother, this profession I've chosen."

"Whoa, whoa, whoa. Slow down. You're handing this trial brilliantly."

"I'm not so sure. Didn't you see some jurors in tears when Montrel told Leroy's life story?"

"But look what you did this afternoon. You dropped a bomb and surprised the jurors when you talked about Daphne. You showed them her picture with Leroy. Didn't you see the shocked expressions on some of the jurors' faces? Now the jury knows that Daphne is not a fictitious character you created. They must also know how McNeil must have felt seeing that picture."

"I still haven't been able to prove that Daphne was also kidnapped by Leroy. I believe if I could connect the two kidnappings, the jury might accept that the judge felt both his life and his daughter's life were in danger."

"They will. You haven't even started the defense's case yet."

"I know. But I'm upset that the jury heard what Keshan's mother said to me before she left the courtroom. I'm dying to know what they're thinking about her statement."

"Oh, those were just angry words from an uneducated woman."

"She called me a bitch. Suppose some of those jurors feel the same way about me anytime I crucify one of the prosecutor's witnesses?"

"It's your job to defend your client."

"That's exactly my point when I say I'm contemplating this *profession* I have chosen."

"You've always enjoyed being a criminal defense attorney. Why is this trial different from your other cases?"

"I feel like such a *hypocrite*. A part of me wants to defend Leroy. After all, I have represented many Leroys over the past five years. I've stood before judges, telling them about tragic events in my clients' lives and why they did what they did."

"Are you telling me that what Leroy did to Judge McNeil is okay with you? For God's sake, he even kidnapped you."

"No, what he did to the judge was horrible, and he should've been punished for it—by any punishment short of dying."

* * *

The next morning, Denis Gray submitted the government's 119 exhibits and informed the court that the people rested.

When Amanda approached the bench, Judge Hutchinson could tell she had a motion to argue. He put the husher on so that the jury and the audience could not hear the attorneys' legal arguments. Amanda asked the judge to dismiss the murder-one charge against her client.

"Your Honor, the prosecutor has not proven each and every element of the offense of murder one beyond a reasonable doubt. Furthermore, he has not submitted any evidence that my client was armed with a deadly weapon. According to the laws of this jurisdiction, this is an affirmative defense, and therefore the charge of murder in the first degree should be dismissed by this Honorable Court."

"Ms. Perkins, I see your point, but right now, I don't want to confuse the jury. If I give them a curative instruction, they may feel that now that murder one is out, they should convict him of murder in the second degree. I will review your motion for judgment of acquittal at the end of the trial. You can call your first witness."

The defense's first witness was Tonya Henderson. Aristo had arranged for her trip to Denver and gotten her a nice hotel room. Amanda had prepared Tonya for her testimony and had advised her to dress conservatively. In the past, several of her witnesses had shown up before the judge and jury in inappropriate outfits. She had learned from bad experience to warn them ahead of time. "Whenever you come to court, dress as if you're going to church or a funeral," she now instructed them. She was very pleased when Tonya arrived wearing a dark business suit.

When Tonya entered the courtroom and saw Judge McNeil for the first time, she froze. Then she became emotional and burst into tears. She cried quietly all the way to the witness stand. As she raised her right hand and swore to "tell the truth, the whole truth, and nothing but the truth," she wiped her tears with a tissue.

After Amanda established Tonya's employment relationship with McNeil, she asked and received the court's permission to approach the witness with a picture in her hand.

> Amanda: Ms. Henderson, I am showing you Defense Exhibit 27. Would you please take a look at it and tell the jury if you recognize anyone in that picture?

Tonya got emotional again and cried softly.

> Amanda: Would you like some water?

> Witness: No, thanks. I'm sorry for being so emotional today. This is a picture of Daphne. I haven't seen her in years, and she's grown up so much.

> Amanda: In addition to Daphne, whom do you see in the picture?

> Witness: Leroy holding a baby.

> Amanda: Who's Leroy?

> Witness: Leroy is the man who mowed the lawn for Judge McNeil.

> Prosecutor: Objection.

> Court: What are you objecting to, Mr. Gray?

Prosecutor: The witness is using the defendant's title. We have discussed this before. He's a defendant in this court, not a judge.

Court: He was her employer. Maybe this was the way she addressed him.

Prosecution: I still object.

Court: Overruled.

Amanda: How did the judge employ Leroy?

Witness: Leroy was mowing the neighbor's lawn, so when the old man who used to cut the grass for us got sick, Judge McNeil hired Leroy.

Amanda: Did the judge have face-to-face contact with Leroy?

Witness: No. He hired him on the phone when our neighbors gave good recommendations.

Amanda: What time of day did he come to cut the grass?

Witness: He would come early in the afternoon and leave before five.

Amanda: When did the judge come home?

Witness: Court usually finished at five, so by the time the judge would get home, it was six o'clock.

Amanda: So who was at home when Leroy was mowing?

Witness: Me and Daphne. But sometimes Daphne would bring her friends home to do their homework together.

Amanda: How was Leroy's relationship with you and Daphne?

Witness: I didn't like him because the first time he stepped inside the house, he got fresh with me. But he talked to Daphne a lot. She was a sweet angel. She liked everybody. Sometimes she would serve him cold lemonade.

Amanda: When was the last time you saw Daphne?

Witness: Five years ago.

Amanda: When was the last time you saw Leroy?

Witness: The same time. When Daphne disappeared, Leroy disappeared too.

Amanda: Did you know that the baby in Leroy's arms in that photograph was his and Daphne's baby?

Prosecutor: Objection.

Court: Sustained.

Amanda: No further questions.

Court: Mr. Gray, your cross-examination.

Prosecutor: Thank you, Your Honor.

Denis Gray walked to the jury's box and stood near juror number six.

Prosecutor: Ms. Henderson, you were more than an employee to the defendant. You had an affair with him, didn't you?

Amanda: Objection.

Court: Overruled.

Amanda knew that she couldn't object to the prosecutor's question. It was his job to establish before the jury that Tonya had a bias in favor of the judge. Denis Gray was trying to dismiss Tonya's entire testimony by telling the jury that because of her romantic relationship with the judge, she would say and do anything to get him free.

Witness: I was not married, and he was a widower. I don't call that an affair.

Prosecutor: So you admit you slept with him.

Witness: We dated.

Prosecutor: It was more than dating. He paid for your apartment in a fancy area in Washington, didn't he?

Witness: Yes, he did.

Prosecutor: You mentioned Daphne disappeared. Isn't it true that she flew to Madison, Wisconsin, to stay with her aunt Margaret?

Witness: I don't know nothin' about flying.

Prosecution: You knew the defendant had a sister living in Madison, didn't you?

Witness: Yes, but I don't know nothin' about flying.

Prosecutor: The defendant's sister called and told him that Daphne was with her, didn't she?

Witness: Yes, she did.

Prosecutor: So Leroy couldn't have kidnapped Daphne.

Witness: How do you explain that picture and their baby?

Prosecutor: That picture is a recent picture.

Amanda: Objection. The prosecutor is testifying.

Court: Sustained.

Prosecutor: Your Honor, may I borrow Defense Exhibit 27 and approach the witness?

Court: You may.

Amanda handed the picture to the prosecutor.

Prosecutor: Ms. Henderson, in addition to Leroy, his baby, and Daphne, do you see another individual in this picture?

Witness: A little boy.

Prosecutor: A little blond boy who is holding Daphne's hand, correct?

Witness: That's correct.

Prosecutor: Daphne had a boyfriend named Justin, didn't she?

Witness: Yes, she did.

Prosecutor: Isn't it true that the little boy is Justin's?

Witness: I don't know nothing about no little boy.

Prosecutor: Isn't it true that after Daphne told her father about the pregnancy, he kicked her out of his house?

Witness: I never knew about Daphne's pregnancy. He didn't kick Daphne out. He's the kindest, the most wonderful father—

Prosecutor: Answer the question. Isn't it true that he kicked Daphne out?

Amanda: Objection. He's badgering the witness.

Court: Overruled.

Witness: He would never do that. He loved Daphne more than life itself.

On redirect, Amanda was able to establish for the jury that the last update McNeil had received from his sister was that Daphne had been seen in Madison with an African American man who was built like a football player.

Amanda: Did it ever occur to you that the individual who looked like a football player could be Leroy?

Witness: No, how could it? The man was just cutting grass. He was twice Daphne's age. I could never imagine that Daphne would associate with someone like Leroy.

Amanda: Did the judge suspect anything?

Prosecutor: Objection, asks for speculation.

Court: Sustained.

Amanda: Did the judge talk about Daphne's disappearance?

Prosecutor: Objection, hearsay.

Court: Sustained.

Amanda: How did he look to you after his daughter's disappearance?

Witness: He was devastated.

Chapter 40

Detective Prez was messing up the DC murder investigation by interviewing the wrong people, so Aristo needed to fly back to Washington. Besides, he also needed to meet with FBI agent Ralph Brown, who had located Daphne. She was living with her boyfriend and two children in a high-rise apartment building in the Chevy Chase area, not too far away from her father's house.

After another chat with the DC chief and another confrontation with Prez, Aristo gave them an ultimatum. "If he messes up two years of my investigation, I'll quit."

The chief assured him that he would monitor Prez's actions, but Aristo was frustrated. He couldn't afford to worry about Prez when he had to concentrate on McNeil's case.

* * *

"Our investigation shows there was no sign of kidnapping," Agent Brown told Aristo as soon as he showed up in his office. "Here's my report." He handed a folder to him.

"But she was fifteen. She couldn't have legally consented to anything—leaving town *or* sleeping with him. We don't know if he raped her or not. We only know that they have a baby."

"According to Daphne, they had sex when she was over eighteen."

"You believed her?"

"Why would she want to protect the man if he raped her? We found no evidence of captivity. She said she was free to date anyone she liked

182

when she lived with Leroy. I believe her because she's living with her new boyfriend now."

"Was she ever taken to Denver?" Aristo asked.

"No, just from DC and then from Madison back here."

"How did she get back here from Madison?"

"Leroy drove her, but he didn't kidnap her."

"Now I can understand why she told Amanda Perkins that her testimony would not help her father."

"She contacted her father's attorney?"

"Yes, she did. Let me ask you another question. Did Darnell and Melvin help Leroy in transporting Daphne to Madison?"

"No, they were still in jail. Look, Daphne's an adult now. We can't arrest her because she hasn't broken any laws. Leroy is dead, so we're not going to waste our time investigating this case anymore. We're letting you and your detective friends at DCMPD handle this case. If you need her as a witness in the judge's trial and she won't come voluntarily, you know the rule. You can subpoena her … get a warrant for her arrest to assure her presence in court. It's your call."

"I don't think we can use her as a witness now."

"Call me if you have any more questions. We're now concentrating on our search for Darnell—the kidnapper who escaped."

"Have you got any leads?"

"Not yet, but we'll find him."

"Thanks for everything. One last request."

"What's that?"

"Please don't talk about this case to a detective named Prez in DCMPD."

"Why not?"

"This is my investigation. He'll mess things up."

"Okay. Don't worry, we won't."

* * *

Aristo took Daphne's address and drove to Chevy Chase. He sized up the huge high-rise building, which seemed to contain more than three hundred apartments. He showed his badge and Daphne's picture to the security guard.

"Do you know this young lady?" Aristo asked.

"Oh yes. A very pleasant girl."

"Do you know about her comings and goings?"

"She usually takes her children to a nearby park around noon and comes back an hour later."

"What do you know about her boyfriend?"

"Are these kids in trouble? First the FBI guy, now you?"

"Don't worry; Daphne is the daughter of a client I'm helping. We're trying to make sure she's okay."

"The young man has the lease. He's in his midtwenties and getting a master's degree at American University. You know the address?"

"I know where the university is located. I'm not going to talk to him. My concern and my client's concern is Daphne. Does she seem happy with her boyfriend?"

"Oh yes, they're in love."

Aristo sat in one of the comfortable chairs in the building's luxurious lobby. As the security guard had indicated, Daphne showed up in the lobby at noon. She was pushing Malcolm in a stroller and holding a little blond boy's hand. She wore blue jeans and a flowered spring jacket.

"Daphne," Aristo called out. "Can I talk to you for a minute?"

Daphne turned her head in the direction of the voice, but as soon as she saw Aristo, she turned the baby stroller around quickly, pulled her boy's hand, and ran toward the elevator.

"Daphne, please wait," Aristo shouted. "I'm not from the FBI," he said as he ran after her. "Please wait. I am working with Attorney Perkins. We're trying to get your dad out."

Daphne looked at him suspiciously. "You want me to testify at his trial?"

"No. Your dad's attorney has changed her mind. We only need to know that you're safe."

"If you give my address to the attorney or my dad, I'll move again."

"Daphne, your dad is fighting for his life. He's not in any position to hire people to spy on you."

"He sent the FBI after me. The FBI man was following me for weeks."

"Your father never wanted to have the FBI involved. They had to investigate your father's kidnapping and also your disappearance."

"Okay, now that you know I wasn't kidnapped, could you please leave me alone?"

"Daphne, your father is in jail. After all the torture Leroy put him through, he was stabbed in jail. He almost died. Don't you feel sorry for the man?"

"He killed Malcolm's father, didn't he? After what he's done to me, I don't want to see him ever again."

"What has he done to you that's turned you so against him?"

"Why don't you ask him?"

* * *

For several days before flying back to Denver, Aristo pondered whether he should let the judge and Amanda know about the FBI's findings and his encounter with Daphne. On one hand, he knew the judge would be relieved to know that his daughter was living a normal and happy life with her boyfriend and her children. On the other hand, the news would weaken Amanda's argument that Leroy had also kidnapped the judge's daughter. Amanda was ethically obligated to reveal the truth to the prosecutor and the jury.

After weighing his options, Aristo decided not to disclose the information he had gathered until after Judge McNeil's testimony. He postponed his trip and kept telling Amanda over the phone that he needed a few more days in Washington to handle some of his old cases.

He was relieved to see that Daphne was safe, but he was still burdened by her not wanting to share what her father had done to alienate her so much. He began thinking that Amanda had been right in calling Daphne cold and distant. His detective mind wondered how a woman like Daphne could be interested in a criminal like Leroy and have a baby with him. Was this Daphne's revenge for what her father had done to her? But what had McNeil done to deserve this? Daphne's voice kept echoing in his head: "Why don't you ask him?"

Chapter 41

The two individuals who had terrorized her were behind bars, yet Amanda still feared going places alone. The sound of her car exploding and the images of the flames coming out of her living room windows haunted her night after night.

After living in a hotel for a week, she returned to her townhouse, where the repairs had been finished. Her aunt and uncle helped her replace the burned and damaged furniture. She rejected their invitation to live with them. "I'm a big girl. I can take care of myself," she said. "Besides, Aristo has installed a very good security system."

One afternoon, when Judge Hutchinson recessed the trial early, Amanda took a cab and headed for her office. During the trial, she had been relying on her secretary and the law clerk to handle her other cases, but there was still a pile of work on her desk. She missed having Aristo around. He had acted as her liaison between court and her office. She had also become accustomed to sharing her day with him and asking him his opinion on witnesses' testimonies, the jury's reaction to each testimony, and so forth.

Once in her office, she rummaged through her mail, pulled out the important pieces of mail from the courthouse, and put them in her briefcase. She then noticed a medium-sized yellow envelope with a postmark from Prince George's County, Maryland. She opened it immediately, out of curiosity, because she didn't know anyone in Maryland. Inside the envelope was a folded letter addressed to her and a regular white envelope addressed to Judge McNeil.

Amanda opened the folded letter addressed to her first. She froze for a moment when she saw Darnell's name at the end of the letter. She read in a hurry.

Dear Ms. Perkins:

When I was released from jail, I was hoping that one day I could find you and thank you for your help with my appeal case, though we lost it. But I never imagined I would see you tied to a chair by the two idiots who talked me into kidnapping a judge. Please forgive me for doing something so stupid. I want you to read the letter I've written to Judge McNeil and deliver it to him.

Many thanks,
Darnell

Amanda opened the envelope, took the letter out, and began reading.

Dear Judge McNeil,

I've followed the news and know that you've been charged with Leroy's murder. He finally got his wish and put you in jail—but for murder, not for selling drugs.

During those occasions you reminded me of my dream and medical school, I expected you to ask me why I helped Leroy and Melvin, but you didn't. I believe you deserve to know the answer.

After spending so many years in jail and losing all your loved ones, you become numb. Nothing matters or scares you anymore, because you have seen the worst. You have nothing to lose. I think I told you this before. I'm repeating myself. Since I was the youngest in the group, Leroy assigned me to dig a hole—your potential grave. I hated every moment of it, but I think I was destined to find the treasure trove buried there. The owner of the home in Lakewood was a kingpin serving twenty years in jail. He asked Leroy to look after his property. Apparently, he had hidden tons of drug money from the feds in a box in the area I was digging. One dark night, I found the box, brought it to my room, and hid it under my bed. My first thought was to escape as soon as possible, but I waited for you to get arrested. I had planned to escape to Mexico, call the authorities from there, and tell them that you were kidnapped. But when they kidnapped Ms. Perkins too, I knew that I had to run. I bought a suitcase and told Melvin it was for our trip to Mexico. I hid the money in the suitcase and covered it with my clothes.

The money I found will help me live luxuriously for the rest of my life. You might think, "Once a thief, always a thief." I stole a few vials of morphine to save my dying father. This is my second and my last theft, but I'm going to pay back my debt to society by helping the poor.

Despite my horrible act of kidnapping, I feel happy that I could save you from having cardiac arrest several times. When I called the police, I thought the tragedy would be over. Both you and Ms. Perkins would be saved. I never anticipated Leroy's death and your imprisonment on a murder charge.

I know you are obligated to give this letter to the police. But even if you do, they won't be able to find me. I'm thousands of miles away in hiding, and I know how to spend my money so that no one can ever find me. I hope Ms. Perkins wins your case.

Regards,
Darnell

* * *

Aristo was still in Washington, so Amanda felt relieved that she didn't have to share the news with him. She showed the letter to Judge McNeil the next day but told him she had decided not to tell Aristo about it. "I feel awful keeping something like this from him, but he's a detective. He may feel compelled to notify the authorities."

"I agree with you," the judge said. "Darnell deserves a second chance. He saved my life and yours."

Back at the trial, Amanda's morning witnesses included several members of the Jefferson County sheriff's SWAT team—the team that had raided the ranch above Lakewood. The last witness was a deputy who had investigated her kidnapping.

> Amanda: What made you decide to raid the house in Lakewood?
>
> Witness: We received a call from the Denver chief of police telling us that two individuals, a man and a woman, had been kidnapped and were being kept captive in that house. The chief asked us to allow a detective from DC to join us and identify the kidnapped victims.
>
> Amanda: Do you remember the name of that detective?
>
> Witness: Yes, his name was Detective Manfredi. He worked on the kidnapping of the judge's daughter.
>
> Prosecutor: Objection, move to strike the part related to the kidnapping.
>
> Court: Sustained. Jury should disregard the last part of the witness's statement.
>
> Amanda: Without telling us about the information you received, what was your impression as to *why* you had to work with a detective from DC?
>
> Witness: He could identify the female victim because he had investigated her kidnapping.

Prosecutor: Objection, move to strike.

Court: Overruled. The witness should be allowed to testify as to his own thoughts.

Amanda: Tell us what happened next.

Witness: We surrounded the house. Detective Manfredi got inside through an open window at the rear of the house. We used a loudspeaker and directed the kidnappers to free their hostages.

Amanda: Did they?

Witness: No. At the time, we didn't know that there was only one kidnapper and one victim in the house.

Amanda: Which victim?

Witness: The female victim.

Amanda: When did you learn that there was only one victim and one kidnapper?

Witness: We were notified by the Denver police that one of the victims, by the name of McNeil, was already in police custody, and one of the kidnappers had been killed.

Prosecution: Objection, hearsay.

Court: Sustained.

Amanda: Without telling us about your conversation with the Denver police, what was your impression of the situation at that time?

Witness: As I said before, at first we thought there were several kidnappers and two victims. That's how we were ordering them to come out. But once we knew that there was only one kidnapper and one victim, we ordered him to let his female victim come out first.

Amanda: How many kidnappers did you eventually find in that house?

Witness: We expected more than one because the anonymous caller who called the Denver police—

Prosecution: Objection, double hearsay.

Court: Sustained.

Amanda: Please just answer my question. How many kidnappers did you find in the house?

Witness: Only one.

Amanda: Did you arrest him?

Witness: We didn't need to. He attempted to escape. He shot and wounded one of our team members in the shoulder and fired shots like crazy. We had to shoot him. He was killed.

Amanda: Did you rescue the kidnapped female?

Witness: Detective Manfredi did. He overpowered the kidnapper before he ran outside.

Amanda: Who was the female victim of the kidnappers?

Witness: It was *you*.

There was a murmur in the audience. Amanda intentionally paused for a moment and enjoyed watching the reactions of the jurors. Some of them had leaned forward. Some were looking at each other as if asking, *Can you believe this?* Some in the audience were whispering. But Judge Hutchinson didn't have to use his gavel. The audience became silent fast.

"Your Honor," said Amanda, "as I alerted the court beforehand, we need Your Honor's *curative* instruction."

Over the next few minutes, the trial judge explained to the jury why the defendant's attorney could not testify as a witness. He also explained that because Detective Manfredi had been present in the courtroom almost every day and had heard many witnesses' testimonies, he could not testify either.

Through subsequent questions, Amanda provided the details of her own kidnapping. She introduced into evidence the pictures she had taken, as well as those of her damaged car taken by the crime-scene photographer.

Denis Gray really didn't have any meaningful questions to attack the credibility of Amanda's witness, but he posed a series of questions to the witness to prove to the jury that the witness's testimony was irrelevant because the deputy was not an eyewitness to the real crime—the killing of Leroy. Amanda objected each time the prosecutor's questions were not within the scope of the defense's direct examination. And when Judge Hutchinson sustained every objection, Denis Gray gave up and said, "No further questions."

In the afternoon, Amanda called two doctors to the witness stand. Through their testimonies, she drew a painful picture of the judge's battle against the drugs he had been forced to take. She also called a third doctor, who informed the jury of the judge's treatment after he had been brutally stabbed in jail by a friend of Leroy's.

Amanda's last witness for the day was the detective who had investigated the judge's stabbing. His testimony revealed that Lionel Warrenton—the man who had stabbed the judge—was a good friend of Leroy Walker. He had sold drugs in Denver to intentionally get arrested and be placed in jail.

> Amanda: Do you know how Mr. Warrenton obtained the knife?

Witness: We're still investigating that.

Amanda: Has he made any statement?

Witness: He immediately retained an attorney, so we couldn't talk to him.

Amanda: Was he willing to talk to you in the presence of his attorney?

Witness: His attorney is negotiating a plea—

Prosecutor: Objection, hearsay.

Amanda: Your Honor, I'm not asking the witness to tell us what the attorney is saying. Besides, the court can take judicial notice that no trial has been set.

Court: Ms. Perkins, do you have any more questions for this witness?

Amanda: No, Your Honor. Thank you.

Court: Good. The court is adjourned.

Chapter 42

Despite her long day in court, Amanda managed to spend two hours with Judge McNeil to prepare him for his testimony the next day.

"You've handled everything brilliantly. Do you really think, after so many witnesses, you still need me to testify?" McNeil sounded tired.

"You're the star witness in this murder trial. I put three doctors on the witness stand. They talked about their diagnosis and your treatment, but they couldn't talk about your pain. Only you can tell the jury about the pain and the suffering you endured as a result of your addiction, your time in captivity, and the stabbing. And most significantly, you're the only one who can tell the jury what happened between you and Leroy that forced you to push him into the street."

* * *

That evening, when Amanda arrived at her home, she found Aristo in the kitchen preparing dinner for her. She almost screamed. "Oh my God! When did you get back?"

Aristo took her in his arms and gave her a long kiss. "I missed you, and I couldn't stay in DC anymore."

"We had some good witnesses today. Why didn't you come to court?"

"I arrived late in the afternoon. I wanted to surprise you. Thought you could use a romantic candlelit dinner."

"I certainly can, but first, please tell me about Daphne."

"She's fine. She lives in Chevy Chase. She doesn't want to talk to you or the judge. We can talk about Daphne later. But tonight, we're having chicken pasta, one of my specialties," Aristo said and then took a bow like a waiter pouring wine.

"When did you find time to learn how to cook?"

"My father started teaching me when I was a teenager. Of course, by favoring Italian food, I disappointed my mother. She wanted me to love Greek food."

"I'd love to meet your parents sometime."

"Well, they've been dying to meet you for a long time."

"You've told them about me?"

"Yes. Unlike someone who's been hiding me from her family, I told my mother about you during my trip to Wisconsin. My father was visiting his relatives in Italy, but I'm sure my mom has called him. By now, everyone in my father's little town probably knows about you. My mom has been worried about my future since Mary was killed."

"Are you telling me you haven't had any girlfriends for that long?"

"Don't get me wrong—I dated a lot. But no, no girlfriend."

"How come?"

"Because I had a crush on a feisty attorney who crucified me on the witness stand every time I testified against her clients."

Amanda walked toward Aristo with a loving smile, put her arms around him, kissed him on the lips, and said, "I didn't know you felt that way about me. And I'm sorry I had to impeach you in order to defend my clients."

"You don't have to be sorry. I understood your dilemma. We always worked on opposite sides," Aristo said, walking to the kitchen to bring the food to the table. "Boy, am I glad we're on the same side this time."

"Me too."

"So when am I going to meet your aunt and uncle?"

"After the trial. I hope you understand. I can't concentrate on anything but McNeil's case."

"Believe me, I understand. This case has priority over my other cases too," Aristo said, placing Amanda's plate in front of her.

During dinner, Aristo briefly talked about the difficulties Detective Prez had created for him in the office and how he'd had to reassure his boss that Judge McNeil's case was not interfering with his detective duties in DC.

The unexpectedly delicious food, the wine, and the music of Verdi helped Amanda forget about the trial. All she could see or think about was the man sitting across the table—the man she loved, the man she wished she could keep in Denver forever.

Amanda's romantic evening didn't last long, though. As they were finishing dinner, she received a call from jail—a collect call from Judge McNeil. "Ms. Perkins, I don't think I'm ready to testify. Please come and see me tomorrow morning before you go to court."

"Oh my God," Amanda uttered. She knew the judge had to testify. Her past experience had proven that the jury always wanted to hear from the defendant—especially in a self-defense case.

Chapter 43

When Amanda saw Judge McNeil at the detention center, he looked as though he was about to have a panic attack. "What's wrong?" she asked him immediately.

"I'm afraid I won't be a good witness for you. I might ruin all the good points you've made so far."

"You've handled hundreds of trials. You know that the jury needs to hear your side of the story. You also know that in a self-defense case the jury should know about your state of mind. And if you don't testify, they'll think you're guilty."

"Ms. Perkins, you're right. I've handled many trials, but as a judge, not as a witness. I don't think I will make a good witness for you. You have to put someone else on the stand."

"How can I find a witness who can describe to the jury your state of mind at the moment you pushed Leroy to the street?"

After failing to convince McNeil of the significance of his testimony, Amanda called Judge Bowen at his hotel and asked for advice.

"File an emergency motion to continue the case. Tell Judge Hutchinson your client is sick."

"I've already given Hutchinson such a hard time, insisting on my client's constitutional right to a speedy jury trial. I'm afraid he's going to laugh if I ask for continuation."

"Put me on the witness stand, as a character witness."

"The prosecutor is going to tell the jury you're the judge's friend and have bias in his favor."

"The hell with him. Let me tell the jury McNeil's an honest man, not a murderer."

Amanda knew Judge Bowen's testimony would not take more than thirty minutes. What was she supposed to do with the jury for the rest of the day? She called Aristo and told him about her client's last-minute panic. She also told him about using Judge Bowen as a good-character witness. But she emphasized that Bowen's testimony would be effective only if McNeil's testimony followed.

"Wait a minute. I think I can bring you a witness," Aristo said with some hesitation in his voice.

"Who?"

"He's a homeless man, drunk most of the time—that's why I thought the prosecutor would attack his credibility. But he says he heard the judge tell Leroy, 'Leave me alone,' before he pushed him."

"God, you're a lifesaver. Please bring him to court."

Before trial, Amanda talked to her new witness for twenty minutes at the courthouse and found him credible enough to testify.

In court, after she established the witness's identity, she asked him whether he had seen McNeil before.

Witness: No. I only saw him on the day of the accident.

Amanda: How far were you from my client?

Witness: I was on the same sidewalk, maybe a couple of feet away.

Amanda: What did you see?

Witness: I saw a large man pulling your client's arm, and when your client got his arm free, the big guy grabbed him by the shoulders and pulled him toward the curb.

Amanda: Could you please describe the "big guy's" physical appearance?

Witness: He was about six three or six four and weighed about 300 pounds.

Amanda: Your Honor, may I approach the witness?

Court: Yes, you may.

Amanda: I'm showing you what has been marked as Defense Exhibit 27. Could you please take a moment and describe it?

Witness: It's a picture.

Amanda: What do you see in that picture?

Witness: An African American man with a baby in his arms.

Amanda: Is this the same man you saw on July 31, pulling my client's shoulders?

Witness: Yes, that's him.

Amanda: Did you hear what he was saying?

Prosecutor: Objection, hearsay.

Court: Sustained.

Amanda: Could you see the man's face?

Witness: Yes, he was very angry.

Amanda: Did you hear what my client said to the big man?

Prosecutor: Objection, hearsay.

Amanda: Your Honor, we are not offering the statement to prove what actually happened. This is to show my client's reaction, his state of mind.

Court: Proceed.

Amanda: Without telling us what my client said, what was your perception?

Witness: Your client wanted to be left alone.

Amanda: What happened next?

Witness: The big guy kept pulling your client toward the curb. At first, I thought the big guy was gonna throw him in front of the moving cars. But then your client pushed him away, and he fell backward into the street.

Amanda: No further questions.

Denis Gray stood up for his cross-examination. He smirked for the jury before cross-examining the witness.

Prosecutor: Mr. Baker, what's your occupation?

Witness: I have no job. I'm homeless.

Prosecutor: Where do you live?

Witness: I don't have a fixed address. I live in different shelters.

Prosecutor: In which shelter are you living now?

Witness: The First Baptist Church shelter in Aurora.

Prosecutor: What were you doing on Colfax Avenue?

Witness: I got off the bus to go to the courthouse.

Prosecutor: Did you have a pending case in this courthouse?

Prosecutor: No, sir. I was going to see a friend who works there.

Prosecutor: A homeless man who has a friend in this courthouse. Is he homeless too?

Witness: No, he works for the clerk's office. I was going to borrow some money from him.

Prosecutor: Mr. Baker, isn't it true that you're drunk all the time?

Witness: I'm a Vietnam vet with two years of college. Wouldn't you get drunk if you had ended up like me?

Prosecutor: Are you sure you weren't drunk on the day you saw the defendant pushing his victim to the street?

Witness: I was not drunk then.

Prosecutor: If you weren't drunk, why did you hear only the defendant's words, not his victim's?

Witness: He was speaking angrily, but the noise from the traffic drowned out his voice.

Prosecutor: How did the noise from the traffic drown out the victim's words, yet conveniently not drown out the defendant's?

Witness: The traffic light must have turned red, and the cars must have stopped down the street. That's why I heard this gentleman's words but not the other guy's.

Prosecutor: Did the defense promise you something in exchange for your testimony today?

Amanda: Objection.

Court: Overruled.

Witness: The detective who gave me the subpoena told me he would buy me lunch.

Amanda saw the grin on the prosecutor's face. With one look, he essentially told the jury that they should disregard the witness because he had been paid by the defense. Amanda was ready to wipe that grin off Denis Gray's face. She jumped to her feet without waiting for the judge to allow the redirect.

Amanda: Mr. Baker, you said you're a Vietnam veteran with two years of college education. How did you become homeless?

Prosecutor: Objection. Not within the scope of the direct examination.

Court: Mr. Gray, you made such a big deal about the witness's homelessness, even I'd like to hear why he's homeless.

Judge Hutchinson swiveled in his chair, turned his head toward the witness, and waited for his answer.

Witness: I'm diabetic. I lost my job due to poor health, and when my wife divorced me a few months later, she kicked me out of her house. My government check is not enough to pay for an apartment.

Amanda: Mr. Baker, did you come here today to lie to the jury because Detective Manfredi promised you a lunch?

Witness: No, I get lunch at the shelter every day. I'm telling you the truth. I told the same thing to the police and to a young prosecutor I talked to.

Amanda: You mean you met with a prosecutor at the district attorney's office?

Witness: Yes, ma'am.

Amanda: And you told him what you told us here a few minutes ago?

Witness: Yes.

Amanda: And what did the prosecutor tell you?

Witness: A police officer told me a week later that the prosecutor had found another witness and they didn't need me to testify.

Court: Mr. Baker, you're excused. Counselors, please approach the bench.

Judge Hutchinson put the husher on, and as soon as the two attorneys approached the bench, he spoke. "Ms. Perkins, I'm not going to declare a mistrial because I don't believe that your client *has been* prejudiced, so save your breath. But Mr. Gray, this is very disturbing to me. Your office has withheld exculpatory evidence from the defense. How do you explain that?"

"Your Honor, this was during the time my younger colleague was handling this case."

"Your office has a continuous obligation to provide exculpatory evidence to the defense, notwithstanding who the prosecutor is. Ask your supervisor to call me immediately. I'll recess for lunch and resume trial after I talk to your boss. This is prosecutorial misconduct." There was unmistakable anger in the judge's voice.

The spectators were still chatting when the judge turned off the husher. He banged his gavel. "This court is adjourned for lunch break until 2:00 p.m."

During the lunch break, Amanda filled in McNeil on the bench conference. "I've written my motion to continue the case for a day or two, but your testimony would be so effective after the jury heard Mr. Baker's version of what happened between you and Leroy."

"Okay, I'll do it. Put me on the witness stand."

"Are you sure you're ready?"

"Yes, I'm sure."

* * *

Amanda was happy and relaxed in the afternoon. Her last two witnesses were two judges with years of trial experience. She'd had to prepare McNeil for the prosecutor's expected brutal cross-examination, but she didn't have to worry about Judge Bowen's testimony. He knew what character witnesses had to accomplish. Besides, he was a likable person who could charm the jury in a few minutes.

Amanda: Please state your full name for the record.

Witness: My name is Fredrick Craig Bowen.

Amanda: What's your occupation?

Witness: I'm an associate judge in the DC superior court.

Amanda: How long have you worked as a judge?

Witness: For sixteen years.

Amanda: Do you know my client?

Witness: I've known Judge McNeil—

Prosecutor: Objection.

Court: Please refer to the defendant by his name.

Witness: Yes, Your Honor. I have known Walter McNeil since we were six years old. We both lived in the same neighborhood in Madison, Wisconsin. We went to the same schools. Then we went to the same college and the same law school.

Amanda: What's my client's occupation?

Witness: He's a judge, like me, in the DC superior court.

Amanda: How long has he been a judge?

Witness: Like me, for sixteen years.

Amanda: During all the years you've known him, has he ever committed any violent act or displayed any violent tendencies?

Witness: No. Never.

Amanda: Is he known in the community for his truthfulness and veracity?

Witness: Yes.

Amanda was relieved that as a judge, Bowen knew the significance of truthfulness and veracity. With ordinary witnesses, she always had to explain the formula.

She was surprised at the end of her questioning to see Denis Gray coming to the well of the court, getting ready for his cross-examination. What could he possibly accomplish by questioning Judge Bowen? The judge had overseen many jury trials for sixteen years and had listened to many prosecutors' cross-examinations.

> Prosecutor: You testified that the defendant is your childhood friend. You like him, don't you?
>
> Witness: If you are referring to Judge McNeil, yes.
>
> Prosecutor: You wouldn't say anything to hurt him, would you?
>
> Witness: No, sir.
>
> Prosecutor: In fact, you don't want to see him convicted for the crime he committed?
>
> Amanda: Objection.
>
> Court: Overruled. Mr. Gray can establish bias. The witness can answer the question.
>
> Witness: The jury has not decided whether he has committed a crime.

Judge Bowen looked at the jury and smiled. Some jurors smiled back. Amanda knew what Bowen was doing—he was charming the jury, telling them it was *their* job to convict or exonerate the defendant, and the prosecutor could not assume that they already had.

> Prosecutor: You don't want to see your friend get convicted, yes or no?
>
> Witness: Of course not.
>
> Prosecutor: On July 31 of last year, you were not anywhere near Colfax Avenue, were you?

Witness: No, I was not.

Prosecutor: So you didn't see your friend throwing his victim in front of rows of speeding cars?

Witness: No, but I didn't see what your so-called victim had done to my friend either.

Prosecution: Move to strike the witness's comment.

Court: Overruled. You're asking for his observation, and he's telling you the truth.

Amanda saw some jurors smiling. Denis Gray's effort to dismiss Judge Bowen's testimony wasn't working, but he wouldn't give up.

Prosecutor: You socialize with your friend outside the courthouse, correct?

Witness: Yes. Before his wife passed away, my family and the judge's family had many dinners, even trips, together.

Prosecution: What happened after his wife died?

Witness: We still had lunches together and dinner once in a while with my family.

Prosecution: Isn't it true that when his wife died, he became an angry man?

Witness: I wouldn't say angry. He became a sad man because he loved his wife. After she died, he was left to raise his six-year-old daughter all by himself.

Prosecution: No further questions.

Amanda had to ask Judge Bowen more questions. Otherwise, the jurors who hadn't smiled could side with the prosecution and not believe a word of his testimony.

> Amanda: You said, after his wife's death, my client became a sad person. Could that loss have turned him into a murderer?

> Prosecution: Objection. This witness is not a psychiatrist.

> Court: Sustained.

> Amanda: Judge Bowen, did you travel all the way from Washington, DC, to come here and lie about your friend and colleague under oath?

> Witness: No.

Bowen looked directly at the jury. "I came here to tell the jury that my friend has a good reputation in his community for truthfulness and veracity."

> Amanda: No further questions.

Chapter 44

With his suit, tie, and trimmed beard, McNeil looked very distinguished on the witness stand. He raised his hand and was duly sworn in by the courtroom clerk.

Amanda: Please state your full name.

Witness: My name is Walter Scott McNeil.

Amanda: What's your occupation?

Witness: I was a judge at the DC superior court before I was abducted in July of last year.

Amanda: How long did you work as a judge?

Witness: For sixteen years.

Amanda: Where did you live in DC?

Witness: Off Connecticut Avenue. Northwest area.

Amanda: How did you commute to work?

Witness: By train. I took the Red line metro, which stops at Judiciary Square—a block away from the courthouse.

Amanda: Do you own a car?

Witness: Yes.

Amanda: Why didn't you drive to work?

Witness: It would take me thirty to thirty-five minutes to drive in rush hour. The train took only fifteen minutes and gave me a chance to read or write.

Amanda: Are you the only judge who commuted by train?

Witness: No, I know at least a half dozen of my colleagues who commute by train.

Amanda: Drawing your attention to Friday, July 2, 2010, do you remember that day?

Witness: How can I forget? I was kidnapped that Friday.

Amanda: Please tell the jury what happened to you.

Witness: After I finished my court calendar, I went to my chambers and reviewed several motions filed on behalf of Keshan Walker.

Amanda: Who is Keshan Walker?

Witness: He is a seventeen-year-old juvenile who was being charged as an adult in a triple-murder case.

Amanda: Were you the judge assigned to try that case?

Witness: Yes, the case was set for trial in early August.

Amanda: When did you leave your chambers?

Witness: A few minutes before 8:00 p.m.

Amanda: Was it dark outside?

Witness: No. There was still daylight. We have long days in July.

Amanda: What happened next?

Witness: I left the courthouse and walked along Indiana Avenue toward the Judiciary Square metro station. I was crossing the street when a large black Pontiac stopped me right in front of the DC police headquarters. A passenger from the backseat came out with a map. He said they were lost—

Prosecution: Objection, hearsay.

Court: Sustained.

Amanda: Without telling us what he said, tell us what impression you got.

Witness: They were lost and needed directions to Union Station. As I was looking at the map, trying to find Union Station for them, I felt the muzzle of a gun in my back. The man with the map said, "Get inside quietly, and—"

Prosecutor: Objection, hearsay.

Amanda: Tell us what you thought.

Witness: I knew something terrible was going to happen when he pushed me into the backseat. I was held by him and another man. I asked who they were. He said, "Shut up and you'll be—"

Prosecution: Objection, hearsay.

Court: Counselors, approach the bench.

Judge Hutchinson put the husher on to prevent the jury from hearing the sidebar conference. "Ms. Perkins, you know that the prosecutor is going to object to hearsay. Why can't you pose a question that doesn't elicit out-of-court conversation?"

"Your Honor, this is my client's first and last opportunity to tell his side of the story from the beginning. The words of the kidnappers are significant in showing my client's state of mind. Your Honor, I can find exceptions to the hearsay rule, like present sense impression, excited utterance, unavailable declarant, et cetera. Or I can continue telling my client, 'Don't say what they said; just tell us what you thought.'"

"Your Honor," said Gray, "two of the kidnappers, including the victim, are dead, and the third one has escaped. If you allow the defendant to tell the jury what they said, there's no way for me to impeach him. And the jury will take the defendant's word because there's no other witness to refute it."

"If you eliminate the words of the kidnappers and have the defendant tell the jury what he thought after every conversation, then there are lots of gaps for the jury to fill. On the other hand, I see the problem of absent kidnappers," Judge Hutchinson said.

"Your Honor, if this were the kidnapping trial of Leroy Walker, his attorney wouldn't allow him to take the witness stand to incriminate himself, and then Judge McNeil, as a victim, would tell the whole story," Amanda pointed out.

Judge Hutchinson sighed. "Mr. Gray, I can sustain as many objections as you want me to, but I'm warning you, the jury is not going to like it. After all the witnesses they've heard, they want to hear the judge's side of the story, and every time you cut him off, they're going to hold it against you."

"Your Honor, Mr. Gray can challenge my client's statement during his cross-examination. He can argue to the jury in his closing argument that my client made up all those conversations. After all, the jury is the fact-finder; let them sort it out. Let them decide whether my client is telling the truth."

"I will give the jury the definition of hearsay and then rule on each statement and each objection as I see it," the judge decided.

Amanda and Denis Gray went back to their tables while the judge addressed the jury. "Ladies and gentlemen, you have been hearing objections from both attorneys throughout this trial whenever there is a hearsay problem. I'm going to give you the definition of hearsay. It's a statement made by someone other than the person who is testifying at the trial, and it's offered in evidence to prove the truth of the matter asserted. There are exceptions to the rule against hearsay. They will be too confusing for you to learn, no matter how well I explain them to you. And believe me, sometimes it's even hard for the lawyers to understand. So if I make a ruling from the bench agreeing or disagreeing with the attorneys, please concentrate on what's admissible, and don't try to question why certain statements can come into the record and certain statements cannot. These are procedural rules that the court has to decide. You are the fact-finders. With that, I will ask Ms. Perkins to resume her direct examination of her client."

Amanda: You testified that you were pushed into the backseat of a black Pontiac. What happened next?

Witness: The driver sped off. The passenger to my left shoved a piece of cloth into my mouth, pinned me down, and held a bottle of ether against my nose.

Amanda: What happened next?

Witness: I was gone immediately—and I don't know for how long because when I woke, I was hooked up to a dripping IV bag. At first I thought I was in a moving ambulance. But then I saw two of the kidnappers standing at the foot of my bed. They told me—

Amanda: Please don't tell us what they talked about. Tell us what your understanding was at that moment.

Witness: I was in a mobile home hundreds of miles away from DC.

Amanda: You talked about two kidnappers. How many were there?

Witness: Once they took me to that house, I saw three. I think the third one was the driver of the Pontiac.

Amanda: Your Honor, may I approach the witness?

Court: You may.

Amanda picked up two enlarged photos mounted on a tripod and approached Judge McNeil.

Amanda: I'm showing you what have been marked as Defense Exhibits 68 and 69. Could you please take a look at them and tell the jury what they are?

Witness: Exhibit 68 shows the aerial view of the DC superior court, district court, DC police headquarters, and the Judiciary Square metro station. Exhibit 69 shows the front of the DC superior court building, the police headquarters, and the Judiciary Square metro station.

Amanda: When you left the courthouse, did you see anyone in the street?

Witness: No. There are several courts in that area, and they all close at 5:00 p.m., so by 8:00 p.m., the street is usually deserted.

Amanda: Are there any businesses around the courthouse?

Witness: Only a few sandwich shops, and they close at 5:00 or 6:00 p.m., because their customers are usually court employees, jurors, or those who have pending matters in the court.

Amanda: Are you suggesting that no one saw you being kidnapped?

Witness: I don't know whether someone was behind me or not, but everything happened so fast. One minute I had a map in my hand; the next minute I was pushed into the car.

Amanda: I assume you didn't scream?

Witness: I think I was too shocked to do anything. I had walked from the courthouse to the Judiciary Square metro station for sixteen years, and nothing had ever happened to me before. In any event, what I'm trying to say is, I've never been in a situation that required screaming. Besides, I don't know how to scream.

Amanda: Could you please put a letter "C" for "court," indicating which building is the courthouse, and also a letter "P" for the police headquarters? Would you also use arrows showing the path you took?

Amanda approached the witness chair and gave Judge McNeil a highlighter. After he made his marks, she asked the trial judge's permission to show the two pictures to the jury. She then entered the two exhibits into evidence.

The next exhibits were two identical, enlarged pictures taken at night.

Amanda: I'm handing you what have been marked as Defense Exhibits 70 and 71. Could you please tell the jury what they are?

Witness: Exhibit 70 is identical to Exhibit 68, showing the aerial view of the DC superior court, district court, DC police headquarters, and the Judiciary Square metro station.

Amanda: What's the difference between the two pictures?

Witness: The only difference is the time that the pictures were taken. The earlier exhibit was taken in daylight. This one is the night view of the area.

Amanda: What about Exhibit 71?

Witness: Exhibit 71 shows the front of the DC superior court building, the police headquarters, and the metro station at night.

Amanda: Do you see any difference between the pictures that were taken during daytime and those that show the area at night?

Witness: The daytime pictures show many people in the street, but the night pictures don't show any individuals.

Amanda: Is this the typical day-and-night scene for the area?

Witness: Yes. But some nights you see one or two drunk or homeless individuals walking around.

After getting Judge Hutchinson's permission, Amanda showed the pictures to the jury. She then asked the judge to admit them as evidence. All four pictures were admitted without objections.

Amanda: Do you know when you arrived in Denver?

Witness: No, but I had a law clerk once who was from the Denver area. He told me that it took him twenty-six hours and thirty minutes to drive to DC.

Amanda: So when did you find yourself in that Lakewood house?

Witness: They didn't tell me where I was. When I woke up, I had a severe headache and a dry mouth and was in a lot of pain. I was in a small, windowless room, more like a walk-in closet.

Amanda: Your Honor, may I approach the witness?

Court: Yes, you may.

Amanda approached Judge McNeil with a large picture in her hand.

Amanda: I'm showing you what has been marked as Defense Exhibit 21. Could you please take a good look at it and see if you recognize it?

Witness: This was my room for the entire time I was kept in captivity.

Amanda: Your Honor, may I publish the picture to the jury?

Court: Yes, you may.

Amanda paraded the picture in front of the jury, moving from one end of the jury box to the other. She then submitted the picture to the court as Defense Exhibit 21.

Amanda: Tell us what happened next.

Witness: I kept asking them who they were and what they wanted from me.

Amanda: Did they give you an answer?

Witness: No. Instead, they showed me a big hole and told me—

Amanda: Don't tell us what they said. Tell us what you understood.

Witness: That the hole was dug to be my grave if I didn't cooperate.

Amanda: Your Honor, may I approach the witness?

Court: Yes, you may.

Amanda handed a picture to Judge McNeil.

Amanda: I'm showing you a picture marked as Defense Exhibit 22, already admitted by the court as defense evidence. Could you take a look at it and tell us what you see?

Witness: This picture depicts the backyard of the Lakewood house and shows that hole, which was intended to be my grave.

Amanda: You said earlier that you were supposed to cooperate with them. Cooperate with what? Again, please don't tell us what they said. Tell us what you understood you were supposed to do.

Witness: They didn't tell me anything specific on that day, but the day after, they ordered me—

Prosecution: Objection, hearsay.

Court: Overruled.

Amanda: You can answer the question.

Witness: They ordered me at gunpoint to make rulings in favor of the defense motions in Keshan Walker's murder case in DC.

Amanda: Did you?

Witness: I had to. One of the kidnappers always had a gun pointed at me. They forced me to use my laptop and e-mail my decisions to my law clerk.

Amanda: Do you know the names of your kidnappers?

Witness: They addressed the heavy kidnapper as—

Prosecution: Objection, hearsay.

Court: Overruled.

Amanda: Please go ahead and complete what you were about to say.

Witness: They called the big kidnapper Boss; another kidnapper was referred to as Doc, because he had finished a year in medical school; and the short one was called Shorty.

Amanda: Did you find out why they were interested in Keshan Walker's trial?

Witness: I asked them if they were related to him. They didn't respond.

Amanda: Were they satisfied when you e-mailed your ruling?

Witness: They were happy with my favorable ruling for a short period of time, but then when the DC prosecutor appealed my decisions and the court of appeals reversed me, they got mad.

Amanda: What happened next?

Witness: They kept showing me my grave in the yard and then pumped drugs into my body.

Amanda: Did you resist?

Witness: Yes, at first. But then the pain of living in a closet-sized, windowless room became so unbearable that sometimes I welcomed the drugs because, at least momentarily, they would knock me out and make me forget what I was going through.

Amanda: Were you allowed to get out of your room once in a while?

Witness: I was always tied to a chair, and at night they would lock the door to my room. But once a day, the short kidnapper would take me to the yard and let me walk. But he kept his gun pointed at me.

Amanda: Do you know how many drugs they gave you?

Witness: When I was a judge, I had many drug cases tried before me and heard many chemists talking about them. Based on my knowledge, my body reactions, and the appearance of the drugs they gave me, I believe I was forced to take marijuana, cocaine, crack cocaine, heroin, PCP, and LSD.

Amanda: Did you develop any tolerance to any of those drugs?

Witness: I hated the drugs' side effects—muscle pain, diarrhea, stomach cramps, the sweating and shivering. But when I became addicted to heroin, I craved it, and sometimes, when the withdrawal became unbearable, I begged them to give it to me.

Amanda: Your Honor, may I approach the witness?

Court: You may.

Amanda: I'm showing you Defense Exhibits 72 and 73. Could you please describe them for the jury?

Witness: Exhibit 72 is a mug shot of me, taken by Denver police when I was arrested. Exhibit 73 shows my arms, including the spots that show where they had injected the drugs in my veins.

Amanda: Could you describe your face in Exhibit 72?

Witness: I look like a homeless drug addict.

Amanda showed the two exhibits to the jury and enjoyed the shocked expressions on some of their faces when they first saw the judge's picture. She then asked the court to admit the two exhibits as evidence for the defense.

Amanda: Could you tell the jury about your first arrest in Denver?

Witness: They dressed me like a homeless man and put me on the street with drugs in my pockets, to make it look like I was selling drugs. I got arrested, but the arraignment judge released me on personal recognizance because I didn't have any criminal record.

Amanda: Did you give the police your real name?

Witness: I was instructed to use the name John Smith.

Amanda: Why didn't you tell the authorities who you were?

Witness: The lead kidnapper, called Boss, threatened that he would kill my daughter. I was shocked to learn my kidnappers had my daughter in captivity too. I knew that if I messed things up, Leroy would kill my daughter.

Amanda: Before your arraignment, did you have to wait in a cellblock for some time?

Witness: Yes.

Amanda: While in the cellblock, did you see someone you knew?

Witness: Yes, I saw *you* talking to an inmate.

The audience moved in their seats, talking among themselves. Judge Hutchinson's gavel came down and silenced the spectators. Amanda paused for a moment to set the stage for telling the jury about her encounter with McNeil, and later with Leroy.

Amanda: Did you ask me for something?

Witness: Yes. You didn't recognize me. I asked you for some paper and a pen. I wrote a note to you and told you who I was. I asked for your help. I'm so sorry for putting you in danger.

Prosecutor: Objection. Your Honor, please ask the witness to cut the theatrics.

Court: Sustained.

Amanda: What happened that night?

Witness: Leroy, or Boss as I knew him, was angry. After I came out of the courthouse, he dragged me to his Pontiac and drove off like a madman. Back inside the house, he tied me to a chair and then went out again with the short kidnapper.

Amanda: What happened next?

Witness: Then they brought you in and tied you to a chair.

Amanda: What did you think when you saw me?

Witness: I assumed they'd caught you because you followed us.

Amanda: What happened next?

Witness: They were mean to you. They asked you questions. They pulled out all your ID cards from your wallet and discovered who you were.

Amanda: Without telling us about their conversation with me, what was your understanding of the situation?

Witness: Leroy had caught you taking pictures of the house. He and Shorty had captured you and dragged you inside the house.

Amanda paused for a few seconds and let the jury absorb the significance of the event. She had already established through the testimony of a deputy sheriff that the police had found her tied to a chair in the Lakewood house. But since, as Judge McNeil's attorney, she couldn't testify, she had to let the jury know she had been taken to the house by force.

Amanda: What happened the next day?

Witness: They dressed me again like a homeless man, but this time they put more plastic bags of marijuana, cocaine, crack cocaine, and heroin in my pockets. Leroy's goal was to get me arrested for felony distribution. He assumed that I would get lengthy jail time and he could enjoy his life in Mexico.

Amanda: Did Leroy threaten you with anything?

Witness: He was constantly threatening me, whether it was related to my rulings on Keshan Walker's motions or selling drugs for him.

Amanda: When was the last threat?

Witness: He told me if I didn't get arrested as he had planned, he would kill me and my daughter both.

Prosecution: Objection, hearsay.

Court: Overruled.

Amanda: What was your reaction?

Witness: I was shocked. I asked him how he knew my daughter. That was when he told me about his cover using the lawn-mowing business and how he had befriended my daughter, Daphne.

Amanda: Had you seen Leroy during the period he mowed your lawn?

Witness: No. He had purposefully chosen times he knew I was in court.

Amanda: Who was with Daphne during those days she came home early?

Witness: My employee, Ms. Tonya Henderson, and occasionally some of Daphne's friends.

Amanda: Did Leroy give you more information about Daphne?

Prosecution: Objection.

Court: Sustained.

Amanda: Without repeating what he said, please tell the ladies and gentlemen of the jury about your thoughts and your feelings.

Witness: He shocked me again with a picture of Daphne, with him, a little boy, and a seven-month-old baby. I found out the baby was theirs. I accused him of kidnapping and raping my fifteen-year-old daughter.

Amanda: Why do you think he was the one who kidnapped your daughter?

Prosecution: Objection. Defense has not offered any evidence of Daphne's kidnapping.

Court: Overruled.

Witness: The timing. When Daphne disappeared, the man who mowed the lawn for me disappeared too.

Amanda: Your Honor, may I approach the witness?

Court: You may.

Amanda: I'm showing you Defense Exhibit 27. Is this the picture Leroy showed you?

Judge McNeil bent his head, trying to hide the pain on his face. He covered his eyes with the palm of his left hand while holding the picture in his right hand. He sighed, and then he began crying quietly.

Amanda took the picture away from the judge and paused until he regained his composure. The courtroom clerk gave him a box of tissues, and he wiped away his tears.

Amanda: Tell us what happened after Leroy brought you to the same spot to sell drugs again.

Prosecution: Objection, leading.

Court: Overruled.

Witness: He was watching me from across the street.

Amanda: What were you doing?

Witness: I could not get the image of my daughter in that picture out of my head. I had not seen her for four years. I thought Leroy had kept her in captivity too. I opened a Ziploc bag of cocaine and snorted it. I wanted to forget my pain.

Amanda: What was Leroy's reaction?

Witness: He was angry with me. He charged across the street, dodging cars, and came at me using profanity I cannot repeat here. He told me if I messed up again, he would kill me—

Prosecution: Objection, hearsay.

Amanda: Your Honor, I'm establishing my client's state of mind.

Court: Objection overruled.

Amanda: What happened after he said that he would kill you?

Witness: He pulled my arms, and when I pulled away from him and told him to leave me alone, he grabbed me by the shoulders and kept pulling me toward the curb.

Amanda: At the moment you pushed Leroy to the street, did you fear imminent danger of serious bodily injury or death?

Prosecution: Objection. Leading the witness.

Court: Overruled.

Witness: I had been fearful for my life since the kidnapping, but at that moment, not only did I fear that he was going to throw me into the street; I also feared for the safety of my daughter.

Judge McNeil became tearful again, picked up another tissue, and wiped his tears. Amanda paused for a moment and let the jury see the agony painted all over her client's face. Then she said, "No further questions."

Chapter 45

Denis Gray angered Amanda by asking the court for a day of recess. He told the judge he was waiting for a report that would help him cross-examine the defendant.

Judge Hutchinson asked McNeil to return to the defense table so the counselors could have a bench conference. As the attorneys approached the bench, he put the husher on and asked Amanda if she would object to the continuation of trial.

"Yes, Your Honor, we object," Amanda said. "Mr. Gray has seen the impact of my client's testimony on the jurors. He just wants to undo the damage done to his case by delaying his cross-examination."

"Mr. Gray, until you tell me what this report is all about and what connection it has with the defendant's cross-examination, I cannot allow any delay in this trial," Hutchinson said.

"Your Honor, I have to discuss this ex parte."

Amanda went back to the defense table; worried about the information the prosecutor was hiding from her. After a short bench conference, Denis Gray went back to the prosecution's table and sat in his chair.

"Ladies and gentlemen," Judge Hutchinson said, addressing the jury, "the prosecutor needs to interview a witness before cross-examining the defendant. So we're going to have a recess until Monday."

Amanda was furious; it was Thursday morning. The judge had given Denis Gray three and a half days. Amanda knew that by Monday, chances were the jury would have forgotten Judge McNeil's fears, tears, and pain.

* * *

Amanda had been surprised not to see Aristo in the courtroom during McNeil's testimony, so as soon as she saw him waiting for her outside the courthouse, she questioned him. "I thought you would be interested in listening to McNeil. Where were you?"

"I had some important things to do. How did it go?"

During the car ride to Lakewood, Amanda described McNeil's emotional testimony and kept talking about Denis Gray's tricky way of delaying the trial. Aristo listened as he drove without making any comment. But at home, during dinner, when Amanda started a guessing game about the prosecutor's mystery report, he spoke up.

"I know what report he's talking about and who his mystery witness is."

"He has used up all his essential witnesses. I can't think of any other witness. Who is it?"

"I'm sorry for not sharing the details of my trip with you."

"What details?"

"I've kept some information from you, and I believe it may come back around to bite us."

"*What* information?"

Aristo disclosed the contents of the FBI report and his meetings with Agent Ralph Brown and Daphne. "I think he's going to use the FBI's report and have Agent Brown as a rebuttal witness."

"Oh my God! You talked to the FBI agent? Why didn't you tell me?"

"I'm so sorry. If I had told you, your theory about Daphne's kidnapping would've fallen flat. I couldn't tell McNeil either. You just told me how emotional his testimony was when he talked about Daphne. You told me how some jurors reacted when they saw a powerful judge crumble and cry on the witness stand because he thought his daughter had been kidnapped and raped."

"You're right about that, but the impact of that heartbreaking testimony will be gone by Monday."

"You never know. Some jurors may remember the judge crying."

"Aristo, under normal circumstances, I would be really mad at you. But I've withheld some information from you too."

"What?"

Amanda went to her briefcase, pulled out Darnell's two letters, and gave them to Aristo, who began reading them immediately.

"Wow!" Aristo said when he was done. "And I assume both you and McNeil have decided to keep this information from the authorities?"

"Yes."

"McNeil's career is over, but you ... you've just started practicing here in Denver. The Colorado Bar Association doesn't know you well. If you want to be disbarred, go ahead, be my guest."

There was a long pause. For the first time in her career, Amanda was not able to counter-argue.

The next day, she mailed Darnell's letter to Denis Gray, saying that because of her trial schedule, she hadn't read her mail every day. She knew that the letter would be faxed to the FBI immediately. She hoped they never caught Darnell.

Chapter 46

Daphne was walking with her kids to the park when a *Washington Post* headline on a newsstand near Chevy Chase caught her eye: "Judge Cries While Testifying about Daughter's Kidnapping."

She bought the newspaper and took her kids to their usual playground in the park. She sat on a bench and read the entire article. The reporter had written an emotional story, and it was hard to ignore the words describing her father's testimony. She felt a twinge of pain in her heart, and before she could stop them, tears ran down her cheeks. She wiped her face, got up, and hailed a taxicab. She put her children and Malcolm's stroller into the backseat of the cab, climbed in with them, and gave the cab driver an address on Connecticut Avenue—her father's home, a place she hadn't visited since 2006.

Her keys didn't work. She couldn't open the front door. She walked to the backyard and tried the back door. When she didn't have any luck getting inside the house, she assumed someone had changed the locks.

She took her children to the area in the backyard where her tree house and swing remained intact. Sean's laughter on the swing brought back memories of her mother and how she used to do the same with her. Memories of the carefree days she'd spent with her parents brought a smile to her face—especially those memories with her father. After all, he was the single parent who had raised her. But the good memories soon disappeared, like the sun being covered by clouds, when she remembered the anger and rage she felt against her father for the crime he had committed before her eyes—and the guilt she felt for keeping her silence.

Her kids were now running around, making cheerful noises, as Daphne remembered her own faults. To punish her father, she had lived a wild life with three college boys, used drugs and alcohol, and gotten involved with a man twenty years her senior. Why had she had a baby with Leroy when she didn't even love the man? Daphne was now questioning, for the first time, whether she was a fit mother to raise Malcolm. With Sean, she hadn't had a choice, but *she* was responsible for bringing Malcolm into this world. How could she explain to him one day that his grandfather was the one who had killed his father?

She stood and looked around one more time as though she were saying good-bye to every tree, every bush, and every bench in that backyard.

* * *

Back in Denver, Amanda received a phone call from Judge Hutchinson's secretary. "The judge wants to see you and Detective Manfredi in his chambers at four o'clock."

Amanda panicked. It was Sunday, the day before Judge McNeil's cross-examination by the prosecutor. Aristo reassured her that Denis Gray had probably made a big deal out of not being informed of Aristo's meeting with the FBI in DC.

They arrived at the judge's chambers a few minutes before four o'clock, and Amanda was surprised to see that Denis Gray was already there talking to the judge.

"Please have a seat," Judge Hutchinson said, showing them two empty chairs. "I believe you two know why we are here."

"No, Your Honor, we do not," Amanda answered.

"Ms. Perkins, despite the fact that you are Judge McNeil's attorney, you're still an officer of the court. How could you let your client testify about the kidnapping of his daughter, knowing full well there was no kidnapping?"

"Your Honor, I probably know why we are here," Aristo said. "I believe Mr. Gray has contacted the FBI agent I met during my recent trip to DC."

"You're damn right," Denis Gray said, anger in his voice.

"Your Honor, Attorney Perkins and Judge McNeil had no knowledge of the report I received from Agent Brown. They didn't even know that I had talked to Daphne."

"Why didn't you share the news with them?"

"Your Honor, Daphne lives with another man. Judge McNeil has been so emotional and has gone through so much pain, and I didn't want to add to his problems."

"I believe he would be happy to know that his daughter is not held hostage somewhere and, in fact, is doing well."

"Not if I would have told him she hated him and never wanted to see him again."

"I can charge you with obstruction of justice among other charges, you know," Denis Gray said. "But more significantly," he said, turning and pointing to Amanda, "I can report you to the bar for allowing your client to perjure himself, and I can bring perjury charges against him as well."

"Mr. Gray, stop using your office's power to harass people in my chamber," Judge Hutchinson said, admonishing the prosecutor.

"Your Honor," Amanda said, addressing the judge, "as Detective Manfredi told you, neither Judge McNeil nor I was aware of the FBI report or Daphne's whereabouts. Besides, Judge McNeil's testimony was about his state of mind at the time Leroy showed him the picture of his daughter and gave him the shocking news about having a baby with her. Leroy didn't tell Judge McNeil where Daphne was. He kept threatening that Daphne's life was in danger if Judge McNeil didn't sell the drugs. And finally, moments before his death, Leroy threatened to kill him *and* his daughter if he messed up his plan."

"Mr. Gray, I'm afraid I have to agree with Ms. Perkins. You can go ahead and read the transcript again. Ms. Perkins didn't ask her client whether he thought his daughter was captive today. Judge McNeil talked about what was going through his mind on July 31 of last year. This is April—eight months later. The information you have obtained now was not available to the defendant on July 31 of last year when he pushed Leroy—"

"Your Honor, you mean when he *killed* Leroy."

"Mr. Gray, that's for the jury to decide."

"Your Honor, if the detective had provided this information to the judge, the defendant wouldn't have been able to create the theatrics he did on the witness stand."

"Your Honor, I will inform my client of the information we have on Daphne, and Mr. Gray can bring it up during his cross-examination tomorrow," Amanda said.

"Your Honor," Aristo added, "I'm a detective working for the defense. I'm surprised that Mr. Gray believes I have a duty to inform *his* office of the information I have gathered for the defense. The DA offices all over the country have good relationships with the FBI. All they have to do is make a phone call and request the FBI's report on anything. Mr. Gray's office knew that the FBI had been investigating Daphne's disappearance for years."

"I'm still going to review this matter and bring appropriate charges against you," Gray said to Aristo.

"Mr. Gray, if you do that, I'll report you to the Colorado Bar for withholding exculpatory evidence from the defense," Amanda warned. "The homeless witness you hid from us? Remember?"

"My boss told the judge that it was an oversight by our office."

"Fine. I'll let the Board of Ethics decide whether crucial evidence in favor of a defendant can be withheld due to an 'oversight,'" Amanda said to the prosecutor.

She was grabbing her briefcase to leave when she was addressed by Judge Hutchinson. "I'll see you in court tomorrow morning."

"Yes, Your Honor."

* * *

On their drive back home, Aristo tried to convince Amanda that the prosecutor's cross-examination would not damage the judge's powerful testimony. "No matter how hard he exaggerates the fact that Daphne wasn't kidnapped, he cannot change the fact that the judge *was* kidnapped, drugged, and tortured."

"Aristo, you were not in the courtroom. You didn't see how sympathetic the jury was when the judge started crying. Now, a few days later, the prosecutor is going to tell them that the judge lied on the witness stand and his tears were all part of a game."

"He wouldn't dare."

"You watch him. He's not the nice, soft-spoken man I first met. He has become so cruel to Judge McNeil. He doesn't have any respect for me either. How dare he threaten to report me to the Colorado Bar?"

"He has no mercy for you because he feels he's losing the case. As for cruelty to McNeil, the harsher he treats the judge, the more jurors are going to hate him."

"He's not losing. I may have made some jurors uncomfortable here and there, but I don't think I have a unanimous verdict of not guilty."

"You will win this case."

"How can you say that? Have you forgotten some of the jurors' poker faces?"

"Forget them; do you want me to take you to jail to talk to McNeil?"

"I'm tired, I'll talk to him early tomorrow morning."

Chapter 47

The next morning, Denis Gray acted like an angry soldier, ready to shoot anyone and anything in his path. Amanda was not concerned about him anymore, though. He was not the courteous prosecutor she had met a few weeks ago. He had shown his true colors.

Denis Gray stood next to the jury box, wearing his hatred for the defendant on his face. He took a short breath and shot his first question.

Prosecutor: When was the first time you planned to kill Leroy Walker?

Amanda: Objection.

Court: Overruled.

Witness: I didn't plan to kill anyone.

Prosecutor: Are you telling us that during your month-long captivity, you never intended to kill your kidnappers?

Witness: I only felt the urge to attack Leroy once.

Prosecutor: When was that?

Witness: The first time he showed me his picture with my daughter and threatened that her life would be in danger if I messed up his plan.

Prosecutor: And what plan was that?

Witness: He wanted to get me arrested and then go to Mexico.

Prosecutor: Is this the same daughter you told the jury Leroy kidnapped and raped?

Witness: I told the jury I accused him of rape and kidnapping, but he denied it.

Prosecutor: Did you ever report to the police that she was missing?

Witness: No.

Prosecutor: Did you ever get the FBI involved?

Witness: No, not immediately, because I had hired two retired DCMPD detectives to find her. I was afraid that the FBI would scare her. But later I got them involved.

Prosecutor: Isn't it true that there was no kidnapping and you knew that your daughter was living in DC, not too far away from your house?

Amanda: Objection.

Court: Sustained.

Prosecutor: Did you or did you not know that your daughter was never kidnapped?

Witness: I always thought that my daughter had been kidnapped from Madison, but my attorney informed me last night that a recent FBI report ruled out the kidnapping. But—

Prosecutor: You cried before the jury the other day when your daughter's name was mentioned, while knowing she was safe and living in DC, didn't you?

Witness: When I testified the other day, I didn't know that. All I knew was that my fifteen-year-old daughter had disappeared and that, years later, my kidnapper showed me her picture with him and a baby. I had no choice but to believe that Leroy had also kidnapped my daughter … the timing … When Leroy told me about his business mowing lawns as a cover to get close to me, I remembered that the man who mowed the lawn for me had disappeared the same time my daughter did.

Prosecutor: Your daughter is smiling in that picture and seems very happy. Is that the face of a person who has been kidnapped?

Witness: I thought maybe Leroy had gotten her addicted to drugs the way he did with me.

Prosecutor: Speaking of drugs, you told the jury that your kidnappers forced you to use drugs, yet you used cocaine shortly before you killed Leroy. Did he force you to snort cocaine on the street?

Witness: I told you the pain of seeing my daughter's picture with my kidnapper was unbearable. I had to get rid of the pain. I was also an addict at the time, due to being forced to use drugs during my captivity.

Prosecutor: You also said you sometimes begged them to give you drugs. Isn't that correct?

Witness: Yes. They knew heroin was addictive. They kept injecting it into my arms, and before long, I was addicted. Do you honestly believe I would drive to Denver, a city I'd never visited, to ruin my reputation by getting high or putting holes in my veins?

Prosecutor: Nonresponsive, move to strike.

Court: Overruled.

Prosecutor: You told your attorney that you feared your life was in imminent danger when you killed Leroy. Isn't it true that you knew Leroy was not carrying a gun and never intended to kill you?

Witness: I didn't know that. He had threatened and assaulted me; the short kidnapper always had a gun when he talked to me. I always felt my life was in danger.

Prosecutor: The first time you stood near the courthouse to sell drugs, why didn't you run and cry for help?

Witness: Leroy had threatened to kill me and my daughter. He wanted me to get arrested.

Prosecutor: You got arrested. Why didn't you tell the police you were being kidnapped?

Witness: How many times do I have to repeat myself? He had threatened my daughter's life. I thought he was holding her as a hostage too.

Prosecutor: Okay, you got released, but on the second day, you were shown your daughter smiling in a picture. You had to know that Leroy would not hurt the mother of his child, right?

Witness: No, I didn't know that. I saw him as someone who was capable of doing anything he wanted.

Prosecutor: Isn't it true that you had planned to kill Leroy for a long time, even before he talked to you about your daughter?

Witness: No, I killed the bastard because he threatened to kill my daughter, and he was about to kill me too.

Prosecutor: No further questions.

Amanda held back a breath when she heard the word *kill*. She hadn't wanted her client to utter that word in front of the jury. She relaxed, though, when she saw McNeil emotional again, crying quietly.

She looked at the jury box and noted some jurors' sympathetic reactions. She offered her client a glass of water before she began her redirect.

Amanda: On July 31 of last year, when Leroy pulled your arm and grabbed you by the shoulder, what was going through your head?

Witness: That he would kill me.

Amanda: No further questions.

Amanda informed the court that the defense rested. Judge Hutchinson invited the counselors to the bench to hear Amanda's motion for judgment of acquittal. He put the husher on before she spoke. Amanda renewed her motion, asking Judge Hutchinson to dismiss both murder in the first degree and murder two. She repeated the argument she had made at the end of the prosecution's case-in-chief, stating that since Judge McNeil was not armed, he couldn't have planned or premeditated the killing. As to the charge of murder two, she argued not only that there was enough provocation, but also that her client had a strong self-defense argument.

Judge Hutchinson promised her, as he had at the end of the prosecution's case, that he would consider her motion after the jury's verdict. He instructed Denis Gray to be prepared for the prosecution's rebuttal the next morning. He then thanked the jury and gave them his usual daily instruction that they shouldn't talk to anyone, including fellow jurors, about the case. "You should avoid reading about the case, listening to the news, or watching TV when media is covering the case. You are also not allowed to do any research online about the case."

Chapter 48

The prosecution's first rebuttal witness was a Denver police crime-scene investigator who testified that Leroy didn't have any gun on his person at the time of his death. On cross-examination, Amanda proved that Leroy had a gun readily available to him in his car parked a few feet away from the crime scene.

As Aristo had guessed, the prosecution's second witness was Ralph Brown—the FBI agent he had met in Washington, DC, a week earlier. Denis Gray wore a large smile. It was clear he felt confident that the FBI agent's testimony would prove to the jury that the judge had made up the story about his daughter's kidnapping.

> Prosecution: Could you please state your full name and tell the ladies and gentlemen of the jury where you work?
>
> Witness: My name is Ralph Brown. I work for the FBI in Washington, DC.
>
> Prosecution: How long have you worked for the FBI?
>
> Witness: Two months shy of twenty years.
>
> Prosecution: Were you assigned to investigate a kidnapping case related to the daughter of the defendant, Walter McNeil?
>
> Witness: I started the case last year when the defendant was arrested.

Prosecution: Was that in July?

Witness: No, I started in the second week of August.

Prosecution: When did you finish your investigation?

Witness: About two weeks ago.

Prosecution: What was the result?

Witness: Our office concluded that there was no kidnapping. An individual by the name of Leroy Walker had driven the defendant's daughter to Madison and again, a few months later, had driven her back to DC.

Prosecution: Are you telling us that the defendant's daughter is living in Washington, DC?

Witness: Yes, actually not that far from her father's house.

Prosecution: Did you meet with a detective who works for the defense in Washington about a week ago?

Witness: Yes, Detective Manfredi. I've known him from other contacts I had with DCMPD.

Prosecution: Did he ask for the result of your investigation?

Witness: Yes, he did. We talked about the case, and I gave him a copy of our report.

Prosecution: So when he left your office, he knew that there had been no kidnapping?

Witness: Correct.

Prosecution: No further questions.

Court: Ms. Perkins, you can cross-examine now.

Amanda: Agent Brown, when Detective Manfredi received your report, did he tell you—

Prosecutor: Objection, hearsay.

Court: Overruled. You asked about the agent's conversation with the detective also, so I'll allow it.

Amanda: Was Detective Manfredi planning to come to Denver immediately?

Witness: No, in fact, he stayed in town for several days working on some of his DCMPD cases.

Amanda: You have no knowledge of whether Detective Manfredi talked to my client or me, do you?

Witness: No, ma'am.

Amanda: If a detective works for the defense, does he have any obligation to share the result of his or her investigation with the prosecutor's office?

Witness: I don't think so.

Amanda: Does the FBI have a good relationship with DA offices all around the country?

Witness: Yes.

Amanda: Do you have a good relationship with the DA office in Denver?

Witness: Yes.

Amanda: You said you started working on the judge's daughter's kidnapping case sometime in August of last year. Did Mr. Gray's office ask anything about the result of your investigation at that time?

Witness: No, they asked about the report a few days ago.

Amanda: Agent Brown, when you started the investigation of Daphne's kidnapping, did you also look into my client's abduction?

Witness: Yes.

Amanda: And what was that result?

Witness: Your client was kidnapped by three individuals named Leroy Walker, Melvin Hill, and Darnell Lewis.

Amanda: Thank you. No further questions.

* * *

Hearing Margaret McNeil called as the prosecution's last rebuttal witness surprised Amanda. She asked the judge for a bench conference. "Your Honor, we were not aware that Mr. Gray was putting this witness on the stand because her name was not on the witness list we received. This is a complete surprise to us," Amanda objected.

"Your Honor, this witness is the defendant's sister, for God's sake. The defense has had access to her since the beginning of this trial," Denis Gray responded.

"Ms. Perkins, you cannot object to the prosecution's choice of witnesses for their rebuttal, especially when the witness has been known and available to you," Judge Hutchinson ruled. "I'll give you enough time to prepare for your cross-examination should you need it."

The witness was duly sworn in by the courtroom clerk.

Prosecutor: Please state your full name for the record.

Witness: My name is Margaret McNeil.

Prosecutor: What's your relationship to the defendant?

Witness: He's my brother.

Prosecutor: Do you two have any other siblings?

Witness: No.

Prosecutor: Does your brother have any family members other than you and his daughter?

Witness: He had a wife who passed away many years ago. Now it's just me and Daphne.

Prosecutor: Where do you live?

Witness: I live in Madison, Wisconsin.

Prosecutor: Is that home?

Witness: Yes. I was born in Madison and have lived there all my life.

Prosecution: Does your family live there too?

Witness: Only my husband, who teaches at the University of Wisconsin in Madison.

Prosecutor: Was Madison home to your brother too?

Witness: Yes, until he left for college and then law school.

Prosecutor: Did he come back home when he finished his education?

Witness: No. He got a job in Washington, DC, and lived there.

Prosecutor: Did you visit each other?

Witness: Yes, when my parents were alive and before Fiona's death.

Prosecutor: Who's Fiona?

Witness: My brother's wife. After she died, he changed. His personality totally changed. He became a different person.

Prosecutor: What do you mean by that?

Witness: He became an angry man—an overbearing, overprotective father. I also read in the newspapers that he was a harsh judge, sending—

Amanda: Objection.

Court: Sustained.

Margaret McNeil turned to her brother: "I'm sorry, Walter, but bad things happen to bad people. You—"

Amanda: Objection.

Court: Sustained. Jury should disregard the witness's last two remarks.

Prosecutor: Five years ago, you had a surprise visitor. Daphne came—

Amanda: Objection, leading the witness.

Court: Sustained.

Prosecutor: Did anything interesting happen five years ago?

Witness: Yes, my niece Daphne came to live with me.

Prosecutor: Why?

Witness: She had a fight with her father over a boyfriend and was kicked out of the house.

Prosecutor: Did you call your brother and let him know his daughter was in Madison?

Witness: Yes.

Prosecutor: Did he say anything about Daphne being kidnapped?

Amanda: Objection, hearsay.

Court: Sustained.

Prosecutor: Did you think that your niece had been kidnapped from Washington and brought to Madison?

Witness: No. She was driven to Madison by a friend.

Prosecutor: No further questions.

Court: Ms. Perkins, you can do your cross-examination now.

Amanda: When you talked to your brother, did you ask him what had happened?

Witness: I didn't have to. I believed my niece.

Amanda: So you didn't want to hear your brother's side of the story, right?

Witness: I hadn't talked to my brother in ages. I made a courtesy call just to let him know his daughter was with me. Besides, knowing Walter, I had no doubt that Daphne was telling the truth.

Amanda: Ms. McNeil, isn't it true that Daphne left your house because she also had a problem with you?

Witness: She had befriended some college kids and was partying with them until 2:00 a.m. I couldn't allow that.

Amanda: So when she was forbidden from going to those college parties, she left your house, didn't she?

Witness: Yes.

Amanda: Did you know where she went to live after she left your house?

Witness: She lived with some college boys.

Amanda: Did you notify your brother that she was no longer living in your house?

Witness: No.

Amanda: Why not?

Witness: I was not going to baby-sit his fifteen-year-old daughter. Besides, he didn't care what happened to Daphne.

Amanda: How can you say that? You just said that he was an overprotective father.

Witness: All I know is that my brother is a selfish man who only cares about himself.

Amanda: You know your brother worships Daphne—his only child.

Witness: No, I do not.

Amanda: Isn't it true that you have resented your brother all your life?

Witness: I didn't resent him.

Amanda: You resented him because your parents loved him more, because he got an education from Harvard and you didn't even finish college.

Prosecutor: Objection. Defense attorney is testifying.

Court: Sustained.

Amanda: Ms. McNeil, isn't it true that you hated your brother because your parents bequeathed 60 percent of their assets to him and only 40 percent to you?

Witness: They thought he would take care of me.

Amanda: And he did, didn't he? Didn't he buy you a house, a car, and a studio for you to do your painting?

Witness: He should have done more.

Amanda: Are you here for revenge?

Prosecutor: Objection.

Court: Overruled.

Amanda: Did you tell your brother that Daphne was living with three college boys?

Witness: No.

Amanda: Why not?

Witness: I was hoping she would come back to my house.

Amanda: You found her behavior unacceptable, didn't you?

Witness: Yes.

Amanda: Then why are you saying that Daphne's running away from home was your brother's fault?

Witness: Because it was.

Amanda: Do you have any children?

Witness: No.

Amanda: But you know that in order to raise a child properly, parents sometimes have to use rules or set some boundaries, don't you?

Witness: My brother had harsh rules, like the way he sentenced defendants in his courtroom.

Amanda: Objection, move to strike.

Court: Objection sustained. Jury should disregard witness's last comment. Ms. McNeil, your testimony today is not about your brother's rulings as a judge. It's about his daughter's visit.

Witness: Your Honor, I'm a member of the Justice for All Project. We're trying to get people out of jail. How can I tolerate a brother who puts everyone *in jail*?

Court: Madam, your work is admirable, but this is not the forum to promote your organization and its activities. The jury should disregard the witness's statement about her brother's rulings as a judge.

Amanda: Your organization is trying to get prisoners who have been wrongfully convicted out of jail, correct?

Witness: Yes.

Amanda: Your brother is in jail too, accused of murder. Isn't it hypocritical of you, coming here today and testifying against him?

Amanda heard some noises from the audience. Hutchinson banged his gavel and restored order. Margaret McNeil paused for a few moments and then replied, "My brother is an angry man capable of doing anything."

Amanda: How can you sit there and tell the ladies and gentlemen of the jury that you get innocent people out of jail while you are helping the prosecution to keep your brother *in jail*?

Witness: He deserves to taste life in prison.

Amanda: You were not present at the crime scene. How can you judge him?

Prosecution: Objection, Your Honor. Ms. Perkins is badgering the witness.

Court: Ms. Perkins, move on to your next question.

Amanda: Didn't you talk to the three boys who lived with Daphne?

Witness: Yes.

Amanda: Didn't you threaten to bring statutory rape charges against them because Daphne was fifteen?

Witness: Yes.

Amanda: Weren't those *your rules* and boundaries, telling Daphne that a fifteen-year-old could not live with three college boys?

Margaret did not answer but showed frustration by moving in her chair several times.

Amanda: Let me ask you another question. After you scared the college boys with a statutory rape charge, they kicked Amanda out, didn't they?

Witness: Yes, they did.

Amanda: Did you notify your brother of what had happened?

Witness: No.

Amanda: Why not?

Witness: I was hoping she would come back and live with me.

Amanda: Did she come back to your house?

Witness: No.

Amanda: In fact, she ran away with an African American man twenty years older than her, didn't she?

Witness: I found out about it through the college kids.

Amanda: And that's exactly what you told your brother— that Daphne had left Madison with an African American who looked like a football player, didn't you?

Witness: Yes.

Amanda: Did you know that Daphne was pregnant?

Witness: No.

Amanda: No further questions.

On redirect, Denis Gray asked his witness certain questions intended to prove that Daphne had never been kidnapped.

Prosecutor: Ms. McNeil, you threatened the college boys that you would bring statutory rape charges against them, correct?

Witness: Correct.

Prosecution: So if you knew your niece had been kidnapped, you would have notified law enforcement—

Amanda: Objection, leading the witness.

Court: Sustained.

Prosecution: If someone had kidnapped Daphne, what would you have done?

Witness: I would have called the police and the FBI.

Prosecution: But you didn't. Why?

Witness: Because Daphne had a friendly relationship with the man who took her out of Madison.

Prosecution: No further questions.

Chapter 49

Amanda met with Judge Bowen in the lobby of his hotel. He had stayed in Denver to be with his friend, Judge McNeil, during the last stage of the trial. She showed him the rough draft of her closing arguments and asked for his advice. "Is it okay?"

He took a few minutes to read the draft and said, "It's perfect. I wouldn't touch anything. What does Walter think?"

"Like I've told you before, he's withdrawn. He leaves everything to me. I've never had a client so uninvolved and indifferent. Sometimes I feel he really wants to be found guilty and punished for something. But I don't know what that thing is!"

"Ms. Perkins, the man spent a month of horror in captivity, where he was tortured and drugged. And so far he's endured nine months in jail, not to mention a painful near-death experience when he was stabbed. What do you expect?"

"I know all of that, but he is a highly intelligent man. He can rise above it. This is his *life* we're talking about. He has to fight for it."

"I think this is the impact of all the drugs they gave him."

"I've had so many clients with drug problems. I know what drugs can do to a person's brain. But with Judge McNeil, I think it's more about Daphne than drugs."

"What about Daphne?"

"It seems to me he feels that he's committed a crime against her and should be punished for it."

"You know he raised Daphne all alone after his wife died."

"I know that."

"The poor man had only one other family member: a sister who acted more like an enemy. Daphne is the love of his life. I think he feels horrible because his anger drove his only child away forever."

* * *

Amanda listened to the prosecutor's boring closing argument for ninety minutes, taking notes. Denis Gray examined and analyzed the testimonies of all the prosecution's witnesses, as well as the witnesses who had testified for the defense. He dismissed Judge McNeil's testimony as "self-serving."

Gray concluded, "Ladies and gentlemen, this defendant is lucky, because one of his kidnappers has escaped, and the other two are dead—one killed by him, I should add. So when he tells you they forced him to take drugs, we have no way to know how much of that is true. Yes, there was some evidence that he had used drugs, but we don't know whether he did that voluntarily or not. You heard from him that when he was standing on the street to sell drugs, he opened a Ziploc bag of cocaine and snorted it. He wanted to forget his pain.

"You heard testimony from witnesses that proved to you that the judge's daughter was never kidnapped. She left DC because she had a dispute with her father. Ladies and gentlemen, I have to remind you, again and again, that this trial is not about Leroy's kidnapping of the defendant or the made-up story about the kidnapping of his daughter. It's about a *murder.*" Denis Gray walked to the defense table and pointed to Judge McNeil. "A murder committed by *this* defendant. If Leroy Walker had not been murdered, our office would have punished him for his crime. But he's dead. So now, I want you to do me a favor. When you go to the jury room, please try to remember the testimonies of all the defense witnesses. Let us start first with the defendant himself. Of course, he tells you anything to prove he's innocent. Then you have his girlfriend-employee, whom the defendant paid not only for the services she provided in his home, but also for comforting him.

"Another defense witness was the defendant's best friend, Judge Bowen, who told you that the defendant is known for his truthfulness and veracity in the community. You also heard from the defendant's sister, who testified for the prosecution. Whom do you believe? Who do you think knows the defendant better, his friend or his sister?

"The testimonies of the defense witnesses were mostly related to the kidnapping. I have repeated this several times, and I have to repeat it again, ladies and gentlemen: this trial is not about the kidnapping. The defense's star witness was a drunken homeless man who had just heard the defendant saying, 'Leave me alone.' That doesn't prove anything. We brought you five eyewitnesses who testified that they saw the defendant throw Leroy Walker in front of cars on a busy street.

"Ladies and gentlemen, your duty is not to decide based on sympathy, and you should not be intimidated because the defendant used to be a judge. Therefore, you should not focus on the kidnapping because this trial is about the murder committed by Walter McNeil. Your job is to weigh the evidence and to convict Walter McNeil—because he planned, plotted, and premeditated to kill Leroy Walker. We have met our burden, and we have proven beyond a reasonable doubt all the elements of murder in the first degree. So you should find him guilty of the charge accordingly. Thank you for your time and attention."

Amanda took a sip from her water bottle, straightened her jacket, and walked toward the jury box. She stood a few feet away, making sure every juror could see Judge McNeil. She smiled at them and began her closing statement. "Ladies and gentlemen, good morning. This is my last chance to talk to you because after I finish, the prosecutor has the right to come back and attack my closing argument. He gets two bites of the apple.

"Mr. Gray wants you to look at this case from the moment Leroy was pushed to the street. He wants you to ignore that Leroy had planned for years to kidnap and torture my client. He wants you to forget that Leroy and two other kidnappers tied my client to a chair and pointed a gun at him for a month.

"He wants you to forget how my client was forced to make decisions in favor of Leroy's nephew, Keshan Walker, who was—and still is—in jail, facing a triple-murder charge in Washington, DC. He wants you to believe that a law-abiding citizen—a prominent judge who had never visited Denver—decided to come here, befriend three convicts, and enjoy their wild drug parties. He wants you to accept that my client was the one who put needles in his arms and that he *enjoyed* visiting his potential grave every night.

"It's true that my client's daughter was not kidnapped, but that information was revealed to my client only a few days ago. He heard from his sister in 2006 that Daphne had last been seen in Madison with an African American man who looked like a football player. Remember Ms. Henderson's testimony? She told you that when Daphne disappeared, the man who mowed the lawn also disappeared.

"Contrary to what Mr. Gray said, my client did report the kidnapping to the FBI—but not immediately. He told you that he hired two retired detectives to do their investigations first. He was afraid the FBI would scare his daughter.

"This was my client's state of mind—that his fifteen-year-old daughter had been kidnapped by the man his sister had described. By showing Daphne's picture to him, Leroy left no doubt in my client's mind that he had kidnapped and raped my client's fifteen-year-old daughter.

"Leroy shocked my client by revealing to him how he had fooled him with his phony lawn-mowing company and how he had befriended his daughter. He shocked him once more, by showing him the picture of Daphne with their baby. For those of you who have children, could you please think for a moment and put yourself in my client's shoes? How would you feel about your kidnapper if you learned that he also had control over your child's life?

"Mr. Gray is asking you to forget about the kidnapping. He wants you to believe that Leroy invited my client to the Lakewood house and treated him like a guest. But the truth is, my client was assaulted and threatened constantly. Ladies and gentlemen, according to criminal law, every unwanted touch is assault, every push and shove is assault, and forcibly pumping drugs into someone's body is *definitely* assault. As you see, everything that Leroy did to my client was pointing my client toward one conclusion—that his life was in danger.

"The prosecutor tells you that Leroy never intended to kill my client because he didn't have a gun on his person. But for almost a month, he had made my client taste death every day by showing him his potential grave, by tying him to a chair, and by forcing him to use drugs, all at gunpoint.

"Leroy Walker repeatedly threatened my client. He told him twice that if he didn't succeed in getting himself arrested, his daughter's life would be in danger. And a few minutes before he was pushed by my client, Leroy threatened, once again, to kill him if he messed up his plan.

"I remind you of the testimony of the homeless veteran who heard my client telling Leroy to leave him alone when Leroy continued to pull and drag him. My client wanted to get rid of him. He pushed him in self-defense. He didn't have a gun on him, he didn't use excessive force, and he hadn't premeditated to kill Leroy. This was a classic case of self-defense. For that reason, I'm asking you to come back with the verdict of not guilty. Thank you."

Denis Gray stood before the jury box for his rebuttal argument. This time, his tone was not angry. He attacked Amanda's argument again and concluded that it was not a killing committed in the sudden heat of passion. Going further, he argued, "If the defendant had killed Leroy after Leroy showed him his daughter's picture, you could say Leroy had provoked the defendant to the point that he was overcome by an irresistible passion to kill him. But the killing occurred a day later. Even if you believe that provocation occurred forty-five minutes before the killing, there was an interval sufficient for the voice of reason. In other words, the defendant had enough time to cool off.

"As I have explained to you repeatedly, this trial was not and *is* not about the kidnapping. Nor is it about how many times the defendant was assaulted. This was a premeditated murder. We have proven every element of the crime beyond a reasonable doubt; therefore, the only thing left for you to do is find the defendant guilty of murder in the first degree."

Chapter 50

It was 2:00 p.m. when Judge Hutchinson began his jury instruction. He repeated some of the issues he had discussed with the jury before. He emphasized the roles of the jury, the judge, the prosecutor, and the defense attorney.

He told them that after weighing all the evidence provided to them by both sides, they should either exonerate the defendant by a unanimous vote or find him guilty beyond a reasonable doubt—the standard used in criminal law cases. But he added that "beyond reasonable doubt" did not mean beyond *all* doubts.

He went over the elements of murder in the first degree and differentiated it from murder in the second degree. He instructed them that they should select a foreperson who would be responsible for all the jury communications with the court. He told them that if they ran into the prosecutor or the defense attorney in the hallways or the elevators, they should not talk with them. "And if you notice that they ignore you when they see you outside the courtroom, that doesn't mean they are mean individuals. They're not supposed to communicate with you."

He instructed them, again, that they should not talk to anyone about the case, including fellow jurors, until the case was submitted to them for their deliberation. He also reminded them they should not read, listen to, or watch any news related to the case. Judge Hutchinson finished delivering his jury instructions at 2:45 p.m. He then asked his courtroom clerk to lead the jurors to the jury room to start their deliberation.

Amanda saw relief on Hutchinson's face when he left the bench. The bailiff took Judge McNeil back to the adjacent cellblock, but Amanda didn't leave the courtroom with Judge Bowen and Aristo. She used the presence of the media reporters outside the courthouse as an excuse and stayed behind, promising to join them later in Judge Bowen's hotel for a cup of coffee.

Everyone, including the courtroom staff, had left now, but Amanda remained in her chair at the defense table. Her head ached, like she had just gone through brain surgery. Feeling exhausted, she sat there and stared at the empty jury box. Obviously, Judge Hutchinson would grant a motion to dismiss the greater charge of murder one because her client was not armed. But what if the jury found him guilty of murder in the second degree? Suddenly, she panicked, having realized that the trial was over and her client's fate was in the hands of seven men and five women. There was nothing more she could do now except renew her motion for judgment of acquittal and eliminate murder one.

Amanda looked at her watch; it was 3:15 p.m. She gathered her files and put them in her briefcase. She tucked some more files under her arm and began walking toward Judge Bowen's hotel. She thought about her next move—an appeal. But Judge Hutchinson had not made any procedural errors. She couldn't even argue prosecutorial misconduct. Even though the prosecution had withheld exculpatory evidence from them, the homeless veteran had testified before the jury about Judge McNeil's last statement—"Leave me alone." All she could do at that point was appeal the conviction by claiming the prosecution had not provided sufficient evidence to the jury to get a conviction.

Amanda was so lost in her thoughts that she was surprised when she realized she'd already reached Judge Bowen's hotel. Aristo was waiting for her in the lobby. "What happened to you?"

"I was nailed to my chair behind the defense table; I couldn't move."

Aristo led her to the hotel's coffee shop, where Judge Bowen was waiting for them. "What's with the worried face?" Judge Bowen asked as soon as he saw Amanda.

"I just realized it's over."

"You should be relieved."

"What if they convict him?"

"They won't. You put an excellent self-defense argument before the jury."

"They may believe Mr. Gray; they may believe that this was not killing in self-defense or the heat of passion—"

"Amanda, stop thinking negative," Aristo interjected. "Look, you established for the jury that your client didn't have a gun, but Leroy had one readily available to him in his car a few feet away."

"I have to agree with Aristo," Bowen said. "Besides, this jury should be fed up with Leroy and his coconspirators for tying the judge to a chair, holding him at gunpoint every waking hour, and pumping him full of drugs."

"I hope you're both right. But did you notice the jury's poker faces during the closing argument? In past trials, anytime a juror or a few jurors have nodded in agreement with me, I've won the case. Today, none of the jurors nodded, even when I put forth my strongest argument defending McNeil."

"You're right," Aristo agreed. "But I have observed this jury for many days. I have seen them agonize; move uncomfortably in their chairs. You told me some were in tears when McNeil testified."

"Aristo is right," said the judge. "I don't think this jury has the heart to convict Walter of first-degree murder."

"But Judge Bowen, that's exactly what I'm afraid of. If the jury is confused between the elements of murder one and murder two, they may convict him of a lesser included crime."

"Ms. Perkins, if the jury is confused about something, they'll send a note to the judge and ask him for more instruction. The case is out of your hands now. You should rest for a few days. They have more than a hundred exhibits to review," Judge Bowen said. Then he turned and called a waiter and ordered three coffees and assorted desserts.

The trio continued their discussion for a while. Amanda hadn't finished her coffee when her cell phone vibrated; Judge Hutchinson's courtroom clerk was calling. She answered immediately.

As the clerk delivered the message, Amanda looked up at Aristo and Judge Bowen. "Oh my God! They've reached a verdict." Amanda thanked the clerk and hung up, a worried expression on her face. "This is not good. It only took them two hours and fifty-five minutes to find him—" Amanda couldn't finish her sentence. She was scared to use the word *guilty*.

"I have to agree. A quick verdict is usually a guilty verdict," Judge Bowen said, shaking his head.

Aristo took Amanda in his arms and gave her a firm hug. "Hey, you can appeal this."

"Judge McNeil cannot survive another lengthy legal battle sitting in jail."

"Maybe you can get him released on bond this time."

* * *

The trio rushed back to the courthouse. When they arrived, Judge Hutchinson was already on the bench. Amanda looked at her client's pale face and forced a smile.

"It takes at least twenty minutes to choose a foreperson," McNeil commented. "How could they reach a verdict so quickly?"

"I have no idea. Maybe—" Amanda had to stop talking because the jurors entered the courtroom, and everyone had to rise.

Her heart was beating fast, the same way it had when Melvin put a gun to her head and when she saw her living room in flames. She looked back to see who was in the audience. To her surprise, the courtroom, which had been fully packed day after day during the two-week trial, was almost empty now. Judge Bowen and Aristo were the only two audience members sitting in the courtroom. Apparently, no spectators or members of the media had anticipated a quick verdict either. Amanda sensed that Judge Hutchinson preferred it that way.

She looked at the jurors' faces. They seemed to be relaxed, but no one was smiling—another bad sign for the defense.

The trial judge asked the jury to identity their foreperson. It turned out to be juror number seven—an African American US Postal Service employee. Amanda had always thought number seven was her lucky number, but she already knew the jury had convicted her client; no jury could deliberate a murder case in just two hours and fifty-five minutes.

Amanda had always had a good experience with postal service employees as witnesses in her trials. For some unexplainable reason, she sensed that juries loved mail couriers. She remembered that during the voir dire juror number seven had disclosed that she had a cousin who was a police officer. When Amanda inquired whether she would be fair to a defendant accused of murder, despite her association with a cop, she had responded, "I'll be sitting in the jury box, not my cousin, and I'll make the decision, not him." Amanda liked her answer and hadn't used her preemptory strike to eliminate her, but now she wondered whether she had made the right choice.

The bailiff took the verdict from the foreperson and handed it to the judge. Hutchinson looked at it and, without showing any reaction, handed it over to his courtroom clerk and asked her to read the charges against the defendant.

"Would the defendant please rise?" said the clerk.

Both Amanda and her client stood and looked at the jury box.

The clerk continued. "Madam Foreperson, in the case of People versus Walter McNeil, felony number 2317, for the charge of murder in the first degree, how do you find the defendant: guilty or not guilty?"

"Not guilty," answered the foreperson.

Amanda exhaled and took Judge McNeil's hand.

"For the charge of murder in the second degree, how do you find the defendant: guilty or not guilty?"

"Not guilty."

Amanda took a deep breath and tried to maintain her composure. She turned to her client to give him a congratulatory handshake, but the tearful Judge McNeil opened his arms and gave her a long hug. She fought her tears and whispered, "The nightmare is over."

Amanda looked at the trial judge, waiting for him to order her client's immediate release. But before Judge Hutchinson got a chance to say anything, Denis Gray asked the judge to poll the jury—a process in which every juror individually had to utter his or her vote. The judge granted the prosecutor's request.

Amanda saw how Denis Gray was studying every juror's face to make sure no one had been intimidated to vote against his or her will. He was also watching for any sign of hesitation by any juror while the juror recounted his or her vote. His defeat was even more obvious when the court heard the words *not guilty* twenty-four times, in the polling for both counts.

Judge Hutchinson thanked the jury members for their service and informed the attorneys that the jurors did not wish to discuss their decision with them. Although happy with the jury's verdict, Amanda was disappointed that they didn't want to talk to her or Denis Gray. In the past, she'd found the conference with the jury at the end of every trial educational. Attorneys on both sides could learn about their weak or strong arguments. Most significantly, the jury would tell them what had made them angry or happy or had swayed their votes.

After the jury left the courtroom, Hutchinson looked at the defense table with a judicial smile. "Judge McNeil, you'll be released from the detention house once the paperwork is ready. Have a safe trip to Washington."

"Thank you, sir," Judge McNeil responded over a lump in his throat.

Amanda appreciated Judge Hutchinson's kind gesture and the fact that after such a lengthy ordeal, her client was able to hear another judge address him by his professional title. As soon as Hutchinson left the courtroom, Amanda rushed to Aristo. She needed a hug. She needed to be in the arms of the man who had helped her and loved her throughout the nerve-racking trial. Aristo showered her with a flurry of quick kisses and then a long, passionate one.

"Hey, you two, get a room," the courtroom clerk yelled, smiling.

Amanda turned around to respond to the clerk, but she forgot what she was going to say when she saw a tearful Judge Bowen hugging and comforting his childhood friend.

Denis Gray and his law clerk left the courtroom without saying a word to anyone.

* * *

Judge Bowen invited everyone to dinner at the luxury restaurant in his hotel. After the first round of champagne, Amanda noticed that although McNeil was smiling a lot, he was millions of miles away.

"How does it feel to be free?" she asked him.

"I feel like someone has removed a cancerous tumor from my brain so that I can live. But that's the scary part—*to live.*"

"Walter, you need a period of adjustment. You need some time to heal. I'm sure you'll be okay in no time," said Judge Bowen.

"I killed a man. Maybe the prosecutor was right and Leroy wasn't ever going to kill me. Maybe I had become so paranoid that I didn't see that. How can I be okay? How can I forgive myself?"

Judge Bowen put a hand on his friend's shoulder. "I suggest, every time you think like that, start remembering what Leroy did to you—the beating, the pumping your body with drugs, then forcing you to sell drugs, and finally, causing you to spend almost a year in jail."

"I agree with Judge Bowen," Aristo said.

"You'll go back to DC tomorrow, so please, try not to think about Leroy, at least for tonight," Amanda suggested.

"It's not easy. No matter how I try to justify my actions, I can't change the fact that I killed a man."

"Don't worry, you're going to be my roommate tonight, and I'll keep your mind off Leroy," Bowen said.

When everyone was ready to leave, McNeil asked Bowen and Manfredi to give him a few minutes to talk to Amanda alone. Once the other two had left the area, McNeil spoke. "Ms. Perkins, I've been meaning to tell you something, but I wanted to wait until the trial was over."

"What about?"

"About your client, Damian Lewis, the juvenile I sentenced so harshly the day I was kidnapped."

"What about him? Is he in trouble again?"

"No. After I slammed the door in your face, I felt so ashamed of my behavior that I couldn't continue reading Keshan's motions anymore. So I read your two-page motion, and I decided to grant it."

"Oh my God, why didn't you tell me?"

"Well, I was too tired that night. I was going to write my ruling on Monday, but then I got kidnapped. One day during my captivity, when Leroy was in a good mood, I asked for his permission to write an opinion to grant a motion. When he realized Damian was seventeen years old, like his nephew, Keshan, he let me."

"I didn't hear anything about this."

"My law clerk must have sent my order to your DC office address, but you were here."

"Oh my God, Damian is free? Thank you so much," Amanda said, grabbing Judge McNeil in a heartfelt hug. Suddenly, she pulled away. "Wait a minute. Why did you keep this from me for all these months?"

"I expected you to say something. When you didn't, first I thought the reason you didn't mention it was that you were still mad at me. But then, once we'd had hours of discussions about everything, I assumed that you must not have known about my decision."

"When did you send your decision?"

"It was long before I saw you in the cellblock. Another reason I didn't talk about it was because I didn't want you to accept my case only because you felt you owed me anything. But after all these months and the zealous way you advocated for me, I have to confess, Ms. Perkins, you're a class act."

McNeil was tearing up, so Amanda gave him another hug. "Thank you so much. I'm going to call Damian tomorrow. Please get a good night's sleep tonight."

* * *

Back in Amanda's bedroom, Aristo put on some soft music and asked Amanda to wait for him to take a quick shower. "I won't have time in the morning. I have to meet someone in Boulder at eight o'clock."

He was glad the verdict had put Amanda in such a euphoric mood that she didn't ask any questions about his early-morning trip. He had made several trips to Boulder during McNeil's trial and each time had told Amanda that he was investigating an old case. She'd been so preoccupied with her murder trial that she'd never asked him the nature of his investigation in Boulder.

When Aristo came out of the shower, he found Amanda in bed, wearing a sexy negligee—and sleeping deeply. Aristo chuckled and shook his head. "Too much champagne," he said as he pulled the cover over her and kissed her forehead. He crawled onto the other side of the bed and smiled. He only hoped he could bring her more good news from Boulder.

Chapter 51

Judge Bowen and his wife had several plans for McNeil to help him adapt to his new life in Washington. Their first suggestion was that he stay in their house for a week or so, which he politely rejected. The second one involved getting him a gun so that he could protect himself at home. The third suggestion was that he erect a tall fence around his large yard.

"I cannot live the rest of my life in fear," he told the Bowens. "I have a few plans of my own. The first one is to get my daughter back, although at this point, I know getting Daphne back may only be a dream."

Judge McNeil made up an excuse to leave the Bowens' home. For two days, they had overwhelmed him with kindness that he couldn't handle and had comforted him with the kind of love he hadn't felt since his wife's death.

Back home, the first thing he did was visit Daphne's room. Since her disappearance, he had kept her door locked, as though the room were a crime scene. After opening all the windows, he made Daphne's bed. He picked up the nightgown she had worn during her last night at home and hung it in her closet. He then quickly left the room. After the torture he had endured in the Lakewood house and after spending many months in jail, he had thought he could handle anything—including visiting Daphne's room. But he was wrong.

McNeil took off his tie and suit, put on his jogging clothes and a baseball hat, and walked toward Connecticut Avenue. He felt like a stranger in a new town. Every few minutes, he looked over his shoulder to see whether someone was following him. After about ten minutes of walking, he relaxed. No one had recognized him on the street. After all, a bearded man with a baseball cap didn't resemble the easily recognizable photos of a clean-shaven judge, seen all over newspapers and TV.

McNeil stopped walking when he found himself across the street from Daphne's apartment building. He waited there for a while, watching the revolving door, hoping to see her walk out. But Daphne didn't show.

That afternoon, he drove to the cemetery and spent some quiet time at Fiona's grave. He sat on the stone bench and stared at the grave. "Fiona, I'm back home. I should be happy, but I'm not. Daphne doesn't want to see me."

That evening, about ten of his neighbors showed up at his home with flowers and lots of food. He was overwhelmed by their gesture. For the first time, McNeil felt he had really left the Denver detention center—he was free and in his own home.

For the next two weeks, every day, he stood across the street facing Daphne's building around the time Detective Manfredi had seen her, but Daphne never showed.

Then one day he stopped making his daily trip. Daphne must have known that the jury had exonerated him. She must have read the details in the paper. She was sending him a silent message; she didn't want anything to do with him. It pained him to admit he had lost his daughter forever.

Many years before, McNeil had purchased a good printed copy of Edvard Munch's *The Scream*. It was suspended on the wall above the fireplace in his living room. Since his return from Denver, every time he looked at the painting, he felt the artist had painted *his* silent scream. Next to the painting was a large picture of a happy five-year-old Daphne with her mother. One day, he stared at the picture for a long time. Then, when tears formed in his eyes, he left the room. He thought about another father who had lost his daughter—Leroy.

McNeil wiped his tears, went to his study, pulled an address book from his desk drawer, and dialed a number. "May I speak to Mike Franklin?"

"Speaking," the voice said.

"Mr. Franklin, this is Walter McNeil—"

"Your Honor. Hi, how're you doing? I'm so sorry for what happened to you."

"That's very nice of you. I know you're the best investigator working for the Federal Criminal Defense Program. I want to hire you to find someone for me."

"Thanks for the compliment, Your Honor."

"First of all, I'm no longer a judge, so you don't have to call me 'Your Honor.' Second, I have seen you work with Attorney Perkins. You've testified in many trials before me, so when I say you're the best, it's not a cheap compliment."

"Give me a little information, Judge. I'll start right away."

"Her name is Samyra Walker."

"Any relation to the man who kidnapped you?"

"Yes. It's his missing daughter. She's twenty. You can get more details about her from Keshan Walker's mother and a friend of Leroy named Montrel. But no one has to know you've been hired by me."

"Will do."

McNeil dialed another number and asked to speak to attorney Debbie Newman.

"Speaking," a voice responded.

"Ms. Newman, this is Walter McNeil. I need to see you to discuss a matter."

"Your Honor, I'll be more than happy to meet with you, but I'm representing Keshan Walker, and this is kind of—"

"It seems odd, but there's no impropriety on your part. I want to help Keshan."

"But his uncle kidnapped you and then was killed—"

"Leroy had three wishes: to put me in jail, which he did; to find his daughter; and to help Keshan get out of jail. I'm trying to fulfill his other two wishes."

Chapter 52

Debbie Newman reluctantly took Judge McNeil to the DC jail and introduced him to the authorities at the entrance door as her new paralegal. The judge used his new driver's license, with the photo that showed him bearded and with longer hair. Even if the DC jail guards had seen his picture in the newspapers, they couldn't have recognized him.

At first, when Keshan saw McNeil, he thought his attorney had hired a new investigator. "What happened to the other investigator?" he asked his attorney.

"Keshan, this is Walter, my research assistant. He knows a lot about murder cases like yours."

McNeil had three lengthy visits with Keshan and his attorney at the DC jail. When Keshan showed some signs of trust and gratitude, McNeil stopped visiting him. He was afraid someone would recognize him, and he had accomplished his goal in the three visits.

Keshan liked the new paralegal, and when he stopped coming to the jail, Keshan noticed immediately. "Where's Walter?" he asked his attorney.

"He's busy researching and preparing for your trial."

And she was telling the truth. Judge McNeil was researching the case laws, not only for the murder trial but also for the possibility of an appeal, in case the jury found Keshan guilty.

Attorney Newman was apprehensive that she would lose her two essential eyewitnesses. "Either the codefendant's friends will scare them, or they'll kill them before the trial," she told McNeil.

"Where are they now?"

"Hiding in their relatives' homes in PG County."

"I have a house in Rehoboth Beach. Would they be willing to live there for a few weeks until trial? I'll pay for their expenses."

"Would you really do that to help Keshan?"

"Yes, I believe he's innocent. The evidence proves that he couldn't have killed those three girls. I want to help."

Newman stared at Judge McNeil for a long moment. "I can't believe this!"

"I know it's a cliché, but I'm a changed man. I'm not the monster you defense attorneys used to gossip about."

"I don't know what to say."

"You don't have to say anything. I can drive them up there."

"I don't know them well. What if they steal your belongings?"

"There's not much there—just some pieces of furniture. I don't care."

"What if they take off and never show up in court?"

"That's your responsibility—to make sure they understand they're under subpoena, and if they don't come to court, a US deputy marshal will find them and arrest them. You can also tell them that we have some money reward for them."

"How much are we talking about?"

"I don't know, maybe a thousand dollars each."

"That'll do it. I'm going to talk to them. I'd like to come with you, if that's okay?"

"Sure. I could use your company on the drive back."

"I have a lot of questions for those two guys. Maybe during the trip, I can prepare them for their testimony, and you can tell me whether I'm asking the right questions."

* * *

McNeil's property in Rehoboth was a two-level, three-bedroom house with an ocean view from every window. One of the first things Debbie Newman noticed was a large framed picture of the judge's wife and daughter hanging in the family room. "You have a beautiful family," she said.

"I used to, not anymore."

"How come?"

"My wife died when Daphne was six years old, and I'm sure you have read about Daphne and her relationship with me in the newspapers."

"I'm sorry about your wife, but I'm embarrassed to admit I was too busy with Keshan's trial to read the newspapers. But I saw bits and pieces of your trial on TV."

Once they got to his house, McNeil played a judge watching a mock trial and let Attorney Newman examine her witnesses. He gave the two witnesses some advice about their demeanors on the witness stand and warned Attorney Newman against some open-ended questions she had posed to her witnesses. After he served his guests pizza and ice cream, he walked to the beach. Ms. Newman followed him. "Do you mind if I join you?" she asked.

"Please do. I enjoy your company."

"If I had a beach house like this, I would escape from DC every weekend and come here to relax. My life is really depressing—just a lot of crime scenes in Washington and trips to the DC jail."

"It has a heavy mortgage; now that I've retired, I don't know how long I can keep it. But as long as I have it, you're welcome to use it whenever you want."

"That's very generous of you, but these days, I have to concentrate on Keshan's trial."

"I used to come here with Daphne and her friends a lot; after she disappeared, I stopped coming."

"Who would've ever thought that one day I'd be a guest in Judge McNeil's beach house? You really have changed."

"I'd like to help your client, as well as find Samyra."

"After what Leroy did to you, I still can't believe you want to do all this for him."

"I sympathize with him. He was a father searching for his missing daughter, like me. And let's not forget, I killed the man."

"It was in self-defense."

"That's just a legal argument. I still can't believe I killed a man, even if it wasn't on purpose."

"I dealt with Leroy a few times. He was a demanding and angry man. He treated me like an employee—as though *he* were paying me to represent his nephew. To be honest with you, I was afraid of him."

"I agree with you; he was an angry man. But I put him away for a long time and destroyed his family. And he didn't deserve to die."

"You talk as though he had nothing to do with all his criminal activities."

McNeil didn't answer and resumed walking. "Do you mind if I spend some time here—alone?"

"Not at all. I better go back to my witnesses."

He continued walking and reminiscing about the time he had spent with his family and friends in Rehoboth. He had fond memories of the beach, except one dark memory he could never forget: the night he and his wife, Fiona, had had a fight. Afterward, she had run out of the house, and McNeil hadn't seen her for the rest of the night.

She came back the next morning, still drunk and crying. She had picked out a man at a bar and spent the night with him. McNeil felt like someone had put a bullet in his head. Fiona begged for forgiveness. At first he thought that one-night affair had ended his marriage. But he loved Fiona too much; he couldn't live without her. When Fiona discovered she was pregnant, he forgave her. He couldn't let her go. His worst nightmare came true when he found out that the baby was not his; the father was the nameless stranger from the bar. Fiona didn't know anything about the man. McNeil promised her that he would never tell anyone about her one-night affair, not even his best friend, Fredrick Bowen. He promised that he would love and raise the little baby girl as his own. And he had kept his promise. As Daphne grew older, she resembled Fiona more than ever. She also developed her mother's characteristics. McNeil was happy there was no trace of the biological father in Daphne.

When Daphne ran away, something died in McNeil's heart; it was like losing Fiona all over again. Nothing, not even his hectic court schedules, could make him forget about her. Daphne was living in every corner of the house and in every moment of his life. He missed seeing her beautiful face and hearing her voice. There were days he dreamed that Daphne would just walk into the house and call out, "Dad, I'm home!" Daphne was a gift that Fiona had given him. How could he live without her?

Walter McNeil sat on a large rock and stared at the waves for a while. The sun was kind and the ocean kinder. He thought the sounds and the smells of the ocean would bring him peace, but instead, he kept remembering the Lakewood house, his drug addiction, his days in jail, the stabbing, and his empty life without Daphne. The void he felt in his heart was as big as the ocean. Rehoboth Beach resembled another planet.

Chapter 53

After returning to DC from his beach house, McNeil visited Judge Bowen. He shared his weekend experience with him and the plans he had to help Keshan and find Samyra. His enthusiasm disappeared when he received harsh criticism from his childhood friend.

"You're ruining a brilliant legal career. You can still apply for a senior judge position. But with this kind of activity, the Judicial Nomination Committee may not approve you."

"I'm not going to take the bench again. I don't care what the committee thinks. I won't be seeking a senior judge status."

"What about me? Are you researching how to appeal my rulings on the Walker case as well?"

"You're an outstanding judge who doesn't make procedural errors. If Keshan loses, I have DC Court of Appeals and Supreme Court cases that can prove the jury didn't have sufficient evidence to find him guilty beyond a reasonable doubt."

The next morning, McNeil was still ruminating about his best friend's criticism when Mike Franklin called and gave him some good news.

"I've located Yvette, Leroy's girlfriend. She's working in a topless club on U Street, Northwest."

"Wonderful. What about Samyra?"

"Some people spotted her a few months ago standing on Fourteenth Street."

"You mean soliciting?"

"Unfortunately, yes."

"When can we talk to them?"

"Judge McNeil, I have a murder trial to investigate. I'll get you more information in about a week."

McNeil didn't have the patience to wait a week. He asked about the exact location of the club. He was on a mission to find Yvette and Samyra.

* * *

He arrived at the U Street club at 9:00 p.m. The noise was unbearable and the music deafening. He saw three topless dancers swinging back and forth from three metallic columns. Colored lights danced over their naked bodies. He felt uncomfortable; he had never been in this kind of place before. He asked the bartender if he could talk to Yvette.

"You mean Tasha, right? Her stage name is Tasha."

"Okay, Tasha. May I see her for a few minutes?"

"She's off tonight, but you can come back tomorrow."

"What time does she start?"

"Around six."

McNeil took a cab and asked the driver to take him to Fourteenth Street, Northwest. When the driver asked him for a specific block number, he explained that he was trying to locate one of the ladies of the evening.

"Are you crazy? Fourteenth Street is full of cops. I'm not gonna go to jail just because you feel horny tonight."

"Please, I'm not looking for sex. I'm trying to help a young lady."

The driver gave him a strange look and drove to Fourteenth Street and Rhode Island Avenue. "There. You can see a few of them working."

McNeil paid the fare and gave the driver a big tip. "Can you come back and pick me up in ten minutes?" he pleaded.

"I don't know," the driver said, and he sped off.

McNeil stood there for a few minutes, not knowing what to do. Three African American women were talking loudly to each other. Another young woman wearing short shorts and a tank top noticed him. She approached him, smiling. "Looking for a date?" she asked in a coquettish voice.

"I'm looking for a girl named Samyra. Do you know her?"

"Maybe I do. Maybe I don't."

"How can I find her?"

"It'll cost you."

"How much?"

"Fifty bucks."

McNeil took a hundred-dollar bill out of his wallet and showed it to the girl. "It's yours if you give me her address."

The girl scratched her temple as if she were debating. McNeil extended his hand holding the money. "It's yours. Please help me find her."

Suddenly, the other prostitutes screamed and started running. Before he could figure out what was happening, his hands were pulled forcefully behind his back and put in handcuffs. Turning his head, he saw two uniformed police officers behind him and a police cruiser that had quietly parked near the curb. "You're under arrest for solicitation. You have the right to remain silent. Anything you say can and will be used against you in a court of law. You have the right to have an attorney …"

McNeil didn't hear the rest of his Miranda rights as the other officer pushed him into the police cruiser. He finally realized what had happened, though. The young girl posing as a prostitute was an undercover police officer. By scratching her temple, she had given the signal to the arresting team that a john had just offered her money in exchange for sex.

Chapter 54

Aristo was in his office listening to his phone messages when he heard a familiar voice yelling, "Officer! The young lady made a mistake. I didn't solicit."

He turned his answering machine off, came out, and followed the direction of the voice. He jumped out of his skin when he saw McNeil handcuffed, sitting in a chair a few feet away. He was being questioned by a young DC officer.

"What's going on here?" he asked the officer.

"Am I glad to see you," McNeil said excitedly before the officer got a chance to talk.

"He's booked for solicitation."

Aristo took the officer away from his desk and talked to him about the identity of the man in handcuffs. He then went to McNeil and asked for his side of the story. When Aristo went back to talk to the arresting officer again, the officer insisted that their undercover officer was reliable and would not lie.

"Let me talk to her," Aristo said.

The officer dialed a number, and after a few minutes, the undercover officer showed up, still in her prostitute outfit and makeup. Aristo knew her well. She was a twenty-five-year-old, good-looking rookie who had gained a reputation for getting ten to fifteen men arrested every night she worked undercover.

Aristo took her to his office and disclosed that her john was a judge. "Now can you tell me the real story?"

"He offered me a hundred dollars."

"For sex or for information?"

"What difference does it make? He was asking for Samyra. If she was there, he would've given her the money."

"I know your team is very proud of you for the number of arrests you make every night, but that doesn't and shouldn't give you the power to interpret the law. The DC code specifically says 'money in exchange for sex.' What we are doing using female undercover posing as prostitute is called entrapment. We're lucky the Supreme Court has sided with us so far, but that doesn't mean we should abuse the power."

The undercover agent looked nervous. She turned around and left Aristo's office. "I don't need your lecture," she said, shaking her head as she left.

Aristo asked the arresting officer to take McNeil's handcuffs off. "I'll take you home," he told the judge.

When they exited the DC police headquarters, McNeil asked Aristo to walk with him toward the superior court building. "I'm still afraid to go there alone. The horrible experience still haunts me. And the events of that night keep playing in my head like a movie," he said as they walked. When they stood in front of the superior court building, McNeil pointed to a window. "Detective, that's the window to my chamber. I never thought I would miss the courthouse so much," he said, sighing. "I miss the employees, the judges, the officers, and believe it or not, even the defense attorneys who quarreled with me every day."

"You can always come back as a senior judge."

"I'm done here as a judge."

"Why is it so difficult for you to accept the fact that you didn't kill Leroy intentionally?"

"How can I ever sentence a defendant when I have committed a crime myself? Besides, the Judicial Committee isn't going to approve my application for a senior judge position."

"You don't know that until you apply."

"Don't you remember Judge McKinley and the famous neglect case that ruined the man's career? He gave weekend visitation rights to a mother in a neglect case after the social worker recommended that the mother was fit to have unsupervised visitation. The child fell down the staircase and died. They blamed the judge more than they blamed the mother. He didn't kill anyone, but they denied his application because they felt his wrong judgment had killed a child."

When they got into Aristo's car, McNeil told him in detail about his efforts to help Keshan and find Samyra. He asked Aristo to take him to the U Street nightclub. "The bartender told me that Yvette would be there tomorrow, but I don't believe him. Please help me talk to her. I'm afraid if I go there alone, someone will arrest me or kick me out."

"Judge McNeil, haven't you had enough excitement for one night?"

"Detective, I'm so grateful to you for finding me in Denver, for assisting Ms. Perkins during my trial, and for getting me off the hook tonight. You have no idea how I panicked when they arrested me. When I sat as a judge in arraignment court some Saturdays, I saw a few congressmen and some foreign diplomats arraigned for solicitation. I saw how embarrassed they looked. I just imagined myself standing before another judge, feeling humiliated. Thank you so much for saving me tonight. I'm eternally in your debt. But please, you've got to help me find Samyra."

"The jury found you not guilty. What's this obsession you have with finishing what Leroy started?"

"Detective, I killed the man. Despite all the horrible things he did to me, he was a father looking for his missing daughter. If I hadn't given him so many years in jail, his daughter wouldn't have been raped, wouldn't have contracted HIV—his life wouldn't have fallen apart. I'm the father of a missing daughter too. I know how Leroy felt."

"I thought you were going to use all your efforts to get Daphne back."

"She knows I'm back in DC. She has made it clear she doesn't want to see me. As far as she's concerned, I'm dead."

* * *

They arrived at the nightclub just as a topless dancer was crawling on the stage. The combined noise level of the music and the applause was unbearable. "That must be Yvette," Aristo said, pointing to the woman on the stage. "She looks like one of the pictures we found in Leroy's suitcase in the Lakewood house."

They chose a booth and waited for Yvette to finish her dance. When she had collected the money tossed by the boisterous drunk customers and left the stage, Aristo showed his badge to the club manager and asked if he could talk to her.

"What's this all about?" he asked Aristo.

"Don't worry. We're here to help her."

They were led backstage. Yvette was wearing a robe and sitting at her dresser, removing her makeup. She jumped when she saw two strange white men with her manager. "What do they want?" she asked the manager.

"They just want to talk to you. I'll be outside if you need me."

Aristo stepped inside the room and introduced himself. He then pointed to McNeil and said, "This gentleman is here to talk to you. His name is—"

"I know who he is," Yvette said, cutting him off. "He's the judge who killed Leroy. I can recognize him even with his beard and mustache."

McNeil stepped inside the room and said, "I'm sorry for what happened. You can hate me all you want, but it really was an accident."

"I don't hate you. Actually, you gave me my freedom. I was in hiding for years. I came back to DC when I read in the paper that he died."

"Aren't you afraid of his friends?" Aristo asked. "You must know that one of them committed a crime just to go to jail to stab the judge."

"I've made my peace with them. Besides, my manager and his employees protect me like bodyguards."

"Where's your daughter?" McNeil asked.

Yvette stared at a baby picture on the wall and then closed her eyes and whispered, "She's gone."

"Where?" Aristo asked.

"She died three months ago," Yvette said, fighting tears she couldn't stop. The tears washed mascara down her face, and her pain was visible under the rest of her heavy makeup.

"I'm so sorry," McNeil said.

"What happened to the money you got after you sold the house?" Aristo asked.

"When Leroy went to jail, I was a part-time waitress taking care of a sick woman and two children. The money was not enough. I started seeing men. One of them messed with Samyra when I wasn't home. When I found out my baby had HIV, I went crazy. I took care of Leroy's mama for a long time, but then I just got tired. I put her in a shelter. I thought her husband's pension was enough."

"But she had to have kidney dialysis twice a week. Who was supposed to take her to the clinic?" Aristo asked.

"I gave a lot of money to one of the staff at the shelter. He promised me he would take care of Doris. I'm sorry. I had to save my child. The house sold for three hundred thousand dollars. I took Samyra to Johns Hopkins Hospital, then to Anderson Center in Houston. I spent the money trying to keep my baby alive. But it didn't last long. The doctors and the medications kept her alive for only ten years. She died a few days after she turned twenty."

Yvette began crying again, causing black mascara to run even farther down her face. She wiped her tears, pulled out her drawer, and took out a picture. "This is her last picture, taken on her birthday," she said as she handed the picture to Judge McNeil.

McNeil looked at the picture. "She's a beautiful young lady." He thanked Yvette for talking with him and apologized for his role in sentencing Leroy harshly and causing pain for his family.

"It's not your fault. My baby died because of my sins, and I have to live with it."

"I'm so sorry for your loss."

* * *

After he dropped McNeil in front of his home, Aristo called Judge Bowen and gave him the details of the day's events. "He's forgotten all about Daphne and is only concentrating on Leroy's family," he told Bowen.

"He's losing his mind. I think it's the guilt that's killing him. Detective, I am very busy with Keshan's murder case. Could you please keep an eye on him until I finish this trial?"

"Of course."

Chapter 55

For a week, Aristo followed Judge McNeil, using different disguises. He felt sad when he saw him every day around noon, standing a hundred feet away from Daphne's apartment building. Some days, Daphne would walk outside with her children, and the judge would hide behind a tree and follow their path with his eyes until they were no longer visible. Some days, he would walk back home looking sad because she had not shown up.

Aristo was about to quit his mission, but one day, he saw McNeil leaving the office of Dr. Carter, a psychologist who worked for the DCMPD. Aristo was there because he had a meeting with Dr. Carter to discuss the progress of one of the officers under his supervision. The officer had beaten up a suspect during his arrest, after which he had been suspended for a month and ordered to seek psychotherapy with Dr. Carter.

Aristo hid in his car until McNeil drove away. At first, he was surprised, but then he thought therapy probably was a good idea to help the judge get back to his normal life. But his curious detective mind was telling him that Judge McNeil had a deeper problem he had not shared with him, Amanda, or Judge Bowen.

When Aristo entered Dr. Carter's suite, it was four thirty in the afternoon. He saw a female patient sitting in the waiting room, reading a book. Dr. Carter came out and greeted both Aristo and the female patient. He handed a thick file to his receptionist and told her she could go home. He then asked the female patient whether he could see Aristo first. "Your session is forty-five minutes long, but I need to talk to this gentleman for only a few minutes. Do you mind?"

The patient indicated that she could wait a few minutes longer. While Dr. Carter was thanking his patient, Aristo's gaze followed the file in the receptionist's hands. He guessed it must be McNeil's file. By the time Dr. Carter invited him to his office, Aristo had seen where the receptionist placed McNeil's file—on a shelf in an alcove behind the reception desk.

At first, he was tempted to ask Dr. Carter about the judge's visit, but he knew that doctor-patient confidentiality would bar Dr. Carter from disclosing any information.

"I have good news for you," Dr. Carter said, smiling. "Your officer has finished all his therapy sessions successfully, and he can go back to work."

"Are you sure he won't break anyone else's nose?" Aristo said jokingly.

"I'm sure he won't. Here, this is my complete report for you and the chief."

"Dr. Carter, do you mind if I sit in the waiting room and take a quick look at the report, in case I have some questions?"

"I have to finish with my patient first. Then I can answer any questions you might have. Can you wait another forty-five minutes?"

"Yes, I can, but I may not even have any questions."

Aristo walked to the waiting room and sat in a chair near the reception desk. He pretended to read the doctor's report. The receptionist had already left, so as soon as the female patient entered the doctor's office and the door closed behind her, Aristo got up and walked to the receptionist's area. He easily located McNeil's file, took it back to the waiting room, and started with the last page. The doctor's notes, written thirty minutes earlier, started with a surprising sentence: "The death of Justin—Daphne's boyfriend—is still haunting him."

The subsequent passages didn't make sense to Aristo. The doctor had detailed how emotional McNeil would become whenever he talked about this particular case. Aristo went back to the first pages of the file.

McNeil's first visit with Dr. Carter had been in April 2006—shortly after Daphne's disappearance. Aristo didn't have too much knowledge about Daphne's former boyfriend except his name—Justin. He continued reading the subsequent pages while moving to the edge of his chair. After the last paragraph, he gasped.

Oh my God, he caused Justin's death, Aristo realized. *That's why Daphne disappeared.*

Chapter 56

Leroy's last visit with Keshan had occurred in the DC jail a few days before the planned kidnapping of Judge McNeil. He'd told Keshan he was leaving town for a few months to find Samyra. When Keshan didn't see his uncle for an even longer period of time, he asked his mother about him. "Is he still looking for Samyra?"

"No, baby. I hate to give you the bad news. Your uncle is in jail again."

The news didn't surprise Keshan. Since his early childhood, he had known that his uncle Leroy spent a lot of time in jail, as though jail was his second home. His mother had taken him to the DC jail and to Lorton to visit his uncle several times before Leroy was transferred to Hazelton's federal prison.

During his own incarceration, Keshan didn't have access to the newspapers. His mother asked his attorney, friends, and relatives not to share any news about Leroy with him. So he didn't know about Judge McNeil's kidnapping or the fact that the judge had killed his uncle.

On August 9, when her son was acquitted of all murder charges, Latisha Williams threw a festive welcome-home party for him. In addition to relatives, she invited several neighbors. She requested in advance that no one talk to Keshan about Leroy. "I want my baby to be happy and enjoy his freedom for a few months," she told them. "I have to find the right time to tell him his beloved uncle is dead."

After a week of celebration, Keshan asked his mother if they could drive to Hazelton and visit his uncle.

"He's not there anymore."

"Where's he at?"

"He's far away, in some federal prison in Texas."

"I can take the bus if you let me go."

"He'll be released in six months. Let's wait. I'm sure if he was here, he would tell you to go back to school or get a job, not visit him."

* * *

McNeil invited attorney Debbie Newman to have lunch with him at his home. The purpose of the meeting was to discuss Keshan's future. She was not optimistic about the judge's plans. "With all due respect, sir, you don't know these young defendants the way we do, and by that I mean the defense attorneys. You've dealt with them from the bench, but we've visited them at their homes; we've talked to their family members, friends, relatives, and neighbors. Keshan's mother has told him Leroy is in jail. I'm worried about your safety and his reaction once he finds out you killed his uncle."

"Ms. Newman, I'll be offering him an easy life, a nice car, and a nice home; he may forgive me."

"I can tell him about all the legal help you gave me before and during his trial. I can tell him how you saved the lives of the two essential witnesses for us by hiding them in your beach house. But you have to understand, none of your good gestures are going to change the fact that you killed his uncle, even though we know it was an accident. Leroy was not just a male figure in his life. He was the father Keshan never had."

"But he and I are family now. You must have read about the famous Exhibit 27 during my trial." The judge took a picture from a nearby drawer and handed it to Newman. "Look at it. This is my daughter, Daphne, and her five-year-old son, Sean. That's Leroy holding his baby with Daphne. Malcolm is my grandson. You think Keshan will kill his cousin's grandfather?"

"I don't know, Judge. It's too risky. I just got him out of jail. I don't want to see him charged even with a misdemeanor assault, much less another serious crime."

"So you think he's going to either kill me or—"

"I don't know."

The next week, Attorney Newman reluctantly brought Keshan to Judge McNeil's home. He looked at the yard for a few minutes as though he knew the place. "I think I've been here before," he said. "My uncle had a lawn-mowing business. He brought me to this neighborhood two or three times to help him out."

"Maybe it was our neighbors' yards," McNeil said. "I never saw your uncle here." He was telling the truth; he had never seen Leroy cutting his grass.

They moved inside. McNeil gave Keshan a tour of his home and discussed his plan for him over the pizza he'd ordered. "You will have your own room, your own car, and a modest allowance. I'll pay for your GED if you choose not to go to high school and for four years of college expenses. After that, you're on your own."

"Thank you, Walter," Keshan said, "but my mama ain't gonna let me go. I'm her only child, and after being in jail so long, she wants me home. She's afraid something bad will happen again."

"That's exactly why I want you to come live here. Your codefendant's friends are angry with you and your witnesses. They might try to harm you. Please discuss all of this with your mom and tell her that she's welcome to come visit you here anytime she wants."

* * *

After Keshan and his attorney left, McNeil walked toward Tonya's apartment building. He hadn't seen her since the day she testified for him during his trial in Denver. He needed to see a friend, someone who cared for him deeply and loved him unconditionally. Since his return to Washington, he had stopped by Tonya's apartment building several times. According to the building's receptionist, Tonya had moved out a long time ago, when she lost her job and couldn't afford to pay the rent.

When he arrived at the building's lobby, he couldn't find the friendly receptionist who always gave him information about Tonya. Instead, there was an old woman who didn't even acknowledge his greeting.

"You used to have a tenant here by the name of Tonya Henderson. Has anyone seen her recently?"

"Yes, she was here the other day, asking our florist whether they had a job opening."

"You have a florist here?"

"Yes, in the back of the building, we have a florist, a beauty salon, and a gift shop."

"Did she leave any forwarding address or telephone number with you?"

"No, but you can go and ask the florist."

The old woman gave McNeil directions to the florist's shop. He was surprised she had turned out to be so helpful. He thanked her and walked to the back of the building. He introduced himself to the cashier in the flower shop as Walter, a former employer of Tonya Henderson. "I heard she was here the other day applying for a job. I actually have a job for her. Would you mind giving me her telephone number?"

"Not at all," the receptionist said, looking through a thick spiral notebook. "Here, this is her number."

McNeil wrote the number down and left the shop quickly. He couldn't believe his luck. He opened his cell phone immediately; he was too impatient to go home and make the call. He dialed Tonya's number and had to listen to a popular rap song for twenty seconds before a man's voice came on. "Hey, you know whatchyado. Leave me a number. Love and peace."

McNeil hesitated to leave a message. His bit of happiness had vanished as soon as he heard the man's voice. *This must be her new boyfriend,* he thought as he ended the call.

After a moment, he dialed the number again and listened to the song and the announcement patiently. This time he left a message. "Tonya, this is Walter. I heard from the florist in your old building that you're looking for a job. I have a job for you. Please give me a call or stop by the house."

He walked back toward his home. During the entire twenty-minute walk, he heard a nagging voice in his head telling him he would never have a normal life. He had lost his job, his daughter, even Tonya. He was no longer the powerful judge who ruled and changed people's lives. Now he didn't have any control over his own life.

When he reached his home, he saw a car parked in front of his two-door garage. He didn't see anyone, but he heard the laughter of some kids behind the house. He walked toward his backyard and gasped. Daphne was sitting on the stone bench with her two children.

Chapter 57

"Daphne! Oh my God. I can't believe this!"

Daphne jumped to her feet and raised her left hand as a sign to stop her father. "Stay where you are. Don't come any closer; just listen to me."

"Okay."

"Don't say a word; just listen. You ruined my youth, but I never told anyone what you did. No one knows you killed Justin. This is Sean, Justin's baby"—Daphne pointed to her older boy and then pointed to her younger toddler—"and Malcolm. Remember you killed *his* father too."

McNeil killed a sigh and lowered his head. He didn't hear some of Daphne's subsequent words until she yelled, "Are you listening to me?"

"Yes." He raised his gaze. "You know I didn't mean for Justin to die."

"Stop that nonsense. You banged his head against the wall, hard, and threw him out, knowing—"

"He died because he crashed his car into a tree."

"Just shut up. Don't say another word. You saw how drunk he was."

"Daphne, what did you expect? You came home crying about how he was making out with another girl … and then you shocked me, telling me you were pregnant with his child. Put yourself in my shoes. How—"

"I said shut up and listen. I don't want to talk about that night anymore. Leroy, the man you killed, helped me get my GED, and my boyfriend has helped me get my associate's degree from Montgomery County Community College. American University has accepted me. I want to reclaim my youth; I want to have my life back. Now that you've retired, you raise the kids. I have their clothes and everything they need in two suitcases in my car. I'll come here three times a week to spend time with my kids. Don't even try to talk to me. In fact, get out of my way as soon as you see my shadow. I'll leave you a telephone number. Call me *only* when you have to discuss something urgent related to my kids. Oh, and I need a credit card to pay for my tuition."

McNeil opened the back door, walked inside his house, and retrieved a credit card from one of his drawers. He walked back to Daphne, placed the card on the stone bench, and stepped back. Daphne picked it up and looked at it. "This has my name on it, and it was issued in 2006. How come you never gave this to me before?"

"It was my gift for your sixteenth birthday, but you were gone. I kept it active, hoping that one day you would come back home."

Daphne shrugged, put the credit card in her purse, and walked to her car. She took out two suitcases and left them near the entry door. She walked back to the backyard, kissed her children, and whispered, "You'll stay with Grandpa now. I'll come back and see you in a few days."

McNeil saw his daughter's tears as he fought his. Daphne put her arms around the children and held them for a few more minutes and then walked to her car and drove off.

He followed the car's path with his gaze until it disappeared down the street. Daphne's anger made him wonder whether there would ever be a good time to tell her that he was not her biological father. He had realized the news would devastate her and ruin any happiness she might have in the future. She had gone through so much already; she didn't need more shocking news. He returned his attention to the children, unsure of what to do. Looking at Sean, a blond boy with Daphne's blue eyes, reduced his fear—the boy didn't resemble Justin. It was the same relief he'd felt when Daphne resembled her mother, not her faceless unknown father.

McNeil sat on the stone bench near Sean, scared to talk to him, as if Sean knew about his crime.

The events of that scary night played like a movie in his head. Daphne had come home, thrown herself in his arms, and cried hysterically, telling him she had caught her boyfriend making out with another girl.

It was Justin's prom night, and Daphne had been his date. For a week, McNeil had witnessed his daughter's excitement while she prepared for that night. She had spent days shopping for the right evening gown, shoes, and handbag, with permission to use her father's credit card for a shopping spree.

But when Daphne came home at midnight, she was sobbing, and her body was trembling. She threw herself into the nearest sofa in the living room and told her father Justin had another girlfriend. McNeil didn't know what to do except to grab a bottle of scotch. He needed to calm himself down more than comfort Daphne. At that moment, had Justin showed up at his door, he would have strangled him. A few minutes later, he offered a glass of orange juice to Daphne.

She stopped crying after she finished her orange juice. She looked tired and sleepy. McNeil took her to her bedroom, and when she got into her bed, he gave her a good-night kiss on the forehead. "We'll talk about this in the morning. Get some sleep," he said.

"Daddy, will you please stay with me until I fall asleep?" Daphne asked, sitting on her bed. She hung her arms around her father's neck, swinging her body. McNeil sat on the edge of her bed and tried to wipe her tears. He felt sleepy too. He kissed his daughter on the top of her head and was about to leave when Daphne's bedroom door opened. There stood Justin, distraught and drunk.

"How the hell did you get in here?" McNeil shouted.

"The door was open."

"Daddy, I forgot to lock the door," Daphne said.

McNeil jumped to his feet, grabbed Justin by the shoulder, and tried to push him out of the bedroom. But he froze when Daphne yelled, "Daddy, please don't! I'm pregnant."

McNeil let go of Justin for a moment and looked at his daughter in disbelief. When Daphne said, "It's his baby," McNeil ignored Justin's shouts that he didn't know. He grabbed the teen again and banged his head against the wall several times.

While Justin kept repeating how sorry he was, McNeil dragged him outside, threw him to the street, and locked the door. Through the gate, he yelled at Justin, "If you show your face here again, I'll kill you."

Daphne hurried to the front door and begged her father to let Justin back inside the house. "He's drunk; he can't drive."

McNeil didn't respond when he heard the sound of Justin's car screeching out of their cul-de-sac. He took Daphne's arm and dragged her away. "We'll talk about this in the morning."

The next morning, McNeil woke up early to check on Daphne. He tiptoed up to her door but didn't hear any noise. Assuming Daphne was still asleep, he stepped out to get the newspaper but couldn't find one. While fixing his breakfast, he noticed the paper lying on the dinner table with a note attached to it: "You killed the father of my child." It was Daphne's handwriting. He looked at the paper. A picture of Justin accompanied a headline: "High School Senior Killed in Car Crash."

Years later, when McNeil's kidnappers gave him LSD, he thought he would see gruesome images that would make him forget about the ugly images of the night he'd caused the death of his daughter's boyfriend. He had expected to see decapitated people or lizards chewing people's necks. But instead, he had seen himself stabbing Daphne's body, making her blood splash all over her bed.

He had hated himself for years and uttered the same words in his head many times. "Daphne, forgive me. I didn't want him to die."

* * *

During the drive back to her building, Daphne cried quietly and fought to erase from her mind the confused faces of her children and the painful expression on her father's face. *He was an adult; he should have treated Justin better.* She remembered prom night, how Justin had rejected her love and made out with another girl. His actions had been inexcusable, but her father's actions were criminal—he was the monster who had killed Justin and forced her to run away. But was she the innocent victim?

The sound of Justin's mother crying hysterically on the phone, telling Daphne he had died still echoed in her ears. She felt relieved that Justin's mother thought her son's death was due only to a car crash and didn't know about the role Daphne's father had played.

Why did she have to call Leroy and ask him to drive her to Madison, Wisconsin? Why did she sleep with three college boys? Why did she use drugs and alcohol in Madison? Why did she let Leroy in her life, and why had she made a baby with him? Was she punishing her father? And what about Malcolm? This was the second time that Daphne had wondered whether she was a fit mother. And most significantly, how could she ever tell Malcolm his grandfather had killed his father?

* * *

McNeil looked at Sean and smiled. He took his hands and asked him if he could give him a hug. Sean jumped closer and gave McNeil a big hug. McNeil kneeled and held his grandson while his body trembled. Ignoring the pain he felt in his heart, he forced a smile when he saw the worried look on Malcolm's face. "Come to Grandpa," he said, motioning to the toddler. "We can all hug." Malcolm and Sean both put their arms around him, giving him a collective hug.

He took the children inside and then went back to the yard and grabbed the suitcases. Daphne had left detailed information about her kids—their favorite foods, favorite bedtime stories, good and bad habits, and so on. She had one suitcase full of clothes and toys and a second one full of diapers with a handwritten note: "Malcolm is not potty-trained yet."

McNeil needed Tonya now more than ever. He called her number once more. "Tonya, if I don't hear from you within the next day or so, I'll have to hire someone to help me. You have a job here. Please call me."

The children liked Grandpa's chicken soup. After being bathed, they looked tired. They fell asleep before Grandpa finished one of their favorite bedtime stories.

McNeil walked toward the stone bench and stared at the spot where Daphne had sat. "My dearest Daphne," he whispered, "will you ever forgive me? I'd lost my mind, and I made a terrible mistake." He had rehearsed those lines in his head many times. He remembered how many times he had heard that familiar line—*I made a mistake*—from different defendants who had stood before him during their sentencing. He remembered how he had mocked those attorneys when they said their clients "made a mistake."

Back inside, he checked on the kids. He stared at Malcolm first and then Sean. *How can I ever tell them I was responsible for their fathers' deaths?*

Chapter 58

Keshan didn't discuss Judge McNeil's generous offer with his mother immediately. He had no intention of destroying the chance of a lifetime—the opportunity to live in a fancy area of Washington and drive his own car. He waited for a while, until one day he found his mother in a good mood. When she started talking about GEDs and college, he mentioned Judge McNeil's offer.

"You don't have to live with him. If he wants to help you with your college tuition, he can do it no matter where you live."

"What about a GED?"

"You can get it here in our area."

"What about a car, a job, other stuff he can help me with?"

"You're not gonna live with him, and that's *that*," Latisha said, raising her voice.

"Why *not*?"

"Because this is blood money—because the son of a bitch killed your uncle Leroy."

"What?"

It was too late for Latisha to take her words back. She had blurted out the information she had begged everyone not to share with her son. She reluctantly brought out newspaper clippings she had saved for Keshan to read.

He read the first one and then paused to stare at his uncle's pictures. As he continued reading, one article after another, his face showed his pain and anger. He threw the last article on the table without reading it. The heading read "Judge McNeil Is Finally Free." He ran toward his room, muttering, "I'm gonna kill that motherfucker."

Latisha's heart almost stopped. She followed her son as he walked fast toward his bed. He retrieved a revolver from underneath his mattress.

"Where did you get that gun?" Latisha asked in panic.

"From a friend."

"Please, Keshan, don't do nothin' stupid. You just got out of jail. I'm sorry you had to hear this so soon. Please, baby, don't mess up your future."

Keshan pushed his mother away and ran out of the house. She called Debbie Newman several times before the attorney finally answered the phone. Latisha told her to alert Judge McNeil that Keshan had a gun and was planning to kill him.

Attorney Newman didn't ask any questions. She immediately hung up and called McNeil, but she had no luck; no one picked up the telephone. She called Detective Manfredi and left a message for him. "Detective, this is Debbie Newman, Keshan's attorney. He knows that Judge McNeil is the one who killed his uncle. He has a gun and is looking for the judge. I'm in court and in the middle of a difficult trial. Please alert Judge McNeil, but I'm begging you, *please* don't call the cops. I don't want Keshan to go to jail again."

Chapter 59

Caring for Sean, a well-behaved little boy was easy, but handling eighteen-month-old Malcolm was proving to be a real challenge.

He started crying nonstop on the second morning, as soon as he woke up, asking for his mommy. McNeil didn't know what to do. He offered him candy and gave him his favorite toy, but nothing would stop the crying. Daphne had specifically instructed her father not to call unless there was an urgent matter. Malcolm's crying happened again after dinner: "I want Mommy!" he wailed. Luckily, Sean turned out to be a valuable source of information; he knew how to stop his brother's crying. He told his grandfather that Malcolm liked the swing, so McNeil took the kids outside. It was a humid August evening, but to his surprise, Malcolm did enjoy the swing and stopped crying.

McNeil was more uncomfortable around Sean than around Malcolm, and as he got to know him better, he realized his grandson was an intelligent boy who knew and remembered a lot for his age.

"Do you know your mom's boyfriend's name?"

"I call him Uncle Matthew."

"Is he nice to you?"

"He's the best."

"What does he do for you?"

"He plays ball with me and takes me to the park and ... stuff."

He was scared to ask Sean where his father was, but he dared to probe him about Malcolm's father. "Is Uncle Matthew Malcolm's dad?"

"No. Malcolm's dad is Uncle Leroy."

"You remember Uncle Leroy?"

"Yes, but he died."

"Why?"

"My mom said he got sick and died, but my dad was killed in the war."

"Who told you that?"

"My mom did."

"Did Uncle Leroy's death make you sad?"

"Yeah, but Uncle Matthew said sometimes people die because they get sick or they get old and sometimes when they fight in the war like my dad."

McNeil heard the phone ringing inside the house for the fifth time that evening, but he ignored it. After his return from Denver, he had turned off his answering machine and hadn't felt like talking on the phone much. The media frenzy over his trial had subsided, so most calls he received were from charities or companies that wanted to sell him their products. He answered only the calls that he received on his cell phone because only a few people had the number.

When the telephone rang for the sixth time, he decided to answer it, but he stopped in midstride when he heard someone calling his name. He took Malcolm in his arms and walked fast around the house toward the front door.

"Oh my God!" he said joyfully. Tonya was standing at his doorstep with a suitcase. He put Malcolm down and embraced Tonya in his arms for a long time. "Where have you been all these months?"

"I couldn't afford the rent. I had no job, so I went back to South Carolina and lived with my daughter for a while. When I couldn't find a job there either, I came back to DC."

"I thought you would contact me when you heard I was free."

"I didn't know you were free. The newspapers in our little town don't cover stories from Colorado. We don't get the *Washington Post* neither."

"So did you get my phone messages?"

"Yes, the number you called belongs to my young second cousin. He came to DC last year and was kind enough to let me stay with him until I got a job."

"But I called you several times."

"My cousin's cell phone battery was dead or something. He just gave me the message two hours ago."

Tonya stared at the judge lovingly. "I'm so happy you're back. My life was so miserable without you. I couldn't even talk to anyone about my pain because I had to be discreet."

"Well, that nightmare is over. Now I have another one." McNeil motioned to Malcolm and Sean.

"Who are these two precious ones?"

McNeil told Tonya about Leroy and his relationship with Daphne and their child, Malcolm.

"That bastard molested my precious Daphne," Tonya said. "If he wasn't dead, I'd kill him with my own bare hands. But who's Sean's father?"

"He says his father was killed in the war. I think he must have been one of those men Daphne dated in Madison."

McNeil knew that Tonya had not read the *Washington Post* so many years ago and did not know about Justin's death. He picked up Malcolm in one arm and used the other hand to pick up Tonya's suitcase. It was getting dark, so he asked everyone to come inside. He walked to the telephone table and was pulling out a picture from the drawer to show to Tonya when the front door burst open.

"Don't move, you motherfucker." It was Keshan, with his gun pointing at the judge.

Chapter 60

Although annoyed by the rule, Aristo followed the flight attendant's instruction and turned off his cell phone. It felt good to relax after a long period of hectic work. From time to time, he noticed the smile on his face. This was supposed to be a romantic week with Amanda, and he couldn't let McNeil ruin it. The shocking revelation in Dr. Carter's office had disturbed him for two weeks. On one hand, the judge had obviously committed two crimes: a felony assault and a felony threat. On the other hand, no one had accused him. Without a complainant, even a prosecutor could not initiate a case against him. McNeil's pain and suffering in the Denver jail and Amanda's hard work to get him exonerated kept nagging at him. *I should let McNeil deal with his demons on his own.*

Amanda was supposed to pick him up at Denver International Airport. This was his first trip to Denver just to see her and not to work on McNeil's case. Amanda's face was painted in his mind. He kept looking at his watch as he imagined holding her in his arms and wondered how she would react to the news he had kept from her.

When the flight attendant announced that the passengers could use their electronic devices, Aristo turned on his cell phone, expecting a message from Amanda. Instead, he received a message from Debbie Newman, alerting him that Keshan was on his way to kill the judge. *Damn it, I can't get away from McNeil's drama.* What was he supposed to do, flying thirty thousand feet above the ground and tied to an uncomfortable chair? The call had come in twenty minutes earlier. Aristo took a chance and called the judge's cell phone first, but no one answered. He left a message telling the judge that Keshan was armed and looking for him.

Aristo was certain that McNeil didn't want media frenzy or another criminal case against Keshan. But could he handle an armed teenager? The next step was to contact Judge Bowen. No one picked up at Judge Bowen's house either, and Aristo decided not to leave a message. The last choice was Daphne, but would she answer? To his surprise, Daphne picked up the phone.

"Daphne, this is Detective Manfredi. Please don't hang up on me. I know you hate your dad, but his life is in danger. He doesn't pick up his phone. Keshan is planning to kill him. You live a few minutes away. Please go there and alert your dad. You're the mother of Keshan's uncle's baby. You might be able to change Keshan's mind."

"Oh my God, my children! Matthew, let's go—"

Daphne hung up without asking any questions. Aristo didn't understand what she meant by "my children!" but he felt better that Daphne had agreed to take her boyfriend and go help her dad. Images of McNeil soaking in his own blood washed away the pleasant thoughts of having a romantic night with Amanda. Attorney Newman's message had killed his good mood and ruined his plans for that evening.

Chapter 61

"Keshan, please calm down," McNeil pleaded. "Let's talk."

"You motherfucker, you killed my uncle, and now you're promising me a car, a home, and college. That's blood money."

"Keshan, it was an accident. Please believe me. I never intended to kill your uncle. He kidnapped me and tortured me for a month, and I never did anything to hurt him."

"Shut your big fat fucking mouth. You hurt him plenty. You put him in jail and ruined his family. And mine too."

Keshan's angry face and shouting frightened Malcolm, who began crying. Tonya ran to him and took him in her arms. "Child, put that gun down," Tonya told Keshan in a parental tone. "You don't need no trouble."

"Freeze! Don't do nothin' stupid. I've got no problem killing you too. You're his black whore."

"You punk! Who you callin' a whore?" Tonya took a step toward Keshan and, still holding Malcolm, pointed to the gun. "Put that gun down."

"I ain't listen to my mama. So who the hell you think you are ordering me around, *bitch*?"

"Keshan, you just got out of jail—"

McNeil couldn't finish his sentence because Keshan rushed closer to him, his gun aimed at the judge's face. "Give me one good reason why I shouldn't put a bullet in your head."

"I was about to show Tonya this picture. Please look at it; this is your uncle with my daughter." McNeil took a step forward.

Keshan warned him, "You come closer, you get a bullet between your eyes."

McNeil stepped back again. "Please look at the picture. Your uncle has baby Malcolm in his arms. This is your cousin—my grandson."

Keshan told the judge to throw the picture his way, which the judge did. He picked it up and looked at Leroy and his smiling face. He then looked at Malcolm in Tonya's arms. He lowered his gun as he looked at the picture. Tonya took advantage of his distraction and hurried Malcolm and Sean to another corner of the room. Malcolm had stopped crying now, but Sean was staring at Keshan curiously.

"He's your cousin," Tonya said to Keshan, pointing to Malcolm. "What are you going to tell him when he grows up and learns you killed his grandpa? Put that gun down."

Keshan looked at Malcolm again and then the judge. A painful expression on his face showed that he was debating what to do next. For a moment, he stood there staring at everyone in the room. Then suddenly, he charged against the judge and hit him in the head and face several times with the gun. After the judge lost his balance and fell to the floor, Keshan kicked him in the legs and then began shooting erratically. The bullets shattered a mirror, put a hole in a painting, and broke a window. Keshan ran from the house.

After he was gone, Tonya left the kids, ran to the kitchen, made an ice pack for the judge, and put it on his battered face. McNeil sat up on the floor, checking the swelling on his face. He tried to hide his pain, but every time Tonya touched his face with the ice pack, he flinched and moaned.

Slowly standing up, he walked to the front door and locked it. He put the ice pack on the corner of his left eye and was about to lie down on the couch when the telephone rang. The call was from Attorney Newman. "Is Keshan there?"

"He just left," the judge answered.

"Are you okay?"

"Yes, except for the bruises on my face and body."

"Oh my God. Have you called the police?"

"No, Ms. Newman. Like you, I don't want him to go to jail either. Despite his actions tonight, my offer is still on the table, but he has to change his behavior around my grandchildren."

Tonya grabbed the telephone and asked the caller who she was.

"Debbie Newman. I'm Keshan's attorney."

"You better put a leash on that boy. Next time he shows up here with a gun, I'll be ready for him."

"Who are you?"

"Never mind who I am. Judge McNeil is a noble person, but I'm not. Next time, I'll call the police the minute I see his shadow in the front yard."

Tonya hung up the phone and nodded, clearly pleased with her threats. She took the kids to the kitchen and treated them to chocolate pudding. She then took them to their bedrooms and asked them to play for a while. "I have to take care of your grandpa now."

McNeil was thankful that his immediate neighbors were vacationing; otherwise, they would have heard the gunshots. He took advantage of Tonya's absence and grabbed a rag from a closet. He wiped the areas of the front door that Keshan could have touched during the break-in, eliminating his fingerprints.

Tonya was making dinner in the kitchen now, but every few minutes, she yelled, "Judge McNeil, you need to go to the hospital."

"If I go to the emergency room, I'll have to tell them what happened," McNeil yelled back from the living room. "They are obligated to report it to the police."

He heard some voices outside, and when he looked through the window, he saw two shadows moving toward his house. His heart raced. He thought Keshan had brought a friend to finish what he had started, but when the two shadows stepped closer to the lamppost in the garden, he was surprised to see Daphne and a tall, good-looking man walking toward the house. He opened the door.

"Dad, are you okay? Where are my kids?" Daphne asked in a panicky voice.

"I'm fine; they're fine. They're upstairs."

Daphne ran upstairs to check on her children.

McNeil gestured for the man to have a seat. "You must be Matthew."

"Yes, sir. Sorry that I had to meet you on a night like this."

"That's okay. Nice to meet you, Matthew," McNeil said as he shook his hand.

When she found both Sean and Malcolm asleep, Daphne quickly came back down and checked on her father's bruised and swollen face. "Dad, you have to go to the ER."

Hearing the voices in the living room, Tonya came out of the kitchen. When she saw Daphne, she froze for a moment. Then she ran toward her. "Oh my Lord!" she cried out. "My precious baby. She's back home!"

Tonya's emotional welcome brought tears to Daphne's eyes. After a long hug, Daphne introduced her to Matthew. "This is Tonya. She's like a second mom to me."

"Let me look at you," Tonya said, sizing Daphne up and admiring her looks. "You're so tall, so grown up and beautiful. I missed you like hell. My Lord, I haven't seen you for five years now."

"I missed you too," Daphne said, hugging Tonya once more. She then turned to her father. "Dad, I'm worried about you. You need to get medical care, and we have to call the police and report this."

"He just got out of jail. They'll charge him with felony aggravated assault, burglary, and God knows what else." McNeil rejected the idea with a hand gesture.

"We can call the police and tell them the intruder wore a mask," Matthew suggested.

"That's genius," Tonya said.

Daphne reached for the telephone, but McNeil stopped her. "If you're calling 911, we'd better have a plausible story."

"We weren't here," Matthew said, "so they can only question you and Tonya."

"But the kids were here too," McNeil said.

"Please tell them they were asleep," Daphne begged. "Malcolm is too young to be questioned, and I don't want Sean to have to remember or talk about what he witnessed."

"You should be proud of your little boy," Tonya said. "He stood there and looked at Keshan like he was a stupid man acting crazy."

"He's a wonderful boy," Daphne responded with motherly pride while dialing 911. She told the operator that a masked intruder had broken into the house, injured her father, and taken some cash.

McNeil forgot his pain momentarily. All he could think about was the dreamlike reality of his daughter being back—the loving and caring Daphne he used to know.

Chapter 62

Latisha Williams paced in her room as she waited for the telephone to ring, expecting to hear from Attorney Newman. She hoped she had stopped Keshan before it was too late.

After an hour of waiting, she became impatient and called Montrel, the only person who had some influence over Keshan now. After Leroy's death, Montrel had unofficially assumed Leroy's role. He had visited Keshan in jail every week. He was also the one who had found the two essential witnesses for Attorney Newman—the two witnesses whose testimonies had exonerated Keshan. When the jury returned the verdict of not guilty, many of Keshan's friends and neighbors, who were in court, had congratulated Montrel for winning the case instead of Keshan's attorney.

It took thirty-five minutes for Montrel to drive from PG County to Latisha and Keshan's home in southeast DC. As he parked his car, Latisha waited for him outside.

"Woman, are you crazy?" Montrel shouted as soon as he exited the car. "How could you tell him Judge McNeil was the one who killed his uncle and expect him to stay cool?"

"I'm so sorry. The words just jumped out of my mouth."

Montrel called Attorney Newman several times. But each time, he got her voice mail. "That white bitch has finished the case and gotten her money. She ain't worried about Keshan no more," he mumbled.

When Latisha went inside to call attorney Newman, Montrel kept asking neighbors if they had seen Keshan. Their answers were disappointing. He was about to get in his car and drive to Judge McNeil's house when he saw Keshan walking toward him. "You didn't do nothin' stupid, did you?" he shouted at him.

"He killed my uncle. I should've killed him."

"Where's the gun?"

"In my pocket."

"Give it to me."

Keshan hesitated at first but then reluctantly handed the gun to Montrel.

"What did you do to him?"

"I hit him in the face with the gun."

"Did anyone see you?"

"There were two kids and his black whore. He said the youngest kid, Malcolm, is my cousin—Uncle Leroy's son."

"That's true."

"That's why I couldn't kill him. He's Malcolm's grandpa."

"Did you forget about your life in prison?"

"No, I just lost my head. My mama told me Uncle Leroy was in jail in Texas. Then she tells me the judge killed him. I'm supposed to sit and do nothin'?"

"He's a white man and a powerful judge. If he kills, he gets off the hook. I bet he bought that jury in Denver. We had to find you two eyewitnesses to tell the jury the other dude killed the girls. You're black; you're always guilty until proven innocent. You know that. The judge told the jury he killed Leroy because of self-defense, because Leroy had told him he'd kill him, and the jury believed him. He didn't bring no witnesses, no nothing. They believed him because he was a white powerful judge from DC."

"If he wasn't Malcolm's grandpa, I'd kill him. I don't care if he's white or powerful—"

"That's stupid talk. You should've accepted the motherfucker's offer."

"But that was Uncle Leroy's blood money."

"You should've taken it. It was the least he could do for Leroy after he killed him."

Keshan's mother ran outside. "Attorney Newman called. The judge has not called the police and still wants to help Keshan," she said with a smile.

"Keshan is gonna come and live with me for a while until things cool down," Montrel said.

Keshan went inside the house and packed a duffel bag full of clothes. He hugged his mother and jumped into the front seat of Montrel's car. He waved good-bye to his mother and shouted, "See you next week!"

* * *

Montrel was still lecturing Keshan on how to be smart and stay out of trouble when they crossed Dr. Martin Luther King Avenue, but Keshan had stopped listening. The car didn't have air-conditioning, but he enjoyed the hot summer breeze coming through the open window. He wondered what kind of car Judge McNeil would buy for him. His mother's car was old and always in need of repair. Besides, she never allowed him to drive it because he didn't have a driver's license.

A sound like a tire blowing out interrupted his thoughts. The car jolted, and he heard several gunshots. He felt a sudden burning sensation in his neck and head and heard screeching tires and Montrel's scream. "You motherfuckers, you killed him!" He didn't hear any more.

* * *

When Montrel stopped the car and called 911, Keshan's body was soaked with blood. The ambulance's siren could be heard a few blocks away, but it was too late. Keshan was gone. Montrel held his body, kissed his forehead, and closed his eyes. He then wiped his tears.

Chapter 63

The flight to Denver arrived after a twenty-minute delay. This added to the number of butterflies dancing in Amanda's stomach. She had been awaiting Aristo's return to Denver for weeks now. The trip was special—they didn't have to talk about McNeil's murder case anymore. They had planned a relaxing, romantic week together. For the first time in recent months, she felt she deserved to have a good time and be happy. In the past, happiness had always been something that belonged to her neighbor, her best friend, other people—not her. But now, with McNeil's case over, she had nothing to worry about. She was ready to welcome Aristo to her world.

The trip's other significant issue was Amanda's decision to introduce the man she loved to her aunt and uncle. In the past, every time Aristo had asked to meet with them, she had used McNeil's trial as an excuse. But now she was ready.

She saw Aristo among the passengers heading toward the arrival gate. Her heart pounded like she was a teenage girl on her first date.

"Hello, my love," Aristo said as he gave her a big hug and a few kisses on the cheeks.

"Welcome back," Amanda said, holding his hand. "Is this carry-on the only thing you have?"

"Yes."

"Let's go. My car is parked nearby."

"Amanda, I'm sorry. I can't leave yet. May I borrow your cell phone and make a few important calls? My phone's battery is dead."

"Can you call as I'm driving?" she asked, handing him her cell phone.

"No, I have to talk to you. I may have to fly back immediately."

"I thought you had taken some time off. What's wrong?"

"Please, let's go sit down in a restaurant. I'll tell you what's going on."

They found a quiet area at the airport's nearest restaurant and ordered two cappuccinos. Aristo told Amanda about the disturbing call he had received from Debbie Newman.

"Is McNeil okay?"

"That's what I'm trying to find out. I couldn't get a direct flight. I had three hours to kill before I caught my connecting flight. I didn't bring my laptop this trip because I wasn't planning to work."

"Go ahead and make your call."

Aristo dialed McNeil's number, but no one picked up. He dialed Daphne's cell phone and got her voice mail. He then called Attorney Newman. He didn't have any luck with her either. Finally, he reluctantly called his nemesis, Detective Prez, at the DCMPD and asked him if there was a report on McNeil. He put the speakerphone on so that Amanda could hear the conversation too.

"How do you know about McNeil?"

"Please, answer my question without questioning me," Aristo snapped.

"The judge's daughter called 911 and reported a burglary. They assigned the case to me. I talked to them. I think your good friend—the judge—is lying."

"Why are you saying that?"

"They said that a masked intruder got inside the house and asked for some cash, and when he didn't get enough cash, he beat the judge in his face and head with a gun."

"What part of that is a lie?"

"There are no signs of breaking and entering, no intruder's fingerprints anywhere, not on the door, not even on the drawer where the money was supposed to be."

"Maybe he was wearing gloves."

"Maybe, but the judge's statement proves he's lying. When I asked him why there were no prints on the drawer, he said because he opened the drawer and gave the man the cash himself. No intruder, no robber or burglar, is stupid enough to allow his victim to open a drawer that might contain a gun."

"Prez, why are you telling me this? Are you trying to punish McNeil because I like him?"

"This is obstruction of justice. But don't worry. We're not going to charge him. We know who the intruder was."

"Who?"

"Judge McNeil lives in one of the safest neighborhoods in DC. We haven't had any burglaries or other crimes in that area for years. Who's the judge's enemy? Friends and relatives of Leroy Walker."

"Who's your primary suspect?"

"Keshan Walker, Leroy's nephew."

"Have you arrested him?"

"We didn't have to. We were too late. Someone killed him before we could get our hands on him."

"Oh my God," Amanda gasped.

"Who killed him?" Aristo asked.

"It was a drive-by shooting. We think the killer or the killers were probably friends of his codefendant."

Prez was still talking, but Aristo said a quick good-bye, closed Amanda's cell phone, and left it on the table.

For a few minutes, they sat there speechless, in shock, holding hands. After a while, they looked at each other, but just then Amanda's telephone rang. Aristo looked at the caller ID. It was Attorney Newman. "I have to answer this," Aristo said, turning on the speakerphone again. "Hello, this is Manfredi."

"I'm sorry; I was in trial all day. I just heard some horrible news. Keshan was killed this evening. Montrel just called me."

"Who killed him?"

"Montrel believes it was the friends of his codefendant in the triple-murder case."

"Is he absolutely sure?"

"It was a drive-by shooting. Montrel didn't see anyone, but I believe him. That's not all—" Attorney Newman's voice cracked. After a few seconds of silence, she spoke again. "Keshan's two essential witnesses were also gunned down in drive-by shootings an hour earlier, in different parts of DC. Can I rely on your investigation—"

"I'm so sorry. I'll talk to you later." Aristo ended the call before he could be pulled into something more.

The shocking news caused another long silence. Finally, Amanda asked for her cell phone back. "I should call Judge McNeil. He must be shaken up by today's events."

"Before you call him, I have to tell you another horrible story I've discovered."

For the next few minutes, Amanda sat silently in her chair, listening to the tale of the judge's arrest for solicitation, his meetings with Yvette, the news about Samyra's death, and the judge's efforts to help Keshan. She moved uncomfortably in her chair when Aristo gave her the details of Dr. Carter's notes about McNeil's crime years earlier.

"Oh my God. Are you sure he confessed his crime to his psychologist?"

"No, he told Dr. Carter that he had handled a case that had been haunting him for the past several years. When I put the pieces together, I realized this was what had happened to Daphne's boyfriend. That was the reason Daphne disappeared. Her father had caused her boyfriend's death. She was pregnant ..."

"Are you sure the judge was not actually describing a real case?"

"I love you, but please don't insult me. I'm a detective. I solve crimes."

"During the trial, he kept telling me he had committed a crime against Daphne. I thought he just felt guilty because he was a disciplinarian father who had driven his only child away."

Aristo waited to hear more from Amanda. When she sat quietly instead, drowned in her thoughts, sipping her cappuccino, he asked, "Now what?"

"What do you mean 'now what'?"

"This is a crime. A felony assault, a felony threat—that's ten years. A zealous prosecutor could even charge him with assault with intent to kill. Why am I explaining this to you? A brilliant attorney like you knows all of that."

"I agree about the two felony charges, but where does assault with intent to kill come from?"

"Banging his head against the wall several times. I bet if they'd done an autopsy, that would have been the cause of death, not crashing into the tree."

"I don't know."

"What are we supposed to do with this information?"

"Nothing."

"Is that all you have to say? Nothing?"

"Aristo, what do you expect me to say? You know that as his lawyer, I have to keep all information about my client confidential. If I disclosed any of this, I would get disbarred. Even if I were a prosecutor, I still wouldn't have the heart to see him go to jail again. For ten months, I saw the man die every day in jail. This is Daphne's call. Apparently, she hasn't told anyone; even Justin's parents believe the car crash alone killed him. Now I understand why she didn't come to testify for her father—she said that he was better off without her testimony."

"As much as I hate to sit quietly and do nothing about the judge's crime, I have to agree with you. The decision should be Daphne's, as a witness to the assault, or Justin's parents'—who don't have a clue. I bet the trauma to his head, the alcohol, and the threat of death from McNeil had a lot to do with his crash."

After another long period of silence, during which Amanda kept staring at her cappuccino and sighing, she said, "I wonder how Debbie Newman is handling this. She won a triple-murder case but lost a client and her two essential witnesses."

"Three people dead: that's not winning."

"What a sad ending." Amanda didn't feel the dancing butterflies in her stomach anymore. And she was not thinking about a romantic evening either. Images of three dead bodies and her client's injured face kept flashing before her eyes. She felt nauseated.

Aristo pulled his chair closer to hers and put his arm around her shoulder. He kissed the top of her head. "We'll get through this. I promise."

* * *

That evening, Aristo borrowed Amanda's car to drive to Boulder. He claimed he needed to stay there for a day to finish an old investigation for a friend. During McNeil's trial, Amanda had been too busy to question his Boulder case, but this time she was curious to know who Aristo's friend was. This was supposed to be a no-work trip. As she remembered the number and the duration of the Boulder trips, she became more suspicious. By midafternoon the next day, she was certain that Aristo's "friend" was a female friend.

She didn't blame Aristo for leaving. The news of the murder of three people he knew had been enough to kill his romantic mood. But she was shocked and sad too. He could have stayed and comforted her. The thought of another failed relationship compelled her to share her concern with her uncle. "I don't know what it is he's hiding from me."

"We have a terrible profession, you know that?" Frank chuckled. "We're trained to be suspicious of everything and everyone."

"Why doesn't he tell me about his case and his friend in Boulder?"

"Detective-client confidentiality, you know."

"Do you blame me for being suspicious? He comes here to help me with McNeil's murder trial, and all of a sudden, he has a case in Boulder. Isn't that a little too much of a coincidence? Besides, this trip was supposed to be about us—spending time together."

"Maybe he accepted the case before, and when McNeil's case started, he decided to work on the Boulder case as well."

"I have this gut feeling he's hiding something from me."

"Well, I think the man is crazy about you. I'm sure he has a good explanation for his trips to Boulder. I'll ask him about Boulder over dinner tomorrow night."

That night, Amanda didn't sleep well. It was not easy to forget the deaths of Keshan and his two witnesses. The images of several dead bodies wouldn't go away.

She also thought about her client, McNeil, and the real reason he had become so fearless and unafraid of death. Her train of thought then led her back to Aristo. Yes, the shocking news from DC had been unbearable, but why did he have to leave her immediately to spend the night with a friend? And who was that friend? *He better have a good explanation*, she thought.

* * *

Aristo came back from Boulder in the late afternoon in a good mood, wearing a wide smile across his face. He hugged and kissed Amanda as though he were just seeing her for the first time after a long separation. When she didn't reciprocate his warm embrace, he leaned back and looked sharply in her eyes, trying to read her mind.

"Hey, lady. Our date was ruined last night because of three dead people. But I don't intend to let anything ruin our date tonight, especially when we have such big news to celebrate."

"Who's your friend, and what's this mysterious case you have in Boulder?"

"Hey! If you cross-examined a witness like that, the prosecutor would jump and shout, 'Objection, Your Honor. Compounded question.'"

"We're not in court, and I can ask you any kind of question I want."

"But your body language makes it seem you're cross-examining me."

"Who is she?"

"Excuse me?"

"You heard me. I want to get it over with. Who is she?"

"Oh my God. You think I planned this dream trip and came all the way here just to go to Boulder and see another woman?"

"You're hiding something from me."

"Damn! Do you always have to be this smart?"

"Aha! You just admitted that you're hiding something from me."

"Counselor, since we're in a courtroom asking serious questions, can I ask you one?"

"What?"

"About ten months from now, will you have room for another attorney in your law firm?"

"My uncle is planning to retire after his big class-action lawsuit, so the answer is yes. Who's interested in our law firm?"

"Me."

"You're a detective."

"I was going to share the good news with you over dinner tonight, but your suspicion is scary. I'd better tell you now."

"What good news? Tell me what?"

"After several trips to Boulder and talking to some law professors, I'm happy to report that my application has been approved to finish my law degree at the University of Colorado Law School. They've also given me a fellowship."

"How?"

"They're accepting all the courses I took at the University of Wisconsin Law School, and they're giving me credit for some of the courses I took at the police academy, so I have two more semesters to become a lawyer."

"That's wonderful, but you love being a detective."

"That was another life. I feel like Mary's death turned me into a vengeful man. After I worked with you on McNeil's case, I realized that good people can also get caught in the system."

"Are you telling me that now you're seeing things the same way a criminal defense attorney sees them?"

"Why is this so strange to you? For God's sake, I was in law school for two years. That means I wanted to be a lawyer."

"Oh my God," Amanda said as she embraced Aristo. "I can't believe it! That means you're going to live here in Denver."

"Yes, as long as you live here."

"I'm not going anywhere."

"I have more good news: today, one of the professors who teaches a criminal law seminar asked me to help him teach the law enforcement part of it."

"My uncle and aunt will be thrilled to death to hear about this."

"Would they consider me worthy of you?"

"They know how much you mean to me."

"Maybe they do, but *I* don't know how much I mean to you."

Amanda looked into Aristo's eyes and gave him a naughty smile. She then put her arms around his shoulders and sealed his lips with a passionate kiss. "That much."

Aristo was about to kiss Amanda back when his cell phone vibrated in his pocket. He pulled it out and opened it. It was Detective Prez.

"Prez, this better be quick. I don't have time," he said.

"Don't you want to hear about the burglary investigation?"

"Not really."

"I'm not going to bring any charges against Judge McNeil."

"You said that before," Aristo said as he put the speaker on.

"We know McNeil was trying to protect Keshan, but the boy is dead now."

"Why are you calling me? I've got to go."

"Wait a minute. The burglary investigation is not the only reason I called."

"What else?"

"The chief has not accepted your retirement application because he wants you to handle one last case for him."

"You filed for retirement?" Amanda asked in a hushed tone.

Aristo nodded. "Tell the boss he doesn't have much to say about this. I've worked for eighteen years, and now I want to retire. That's the end of that."

"You may change your mind. He wants you to handle Keshan's homicide. He's assigned me and one other detective to investigate the murder of Keshan's two witnesses."

"Good luck to all of you. My detective years in DC are over. I'm moving to Denver."

"What's so special in Denver?"

"Tell the chief I'm in love with a lady who lives in Denver." Aristo closed his cell phone as he pulled Amanda toward him to finish the kiss that had been interrupted.

Chapter 64

As the days went by, the bruises on Judge McNeil's face faded. He tried to suppress the truth about Justin's death in his mind and enjoy being a grandfather instead, but he kept remembering banging Justin's head against the wall, threatening to kill him, and then throwing him out of his house. Any adult would have known that an injured, drunk boy could end up crashing his car. The blows to his head could have killed him before the accident. Nothing could wash away the ugly memory of that night. Why did he have to drink? He knew that he couldn't handle heavy liquor. *How is a father supposed to handle the news that his fifteen-year-old daughter is pregnant?* he wondered.

In the present day, Daphne had practically moved back home without any announcement. McNeil was so thrilled to see her every day that he was afraid to talk to her or even make eye contact. But he got his share of furtive glances at her anytime she was playing with her kids.

Matthew spent the weekends with them but stayed in his own apartment during the week. He seemed like a levelheaded young man, and his ambition to finish his PhD in psychology had gained the judge's respect. *This family could really use a psychologist.*

September was an exciting month. Daphne started college and in a short period of time had made several new friends. When she joked and laughed with members of her study group, no one could guess her tumultuous past. Meanwhile, Tonya was running the household smoothly and caring for the kids like a seasoned grandmother.

McNeil's pleasant and peaceful life was interrupted one morning when he had a surprise visitor—an FBI agent seeking information about Darnell. "Has he contacted you?" the agent asked as soon as he sat in a chair.

"I wasn't there when he dug the grave and found the money. My information comes from the same letter Attorney Perkins submitted to you a long time ago."

"We have that letter, but do you or Ms. Perkins have more info you want to share?"

"I don't know about Ms. Perkins, but he hasn't contacted me."

"When you were held hostage in that Lakewood ranch, did you hear anything about how the kidnappers got their hands on that ranch?"

"No. But Detective Manfredi's investigation revealed later that apparently Leroy had befriended the owner in Hazelton's prison."

"Well, the owner was a big drug kingpin. He has given us information on a drug tsar we have been after for a long time. We've reached an agreement with him to release him and put him in a witness protection program after his testimony. He tells us that he had a million dollars in cash buried at his Lakewood house. He wants his money back."

"Darnell confessed in his letter that he took the money. But doesn't your kingpin have to forfeit the drug money as required by law?"

"Yes, that's true. We have the authority to confiscate all drug-related money, but we have a deal with him. In exchange for his testimony, which we desperately need, we have promised to give him a small portion of his money back. Besides, we need the money to protect him. The witness protection program is costly. Darnell better have that money when we catch him."

"Do you have any leads?"

"Our informants tell us he's no longer in Mexico, but we'll find him."

"Good luck."

The agent's visit brought back memories that McNeil had tried so hard to forget. He called Amanda and found that she hadn't received any news from Darnell either. He hoped that the FBI would never catch him. After all, Darnell had saved his life. When Leroy and Melvin forced McNeil to use drugs, it was Darnell who had treated him like a doctor trying to ease his pain.

That afternoon, McNeil had another visitor. Unlike his morning visitor, this one was pleasant. Judge Bowen had come with a job offer. "The DC Arbitration Group wants you to join them," he said, smiling.

"I'm flattered, but I'm enjoying my retirement."

"These are mostly retired judges and attorneys you've known for years. It's an easy job—no courtroom drama and no heavy calendar schedules. How can you refuse?"

"Fredrick, I know you have my best interest at heart, and I appreciate your talking to them on my behalf, but I'm really happy just being a grandpa."

"For how long?"

"Maybe for the rest of my life."

"I know you're trying to improve your relationship with Daphne, but that doesn't mean you should sacrifice your whole career."

"She has started college. I have to make sure she succeeds."

"You have given her and the kids a place to live. You have even hired a nanny for them."

"If you're referring to Tonya, she's not a nanny. I've had a relationship with her for many years now." McNeil noticed his friend was not surprised. He paused for a few seconds, and then he spoke again. "I'm sorry you had to hear about it during my trial and not from me."

"You thought I would disapprove?"

"I just didn't feel comfortable talking about Tonya, especially after Daphne's disappearance."

"I'm happy you have someone in your life who loves and comforts you. I think it's time for you to enjoy life again. I believe Fiona would have approved."

"Thanks. You've always been a true friend."

McNeil felt good after Judge Bowen left. He had revealed his true feelings for Tonya to his best friend, but he still had another secret buried in his heart, a secret that he could never reveal to anyone—Justin's death.

That evening after dinner, he took Sean and Malcolm to the backyard. He enjoyed Malcolm's excitement and nonstop giggling on the swing. Tonya was visiting her cousin, and Daphne had gone to one of her group study sessions at a friend's house. McNeil was babysitting the kids when Daphne showed up in the backyard. "What happened to your group study?" he asked.

"My friend who was hosting got sick, so we had to cancel it."

"You're more than welcome to bring your friends here."

"I know, and I'm thankful for all the times you've let me use your home."

"This is your home too."

"Thanks, Dad. I want to talk to you about something else."

McNeil enjoyed the sound of the word *Dad* so much that he forgot to encourage his daughter to talk.

"Do you have a minute?"

"Of course. I'm sorry."

"Matthew pays a lot of money for his apartment. He has a scholarship, so of course, he can afford it. But I was wondering if—" Daphne swallowed her words. The expression on her face revealed doubt or a second thought.

McNeil guessed what Daphne was about to ask. He had expected it was coming for a long time but had been afraid to suggest it to Daphne. He was careful about his conversations with her. He didn't want Daphne to misinterpret any of his comments or gestures as interference with her life. "If what, Daphne?" he asked.

"Is it okay if Matthew moves in with us?"

"Of course it's okay. He's a wonderful young man. But I have to ask you something—"

"Dad, don't worry. We'll get married after I finish college."

"That was not my question."

"Then what?"

McNeil hesitated for a few seconds, lowered his gaze, and asked with a shaky voice, "What have you told him about Sean?"

"I told him that when I was in Madison, I dated a soldier who had just come back from Iraq. After he left for another tour of duty, I found out I was pregnant."

"Did he believe you?"

"I told him my soldier boyfriend got killed in Iraq. That was the end of the story. He never asked me any more questions about him."

"Will you promise me something?"

"What?"

"That you will never, ever tell him or any other soul the truth about Sean?"

"I've made up this story to protect my son, not *you*. I was and still am protecting my son. His life would be ruined if he ever found out that his grandfather killed his father. I could have told Justin's parents about my pregnancy, but I ran away because getting them involved in my child's life would have meant living with Justin's ghost forever. This is a secret that I have to keep in my heart and take to my grave."

"Thanks," McNeil said, turning his head and trying to hide his quivering lips and tearful eyes. He pondered whether this was the right time to tell Daphne that she was another man's daughter—that she belonged to a stranger her mother had met in a bar. Then he remembered his promise to Fiona that he would never tell Daphne about her biological father. *Just like Daphne, I have to take my secret to my grave.*

A heavy weight had been lifted from McNeil's back. So Sean would not find out about his real father, but what about Malcolm? The noisy boy was running around the yard. A chill ran down McNeil's spine when he realized that someday, somehow, someone would tell Malcolm the truth. For a moment, Keshan's angry face and his gun pointed at him flashed before his eyes. Would Malcolm react like Keshan? *Am I raising my future killer?* he wondered.

Chapter 65

Margaret McNeil chose a secluded area of the hotel's restaurant to have her coffee. She needed to be alone to finish her acceptance speech. This evening was going to be a big night in her life. The Justice for All Project was giving her an award for a decade of volunteer work for them. Her relentless efforts in finding attorneys to do pro bono work for the project had resulted in the exoneration of twenty-nine wrongfully convicted inmates who had been imprisoned on charges of rape or murder.

From her booth at the restaurant, she could still see fellow members of her organization walking through the crowded lobby of the hotel. She looked at her speech again and realized it didn't need any changes. The letter in her briefcase was more important.

She put on her cotton gloves and took the letter out. Many years of work with criminal defense attorneys had taught her how to avoid leaving fingerprints on different items. She had used gloves even while typing the letter and fixing the address label on the envelope. She opened the letter addressed to the DC chief of police and reread it.

Dear Chief,

As a concerned citizen, I feel compelled to bring a horrible crime to your attention—a murder, committed in 2006. Since there is no statue of limitation for murder cases, I believe you can still investigate and prosecute the killer. His name is Judge Walter McNeil. Surprised? Yes, it's the same man who killed Leroy Walker in Denver, Colorado, and is now off the hook. He killed his daughter's boyfriend in 2006. You should talk to Daphne.

You might wonder why she hasn't come forward and reported the crime. But remember—she disappeared for four years. Maybe she thought no one would believe her story. How could a prominent member of society—a judge—be capable of committing such a heinous crime? The newspaper reported that after his prom night party, Justin Foster drove his car under the influence of alcohol, and he was killed when the car crashed into a tree near his home. No one knew that fifteen minutes earlier, he had made a trip to McNeil's home to apologize to Daphne for making out with another girl. The judge banged his head against the wall several times and threatened that he would kill him if he showed his face at his home again. An autopsy would have proven this, but since Justin died in a car accident, no one ordered it.

Cordially,
A Concerned Citizen

Margaret folded the letter and inserted it in a prestamped, preaddressed envelope. After finishing her coffee, she left the restaurant and dropped the envelope in the mailbox outside the hotel.

Walking back inside, she wore a naughty smile—her mission was accomplished. No one would guess that a letter sent from Baltimore had actually been written by someone who lived in Madison, Wisconsin.

* * *

Of the thirty days he had stayed in Mexico City, Darnell had spent twenty-nine gathering information about Brazil. His research had revealed that at the time of Brazil's independence in 1822, two-thirds of its population had African or mixed heritage. The most recent statistics showed that 45 percent of Brazilians were considered people of color. He had dismissed publications and discussions about social class discrimination in Brazil. Darnell had found his paradise.

Sitting in a sidewalk café in Cinelandia, Rio's famous square, and sipping on his margarita, Darnell felt good about his adopted country. Now all he needed was to master the language. Whenever his new friends commented on his poor Portuguese, he blamed it on his American mother and Brazilian father, who spoke with him only in English.

He pulled out his new passport from his pants pocket. The plastic surgeon had promised him a Brazilian face, but the man in the picture looked more like an Italian. Darnell didn't mind. With his straightened short hair, new cheekbones, and clean-shaven face, no one would recognize him even if he showed up in his old DC neighborhood. He looked at his name and repeated it in his head: *Ronaldo da Silva*. He liked the sound of it, but he still had to get used to it.

He finished his margarita and walked through Cinelandia Square, smelling and breathing the sweet warm air coming off the ocean. He was loving every moment of his new life. He was too preoccupied with his future to notice the Brazilian man who had been following him all afternoon.